EMBERTIDE

Also by Liz Williams
from NewCon Press

Comet Weather (2020)
Blackthorn Winter (2021)

A Glass of Shadow (2011)
The Light Warden (2015)
Phosphorus (2018)

With Trevor Jones:
Diary of a Witchcraft Shop (2011)
Diary of a Witchcraft Shop 2 (2013)

EMBERTIDE

Liz Williams

NewCon Press
England

First published in June 2022 by NewCon Press,
41 Wheatsheaf Road, Alconbury Weston, Cambs, PE28 4LF

NCP275 (limited edition hardback)
NCP276 (softback)

10 9 8 7 6 5 4 3 2 1

ISBN:

978-1-914953-20-0 (hardback)
978-1-914953-21-7 (softback)

Cover by Ian Whates

Editing and typesetting by Ian Whates

Part 1

Our Thumping Hearts Keep the Ravens In

Prologue

When the woman came out of the wood she could hear the gibbet creaking in the wind. She nudged the grey mare beneath her, keeping the horse steady, but the mare did not falter. The animal was used to death, to the scent of blood, and there was no one hanging from the gibbet, this time. The rough track stretched away along the downland slope, dusty with chalk and banked with thorn brakes just starting to come into bud.

A man was waiting at the gallows tree, perched on the stone at its base and picking his nails with a blade. His horse, bright as a conker, grazed nearby. He looked up as she brought the grey mare forward.

"Oh, hello. I wasn't sure you'd come." A drawling, languid voice. But he did not look languid. He was on his feet, cat quick, by the time she'd dismounted.

"I came," she said. "I got your message last night."

He was taller than she, and masked in silk, jet black. His clothes were autumn colours: deep brown and fawn, white lace peeping at collar and cuffs. Something of a dandy, then, she thought. Behind the mask his eyes were as yellow as a goat's, the pupils slitted. Bronze ringlets fell to his shoulders and when he swept off his tricorn hat she saw that the small coiled horns of a ram nestled among the curls. His smile showed a goat's strong teeth.

"Well, well, well," he said. "I've heard a lot about you. Feldfar, they call you, don't they? The Far Farer."

"I have several names."

"Oh so do all the best people, my dear." He gave a mocking bow, sweeping his tricorn hat. "I certainly do."

"I know. Aiken Drum, some call *you.* I must say, you don't *sound* Scottish."

"I'm not. I took the name some years ago. Many years ago, in fact. You may call me Aiken."

"And they tell me that you run the Lily White Boys?"

He said softly, "One is one, and all alone, and ever more shall be so."

"Is that a *no*, then?"

He laughed. "No, not really. I just don't keep them on a very tight leash, you might say."

"What was it you want of me, Aiken Drum?"

"I want your help," he said.

"To do what?"

"To catch a horse."

"Why? I'm no horse whisperer."

"No." It was not a question. "That's why I asked to meet you here." His yellow eyes gleamed. He shielded them for a moment, looking down the slope. She could not see what was there.

"I don't understand," she said. "And even if I helped you, what would I get in exchange?"

"Safe passage. Spring's coming; tide's changing. It's a strong tide this year, too, stronger than is customary. The drovers will be running soon; some say the Searchers are on the move. Old spirits are waking up. I can protect you. But only if you help me."

She considered this. "I'll think about it."

"Then ride with me a while." He grinned. "You interest me."

"And vice versa, Mr Drum." She took the pommel of the saddle in her hand, put her foot in the stirrup and swung her leg lightly over. "Where to, then?"

"Oh, down aways, along. Up hill and down dale, as long as no church bell sounds. Does that please you, m'lady?"

"We'll see."

He mounted the stallion. "Then follow me, field-farer."

She kicked the mare into a trot. As they headed down the chalky slope, she glanced back over her shoulder. A body swung from the gallows tree in a woodpecker's colours: scarlet and cream and black, and decked with coins and trinkets. She turned away and rode on.

SERENA

The Channel was steel and fire in the late winter light, the water flashing under oncoming rain. Serena sat in a high sided Victorian armchair, looking out to sea. Everything in this hotel was Victorian, including the building itself. It perched like a great red crow between its pallid Georgian neighbours, incongruous and untidy.

Further down the street, most of the windows were overhung with blackout curtains. A little old Ford trundled along the seafront, unremarked by the smart young women in ATS uniforms, the recuperating soldiers and their girlfriends. Brighton had been transformed for the time being into its wartime guise: the film that Ward was shooting (working title *A Colder Day*) was set in the early 40s. Serena had spent the previous evening in a pub in the Laines with the costume department, and had learned a great deal about hats. Perhaps a wartime-inspired collection might be in the offing?

Her previous offer of finance had, perforce, collapsed earlier in the year, but a couple of weeks later Serena had been approached through the fashion grapevine by another backer, this time an American one. Gail Holstein was a brisk, no-nonsense New Yorker in her fifties with a solid appreciation of the nature of the industry and nothing discernibly supernatural about her. Given recent events, Serena thought this was a definite plus. They had met in Milan, liked one another, and Gail had provided the funding for Serena's next collection from a number of business sources with remarkably little fuss and few strings attached: full creative control would be retained by Serena ("not my wheelhouse," Gail had said). It was a relief to have some financial stability, and Serena was luxuriating in it. And it was also nice to be in Brighton, with Ward: the first non-work related break that she'd had this year. It was a good place to come for a dirty weekend, or even a not-very-dirty one.

She watched the seaside at wartime unfold with interest. The clouds were breaking up now, the rain sweeping out towards the invisible Continent, and a wash of pale blue sky appeared in the west. Serena glanced at the clock: it was nearly four. If she wanted to have a walk before meeting Ward in the Black Lion before dinner, now was her chance. She swept up her coat, a belted scarlet mac that reminded her of Red Riding Hood, and went into the lobby, which was decorated with old photographs of the town. Maybe some of those had been taken during the war; Serena reminded herself to take a look. Young men in uniform grinned back at her from the old sea front: Naval officers, RAF. Serena wondered how many of them had made it home again. One young man in particular caught her eye: Serena smiled back at him. *I'd like to have known you*, she thought.

Further along the wall, the war was over but Mods and Rockers still fought eternal battles; skirts and scooters versus quiffs and leather. They took Serena to the doors of the hotel. Outside, there was a fresh and invigorating blast of salt air.

Serena headed west along the sea front, away from the disruptions of the filming towards Hove and the frail ruin of the Victorian pier. It had burned down in the 1990s, the landlady of the Black Lion had informed her, hinting darkly of arson and sabotage from rival piers. Serena had no way of knowing if this was true. Gulls wheeled and cried above it, and this late in the afternoon a black comma curved above the old structure: the murmuration of starlings which used the cage of the pier in which to roost. Serena was used to these flocks in the skies of her native Somerset, but they always fascinated her and she took a moment to watch the twisting, turning shadow of the birds. Then she went briskly down the steps that led from the main road to the walkway along the shore. The tide was in, hushing and booming against the shingle beach, and at length she came level with the spire of the i360, sponsored by British Airways as a local attraction, equivalent to the London Eye. It reminded Serena slightly of the Space Needle in Seattle. The saucer-shaped viewing platform was currently ascending. Serena could see people with drinks in their hands: the saucer contained a rather expensive bar. She knew this as she and Ward had gone up in it over the weekend, rather giggly on champagne and pretending that they were living in the future, that the saucer would take them up to Brighton spaceport. Now, Serena walked past the smart stewardess in her BA uniform handing out leaflets, and on to where the murmuration of starlings was beginning to settle.

Despite the February chill, the walkway was crowded, and Serena made her way onto the shingle and down towards the sea. The clouds had closed over again and she could smell rain coming. She raised her head and sniffed the air, then blinked. For a moment, the old pier had gone, but then all was as before. A herring gull soared up, a vivid white against the clouds.

Hmmm, thought Serena. At the edge of the water lay a long dark bundle. Seaweed, or driftwood? Beachcomber's instincts activated, she went closer to look, and saw a hand, outflung. Serena's own hand went to her mouth. The flesh was blanched and bruised, protruding from a navy sleeve. Serena stood still for a long moment, then forced herself to go closer. The person was very clearly dead. He was young, with a mat of dark hair, and Serena, through a froth of panic, thought that he might have drowned, since she could not see any wound or blood. His sightless blue eyes pleaded with the sky. Confused memories of police dramas produced an instruction: *do not disturb the body*. She had to call 999. When she dialled, however, fumbling with the phone, there was no tone from her mobile, and no signal, either. Maybe get photographic evidence? Serena took a number of snaps with her phone at different angles, trying hard not to flinch. Tears of pity filled her eyes; he looked so young, like the young man in the photo in the lobby of the hotel. Very like, in fact… He was partially wrapped in some kind of greatcoat. Then she thought: *my God, those are RAF wings. It's someone from the movie.*

Serena swore softly and stumbled up the shingle to the walkway, willing the phone to connect. *I wish, I wish I could help you.*

Perhaps you can.

Serena stopped dead. "What? Who said that?" But there was no reply.

When she reached the walkway she was struck by a sudden flurry of rain. The squall was coming in from the north, battering the walkway with big wet drops. Serena's phone pinged, she looked up, and the old pier was ablaze with lights.

But that looks like gaslight, Serena thought, not electricity. And when she looked back, the body had gone. Surf surged up the shingle, and no dark form rolled within it. The gull was still there, hanging on the wind. It screamed once, then dropped like a stone.

The globes along the sides of the pier burned softly, through sudden fog. One of the sea frets of the South Coast had come in, replacing the rain, or perhaps it was just that the time itself had changed. Serena watched a woman in long skirts grip the rail with gloved hands and peer over. She could not see the woman properly: she wore a grey and white coat but her face was obscured by a large and feathery hat.

"Hob! Do come and look!"

A small man stepped to join her. Serena could not see his face either; his back was half turned.

"What is it, my darling?"

"See the dog? What a funny little fellow." She laughed. There was no dog, at least not one visible to Serena.

The couple drifted away down the pier. Serena ran up to the handsome, crenelated entrance and looked through.

"That will be a penny, miss," said a girl's voice.

"Oh! Of course. Here." And Serena searched for her purse and extracted a modern 1p, which she handed over. The girl did not seem to see anything amiss. Serena, in the window glass, saw herself modishly clad in ice blue satin, her fair hair piled up on her head. She went through the gate, onto the pier.

STELLA

"You weren't wrong," Stella said to her friend Evie, dropping the Aldi bags on the deck and rubbing her hands. "Even with the sun out, it *is* bloody freezing."

"Yeah, the river does get a bit chilly. Especially at this time of year. Never mind, it's nice and warm down below. Did you get any cheese?"

"Yes, several kinds. Mission critical, in my opinion."

"Fantastic. More importantly, did you get cat food? Or our names will be mud."

"First thing on my list."

Some time before, Stella and Evie, who had shared an adventure earlier in the winter, had gone out for a drink to catch up, and Stella had mentioned that Ward was moving in with her sister Serena.

"It's a good thing, I think. Be nice for both of them. And Serena's daughter Bella likes him – which is just as well."

"Girls can make a stepdad's life hell."

"Precisely. She says he's 'relevant'. Whatever that means. Sadly, it appears that I no longer speak fluent teenage girl."

"I certainly don't. Mind you, I don't speak famous actor either. You get on with him too, yeah?"

"Yes, very well. Although I'm thinking that in the moving-in slash honeymoon period, I might pop back to Somerset for a bit. So as not to get in the way."

"There's a spare berth on the *Nitrogen*," said Evie, "if you'd prefer to stay in town. I don't mind smoking as long as you go up on deck and I charge minimal rent. It's not everyone's cuppa, living on a barge. And as long as *you're* all right with Rumpole."

"I love cats."

"Then we're good!"

"Seriously?"

"Why not? To be quite honest, Stella, it's a bit tricky expecting a – well, don't take this the wrong way – a *normal* person to put up with some of the stuff that people like you and I have to put up with."

Stella just nodded. "Know what you're saying."

So she had taken a three month lease on a berth in the old barge, now moored along the Thames. Not too far from Greenwich, on the opposite shore. It would be an adventure in itself, Stella thought.

And indeed, it had been. Sometimes a chilly, damp, frankly alarming adventure (Stella now knew quite a lot about bilges), and occasionally a genuine one. She sometimes woke to hear voices crying out at night, far across the river, perhaps from long ago. Evie said that this was not uncommon, and Stella had experience of the river's ways of warning. But no more black-sailed ships had swept down the Thames out of nowhere: the threat of the winter had, it seemed, passed, at least for now. She had heard no more air raid sirens, seen no search lights.

Stella stored the shopping, then went back on deck to find a magpie perching on the rail. It bounced, see-sawing to and fro, and with a flash of light a girl was there. She was dark skinned, pale haired. She wore a hoodie and ripped jeans.

"Mags! Haven't seen you for a while."

"Weather's been shite. I haven't been out much," the angel said. "I didn't know you were living here until Ace said."

"It's my friend Evie's boat."

The angel nodded. "I know. Must be a bit parky, though, living on the water."

"Somewhat. Well, spring's on the way now." It was late, in the city, but Stella had seen daffodils only that morning, lining the edges of Green Park, and the sun was still shining despite the cold.

"I don't have a message, or anything. I just thought I'd pop by and say hello."

Stella nodded. "I saw Ace last week, went for a drink. He says it's all been quiet on the Western front."

The angel grinned. "Yeah, I'd say so. I think the city's a bit stunned after Twelfth Night. Everyone's considering their game plan."

"Have you seen Bill?" Mags worked for the man named Bill, resident in an old house in Lambeth, a man who had once been called William Blake – mystic, artist, visionary – who, remarkably, was still here, looking after the city.

"Not for a while. I like to keep an eye on the old boy, though. Well, I say 'old boy', but I don't think of him like that." Mags turned to gaze out towards Canary Wharf, suddenly misty eyed. "I knew him when he was a little lad."

"Really?" Stella said, intrigued. "Mags, are you immortal, then, or what?"

"No, I was born, or hatched, whatever, and eventually I'll die. Or ascend. Something like that. But I've been around this city for a long long time. I remember it as a handful of huts."

"Bloody hell, Mags. That's what, a couple of thousand years?"

"Then the Romans came from over the sea, and ooh, it was a lovely city then. Great big buildings. Baths and temples and that. Never looked back. Well, there was Boudicca, I suppose. But this city's used to fire and flame."

"You must remember the Great Fire, then."

"And the Plague. That was a shocker. But you know me – I keep myself to myself. Not a lot of people can see me and I prefer it that way."

"My sister's boyfriend Ned remembers Queen Elizabeth," Stella said. "The first one."

"Really? I remember *her*, all right. What is he – a spirit?"

"He's a ghost," said Stella, thinking of Ned Dark, that pearl-earringed nearly-pirate. "He sailed with Drake."

"Oh, did he, now? Drake was a bit of an arse, in my opinion."

"We met," Stella said. "But it wasn't really the time to start questioning him on his dodgy colonial habits." *Wrong but romantic,* she thought, but it was unlikely that Mags had read *1066 And All That.*

"That's the trouble, isn't it? You think of all these things you'd like to say to these historical types if you met them and then you do and it's always more complicated than you think."

"We were on his boat at the time. I didn't fancy getting chucked in the drink."

Mags gave a cackle of laughter, a magpie's raucous cry. "You never know. Might have been the making of you."

"You know, Mags, talking about history, I ought to know more about it. Of this city, for starters. The more that happens, the more I realise how little I *do* know. And since Serena and I seem to be visiting history on a semi-regular basis, I really feel I should do a bit of research."

"What you need," said Mags, "is the *Book of London*."

"Is that a history of the city, then?"

"Sort of. Try the British Library. Although, come to think of it, they may not have it."

"I thought they had everything? Or is that the Bodleian?"

"The Bodleian might have it. Or you could try one of the bookshops."

"Waterstones?"

"No, I was thinking more of the occulty type ones. Ask Ace. He'll know. Well, nice to see you, Stella. I'll keep in touch."

"You too, Mags." She watched as the monochrome arrow shot down the river, skimming low over the choppy water, and then she went thoughtfully back below deck.

Book of London, eh? Surely it would be easier to order it from Amazon. Stella sat down to consult her phone, but she drew a blank. There was *London: the biography*, the *Pop-Up Book of London*, *The Time-Traveller's Guide to London* (Stella ordered this one on Kindle as it sounded particularly relevant) but not the *Book of London* itself. Cursing herself for an idiot in not asking Mags who the author was, Stella phoned the Southwark Tavern, but Ace was not there.

If your mentor is absent, Google will have to do. Stella put *occult bookshops London* into the search engine and came up with two candidates at the top of the list: Atlantis and Treadwells. Both seemed promising. Atlantis was older – it had been in the city for nearly a century. Treadwells was newer, but bigger. Both sold second hand books, which she was beginning to think that the *Book of London* might be, and both were in Bloomsbury. Stella found 5p in her pocket and tossed it: heads, Treadwells, tails, Atlantis. It came up heads so she rang Treadwells first.

"Good morning, Treadwells Bookshop," said a pleasant American female voice.

"Good morning. I'm obviously in search of a book and I wonder if you can help me? I've looked online but I can't track it down. It's called the *Book of London.*"

There was a very slight pause on the other end of the phone.

"Can I ask where you came across the title?"

"Yes, a friend mentioned it to me. Said I ought to take a look at it."

"Okay. Well, we sometimes do have a copy. I'm not able to look for it now – I'm so sorry. Why don't you pop in this afternoon? I'll have tracked it down by then."

"Sure," Stella said. "I can do that. Or I could phone you?"

"No, do come in. We've got so much stock and I can tell you a bit about the book."

"Sure," said Stella again. Why not? A trip to Bloomsbury would be nice, on such a sunny, if chilly, day.

BEE

Spring was on the wind, Bee thought, though the night was winter, still. She had let the dogs out into the orchard and, as if magnet-drawn, had followed them through the French windows into the dusk. There had not been a frost for some time now, after a sharp, chill spell in early February, and the month seemed to be ending in its usual green-grey dampness: some rain, but no more floods; some sun, but a thin and watery version with no heat in it. February fill-dyke, living up to its name. But this evening felt softer, somehow, the light lasting a little longer, and Bee stood, listening, as the spaniels snuffled about the roots of the bare apple trees.

Then, all of a sudden, Dark was at her shoulder.

"Hello!" Bee said, smiling. She reached out and took his hand: it felt firm and warm in her chilly fingers, not like a ghost's hand should be at all, not like smoke or a breath on the breeze.

"Good evening, madam. Have you seen who is walking in your orchard?"

"My dogs?"

Dark laughed. The pearl that hung from one earlobe glimmered above the ivory of his small ruff; he wore his usual clothes, smart Elizabethan attire, though Bee sometimes wondered whether her sailor lover had actually worn this in life, or if he had chosen the black suit of a gentleman once disembodied. She kept meaning to ask.

"Not your dogs. They do not seem to have noticed. But I have noticed. Come and see."

Bee, hand in hand, followed him among the trees. At the far end of the orchard she could see pale shapes and as they drew closer, Dark moving a little cautiously and stealthily, Bee following his lead, she saw that they were stars. A triplicity, three of the star spirits that haunted Mooncote.

"Closer," she whispered to Dark. Letting go of his hand, she crept forwards.

The stars stood facing one another, in conversation, but although Bee could hear their sweet, whispering voices, she could not hear the words and she doubted that she would have been able to understand them. She could see them clearly enough through the branches, however: even in the misty, cold dusk they seemed to cast their own light. Each had the attributes with which they were associated: one had a string of jasper beads in her hair and carried a sprig of plantain; emeralds glinted green fire around the throat of a second, who held a frond of sage, and a third contemplated a small grey ball of granite, balanced in her palm, with a leaf of mugwort tucked behind one ear. Bee knew them all: Arcturus, Spica and Regulus.

Thanks to the instruction of her astronomer grandfather, she also recognised them for their place in the sky: they were the stars of the Spring Triangle, linking the constellations of Boötes, Leo and Virgo. She also knew, due to that same teaching and her own familiarity with the heavens, that the Spring Triangle should be visible overhead now: she looked up, and saw Spica, the blue gas giant, sparkling through the branches of the apple trees as though it might cast its distant light upon its personification below.

"What are they doing?" she murmured to Dark.

"I don't know."

The three stars had linked hands. Whispering, they began to walk, clockwise, but their forms had started to shimmer. Glowing yellow and icy blue, they became indistinct. Someone else stood in the circle of their hands. Bee saw a calm, grave face, golden-red hair swept up into a coronet of curls, a green gown. Roses crowned her brow. Bee had glimpsed her before, walking in the orchard with her upheld skirt full of apples. She was holding something in her outstretched palm: a sprig of apple blossom. She stepped forwards, the stars, now clear once more, fell in behind her. They walked in stately procession along the hedge.

Then all of them were gone, quite suddenly. Bee and Dark stood alone in the orchard, but where the stars and the woman had trod were three faint shapes in the grass, glowing with a little light of their own. Bee ran forwards to see. A snowdrop, poking its spearhead through the dead leaves, and two aconites like small golden cups. Bee and Dark stood contemplating them for a few minutes, before the growing damp caused Bee to give a sudden shiver. She took her lover's hand once more, called to the dogs, and went inside.

After the events of Christmas and Twelfth Night, Luna and Bee had been content to hibernate, not venturing far from the house, with Luna concentrating on her pregnancy and Bee focusing her own energies on renovating the outbuildings. She and Luna's partner Sam had decided to install a cider press, a proper big one, and clearing out the outbuildings and knocking down a wall between them had used up a lot of Sam's time, along with his actual job. For Sam had new employment now. Richard, at neighbouring Amberley, had taken him on to help with the horses after a stablehand had broken his leg.

"It was Cloudy, I'm afraid," Richard and Caro's daughter Laura told Bee. "She kicked him. I think he did something she didn't approve of, the baggage. She's never liked him."

"Oh dear," Bee said. "You never know quite what horses are going to react to. And he should have known better than to get behind her, I must say."

"Especially thoroughbreds." Laura rolled her eyes. "They're all drama queens. But he says he's not coming back, anyway. He seemed to take it a bit personally. He's going home to Ireland so Richard needs someone else to help out. We're placing Cloud Chaser at Cheltenham, Bee, in one of the amateur hunter chases."

"Really? What, at the Festival? I might even see her run. Your parents have invited me up to the races, on Ladies' Day."

"Yes, that's right, and that's when she's due to run so you will have a chance to see her in action." Laura pushed her pale blonde hair from her eyes. "She's an older horse but Dad thinks she's good enough and so do I. She did so well at Wincanton… Dad wants Jason Prior on board. As long as she doesn't kick him, too. She's fine with Sam but he's obviously not a jockey."

"Oh dear," Bee said again. "Well, Sam's always seemed very good with animals to me."

"Sam is excellent with horses. He's got a way with him they really like. Dad's delighted with him so far. Even Cloudy likes him. And we need more people on the premises. Did Dad tell you there was someone prowling round Amberley the other night?"

"I haven't seen him since last week and I haven't spoken to your mother, either. We've been so busy clearing out the barn… But that's not good, Laura. Do you know who it was? Not to do with the stablehand, was it? Someone bearing a grudge?"

"I don't know. They bolted, apparently, by the time Dad got downstairs. I don't want to worry you but I thought I'd mention it. I spoke to Sam and said to keep an eye on his piebalds. Just in case. There was that spate of injuries to horses a couple of years ago and they never found out who did it."

"Yes, I remember that. Awful. I don't know what's wrong with some people, I really don't. I'll keep an eye open, Laura, and thanks for the heads up."

Bee hoped this new employment would induce Sam and Luna to stay at Mooncote a little longer. She preferred to have Luna here, under her watchful eye, at least until the baby was born. It was due later in the year and Luna had already been through quite enough: it was a miracle, in Bee's private opinion, that she hadn't already miscarried.

And now she and Luna were heading over to Amberley, to meet up with Sam and get a lift into Wells, so that Bee could do some banking and collect her boots from the mender.

"Such a nuisance, only having one vehicle," she said to her sister.

"Oh well," Luna answered. "At least they're getting fixed."

The Land Rover had failed its MOT, to no one's surprise, the garage was waiting for a part, and Bee's little car was also in the shop, having its exhaust mended; hence their sudden reliance on Sam and Luna's horse drawn van. But it was not a long walk to Amberley and Bee was grateful for the exercise.

As they passed the churchyard, Luna exclaimed, "Look! Aren't those primroses?"

"Just a few. They're early."

"Serena's seen some in London, in one of the parks. I spoke to her on the phone last night."

"Is she all right?"

"Yes, fine, except Ward's had some not so good news. The theatre where they're putting on *A Midsummer Night's Dream* had a fire."

"Oh no! Bad?"

"The roof's going to need to be replaced but no one was hurt. Poor old Pelican! It's a lovely old building – Serena and I went to see *Measure for Measure* there once. Anyway, the director's determined to treat it as an opportunity and Ward's play is now due to open in June instead."

"That's good, but a shame he's had to postpone. Does he have anything else lined up?"

"Yes, Serena says it was a blessing in disguise – someone really wanted him for a film, and scheduling was proving tricky, but now he's free so he's doing the film."

"In Hollywood?"

"No." Bee laughed. "Brighton, actually. Bit less glamorous. He started shooting this week and Serena went down to the South Coast with him. Says Brighton in February's better than no seaside at all."

"I like Brighton."

"So do I. It's like a raffish old actress. Gone to seed but keeps staging a comeback."

They had passed the church by now and were on the lane that led to Amberley. Bee could see the house, gathered into the hillside. A band of blue-green sky, very pale, hung above it like a banner and up on the hill a white horse ran: Laura must be exercising Cloud Chaser.

"Almost heraldic," Bee said aloud. But Luna was not listening. She paused, her face uncertain.

"What's that?"

Bee was about to reply, "A bird," but she knew it wasn't. The tune threaded through the air, very soft at first, but growing louder.

She did not recognise the melody. It was reedy and thin, and the tune sounded old. Medieval, perhaps? The world seemed to stop around them, the day darkening. Bee reached for Luna's hand and gripped it, fearing separation. But then the tune faded, until it was so faint that Bee was unsure if she might be imagining it.

Then it was gone.

Luna looked at her. "That was a flute."

Bee nodded. She knew what Luna was thinking: a bone flute, a family heirloom, which her mother Alys had gone beyond the world to save. Alys had become trapped in that place beyond a place, and freed with great difficulty, but she had said little regarding the recent whereabouts of the flute and they could not ask her, for Alys was off roaming once more. Not lost, for she had made visits back home, but she was not here now.

"This is the second odd thing since Twelfth Night," Bee said.

"Yes. The nights have been quiet. I keep dreaming about Arcturus. She's always sitting by the side of the bed, with a cat's cradle in her hands. I think I've woken up but I haven't. But that might just be a dream."

Bee smiled. "She's watching over you, Luna. You were always her favourite." This was said without envy, for the star spirits had each adopted a daughter of the house: Algol, the baleful named, bearing diamond and hellebore, watched over Bee herself.

"I hope so," said Luna. "I think we need all the help we can get."

They were at the gates of Amberley now, with a prancing horse carved in stone high on each post before the long drive. And there was Sam with the van and the piebalds in its shafts, ready to collect them. They went to meet him.

Serena

Serena walked the length of the pier, trying not to think about what would happen if it suddenly returned to its dilapidated state in her own time. She did not fancy falling through the metal struts into the water below. But she also wanted to explore: to see the old pier as it had looked in its Victorian heyday. There were not many people about, but those that were looked satisfyingly Dickensian; men in top hats, women in bustles. And then, to her surprise and horror, Serena saw someone she knew.

The woman was standing with her back to Serena, at the entrance to a glassed-in tea room that occupied the central portion of the pier. Fronds of aspidistra framed her figure, which was clad in white and grey. She was the woman Serena had seen looking over the side of the pier and as she turned, Serena saw her face for the first time. Ward's ex-girlfriend, the mad and unpleasant Miranda Dean, whom Serena had last seen in very peculiar circumstances, was now here, in the past, on the pier.

Serena ducked behind a piece of ornamental ironwork before Miranda spotted her. But Miranda's attention was focused on the man at her side, whose arm she now took. Serena saw a crescent of red hair, a pale pure ginger, between top hat and high collar. As he turned towards his companion she glimpsed a long jawed profile. He was smiling; she could see the glint of teeth. Miranda gave a delighted, affected laugh, almost a squeal, and gripped his arm more tightly. Then they moved on, down the pier.

Serena remained where she was.

The last time she had encountered Miranda had been back in the winter. The actress had been a spectator in an audience of people who were both unusual and cruel, at a show organised by a man who had tried, essentially, to murder Serena herself. Serena thought, then and now, that Miranda would have been pleased if he had succeeded. It seemed that the hooks she had placed into Ward were now gone, but Serena could not be sure: she disliked and distrusted the actress. Who was, infuriatingly, an outstanding presence on screen. Serena had seen films in which Miranda had played the heroine, and despite herself had rooted for Miranda's character all the way.

"That's because you're innately fair minded," Ward had said, when Serena pointed this out.

"Unfortunately it's actually because she's very good."

For a moment, Serena wondered if this was just a movie and she had somehow wandered onto another set. Then she told herself not to be stupid. No one on *A Colder Day* had mentioned another shoot in town and actors were the worst gossips. Ward would surely have mentioned it if he had known Miranda was around. And anyway, what movie company would build an entire pier? And could have replaced the old one in the blink of an eye? She took a breath and made her way down the walkway. Miranda and her companion were no longer in sight, but apparently Serena had come equipped with a shawl. She pulled it up to cover as much of her face as she could, just in case. At the end of the pier was another long building, beneath a dome. There were dancers within, circling demurely to the strains of a string quartet. Serena looked back and found that the seafront was only dimly visible, as a series of lights in the fog. She was almost at the limits of the pier, now; it was time to go back.

For a moment she thought again about time changing, spinning forwards to send her plunging down through the empty struts to the salt water below. She swallowed hard. A great wave crashed against the end of the pier, sending cold water spattering against Serena's face. She walked back, past the circling dancers and the tea room. There was a flicker of white and Miranda was once again ahead of her, coming out of the tea room. Serena dodged behind a small pagoda-like hut.

"Do you know, darling," Miranda said to her companion, loudly and clearly, "it's almost as though I'm being watched. Silly, I'm sure." She began to walk towards the hut, swinging her parasol. Serena glanced behind her. There was the railing, and then the sea.

"I must be fancying things," Miranda said, sing song, still walking, still swinging the sharp-tipped parasol.

A door in the side of the hut sprang open. Serena's arm was seized by a small strong hand and she was pulled inside.

STELLA

It never failed to intrigue Stella how different the London districts were. Here in Bloomsbury, even this more modern bit of it, she had a sense of order and class, with a slightly rakish Bohemian air. It might have been the solid regularity of the Georgian fronts, each with a plane tree outside, now just on the point of bursting into new leaf so that their ugly bone-like trunks would become arbours of green shade. Or perhaps it was the presence of the British Museum, whose impressive Classical façade was not far away. Stella felt that Bloomsbury provided a much-needed refinement to the city.

Store Street. She checked her phone: yes, this was the right address. She set off down the street, passing a Thai restaurant, a Greek café and several pubs. And there was the bookshop, on the right hand side, with a telltale rack of second hand books outside. Stella stepped through the door and found herself in an immediate hush of old books and antique carpets and a light, sweet drift of incense. Classical music was playing.

The shop was empty except for a woman in black linen with brown bobbed hair, sitting behind the counter and busy on a laptop. She looked up as Stella came in.

"Hi! Can I help?" An American accent.

"I hope so – I rang the shop this morning. My name's Stella. About the *Book of London?"*

"Oh, yes, hi! Great that you made it," the woman said earnestly. "I'm Christina."

She had a penetrating look, not unnerving but definitely appraising.

"Did you manage to find it?"

"Okay, so, this is going to seem a bit weird."

"I'm used to weird?"

"*How* 'used to weird' are you?"

My sister can turn into a hare?

Her ex-boyfriend was abducted by sort-of fairies and nearly slain by a minotaur?

Trees sometimes speak to me?

My best friend's been dead since 1956 and lives with a goddess?

"I would say I'm, yeah, pretty used to it," said Stella.

"Come and have a look at this shelf here, would you?"

Stella followed her and watched as Christina unlocked a glass case. The books in here were old, with gold tooled leather spines; some of them, in fact, looked very old indeed.

"These look valuable," Stella said.

"Most of them, yes. A couple are seventeenth century, most are eighteenth."

"And is the book in here?"

"Just take a look. At anything you want."

Oh well, Stella thought. If Christina was happy to have Stella's hopefully not too grubby mitts all over her stock, then she was always pleased to rummage through some old tomes…

Carefully, she lifted a couple of books out to see the spines more easily. Both titles were in Latin, in which Stella was not fluent: she had taken the option of Spanish at school. She replaced them, and then found that her hand was hovering over a volume.

Book of London, it said. Bingo! There was no author's name on the spine: it was a square, black-bound book with the lettering stamped in gold, a handsome, if worn, thing. Stella looked up. Christina was in conversation at the end of the bookshop with a tall man, presumably friend or customer. And Christina had invited Stella to peruse the shelves, so… Opposite the bookshelf was a chaise longue, upholstered in dark green velvet, with some cushions on which a small hairy dog was ensconced.

"Scuse me," said Stella to the dog. It wagged its stump of a tail so she took this as invitation and sat down with the book. She opened it cautiously: that spine looked a little infirm. Inside was a set of marbled endpapers in crimson and indigo, reminiscent of stormclouds, and then on the next fragile page the title but no date. There was no note, either, as to which edition this was, but conscious that the thing at least looked over two hundred years old, Stella tried to handle it delicately.

She thought it began with the founding of the city by the Romans: it was strangely gripping, though not written in a modern style, and it swept Stella along like the river itself, a confusing medley of places, dates and battles. People swam up from its pages: she looked into a warrior's eyes as the woman twitched aside her skirt and a hare ran free across a ploughed field. Henry VIII's fleshy, disapproving countenance loomed at her for a moment, ruddy with heat or anger, and she saw Elizabeth's icy crescent moon of a face, her hair flaming, her jewels sparkling. Then another face, also surrounded by firebright hair, with grass-green eyes that looked straight through Stella. She nearly snapped the book shut, startled, but then the woman's hair turned to actual flames; she saw a tall spire, smoke and fire billowing around it, so vivid that she could smell the acrid stench of burning. Stella sat up, the spire crashed down, she saw molten lead pouring out of the gutters and the smoke formed a dome, grey and pearly, rising out of the devastation below. The golden cross at its summit winked at her and it was gone, but Stella recognised the dome: any Londoner would. St Paul's Cathedral.

"The spire belonged to the old cathedral," Christina said, over coffee in the café next door. Stella had felt in need of caffeine after all that. And cake. "It was struck by lightning, they never restored it. Then later on Wren submitted his plans for the new church with the dome and about a week after *that* the Great Fire of London happened."

"So it wasn't too awful that the cathedral burned down?" Stella said. "If it had already been damaged and they were going to rebuild it anyway?"

"Well, I expect it was pretty horrible, but at least they had a plan for what was to come next."

"That book, though," Stella said. "It was so vivid. As though I was there."

"And did you look at the pages after that?"

"Yeah, I tried, but there didn't seem to be any. Or they were blank. I can't quite remember. There must have been pages, though

– it was quite a fat book." She didn't even recall rising from the couch and placing it back on the shelf, but she must have done so.

"The book shows you what you need to see."

"I could go back and have a look, if it's all right with you?"

"Okay, so," Christina said. "The thing is, the book probably won't be there. I wasn't even sure if it was going to show up this morning."

Stella gaped at her.

"But it's your book. In your bookshop."

"It *is* my bookshop," the American said, apologetically, "but the book isn't always there. And it's not really my book. It comes and goes."

"Where does it go when it's not in your shop, then?"

"We're not quite sure about that. Although my friend James – the guy I was talking to in the shop? – once found it in Gladstone's in Wales, so maybe it does the rounds."

"So is there like a timescale of when it shows up?"

"No, that's the thing. Occasionally someone will come in and ask if they can look at those shelves and I know they're looking for it, but they go away disappointed. And once it actually popped up in the middle of the cookery section and scared the hell out of this young woman who started looking at it – but it obviously had something to say to her, or it wouldn't have manifested. Anyway, I'm really pleased it showed up for you."

"Yes," said Stella, rather flatly. The memory of the smoke and flames was still very vivid. She'd had no idea that research could be so exciting.

"So you know what you have to do now, right?"

Stella nodded. "Go to St Paul's."

LUNA

It was amazing what accumulated in houses, Luna thought. This was one of the reasons she liked living in a van: you had to give real thought to what you bought and what you used, and why. She liked the occasional sparkly thing, but she and Sam didn't have much and she preferred to keep it that way. Living light. At least until the baby arrived and then, presumably, she would need some stuff. She planned to ask Serena and Ver, Sam's nan, about all that, and her own mother, if Alys showed up in time. She did not intend to have that American import, a baby shower. Women had managed perfectly well in the Middle Ages, Luna told herself, sternly.

Mind you, in the Middle Ages the infant mortality rate hadn't been all that special.

With a small sigh of effort, Luna put a hand on the hay manger and hauled herself to her feet. She had offered to help with clearing the barn for the cider press; they had reached the back of it now and Luna felt a definite sense of achievement.

Most of this stuff could go to the tip. She picked up a crate and lugged it to the entrance of the barn. The sky seemed to be a little lighter, this late in the day, and Luna's spirits rose. She could smell fresh grass. Sam had mowed the lawn that morning, for the first time this year.

"What's that?" Bee said.

"Crap."

Bee looked into the box, sifting briefly through old wooden slats, a broken toy, the torso of a plastic duck.

"God, it really is a load of old toot, isn't it? What that mate of Sam's calls Somerset Heritage Information Trust material. Onto the bonfire, then. How much more is there?"

"Not a lot but some of it won't burn – it'll need to go to the tip. But didn't Grandfather chuck *anything* out?"

"Apparently not. I wish Mum was here. She might know what's in those boxes without us having to trawl through them. I am definitely in need of a bath." She eyed Luna. "And so are you, young lady."

"I feel filthy," Luna said. "But there really isn't much more. Some boxes with bricks in – I don't know what they were for. And there's an old suitcase which I can't open."

"Intriguing!"

"I thought so. Want to look?"

"It's quite heavy." Back in the barn, Bee lifted the suitcase and gave it a little shake. "The lock has rusted shut."

"It's all battered. You'd have a job closing it again even if you did get it open."

"What you're saying is: we should just bust the lock."

"Yes."

Bee found a hammer and chisel and after some effort, sprang the lock. The lid of the case came free and Bee jerked her hand back, flipping the lid up.

"It moved!"

Luna grabbed her sister and pulled her back. They both stared, warily.

"It's not moving now," Luna said.

"No, maybe I imagined it."

It was a strip of soft, pale brown fur, backed with what looked like suede. There was a tag attached: *property of Stella Fallow.*

"No way is this Stella's," Luna said, puzzled. "It's one of those things you put round your neck, isn't it?"

"Yes, in like the nineteen thirties. I agree, I don't think this can be Stella's – she's been a vegetarian for years. And it's not her writing. More like Serena's sort of thing. But it says 'property of'. Maybe Grandma left it for her? I wonder why, though. At least it doesn't have bloody moth. It looks as good as new."

Moths had been the bane of Bee's life recently: the house was now endowed with pheromone traps and Luna knew she had involuntarily sacrificed an old and beloved woollen shawl.

"We could wrap it up and post it to her, just in case. What about the suitcase? I'd say that was pretty much buggered."

"Yes. Buggered is right. Onto the bonfire with it."

SERENA

"So what happened then?" Ward asked, wide eyed. They were sitting in the back bar of the Black Lion, a pub which erred on the side of lots of gilt and red velvet. Serena had secured a table in a booth and was reasonably certain of not being overheard.

"Inside the hut," Serena paused for effect and took a sip of her Sauvignon Blanc. Now that her adventure was over, she found that she could enjoy it. "*In* the hut, was a woman who reminded me a bit of Vervain March – you know, Luna's Sam's nan – but younger. And there was a pack of cards on a table. But she was not dressed like a Romany tarot reader."

She had, in fact, been dressed as though she had just come from a funeral: all in black except for a purple underskirt. Mourning garb, including the fringes of jet beads. Her hair was black and parted: she was a little like the sour faced woman in the American Gothic painting. But although her expression was chilly and her dress severe, Serena had not been afraid.

"Don't worry," the stranger told Serena. "No one can get into this hut. Unless I want them to." She folded her hands primly at her waist. "My name is Edith Fane." She gave a small formal bow. "Miss."

"I am Serena Fallow. Er, also Miss."

"Please sit down, Miss Fallow. We shall have some tea and I shall, if you wish, read your cards."

"I can't pay you," was the first thing that came to Serena's mind. "I only had a penny for the entrance."

Edith Fane shot her a sharp, dark glance. "And was that the money of your own day, or of now?"

"Oh! My own."

"Yes. You are loose."

Serena thought for a moment that this was some stern moral judgment, but then Miss Fane said, "I mean, in time. Don't ask me how I know; I've always been able to tell. The day falls oddly upon you. And this is a particularly loose day. Time has tides, you know, and some curious things have washed up on time's shores today. For all manner of whens."

"Oh dear!" Serena said. She sat, as instructed, and was handed tea, in a porcelain cup so delicate that the lamplight shone through it.

"What year is this, please, Miss Fane?"

"We are in the year of our Lord 1893. On Brighton pier."

"I know where I am, but not when. I come from over a hundred years in the future."

"Oh, how interesting! I would love to know more but I know from experience that although you may tell me, I should not remember it. So annoying."

"That's really infuriating," Serena agreed.

"It is the way these things work." Miss Fane sighed. "Never mind. You will be here for a reason." She picked up the deck and began to shuffle.

"That woman," Serena said, "The one who was following me. Do you know her?"

"Miss Dean? Indeed I do." Edith Fane's thin lips pursed with disapproval. "Miss Dean and I do not care for one another."

"I do not care for her either," Serena said. "Nor she for me."

"I am glad to hear it. That is why I rescued you. Although she is a bad enemy, but fortunately one with the mind of a moth."

"I gathered that from my – from a mutual friend."

"She finds it easy to hate but fortunately difficult to sustain the efforts that hate requires. Now. Would you like to pick a card?"

"So she did your Tarot?" Ward said.

"Well." Serena took another sip of her wine. "Not exactly."

Her memories of the reading itself were a little hazy. She had an impression of Edith Fane's dark eyes, boring into her own, as she placed the cards deliberately onto the little table, one by one.

"That's the Nine of Sorrows, but that's in the past. All gone now." Miss Fane held up a card: six old women in black cloaks. Above their heads soared great dark wings. "Oh, this is one of the

Major Arcana. The Searchers – you must be very careful of them, Serena."

"The Searchers? What are they?" But Miss Fane was moving swiftly on.

"Ah!" The next card was a woman in a flowery dress, rather like the Primavera, Serena thought. A little whippet danced behind her, in a field of white jonquils. "The White Track. She might help you but she is reversed – you must be careful of her. Or perhaps not you yourself – do you see where she sits, in opposition to the Queen of Suns?" Serena looked. A woman sat in a meadow, next to a beehive, and there was a wren there, too, perched pertly on the hive itself.

The White Horse. The Page of Flames – a young man with red hair and a face like a fox. The Huntsman, the Hound. The images on the cards danced by, leaving dream-like images in Serena's artist's mind. The Map – Serena exclaimed. For a second she saw the young airman again, with an OS map outspread before him.

Then the final card, the Huntress, was placed on the table. Serena looked: an antlered woman, carrying a bow, with a brace of dogs at her heels. Miss Fane gave an exclamation. A gust of the sea wind rattled the pane and swept over the sill, scattering the cards, whirling them up. The little room began to shatter around them, falling into jigsaw fragments. Serena heard Miss Fane cry out. She snatched at the cards but the whole pack was now in the air and Serena flew up with them. She looked into the silvergreen eyes of the girl in the flowery dress, the OS map stretched below her, and then she was sitting down, hard, on the shingle. The ruined pier stretched before her; the lights of the seaside city behind. Further down the shore, to her relief and bewilderment, the body was still not there.

"And that was that," Serena said. "I got to my feet and came straight here."

"You're sure it was Miranda?"

"Quite sure."

"God," Ward said, looking pained. "I hadn't heard she was in town. Maybe she isn't. Not now, anyway."

"Ward, you told me back in the winter, after – well, after all that stuff – that when you were going out with Miranda, you didn't notice anything weird about her."

"Apart from the fact that she is basically barking mad and a bitch, no. She appeared perfectly human. The only thing –" he hesitated.

"Yes?"

"She had a rather odd friend with this sort of truncated name. You said she called her friend 'Hob?'"

"Yes, I think that was what she said."

"Well, that was what this friend of hers was called. Always made me think of an oven. I thought it must be short for something but I never found out what. Reminded me a bit of Tam Stare, come to think of it. Very good looking. Red hair. Rather camp, and quite flirty. Not unpleasant. Actually, he was nicer to me than Miranda was. But they were thick as thieves and he was always round her place in Fulham. She had a flat, on the top floor: nice place, but rather small – when she got her first Hollywood role she moved to that massive pad in Docklands. So I was round there one night, in Fulham, and Hob was there, and we had a few drinks, and I went out into the hall to get my phone out of my coat pocket, and when I went back, Hob *wasn't* there. The thing is, he didn't go out of the front door, because I was standing right next to it in the hall."

"The back door, then."

"Except there wasn't one."

"Maybe he went out of the window?"

"What, like forty foot up? And there wasn't a balcony, or a tree. I'd had a few, as mentioned, so I just shrugged it off. In the morning, I did ask, and Miranda said she didn't know what I was talking about. Then it sort of drained out of my memory. I've only just remembered it."

"Did you see Hob again after that?"

"Yes, several times, but as I said, I'd forgotten about it. Then Miranda and I split up and the last time I saw him, I ran into him in Waitrose and he blanked me. So I assumed he'd taken Miranda's side in the break up, which was reasonable even though she dumped me, since he was her friend, after all. I didn't take it personally."

"And he had red hair, you said?"

"Yes, he did. A very light red, proper ginger. And very pale grey eyes – unusual colouring, I thought at the time. Pale skin, too, and freckles. Not very tall – a little bloke. He used to wear hoodies and track pants, that sort of thing. Bit of a sneakerhead."

"He was in full on vintage tonight, if it was him. Very Victorian dapper."

"I didn't get a bad vibe from him or anything. Rather the opposite, in fact, although he could be a bit of a bitch. Presumably why he got on with Miranda."

"I hope I don't see her again." Serena's gaze wandered around the bar. "Oh! I forgot. I took photos of the – the drowned person." She took her phone from her bag and checked. But it did not surprise her to find that nothing was there. The last pictures on her phone were of the film shoot, that morning, and Ward on the balcony of the hotel.

"I hope neither of us see her again, either. Where would you like to go for dinner? I checked out some places earlier. There's a tapas place round the corner, or high-end vegetarian further down."

"Let's have another glass of wine." Serena, not a big drinker, felt she needed it. "And then we'll decide."

STELLA

St Paul's was more or less on the way home, so Stella did not think that it was too great a detour. The familiar dome rose above the streets as she drew close; once, she thought, this would have dominated the whole London skyline. Funny to think of it as a church with a spire: in the book, it had looked not dissimilar to Salisbury and most cathedrals stayed put once they were constructed, unchanging aspects of the country's cityscapes. Stella was not particularly religious, but the sight of that great spire thundering to earth, the lead streaming in rivulets from the roof, had shaken her. What must it have been like at the time, though? People must have considered it a sign of God's displeasure, that sudden strike from the actual heavens. She remembered seeing a famous photograph of the dome rising out of the smoke of the Blitz: that would have been terrifying, too, but at least this incarnation of the cathedral had survived.

She came to the bottom of Ludgate Hill. The cathedral was before her, and there was some sort of market going on. A book sale, Stella realised, as she passed a stall bearing a range of books that looked very like the ones in Treadwell's glass case. An antiquarian book sale, then. This was turning out to be a theme of the day. A small child ran out from behind the stall, and cannoned into Stella's legs.

"Oops!" she said. "Steady on!"

"God save you, mistress!" the child said. Suddenly Stella was surrounded by children: all little boys, wearing ruffs and smoking pipes.

"What the –?" Stella looked up. To the spire.

A man in a black cape and a soft cap herded the boys out of Stella's way, grimacing as he did so. She had the impression of harassed schoolmaster, rather than someone objecting to her unconventional appearance. She wondered what she looked like to him… From down here, the spire was even more imposing than it had appeared in her vision, but its surroundings were more than a little squalid. Stella trod in something squelchy and winced. The whole place stank: a medley of odours, only some of which were recognisable. Stella tried to work it out: the spire was there, so this must be before the lightning strike and also obviously before the Great Fire, from what Christina had told her. The clothes looked Elizabethan but Stella's sense of costume history was not great; she needed Serena. Little streets marched away from the cathedral close, filled with houses made of grey beams and creamy plaster, not like the sharp black and white buildings that she associated with the period. But they all had the diamond-leaded panes and stepped fronts, the upstairs rooms overhanging the streets, familiar from towns in her own day. There were enough of those buildings still standing in the twenty first century. Despite the filth underfoot she was tempted to explore, but told herself sternly to keep to the mission. The *Book of London* had indicated that she was to go to St Pauls, and to St Paul's she had come. She went up to the great double doors and stepped inside.

Columns marched down the nave like immense waxy trees and the dome was replaced by a ceiling starred with red and gold and blue. It reminded Stella of other Norman cathedrals and abbeys that she had visited: Gloucester, Worcester, Wells. The nave ended in a huge rose window.

Moreover, she was surrounded by people. A woman in long skirts carrying a covered basket knocked into Stella, gabbled an apology, moved quickly on. A group of men were arguing over a handful of coins. Stella caught snatches of conversation but it was a second or two before her ear attuned:

"He is nothing but a huddipick, a common promoter, and I shall not…"

"Caught the French marbles from her and who can be surprised…"

It looked more like a market place than a church. Then a shout went up:

"Look to your purses!"

Stella's hand automatically went to her backpack, but an older man passing down the nave said to her, "Mistress, do not show them where your coin might be! Perhaps you are a stranger and not familiar with these judicial nippers and public foisters! Such a hue and cry is to alert them to the presence of your purse, no more."

"Okay! Thank you!" said Stella. She walked down the nave: there were fewer people here. And it just went to show how little she knew about the history of clothes, Stella thought, because those people looked more Medieval, in their long gowns and weird hats – she looked back. The Elizabethans had disappeared. The cathedral seemed dimmer, different. Stella felt suddenly very exposed. She ducked behind a pillar but found that a woman was watching her from the shadows. She was tall, with elaborately curled hair, bare-armed and dressed in a green gown. She did not look Medieval at all. She nodded to Stella.

"Sit."

There were benches now. Stella did as she was told. The cathedral had gone; she was now within the confines of a temple, made of the same golden-grey stone. Spicy incense drifted through the air, reminding her of the bookshop. A procession was coming up the aisle, but instead of a crucifix the man at its head wore a long draped gown and carried a stag's skull mounted on a spear. Stella watched as they progressed towards an altar and faded out of sight. Someone was sitting beside her: a young woman, younger than Stella, with golden brown hair caught up at the back of her head and a green tunic. A bow rested by her side. Her brown legs were bare and she wore sandals of gilt leather.

"Hello," she said, smiling. "You're new, aren't you?"

"Yes," said Stella, feeling suddenly shy. "A book sent me."

"Ah!" She clapped her hands together. "I *told* it to go and find someone!"

"Is this *your* temple?" asked Stella. The young woman seemed friendly. When Stella looked at her, the word that came to mind was *merry;* an old fashioned thing to think. A pleasant adjective, but there was nonetheless something about her, a wildness, a strangeness that made Stella feel deeply and shakingly afraid.

"Now? Yes, it is. They took me with them when they came over the sea." She laughed. "A lot of them don't like it here. It's too wet and cold and they complain all the time."

"Yes, that's Britain for you. Who are you?"

"I am the Huntress," the young woman said. "I want you to do something for me. Will you?"

"Do I have a choice?"

"Oh yes. I am known as a stern spirit but that's not really true. I'm only stern towards men. When I came here first, I met someone of my own kind. She became my friend, and when my worship died in this city she took my place, with my blessing. My day here was done and she is older than I. She is there in your day, but she needs help. She's trapped, you see, in London."

"I can try to help," Stella said, "but I'm not like a, a superheroine or anything. Where is your friend trapped?"

"In the hunting chases."

"I don't think there are many of those in London, to be honest."

"But that is what she told me. And she and I have slept, but now we wake and she has sent a message. For the tide's on the turn."

"Which tide is that?" Stella thought vaguely of the tidal Thames but the woman said,

"A tide of time. This spring is growing changes."

She reached into the folds of her tunic and pulled out a coin. "Take this. It is my token; if you carry it, you will be recognised as my messenger."

Stella took the coin and held it up: it was a gold coin, and it depicted a woman with a bow, with a dog at her heels. The other side, which should have shown a head, was blank.

"I'll – I'll do my best. But I don't really know where to start looking for her."

The Huntress sprang to her feet and held out her hand. "Now you have my token, *she* can find *you*. Here."

Stella took her hand and was pulled to her feet – but more, tugged through time, voices sounding out around her, snatches of conversation and light and darkness. The pressure of the Huntress' hand abruptly released and she fell back into a pew. The dome of St Paul's arched over her and a throng of tourists consulted their brochures as a guide said, "Of course, there was no church here in

Roman times, but there is a story that when Christopher Wren was investigating the foundations for the building you see here today, he discovered the remnants of a Temple to Diana. We have no way of knowing…"

LUNA

Luna and Sam could tell spring was coming. They didn't need to discuss it. There had been a big storm overnight, a huge Atlantic westerly sweeping in at dusk and scouring the sky so that the stars prickled icy above the black bank of cloud and a line of green light split the west, the last of the winter sun. The storm howled and raged over the chimneys of Mooncote, roaring like an express train over the flat lands of the Levels, thorn hedges and alder brakes hunkering down beneath its lash. In the morning, it had raced east to harrow the chalk downland and a timid dawn crept out, sky the colour of a robin's egg and everything dripping in a stealthy, furtive way. Bee had pulled on Wellington boots and made a quick circuit of the property as soon as it was light enough, taking the delighted dogs with her and returning to report that there were a few branches down beneath the chestnut trees and a loose tile in the middle of the yard, but otherwise no damage.

"We were lucky," she said to Dark, who had joined them in the kitchen. "None of the big trees are down." Luna knew, from a previous conversation, that Dark had spent the night in the house, along with the cats. Might a ghost blow away, she wondered silently, torn ragged on the storm? She thought it might be best to keep that thought to herself. She had been grateful to be in the house. Storms in the van were a little too exciting.

After breakfast Luna and Sam, without saying a word to one another, pulled on coats and boots and headed out, with the lurcher Moth prancing at their heels. They took hay to the horses, checked the gate, then walked up the rain-gleaming road in the opposite direction to the church. Today was Sunday, and once they reached the top of the slight rise where the road joined another, the church bells rang out, faint and sweet across the valley. They turned to look back, to where Mooncote sat amid its trees and Amberley perched on the hillside

"Have you seen Ben Amberley recently, Sam? Is he still at home?"

"Yes. He made me a cup of coffee yesterday morning. Seems more or less all right."

"Has he ever talked about it? The winter? His adventure?"

"No. I'm not sure how much he remembers, Luna. He's not like you and me, I think."

"Maybe. But there's something funny about that family."

Sam laughed. "That was said darkly, if ever I heard it. But you're right. Well, Ward's said as much."

"Mum and Bee tried to talk to Caro Amberley about it, but she sort of clams up, apparently."

"Can't handle it," Sam said. "Can't blame her, either."

The official story was that Ben had had a nervous breakdown following a bad bout of flu and walked out of his Camden flat, stayed with some friends in the north, and Caro'd had some kind of post viral illness.

"The Amberleys move in different circles to your lot," Sam said now. "Society, more like. And even if they didn't, it's a bit tricky to let on to people that your adult son was captured by some fairies and pitted against a minotaur, and you kept having visions of it and cracked up. I mean, it's not the sort of thing you can mention in the aisles of Waitrose."

"Or even Tesco."

"Yeah, no. Anyway, we haven't discussed it and they've got other things on their minds. Someone tried to break into the stableyard again last night."

"Really? No way, that's terrible. Are the horses okay?"

"Yes, but Richard's getting someone in tomorrow to talk about extra security. There wasn't anything on the CCTV and the alarm didn't go off."

"I suppose it was a *human* someone?"

"Well, this is it," Sam said. "I don't know and I can't raise the subject without sounding like a nutter. But I do know that Caro's friend Tessa, the one who rides out at Ditcheat, said they'd had someone snooping about the yard there as well."

Luna knew that Ditcheat, not far away, was home to a racehorse trainer, and a famous one. She disapproved of horse racing, but she loved seeing the string going out through the village, past the old pub, on their daily exercises.

"Those horses are worth a fortune. He's had Gold Cup and National winners," said Luna.

"I know Richard's been talking to Nick Wratchall-Haynes over at Wycholt as well. He's obviously an interested party since he's the Master of the local hunt – even if he hasn't been here that long, he knows everyone with horses round here so he was going to spread the word. It would be unusual for anyone to be after the animals themselves – it's generally horse transporters and equipment that gets pinched. But Richard's suss to all that – he uses padlocks instead of chains, that sort of thing, so they can't use bolt cutters to get in."

"Didn't a famous racehorse get stolen once? I seem to remember Mum and Grandpa having a conversation about it when I was a kid."

"Yes, Shergar. Richard mentioned it yesterday. They never found him."

"It must have been awful," Luna said, "for the people who loved him. I don't know if trainers really love their horses but I know the stable girls do."

"Yes, it's a real obsession for a lot of people. I can understand why. But you're right, there's a lot of money involved and they can't be too careful."

By now, they had come to the road. Sam helped Luna over a stile with a 'public footpath' sign on it, the wooden arrow pointing into a copse. This was a line of woodland that ran along a rise, not really a hill, and down the opposite slope: one of the little parcels of trees that made up the patchwork of the English landscape. Luna knew that most of these were oak and ash, with a scrub of holly and elder below. The autumn leaves were already scurfing into leafmould, the acorns ravaged by squirrels, but there were fat paws of buds on the oak twigs, black hooves upon the ash. Another few weeks and they would burst out into new leaf.

There was a path through the wood, maintained by whoever owned it, and probably kept fresh by badgers, judging from the musty smell. Beneath the gnarled oak roots of one tree was a large dark hole. Moth whined and pawed the earth.

"You're not having it,' Sam said to him. "You wouldn't like it if you met one."

"Has he ever met a badger?"

"I think he must have done but one of our old dogs, called Flea because he had 'em, had a massive fight with a badger outside my gran's van one night. Needed stitches."

"Flea or the badger?"

"The dog. Left off and hid under the van. Badger went off grumbling into the darkness."

"Oh dear."

"That's what Gran said, with a bit more force. He had the scar till the day he died; badgers have teeth that would put a Rottweiler to shame. So you, mate," – this to the dog "– can give it a rest."

Moth, obedient, came to Sam's side and they skirted the tree and the sett, heading deeper into the patch of woodland. Soon, Luna knew, the wood anemones would be poking their heads through the leafmould and then, a little later, the wood would stink with wild garlic and they could come up with a bag and pick its glossy spear-shaped leaves and white flowers for soup.

"Look!" she said, suddenly. "I was just thinking about wood anemones." In a small glade beneath the oaks she could see a few white shoots emerging. Sam frowned.

"Bit early. Must be this global warming."

"There were primroses out in the churchyard. And daffs on the Somerton road before Christmas."

"Those are from the Scillies, though, they're always early. What *are* those?"

With Moth, they went over to take a closer look.

"It's as though something heavy was sitting here," Luna said. "And then lifted up."

In Mooncote's garden someone had moved a small stone urn onto a patch of flowerbed and it had become overgrown. When the plants died back Bec had found it and, with Sam's help a few days previously, moved it. Beneath was a patch of narcissi, coming up but flattened by the urn and a livid, fleshy white in the absence of sunlight. They were gradually beginning to turn green but this handful of shoots, here in the heart of the wood, looked similar, though they were as straight as spears.

"What are they, though?" Sam repeated. The shoots were the thickness of Luna's thumb, stubby but rising to a sharp point.

'They're not toadstools, are they? Before the cap furls out?" Luna poked one experimentally, but it was firmly rooted in the earth and did not stir in response to her prodding finger.

"I don't think so. Oh well. We can look them up when we're back at the house. They might be something someone's planted deliberately."

They went on through the wood and came out onto the long downward slope that led to ploughed fields. A tractor was churning along, followed by a wheeling flock of gulls in from the Bristol Channel, refugees from last night's storm. High in the wood, their dark counterparts the rooks soared up in a sooty handful of confetti and subsided. Sam pointed to the arrowing russet bolt of a peregrine, skimming down the slope and away.

"Hunting."

"What was that?" Luna said. She thought she had heard a voice.

"I don't – oh, there he is."

Far down by the edge of the field stood a figure, waving furiously. He was shouting something, but he was too far away for Luna to hear the words. She waved back, rather impudently.

"He's probably telling us to get off his land," Sam said, philosophical.

"We're not on his land. Well, not on the field, anyway. I don't know who the wood belongs to – might be Nick Wratchall-Haynes, actually. Wycholt's not far away. But I've been coming up here since I was a kid and no one's ever told me to bugger off. Mind you, old Lady Pamela was a real recluse by that point and maybe she didn't care."

"He looks like a gamekeeper type."

Luna thought Sam was right. The figure blended into the greens and browns of the landscape and he was wearing a cap.

"He's not coming up here, anyway." She made a kind of pax gesture: hands up, palms outward, and they retreated further back into the wood. No point in being confrontational, Sam had said, a long while ago. Not when you don't have to.

"Good. That's the only trouble with the English countryside: it's owned by too many people, or too few." It was a conversation they'd had before.

"If we keep to the path, we'll hit the road further down. We can loop back to Mooncote that way, cut across the fields."

"All right." Sam spared her a look. "Are you feeling okay? Not too tired?"

"No, I'm good."

They skirted the edges of the wood, then down along the road. Over another stile, and they would be into the sodden fields that would lead them, eventually, to Mooncote itself. Luna checked for sheep, but they had all been moved inside, or to a drier pasture. She clipped Moth's lead on, all the same. Even the best dog could have a moment's lapse and Somerset girl that she was, she knew that many sheep deaths were the result of heart failure, ewes being prone to panic, rather than mauling. She kept Moth close.

"Where's the stile?" Sam said. "I thought it was here, past that road sign."

"Yes, it's here – oh."

It wasn't. The hedge arched above Luna's head, high and unbroken. It was a thick brake of thorn interspersed with withies of hazel and elder: there was a thin and lovely scattering of blackthorn flowers within it and the first tips of hawthorn buds. Soon, Luna thought, they would be bursting out into the bright green frilly leaves that were still known to some country people as 'bread and cheese'.

"Luna," Sam said. She turned at the warning in his voice. The road sign was no longer there. She spun clockwise and saw the green way reaching before them: a hollow way where the road had been, one of the old sunken lanes. High banks curved up from hoof-churned mud and Luna could see the snaking grey roots that made up the low barriers at the top of the bank: it looked like beech and that, too, was ready to burst into leaf. The ceiling of the cylinder that formed the hollow way was roofed in the spreading branches. It reminded her of some of the Devon lanes, plunging down from the high moor into the narrow valleys around Chagford and Moretonhampstead.

Moth whined and pulled a little at his lead.

"You want to go down it?" Sam asked Luna.

"Well, not much choice unless we turn back –" and she nearly suggested that they should, until she looked over her shoulder and saw that the hollow way stretched behind them, too. They were standing now in the middle of it.

"Okay," said Luna. She reached for Sam's hand and, balanced between him and Moth, felt a little bolder. At least she was not on her own: she had been so before, in this curious otherworld, and coped and triumphed, but now, with her baby well on the way, she could feel an uncertainty within, a quivering cravenness which Luna did not like. She took a breath and quelled it. "Let's go."

STELLA

Stella leaned against the wall and fumbled in her bag for a cigarette. The club was much too hot, a stifling crush, and whether it was living on the river or her age or what, Stella felt an increasing need for fresh air. Even if she was about to pollute it with cigarette smoke. She smoked with an eye on the clock: her second set was still to go. But then a spatter of rain decided the issue. She stubbed out her cigarette and put the butt into the ash canister at the entrance. It was as she was doing this that she became aware of an altercation.

"…not letting you in without a wristband, mate."

"I don't need one, right. I've already told you. I'm a friend of the DJ's…"

Oh really? thought Stella, grinning to herself. If she'd had a pound every time she'd heard *that* one… She went round the corner to the entrance of the Camden club to find Ferdie and Maz, the bouncers, arguing with a slight, wiry young man with spiky hair. Another youth hovered in the background, his face sullen.

"Ah! Stella, do you in fact know this bloke?"

"Sorry," Stella said. "Never seen him before in my life."

"Who are you?" the young man snapped.

"The DJ. You know, your 'mate'."

"Oh, look, fucking forget it, bruv." This was the second young man, who took his friend's arm and pulled. "Let's leave it."

"No, I'm not gonna just…"

He was pissed, Stella could see, from his wavering stance, but there was a febrile energy to him, a kind of greasy auric shimmer, which suggested harder substances.

"Lem, I said *leave* it." Eventually Youth Two dragged his friend away. He spat inaccurately at Stella's feet as he passed.

"Classy!" said Stella to the doormen. "Finishing school obviously failed."

"Yeah, he's well off his tits," Ferdie said in disgust. "Sorry about that. I can't stand liggers."

"Never mind. Goes with the territory." And she went back in to finish the set.

Ferdie and Maz saw her out of the club at the end of the night, and into a taxi, just in case.

"Anyway, you never know who might be bloody hanging about," Maz said.

"Appreciated, chaps. Thank you." It was still raining and Stella was grateful to be on her way home, but she had an errand to accomplish first. The club had paypalled her for the gig and Stella was out of cash: not a disaster these days, as most places took contactless, but she owed Evie some money for the communal housekeeping. At least she'd remembered before she got back. She peered out of the window. There was a church on one side of the road, but they were not far from the improbable turrets of St Pancras Station, so a cashpoint should not be too far away. Stella kept an eye out. They passed shop fronts behind steel shutters, a café, a patch of scrubby waste ground by a wall from which buddleia was sprouting. Then Stella spotted a bank. She leaned forwards to speak to the driver, who was large and impressively bearded, and wore a dark blue dastār.

"Could you drop me at that Lloyds, and wait? I just need to use the cashpoint."

"No worries," the driver said. He waited at the kerb while Stella nipped into the bank's sterile illuminated atrium and used the machine. Forty pounds richer, she went back out onto the pavement.

"Well, look who it is."

Stella had rolled her eyes before she'd turned around. Sure enough, there was Lem and his skanky friend.

"Little Miss Nose in the Air," Lem said. Whatever he was on, he'd had more of it. "Come on, then."

"And do what? I'm certainly not going to fight you," Stella said. "You can barely stand up."

"Oi," the other youth said to her. "Watch your mouth, cunt."

"Or what?" There were people walking past, looking askance, and the cab driver, a large man, was even now getting out of the driver's side, grim-faced. Stella didn't feel she was in a great deal of danger. Lem's friend aimed a push at her arm and nearly toppled over. Stella, grinning, stepped back.

"Yeah, no. Not going to happen."

She wasn't expecting the knife, which was small. Neither was she expecting the weapon to clatter to the floor as soon as Lem drew it. He stared behind her, slack jawed. The passers-by, Stella saw with sudden quivering alarm, had stopped moving and so had the cabbie, paused in time as though someone had pressed the button of a remote.

"Oh," Lem's mate quavered. Something silverquick leaped past her. Stella heard a snarl and saw a long dog's head dip to the wet pavement. It snatched at the knife, as though the weapon were a bone, and swallowed it.

"Hey!" Stella cried. "Hey, don't do that! Drop it!" But the dog turned and she saw wise light eyes in its silver head, blazing with amusement. It looked like something from a Medieval painting, a hunting dog, a gaze hound. Then she saw the woman who stood behind it.

"Oh!" Stella said, echoing the now silent Lem. The woman was tall and her face reminded Stella a little of her own, pale and pointy, but the stranger's eyes were green as summer grass and Stella wondered how, in the rainy London streetlights, she could even notice the colour of a woman's eyes. Her hair was like flame.

"To me." The dog ran back, to flank his partner: another sight hound, as dark as he was silver.

'Two dogs," Stella said, and at once felt like an idiot.

The woman smiled patiently. "Two dogs are better than one."

Stella's next thought, which she managed not to voice aloud, was: *Unusual choice of clothes.* Caro Amberley would approve and so would some of the county set whom her mother Alys knew. Tweed jacket, velvet collared and cuffed in forest green, with a hunting stock at her throat. Jodhpurs, in fawn, tucked into what Stella immediately recognised as very expensive riding boots, the flat heeled kind with a tassle. Country clothes, but for the races or a hunt meet or even a fashion shoot, not the kind with holes in that end up covered in straw.

And when the woman turned her head, Stella saw that she had horns. Very small ones, but horns nonetheless: the pronged antlers of a deer.

The woman was drawing off one of her gloves.

"Distasteful," the woman said, looking past Stella at the cowering lads.

Stella felt a sudden need to be fair. Power radiated from the stranger and her brace of hounds. She reminded Stella of the Behenian stars.

"You don't want to bother with them," she said. "They're not worth the effort."

"All the same." The woman turned her hand palm upwards and blew. A gentle wind, hay-scented, pine-tinged, drifted past Stella. It stirred her hair but Lem and his friend were tumbled away like thistledown, bowled down the busy, frozen street and out of sight.

"Well." Stella said, watching them disappear. "Thank you very much."

"Oh, not at all." The woman was putting on her glove again. "This is my manor, as they say. Now I am awake again, I am responsible for what befalls people here."

"You'd do that for everyone, would you?" Stella had a feeling that plenty of muggings had taken place around St Pancras without supernatural rescue.

"Some people. Your driver, for instance." She nodded in his direction and Stella saw that the Sikh cabbie was now trotting rapidly towards her. "But you carry the Huntress' token. Does your driver have the knowledge?"

Stella, after a second of confusion, realised what she meant. "I should think so – it's a black cab."

"Ah, yes. The knowledge of the roads and the thoroughfares. But I need someone with the *knowledge*. I'll speak to you again."

Stella was about to ask the driver, who had now reached them, but he spoke first.

"You all right, love? That was a right pair of dodgepots – ran off, did they?"

"Yes," Stella said. "Didn't want to mix it up with you, I expect. Cheers!"

"You're welcome. Not having one of my fares molested on *my* watch."

"This woman –" Stella began, but when she turned, there was no sign of the woman, or her black and silver hounds, or anything at all.

Next morning, sitting in the cabin with a mug of tea and the woodburner roaring away, Stella told Evie about the events of the previous night.

"And you've no idea who she is? Never seen her before?"

"No. But I'm assuming she's the 'friend' the Huntress spoke about. Another goddess, or a spirit. Like the star spirits at home. Similar, but different."

"And you said she had dogs with her."

"A pair of greyhounds, or something like that. Quite big, otherwise I'd have said whippets."

"Hmm,' Evie said, frowning at the end of one of her multi-hued dreadlocks. "This is ringing a very faint bell. Do you want me to make some enquiries?"

"Yes, please! And I'm going to do the same."

"Your friend Ace?" Evie asked.

"My friend Ace. I've also got to see someone in Camden at half one, about a gig. I'll be out most of the day."

There had been a mist on the river first thing, shrouding it in a mysterious drifting film, but it had started to lift by the time Stella walked along the dock to the clipper station. She had waited until eleven, being reasonably sure to find Ace in the pub, so had left it to opening hours. It was quicker to go down to Southwark by water rather than the Tube, and, anyway, she liked the journey. The river was London's main artery and Stella was learning its landmarks. She needed to take a bus from their current mooring, but it wasn't a long ride and soon she reached the clipper station for the next boat, coming down from Woolwich. It took her up river to Docklands, then the Tower. Absorbed in checking her phone, Stella did not see the person who came onto the gently rocking deck to stand beside her.

"Excuse me, madam, I think you're in my seat."

"What the fuck, there are plenty of – oh!" Stella looked up to see her sister. "Serena, what are you doing here?"

"Early business meeting. I had to come down the river to see a client." She sank into the seat beside Stella. "Someone in Canary Wharf."

Serena also wore a smart tweed suit today, in shades of heather and rose, and her pale blonde hair was in almost-ringlets. Tweed must be the in thing, Stella thought. Her sister looked a lot more presentable than she did. Stella told her so. Serena made hand waving gestures.

"So how was Brighton?"

"Oh, you know, seaside-y. And interesting." She shot Stella a look.

"I had an interesting night last night myself."

"In a good way or a bad way?"

"In a good way *and* a bad way. You?"

Serena gave a rueful nod. "Same."

"I'm going to Southwark," said Stella. "You want to come?"

Serena opened her mouth and closed it again. "Yes. I think I do. Just let me send Charlie a text. There's some stuff for her to get on with at the studio."

"Fine. We're nearly there." Stella could see the tower of Southwark Cathedral on the left bank and then the clipper was pulling in to the dock. She and Serena hopped off.

"Want to walk through the market?" Stella asked.

"I'm always up for a visit to Borough." This close to lunchtime, the big market was humming beneath its green and white arches. There were daffodils in the grounds of the cathedral, Stella saw, and suddenly it felt like spring. She said as much.

They passed stalls selling expensive cheese, artisanal bread, heaped piles of tomatoes and parsley and porcini.

"I'd pick up something for supper," Stella said, "but Evie might mind if I remortgaged the boat."

"I know, it's pricey, but it's lush. I will actually pick up something on the way back."

"I might go to the cashpoint again and get some more cheese."

At length, they came out of the other side of the market, and the Victorian frontage of the Southwark Tavern appeared.

"Did you tell him we were coming?"

"No. I'm just counting on him being in there. It would be typical if he wasn't, although he practically lives in there."

But Ace – magician, cat fancier, and a lot older than he looked, now that Stella knew he was supposed to have officially died in 1956 – was raising a sardonic glass to the Fallows as they entered.

"Morning."

"Morning! Hoped you'd be in residence."

"I had a hunch you were coming, Stella. I saw your friend Mags yesterday. She agrees with me – the city's on the move. Spring's coming."

"There were daffs in the cathedral grounds," Serena said. She put her gloves and scarf on the table, checking first for spillages. "And that sun's actually got a bit of warmth in it."

"So how are you both?"

"Serena's been to Brighton," said Stella.

"Someone once said that Brighton has the air of a town that's continually helping the police with its enquiries," Ace said.

"So true! Very dodgy, if you ask me."

"I love Brighton," said Ace. "Some really decent boozers there. And of course you're on the coast. Fabulous light." He had, Stella recalled, been a painter and perhaps still was: he had been the youngest member of the Royal Academy, back in the day.

"Ward was shooting a film," Stella said. 'But some other stuff happened."

Ace managed an expression that was halfway between glum and intrigued. "Of course it did," he said. Serena told her story, while

Ace and Stella paid close attention, interrupted briefly by the arrival of some coffee.

"Wow, Serena," Stella said, when she had drawn to a close. "That sounds scary, actually."

"I did once go to the old pier," Ace said. "Many years ago, when it was still a pier and not a total wreck. I took a young lady there, in fact. It didn't end well, but we had a nice time on the actual pier, as I recall. Teas. Amusements. That sort of thing."

"Yes, there was a tea room," Serena said. "And a dance going on."

"It's some time since I've been to Brighton," Stella remarked, "I've had several gigs there, as you might expect – it's such a big clubbing scene. Great town. But as I remember, the old pier was pretty much a skeleton. What happened to it?"

"A ship hit it," said Serena.

"Not enough room in the Channel?"

"I think it was a barge, moored to the end of the pier, and it came loose in a storm. We asked the landlady in one of the pubs and she told us. Then the whole thing just sat there for years like Miss Havisham's wedding cake and there were plans to restore it as a sort of Victorian amusement arcade – much as it had been, actually – but then there was a fire and only the iron frame was left. It's almost gone now. The landlady alluded to the fire being deliberate but wouldn't say any more."

"What, arson?"

"Yes. That was never proved, though."

"I'm not so familiar with the South Coast scene," Ace said. 'Give me a couple of days. I'll ask around."

"Thank you, Ace! Did the card reading make any sense to you?"

"I've heard of the Searchers. Bad news. Give them a miss, if you can."

"Who are they?"

"In ye olden days the Searchers were just women. Old and poor, the very poorest, usually, with no families left to look after them, and they were employed by the parish to search out the dead, specifically, those who died of the Plague. They were like registrars, kind of. They noted the names of the dead, and handed them in to the authorities to write up in what were known as the Bills of Mortality."

"That sounds a bit sad."

"Yeah, it must have been a fucking horrible job."

"You said, *in the olden days*," said Serena, hopefully.

"I've heard rumours that there's a bunch of them still around and they show up before a death, not after it. With a strong suggestion that they cause the death. I've never seen them myself, mind you."

"But listen, Stella," her sister said, "you mentioned you'd had an odd night, too. What happened to you?"

"You know you just mentioned the Huntress, in your card reading? Well…"

And Stella told them.

"Why I came to see you," she said to Ace, "was to ask whether you know who the woman in St Pancras is?" She dropped her voice. "I'm pretty sure about the Huntress."

Ace opened his mouth. Then he closed it again.

"Right. I think I might know. But I'm not a hundred percent certain. She's likely to be one of two people."

"Good people?" Serena asked. "Or not?"

"One of them is – well, 'good' is the wrong word. Wild, perhaps. The other one's similar but not really aligned to humans so much."

"Who's that, then, love?" a voice said, and Stella turned to find Anione, Ace's girlfriend, for want of a better word. Today, her hair was jet black, along with her fake fur jacket, but her lips and her leggings were fuschia.

"Stella met a lady at St Pancras a night or so ago. Couple of dogs with her. Stella says she had very green eyes and a pair of antlers. Said it was her 'manor', apparently."

"Ooh." Anione sat down at the table. "Could I have the usual, please, darlin'?" This was to the barman, who nodded. "Are we on a tab?"

"I'll get them," said Serena.

"No, it's all right. I've got cash. So, Stella. Tell me exactly what madam last night looked like."

Stella did so.

"Well," Anione said, after a long stare into her gin. "That's a turn up for the books. I haven't heard hide nor hair of *her* for a long time and when I say 'hide nor hair' that's exactly what I mean."

"It was the antlers that threw me," Stella said.

"I'm not surprised."

"But does don't have antlers," Serena said. "Only stags, I thought."

"Actually, and here you'll have to forgive me because I'm not exactly David bleeding Attenborough, very occasionally they do. I knew a hunts- a bloke once, down in Windsor Great Park it was, and there's plenty of deer there, and he told me that he'd shot a stag once, but when he investigated, it was a female. It's rare but it does happen. It's a hormone imbalance," she added. "Hark at me, sounding like I know what I'm talking about."

"I'm sure you do know what you're talking about," Serena said.

"They used to say that hare bucks gave birth to the young. And that hares were male one year and female the next. It's not just shapeshifting."

"Oh!" Serena said. 'I don't *think* I'm going to do that."

"You don't know," Stella said. "You might turn out to be genderfluid. I don't think Ward would mind. Anyway, Anione, it also sounds as though you know *who.*"

"Yes. Very old, she is and said to have been sleeping. Mind you, they say that about a lot of people. A spirit. A deer spirit. I know her as Noualen."

"Google is your friend," said Ace.

"All right. I'll do that later. Thanks. Funny place for a deer girl to hang out, though – at St Pancras."

"She's got old links with the area." Anione took a swig of her gin and frowned at the pink smear her lipstick had made. "Before the station, obviously. When it was all just forest, I expect. The story I heard, she came over when the Channel was still a skating rink."

"What, the Ice Age?" Serena said, wide eyed.

"Well, you've met people who are that old," Ace said. "Surprising number of them about. If not older."

"But she's a spirit, not a – anyway, not one of those. And you said she's wild, but not bad."

"The French border stops at St Pancras," Ace said.

"What?"

"I read it in the Standard the other day. It's well known, but I didn't know. Anyway, that's what I read the newspapers for. It's called a *juxtaposed control* and about ten foot of St Pancras is actually, under law, the French border."

"Ace," Anione said. "You're digressing, love."

"I'm just wondering where else it borders," Ace said.

"So who's the other candidate, Ace?" Stella asked.

"Similar. Ancient guardian spirit. But I don't think it is her, from what Anione's just been saying. I'll do a bit of subtle enquiry, though."

"Cheers."

"If she's taken an interest in you, I'd keep an eye out."

"I will."

"Mind you, your surname's Fallow, isn't it? Any cervine ancestry?"

"What?"

"Deer like!"

"I don't think – oh wait."

"Nan," Serena said.

"Nan?"

"She's our American cousin. The one I told you about, who stayed with us in the autumn?"

"Ah yes, you mentioned her a while back. So it's likely that's a *yes*. Have you heard from your cousin recently?"

"Christmas card. It arrived in mid-January, Bee said, because Nan missed the international post. She's expecting a baby."

"A baby, or a fawn?"

Anione cackled. "Bit of a shocker for the old midwife when that pops out."

"She'd be born human," Ace said.

"Well, you say that, love, but I wouldn't count on it. You never know how these things are going to go, believe me. Although I will allow as how it's more common to come out as a human child these days. Used not to be, mind."

"What," Serena said. "People gave birth to animals?"

"Oh yes, happened all the time, with the old bloodlines, but it's not such a thing now. You come out human first and change later. As you've discovered."

Serena looked extremely uncomfortable at this. "Bella was perfectly normal," she said.

"So far. We've got deer, birds and hares in the family tree, then, plus stars. This is so cool," Stella said. "If a trifle peculiar."

"You should see what *she's* got in hers," Ace said, gesturing to Anione.

"I wonder what Ward's got in his?" Serena said.

"Could be bloody anything." Stella finished her coffee. "Listen, Ace, what should I do? Go back up to St Pancras and nose about, or what?"

"I'd just keep doing what you're doing," Ace said. "If she wants you – she'll find you."

LUNA

The hollow way smelled of earth and foxes. The musky scent was familiar to Luna, and also to Moth. He snuffled and sniffed at the high banks of reddish earth that formed the base of the hollow.

"Look," Luna said. Directly ahead of her, in the mud, was a neat cloven hoofprint. "Deer."

"There's some more footprints over there," said Sam. Then the dog's head went up.

"What's that?" Luna could hear distant shouts.

"I don't know! Moth, come here." Sam hauled the lurcher in on his lead. "Come here now!" The hollow way began to drum, the mud shuddering.

"Get off the drove!" The voice came from above, high on the bank. Luna, startled, looked up and saw bright dark eyes beneath a remarkable hat: a kind of bonnet, made from pheasant feathers, wild clematis and moss. The face beneath it, lined and filthy, was male.

"Come on! Get up, get up – quick as you can or they'll run you down."

He reached down a grimy hand. Luna took it, Sam pushed – there was a sudden fluttering inside her, her vision dimmed. For a moment Luna saw the world as a bird, the great dark chasm of the hollow way, the enemy men. A beat of wings and she was up and stumbling amongst the roots, a woman again. Sam was close behind her.

"Crouch down and keep quiet."

Luna and Sam did as they were told. Luna, staring straight ahead, could feel their rescuer immediately behind her. His hand, no more than skin and bone, was nonetheless strong: it held her shoulder with a biting grip. The air filled with hoofbeats. Was it horses? Luna wondered.

Then they came into the hollow way. Luna saw a man, running, huge and dressed in skins. He carried a staff, of a kind she had seen before, with a pinecone crowning its tip. His hair was red, his skin black, and for a moment she met his fiery eyes, but she did not think he saw her; he looked through her into the wood and then he had gone by. Behind him came a herd of cattle. They, too, were enormous. Some were brown, some were moonlight white, and two were mottled like the piebald horses which pulled Sam's van. All had horns, crescent curving. The beat of their hooves and their terrified lowing filled the air like a storm. Luna watched, cowering against Sam, as they thundered past. Last to come were two people who made her gasp with alarm; she had seen them before. Men with long pale faces, lantern jaws, today dressed all in green like the huntsmen they followed. Their hair was afire. One of them flickered before her sight and for a second Luna saw a grim white dog, with a thorny collar and coal-red eyes.

Finally all were gone through, leaving the hollow way steaming with the smell of cattle, the mud churned further into a river of soil and filth. Sam and Luna did not move, and nor did Moth, who stared wide-eyed and alert after the herd.

Their rescuer said, "You'd've been trampled had you not come up. The drove stops for no one."

"I've never heard of, never seen, anything like that,' Sam said.

Luna sat back onto a root. "Those men, they were Hounds, the followers."

"Them as are called the Lily White Boys." Their rescuer spat into the beech mast. "I know 'em both. Bastards."

"Know them well?" Sam asked mildly.

The man held up a hand. His little finger was missing. "Well enough."

"I see."

"Put it this way, I don't want to meet them again, not at close quarters, anyway. But now the herds are on the move. Spring's coming; tide's changing. So the Hounds run with the herds as well as the Hunt."

"And who might you be?" Sam said.

The man stood. He wore boots, trews, a shirt and jerkin, and a coat, but Luna had to look hard to see all these garments, as they were covered in all manner of things: pennies on a chain, feathers, nuts, scraps of cloth like the clootie rags that people still tied to trees for luck, a flint hagstone on a leather thong, and a tiny skein of cowries: not the big tropical shells, but the little pink-tinged delicates that Luna had once found on a Pembrokeshire shore. Beneath, his clothes were multicoloured: red and ivory and black.

He swept off the bonnet and bowed.

"Captain Coral at your service. Kit Coral."

"Pleased to meet you. This is Luna Fallow and I am Sam March. Our real names."

"I can tell. Wouldn't be much point giving me anything else. Good English folk, I see, more or less. Give or take a drop of the blood of the Jenny." He shot Luna a sharp look: he must have seen her brief transformation.

"And yourself?"

"I'm as English a man as they come. What were you doing on the drove road?"

"It came across us," Sam said. "Might you know a woman called Vervain?"

"I don't know her," Kit Coral said, "but I do believe I've heard the name. Your ma, is she?"

"Gran."

"I can't remember what or where. But that's not unusual. A lot of folk about on the ways, after all. The old straight tracks. Especially now the season's on the turn."

"Do you know a woman called Alys?"

Kit Coral looked thoughtful. "What's she look like?"

"She's my mother but we don't look alike: she's tall, white-blonde hair, blue eyes, slim."

"Yes. Yes, I think I might have come across her, by and by. But she didn't give that as her name."

"She might have been using another one," Luna said. It was not the first time that this thought had occurred to her, or that Alys had somehow spun a whole new identity from whole cloth, during her sojourns in this otherplace.

"Woman I met, looks like that, called herself Feldfar."

"Oh. I've never heard that name!"

"Fieldfare, like the bird. The far-traveller, the fallow-farer, used to be called in the olden days."

"Bet that's her," Sam said.

"Your second name is Fallow, you said."

"That's right."

"Hmmm. Well, I don't know a lot about her. She was with some folk I don't care for much. Mind you, there's a lot of those about, too. I keep myself to myself."

"Fair enough," said Sam.

"Speaking of which, we need to get you back onto your road, off the track. Follow me." He spun about and set off through the wood. Dusk was falling, Luna realised. The air was now very still, but not as cold as it had been. A star shivered in the beech branches and she could feel the new of the moon: a moment later it, too, appeared, snared in the crown of an oak but swinging free. Kit Coral strode down a narrow path, shining faintly in the crescent light. Then, further ahead, Luna realised that she could see a warm yellow square: the light of a house.

"Here you go," the Captain said. "Follow the path, don't lose it, don't step off till the wood's behind you."

"Thank you!" Luna said and Sam echoed it.

Kit Coral raised his bonnet and set it once more upon his head. "A pleasure. Perhaps we'll meet again. But stay off the droves if you can, at least till spring's gone."

"We'll try,' said Luna, with sincerity. She had no wish to encounter the giant and his herd again, nor the Lily White Boys, either. She and Sam followed the path until they stood in an open field and heard the sudden shouting of a wren in the hedge. She looked back and saw the wood still behind her. Ahead, the path led to a stile and the pointing arrow of a footpath sign. She knew where they were, now: three fields from Mooncote, and beyond, the golden weathercock of the church, swinging under the moon as the church bells chimed the evening hour.

By the time Luna and Sam arrived back at Mooncote, it was fully dark and rather cold. The new moon had become a bright scythe in the sky and all the stars were prickling out. Looking up, Luna tried to pick out the Spring Triangle: the stars whom Bee had glimpsed talking in the orchard, some while ago. But although she knew the constellations they had not quite risen yet. As she and Sam came into the yard, the kitchen door opened and the spaniels rocketed out, to greet their friend Moth with ecstasy.

"My mates don't say hello to me with that much enthusiasm," Sam said.

"Mine neither."

But Bee was pleased to see them, too.

"Who's that? Oh, it's you two. I was starting to get a bit worried. Sorry, I know it's stupid. You've been gone for rather a long time."

"What time is it?" asked Luna.

"Coming up to seven."

"Oh God, we've been gone for *hours.*"

"Kind of my point! Right, before anything else happens, I need to tell you something – Mum's here."

"She's come home? When?"

"This afternoon, while you were out. Strolled in, cool as a cucumber, says she's staying for a bit. She went upstairs to change. No eldritch appearances, strange lights in the sky, or anything. She just walked into the kitchen and said hello, sorry she didn't give me prior warning and did I want her to go to the shop and pick anything up?"

"Did she say where she'd been?"

"No, she did not." Bee was rather tight lipped, "and frankly, nor did I ask her."

The kitchen was a glow of light and warmth. The Aga roared softly away and Luna could smell something good.

"It's potato and leek soup tonight. I made bread."

"Fantastic!"

"Are you all right, Luna?" Bee looked more narrowly at her sister. "You look a bit pale. Is it Mum coming back?"

"No, it's not. We had – a bit of an adventure."

"Oh!" Bee did not have to ask what that meant. "Are you okay?"

"I think so."

Bee went to the hall door, opened it, and shouted up. "Supper's ready!"

Alys had evidently been drying her hair, for its ends were still faintly damp, curling like fronds of fern. She smiled when she saw her daughters and Sam, and she hugged Luna.

"Hello again. You're back. Did you have a nice walk?"

"Up to the point where it got a bit excessively exciting," Luna said.

"Oh?"

"But it was all right in the end. We were helped, by someone who possibly knows you. His name was Captain Kit Coral."

"I know Kit Coral," a voice said. Luna turned to see Dark, who had not been there a moment ago, sitting at the kitchen table.

"A fellow sea dog?" Sam asked.

"No, I didn't know him in life. After my time. But I've seen him around, with all his feathers and fancies. I like him well enough."

"I liked him, too," Luna said, realising for the first time that it was true.

"I've come across him." Alys' voice was neutral. "An Egyptian, a traveller. A masterless man." She gave a sudden smile. "Can't disapprove of that."

"Masterless man?" Luna said.

"Yes, one of a regiment of such, after some failed rebellion or other. Not the New Model Army. There were a lot of them and after they were put down, some of the participants basically went feral, roamed the country, up to all sorts."

"Like Cock Lorel," Dark said, "the most notorious knave that ever lived. Lord Rascal, closer to my own day."

"Like that. He's supposed to be still around, as well. Didn't he invent thieves' cant, along with a friend?"

"At the Devil's Arse, up Derby way."

"Sounds like he's still roaming," said Sam. "He's come across my nan. Mind you, she knows a lot of people."

"He said you called yourself Feldfar," Luna said. She had to work to keep the accusation out of her voice. She thought she had succeeded, but Alys still looked a little uncomfortable.

"I've always liked them. There was a flock of them out on the lawn earlier."

"A flock – oh, you mean fieldfares." Luna had also noticed the grey and russet birds, fighting and squabbling over the last of the windfalls.

"So I took the name. In Anglo Saxon it means 'Far Farer,' and I thought, well, I am. I didn't want to use my real name."

"Fair enough," Sam said. "This is great soup, by the way."

"Good! So, this Captain." Bee ladelled Sam a second helping. "What did he help you with, exactly?"

Luna told them and there was an uneasy silence.

"I've seen a drove," Dark said. "Best avoided."

"They were big beefy cows." Sam cut himself more bread. "Or steers. I have to say, I was looking at their horns, not anything else."

"They are not cows or steers." Dark spoke quietly, as a ghost should, so that Luna had to strain to hear him. He was staring into the corner of the room. "They are the souls of men."

"I'd heard that, too." Alys was brisker. "They're all right as long as you keep out of their way."

"But, Mum," said Bee. "If they're souls – where are they going?"

"Nowhere good," said Dark. "Nowhere good at all."

Luna had a bath after supper. After the mud of the hollow way, she felt she needed one, but deep down she knew that it was the glimpse of the Hounds that had made her feel unclean. Back in the winter, she had narrowly evaded them, but only just: she still remembered that night flight with Ver March, transformed to birds, fleeing into the sunrise. The memory of the Hound who had tried to snatch her in Chepstow – white faced, dead-eyed, its meadowsweet breath – made her feel weak and ill within. She did not enjoy feeling like this and now she feared for her child. She did not know whether the Hounds were beasts changed into men, or the other way around. She knew that they were chained, enchanted, but in later conversations both Ver and Alys had said that no one seemed to know whether they were truly men or truly Hound, and Ver had told her that some of them were free, had chosen their road, as Ver put it.

There were huge gaps in everyone's knowledge of this patchwork country and Luna wished she could fill some of them. But not too much via personal experience, thank you. The people the Fallows had come to know over the last few months – Ace, Anione, Ver, Nick Wratchall-Haynes, the people at the temple complex in Lydney, the green girl called Aln and her brother, not to mention Luna's own mother and many more – all of them were holders of jigsaw pieces, but no one seemed to know what the full puzzle looked like. Prior to becoming pregnant, Luna might have followed in her mother's footsteps and gone looking, but now her worry for her baby held her back. It would not stop her entirely, though. There were other things she could do.

Out of the bath and in bed, she reached for the notebook that she kept in the bedside table drawer. It was a large, plain notebook and in it Luna had made numerous notes. She might not have got on particularly well at school itself, but that had been more a dislike of authority. If she respected a teacher, Luna had worked, but not otherwise. However, she liked to learn, and she liked working things out: the notebook was proof of that. In it, she had drawn a series of partial maps: of the area around Mooncote and Hornmoon, including the church and the lychgate, of the valley with the stream and the chapel, through which Luna had been chased by the Hunt, then the coracle voyage she had undertaken to the Severn estuary, plus Lydney and Chepstow. In addition to the notebook, Luna kept a road map of southern England in the bedside drawer and she had mapped some of her travels, and those of her sisters, onto it. Serena was doing the same for London, Stella for the Thames Estuary. They were working together as far as they could, and some of what they had found was not to be vouchsafed to Alys. Luna had, growing up, often found herself in opposition to her mother: that was changing, as the child might form a bond between them but – well. There were still some trust issues, thought Luna.

Now, she added the hollow way carefully to the local map with a green felt tip pen, and the place in the wood on the ridge where they had found the strange white shoots, just in case. This accomplished, she turned out the bedside lamp without waiting for Sam, and sought sleep.

And sleep was not far away. She felt exhausted, both mentally and physically, and she dropped into a deep slumber almost at once. But she did not remain asleep. At some point, in the still depth of the night, Luna woke. For a moment, she felt disoriented, as though time had frozen her in the edges of the hollow way. Beech mast crunched beneath her and a chill breath touched her cheek as the branches swayed over her head. Luna listened, knowing that she was in truth warm and safe in her bed, with Sam sleeping beside her and Moth curled up on the rug. Outside, there was no wind.

As she had done once before, in another house, Luna, restless, left her body behind her in the bed and stood. She glided to the window, seeing a gleam of silver beyond, and raised the sash. Outside, the world was shining. Luna took a breath, thought wren. She knew how to do it now, half asleep, perhaps still dreaming. She diminished, shrinking down until her condensed form perched lightly on the sill. Then she spread her tiny wings and shot out. Wrens fly swiftly, like a thrown stone, and soon Luna was in the hedge. She heard herself give that quick, chirping warning cry and then she was hurtling upwards again. She would not, her human mind thought, remembering the old fable, need the lift of an eagle's back.

A huge spine of stone was in her way. Luna swerved, to cling to a curling scroll of toadflax. She was, she realised, on the side of the church spire. She looked up to see the weathercock, gleaming golden although it was quite dark, no moon, no sun; the bird was creaking on his bolt of iron. He dipped his head and winked.

Luna took advantage of the height and looked out. A line of light flared briefly at the edge of the churchyard and ran west. She saw it strike a second tower, a mile or so away: the squatter, squarer tower of Dunmote church in the next village. Then it ran on. And when Luna looked east to where the sun would rise she saw another band of hazy light, cutting through the hedges across the fields. Other roads were visible, too: that was Mooncote land, the field with the shelter where she and Sam kept the piebalds.

"The old straight track," someone said. Luna, still clinging to the stone, half expected to see Kit Coral, sitting on the weathercock, but instead a blue spark of light danced in the air before her. "Granddad!" said Luna.

"Hello, Luna," said her grandfather Abraham's spirit. "Fancy seeing you here." He chuckled. "Wrens are supposed to be tucked up safe in their nests at night."

Luna laughed. "What about women?" she said.

"Maybe not those. See the leys? They're not always visible."

And Luna could see now that the whole landscape was criss-crossed with a web of faint light. One such track ran from the church gate, a dim and livid green, and Luna recognised this for the lych path, the corpse road on which bodies were once carried to the church for burial. This track ran to a dense patch of woodland, too shadowy and dark to see within.

"I need to remember this," Luna said. "I'm making a map."

"You can work it out to some degree. Not the corpse road, perhaps, but the old tracks. Use the churches and the burial mounds, things like that, as your nexus points," her grandfather said. "A ruler and a pencil, that's all you need."

"We did some of that. But do all of them take you into the otherlands?"

"Not all. But some. The corpse path, although I wouldn't take that one – I've spoken to Alys about it. See that?"

It was a very pale gold, barely visible, bisecting the churchyard. "The bee's path," Abraham said. "You should tell your sister. But I don't know all of them. That, for example."

It was a broad track, icy white, running north into starlight. The Great Bear wheeled above Luna, making her dizzy. She almost fell. For a second it illuminated a house: a big place, higher on the hill than Mooncote. She recognised Wycholt, home of Nick Wratchall-Haynes.

"I've only seen that track once before," her grandfather said. "A royal road, I think they're called."

But Luna could feel the sun coming up. The roads were fading. She said as much.

"That's right," Abraham said. "Time for bed."

And Luna dropped from her perch, falling, flying, landing… and woke.

STELLA

After parting company from Ace and Anione and saying goodbye to her sister, Stella felt like a walk. She crossed the Thames, keeping a close eye on the heraldic dragons which were the markers of the City of London, in case one of them had something to say to her. But they were silent and still and the river itself looked normal, a surprising blue in the sunlight. The sun glittered from the golden summit of the Monument and turned the Georgian façades to blinding white. Stella saw a bus with a plate reading *Camden*, and since this was where she was going, pulled out her Oystercard and hopped on. Ace always travelled by bus and Stella could see why. Her favourite seat, the top front, was empty. She watched the city pass by, noting daffodils behind railings and the fat brown buds of the plane trees. Soon enough, the graceful fans of their leaves would be shading the city from the summer heat. The dome of St Paul's came and went behind the roofscape – Stella saluted it, just in case – then Holborn, then Bloomsbury. People were sitting on benches in the parks, enjoying the slight warmth. Then the green expanse of Regent's Park and finally up into Camden High Street.

When Stella had last come up this way, it was to investigate the disappearance of her sister's boyfriend, Ben. The bus swung past the entrance to his street. Earlier in the winter Ben's house had been a wasteland of cobwebs and mould, but Ward had given her to understand that, on the collapse of the enchantment that had ensnared Ben himself, this had disappeared. Ben's Siamese cats were still being looked after by his cleaner, but the place itself was habitable again. Ben himself was still down in Somerset, recuperating with his parents at Amberley. Stella hoped he was on the mend. Despite his treatment of Serena, Stella, in her more generous moments, did not think that this had been entirely his fault. Magic had a lot to answer for, she thought sternly as the bus rolled around the World's End pub.

She got off and took a lungful of grimy air. Her appointment was at the Lock, and she walked slowly up the High Street, noting changes, although Camden mainly consisted of leatherware shops these days, and a few bars. It was in one of these that she had her appointment.

"A veritable pub crawl," she had said to Serena, on leaving the Southwark Tavern.

"Don't get pissed!"

"It's coffee and water all the way, until I get home."

It hadn't been clear from their text conversation, but her appointment, Les, turned out to be a woman, in black dungarees and a stripy top. The sides of her head were shaved, and above nodded a bright pink crest. She looked like a bright eyed, enquiring and slightly mad bird.

"Hello!" said Stella. "Stella Fallow."

"Les Bianco. It's Letitzia, actually – Dad's Italian. Everyone calls me Les. Do you want a drink?"

"Just mineral water, cheers. I do drink but I'm trying to keep it to the evening."

"Oh, me too. I'm getting old."

"Tell me about it! I had this conversation with my sister earlier on."

Les ordered the water, while Stella looked around her. Typical Camden: a surprising number of these bars looked like 1980s student unions. Alys, on being taken into one when Stella moved to London, had come up with this observation, and this particular place was no exception: black walls and orange secondhand sofas. The effect should have been depressing, but Stella liked the rather shabby ambience, and they were playing the Jam. Old school, thought Stella, who had a lot of respect for Paul Weller. Eton Rifles: that class-based classic.

"So, the gig. I'll get straight to the details – I've got to see someone else right after you." Les smiled as she said this, to defuse any bluntness.

"No worries," Stella said. "You said this was an outdoors gig?"

"Yes. It's all legal and everything, no problem on that score. And it's not far out of town so we can pay for your travel or put you up locally if you prefer."

"Okay."

"It's in Windsor Great Park. Here we go," She showed Stella the date on the phone. "Sorry we've left it a bit late to get in touch – Georgina, that's the client, is terrible at communicating. It's not like she didn't know she was going to be twenty-one."

"No, that's fine. And how fab!" Also, the second mention of the Park that day.

"Bit chilly in spring, but they've hired a marquee."

"By Royal appointment?"

"No, although your hostess is in fact a lady. Lady Georgina Hammond."

"I'm going up in the world. Will I need a hat?"

"Oh, I should think so. Hat and heels, please."

"And a Regency frock," Stella mused.

They ran through a playlist: some favourite tracks of Georgina's and the rest left up to Stella's own discretion. She had some ideas, so jotted them down and then sought the ladies while Les texted the client. As she found the door to the toilets, she saw a mirror on the side of the wall, just by the door, and glanced at it to see if she was still presentable. Hair not too much of a mess, no spinach in teeth and so forth.

However, someone was staring at her. She could see him in the mirror, but did not turn round. She made a show of checking her eyeliner and reapplying it, watching all the while. Twenties, perhaps. Quite good looking, clean shaven, in a dark sweatshirt with a colourful abstract pattern across the front and a black beanie hat. Nothing out of the ordinary but his pale eyes were fixed on Stella. She completed the invented repair to her eye makeup and visited the loo, then returned. He would, she thought, be able to see her from where he was sitting, but she could not see him.

She finished her session with Les and they parted company at the door. Stella set off down Camden High Street without a backward glance. But one of the shoe emporiums also had a mirrored door, set catty-corner to its door, and Stella took a good sharp look it in as she passed. Yes, there was Beanie Boy, ambling along behind at a decent distance. Like Stella, he wore Converse. He was quite short, she noticed. Not especially threatening, and perhaps she was mistaken. Then again, perhaps not.

She dodged down into the Tube, crossed the concourse and came up again out of the opposite entrance. Here, she doubled back up Kentish Town Road and after a few minutes, found a café with booths. She selected a seat which faced the front, ordered a cup of tea and clocked the window. By the time she had finished the tea, Beanie Boy had still not put in an appearance. Stella paid for the tea, dived across the road and got on a bus going south.

By this time, she had convinced herself that she was just being paranoid. After all, she wasn't completely repulsive; men did pay her some attention. But something about the episode felt off to Stella and she had learned to take heed; besides, the events of St Pancras were not far behind her. She didn't think the stoned lads had sent someone after her, but who knew? She could not help but feel that the events of the winter had ruffled some feathers. Would a supernatural being wear that kind of hat, though? But Ace didn't really look out of place in the modern world, and Serena had said that their adversary of Twelfth Night, the hopefully late Caspar Pharoah, had looked like a typical businessman. Better safe than sorry, thought Stella.

The bus took her back past St Pancras. On a whim, and perhaps anticipating seeing Deer Girl again, Stella got off and, skirting the station, went into the concourse in front of the British Library. The rather brutal architecture contrasted with the extravagant salmon pink station behind it. Stella located the statue of Newton which stood on the concourse. It had, she knew, been based on William Blake's painting of the great physicist (Stella still found it difficult to think of him as 'Bill'). Newton, bent double from a seated position, scowled beadily down at his compasses. The statue had a kind of brooding power; Stella waited expectantly, just in case it raised its great head, but it did not. At that point, the first drops of chilly rainfall spattered it, cast by a passing cloud, and Stella scurried into the library itself to seek shelter.

The annexe of the library often had exhibitions, and on this occasion it held a display of Medieval miniatures. The annexe was quiet, with only a woman and a couple of small children at the far end. Stella wandered from tiny painting to tiny painting, lost in wonder at the glowing images. It was like looking through a sequence of little stained glass windows. She saw lions and unicorns, reminiscent of the enormous piece of heraldic art that a rock band had painted on the front of what was now Serena's studio, but also orchards and hills, church steeples and ships. She leaned in to examine a woman standing beside a beehive, the bees humming around her head, and wondered if the shop had the image on a card: Bee's birthday was not too far away. Some of the images caused her to smile: had that artist, perhaps short sighted and confined to a monastery, ever actually seen a horse? Let alone an elephant…

The woman and her children had left and Stella was alone in the exhibition room. She glanced up at a wan shaft of sun reflecting from the glass of the display cases, but rain still hammered against the windows. The last case held a charming scene: a man and a woman playing chess in a high castle room. The woman wore green and there were two dogs at her feet, sad Medieval greyhounds, one white and one black. Each had a golden collar. The light changed and shifted, falling over Stella's shoulder and illuminating the miniature, which was no longer tiny, but a full sized window. Stella stood within a chapel, surrounded by images. She turned. The lion and unicorn, larger than life, silver and gold, were locked in battle on the southern glass. In the western window a ship rode a moonlit wave. To the east, an unsmiling sun peeked over a green hill above a city with a dome. Stella turned back to the north, to the tower and the woman and her dogs. The woman's chess opponent, a grave, bearded man, was now looking outwards. He reached up a hand, touched the woman on the wrist as if in warning. But she was frowning at the board and, as Stella watched, she took a piece and moved it. Now that the image was larger, Stella could see that it was not a chess board, but another game, with fewer pieces in unfamiliar shapes.

Someone was standing beside her in the dim shadowy colours of the chapel. She was not surprised to look up and see who it was.

Today, her benefactor wore a dark green coat. Her antlers were barely visible amid the bright fronds of her hair.

"No dogs?" asked Stella. "Or are they in the painting?"

"I left them outside," the woman said. "You can't take dogs into the British Library."

Stella laughed. "But this isn't the library any more. Would anyone notice? Do the library regulations even apply to you?"

"I do try to play by the rules," the woman said. "When I choose, at any rate."

"Same here! Anyway, I looked you up." Stella had to force herself to meet the woman's eyes. Green as a glade in summer and the leaves nodded over their heads, the dappled sunlight falling through.

"Looked –?"

"On Google." *Concentrate, Stella.*

"I'm not sure what that is," the woman said. 'Is it a kind of encyclopaedia? On those machines everyone uses these days?"

"Yes, sort of. It's more the method by which you access many encyclopaedias. I spoke to a couple of friends this morning, and while I was on the bus I looked up deer spirits on my phone. Elen of the Ways popped up. Links with London. Associated with dogs. Also called Noualen. Would that be you?"

"I am worshipped still under many names," the deer spirit said, with a trace of satisfaction. "But that isn't what I want from you."

"Okay. What do I call you? If you are a goddess." She felt absurdly shy as she said this, quite suddenly. But Stella, an inner voice prompted, you met Diana of the Hunt a while ago and you've just been sitting in a pub with a goddess, just this morning. Anione was a lot more human, though. At least these days.

"I am a spirit. Most of us are, though treated as gods."

"I've got a mate like that."

"Oh? What is their name?"

"Anione."

"I know of her."

"She knows of you. I'm not sure if you've met."

"She's from south of the river," Noualen said. "We each have our patch."

Stella almost said, *like gangsters*, but her inner censor had a quick little fit. *No, don't say that! Shut up, Stella!*

"You said, just now, about wanting me for something?" And her friend in St Paul's, perhaps another goddess, had said she was trapped. Might be tactless to mention that, though.

"I do. I need you to find a man."

"A man?"

"I'll show you," Noualen said.

BEE

Bee had decided to clean the kitchen floor that morning. This was a large task: the stone flags of Mooncote's kitchen were old, worn, and had grooves running between them in which detritus gathered. She hoovered, then poured hot water into a bucket, opened the door to let the mild day in and freshen up the place and finally, wrapped in a voluminous apron, located the mop. Sam was at work, and now that one car, at least, had been released from the local garage, Alys had taken Luna to the local cottage hospital for an antenatal appointment (might as well make herself useful now she was back) so Bee had the house to herself. Dark was, she had to admit, an ideal lover in many respects, but not much of a hand with housework despite his intermittent physicality. And why not? Bee thought to herself as she mopped the floor. Surely swabbing a stone floor wasn't all that different from swabbing the deck of a ship? But she hadn't asked him to help and she smiled at the notion. Part of Dark's charm was that he was not part of the everyday world. Then she imagined the Behenian stars helping out, clad in pinnies over their celestial raiment and sparkling jewels, mops and buckets in their hands rather than the fronds of their accompanying herbs, and she laughed aloud.

"Hello?" said a voice and she looked up to see Nick Wratchall-Haynes standing in the open doorway.

"Oh!" Bee said, embarrassed to have been caught laughing to herself like a lunatic. "Sorry."

"Why? You seem to be enjoying yourself."

"I just thought of something funny," Bee said, also conscious that she was enveloped in an apron, with a hole in it, her hair unbrushed and coming out of its scrunchie, and very probably beet-red in the face. An un-vain and practical woman, she was nonetheless aware that the Master of Fox Hounds wasn't the most unattractive bloke she'd ever set eyes on. And what was it with the upper classes? They always seemed to look tidy, even in Barbour and Wellingtons, which Wratchall-Haynes was currently wearing. Was it having manservants or something? Prince Charles, she had once heard, had someone to put toothpaste on his toothbrush for him… Enough of this aristocratic speculation. She wiped her damp hands on her apron and said briskly, "What can I do for you, Nick? Would you like a cup of coffee? Tea? I was just about to put the kettle on."

"Coffee would be lovely, thank you. Black is fine. I just popped in to offer a note of reassurance, actually."

"All right," said Bee, flicking the switch of the kettle. "Reassurance?"

"My estate manager said he spotted a couple of people and a dog, whom I think might have been your sister and her partner, on the edge of the ridge the other day and said he hailed them. That woodland, off the main road, is actually part of Wycholt's land, you see. I hope he was polite. I have to say that Mike can sometimes be a bit abrupt."

"I'm sure he was just doing his job," Bee said diplomatically. "Luna didn't mention it. They're both pretty responsible and Moth – that's the dog – is well behaved. Luna grew up here so she knows about sheep and so forth."

"Okay. I was just a bit worried that he'd been over zealous."

"That's very kind of you," Bee said, handing him the coffee. "A lot of landowners wouldn't bother. You're welcome to sit down, by the way."

"Get orf my laaand," Wratchall-Haynes mimicked, pulling out a chair. "I know. And I have to say, I'm not overly happy about people traipsing willy nilly across the property. It's more the leaving gates open and bothering livestock aspect of it than the nobility clinging on to their ill-gotten territory."

Bee smiled. "Was it ill gotten?"

"Probably. Originally, I mean – I didn't win it at cards or anything. As I assume you know, I inherited it with utmost legitimacy from my Great Aunt Pamela."

"I do know. Lady Pamela was the scourge of village committees in my grandmother's day. I know she was a bit reclusive at the end of her life but I remember her at a large number of fetes in my childhood, wearing a monstrous hat and laying down the law."

"God, I'm so sorry. She terrified me when I was a kid. I hope to be a much nicer lord of the manor. Anyway, as I was on the point of saying, Wycholt's not one of the great estates. I'm not the Duke of Buccleuch or that Drax fellow down in Devon or anything like that. My direct ancestors made their money from the wool trade up north and married into impoverished gentry to improve their social standing. At some point, though, they would have been implicated in the slave trade, and quite possibly clearances of some sort."

"I'm sure that goes for pretty much everyone in this country," Bee said, thinking of Dark and Drake. "So I probably can't throw any stones. And I have to say, I wouldn't be terribly pleased if people started tramping about *my* garden."

"It's a question of scale, though, isn't it? And the right of it – what belongs to whom."

"Yes." Events in the winter had proved that Wratchall-Haynes was, if not on the side of the angels, at least not on the side of the otherworldly Hunt, Master of Fox Hounds though he might be on this side of the fence. So she added, "Luna probably didn't mention it because they had bigger trespassing concerns," and she told him about Kit Coral and the drove.

When she had done so, Wratchall-Haynes was silent. Bee watched him closely. The blue-grey gaze was intent upon his coffee cup. She wondered what was going on in his mind. Eventually he said,

"I know of Captain Coral, though we've never met. As he said to your sister, he keeps himself to himself."

"He saved them from the drove, though. And from the Lily White Boys."

"Yes. He doesn't like the Hunt but it's not clear to me what other alliances, or allegiances, he might have. People in these liminal lands – particularly these edge places – aren't always easy to place. Right and wrong, good and bad – those are human concepts."

"I've been told that," Bee said.

"And you've grown up with it."

"To an extent. It's only recently that it's really come home to roost, one might say."

"If I went down and had a look at the place, the road where your sister and her partner were walking, see if this drove way might be visible, would you come with me?"

"I would," said Bee. She looked him straight in the face. "But I can't guarantee someone else might not come along as well."

Wratchall-Haynes looked nonplussed for a moment and then he said, "Ah. Might that be the Elizabethan gentleman?"

Bee laughed. "He's not a gentleman, actually. A sailor. One of Drake's men."

"Oh, really? That's – that's remarkable. I have seen him, you see, a couple of times. I assumed that either you had a boyfriend who was heavily into re-enactment or that he really was a ghost. Then, the second time, I realised that a hedge was slightly visible through him, which, I thought with my Holmesian powers of deduction, probably ruled out a re-enactor."

"He is my, well, boyfriend, though," Bee said. "God, that sounds so coy."

"No, it's quite all right. I am trustworthy to go gallivanting over the landscape with, in case you had concerns. I am safe in taxis, as they used to say when I was a kid. I have a sort of romantic interest of unusual origins myself."

"Do you, now! Care to say more?"

The MFH smiled. "It's a bit complicated. I will tell you at some point. I mean, if it works out. It might not."

"Good luck," Bee said, with feeling. "Anyway, I need to let this floor dry. Want to get going? And are you on your horse? In which case, I feel bound to tell you that my days of clinging on pillion are possibly over."

"I am in my 4 by 4, you'll be pleased to hear." Wratchall-Haynes stood. "Shall we, then?"

"Let's."

SERENA

After her chance meeting with Stella, Serena went into Borough Market as she had promised Stella and bought bread, cheese, and some doughnuts for later, and a hummus wrap for her lunch, which she ate sitting by the daffodils by the cathedral and watching the tourists come and go. She had, she thought, exercised considerable restraint in not buying everything in the entire market: it was very tempting. But this high bright day was an excellent one for a stroll and, once she had crossed the bridge, Serena turned left and walked in a westerly direction along the Thames. She passed Temple, thinking vaguely of the ancient knights with their red-on-white cross, enjoying the sunshine. Finally she reached the Victoria Embankment Gardens, overlooked by the imposing back façade of the Savoy, and to her delight found narcissi in the borders among the bronze statues of various worthies. Neither Robert Raikes nor Arthur Sullivan had anything to say to Serena. She did, however, pause before the statue of a man on a camel: a monument to the Imperial Camel Corps. The camel's nose was in the air; it had an expression of disdain, as is the way with camels. Serena regarded it for a moment.

From the nearby road, there was a sudden screech of tyres and a thud. Serena looked up in alarm, then ran to see. A cab had swerved to a halt and there was something black lying in the road: an umbrella? A coat? Then it lifted its head and she saw that it was a bird.

"Oh no!" cried Serena. She ran over. The driver was getting out of the taxi.

"Bloody hell! I didn't mean to hit it, love. It was just suddenly there in front of me. Is it all right?"

"It's not dead. I hope it hasn't broken a wing. It's a crow. No, larger than that. Is it a raven?" Serena said, for the bird was very big indeed. She thought of Miss Fane's cards: the Searchers, with the dark bird above their heads. She blinked. For a moment, it was as if a woman stood before her: an old woman dressed in black, with a cold unwavering stare. She looked up at the driver.

"It's got a band round its leg."

"He's a big 'un, isn't he?" An elderly man in an overcoat had paused.

"He really is. I think he's a raven." The bird was on its feet, but it seemed dazed and one wing was slightly extended. Serena was too nervous to touch it, but she needed to work out how to help.

"He is indeed. Shape of the beak. Quite different to a crow. Do you think he's come from the Tower? Or she. Don't know how you'd tell but they do have females."

"I can't think where else it might have escaped from. I thought they clipped their wings, though? I'm wondering if I should phone them."

"Look, sorry, love, but I've got to pick someone up and I'm already running late," the taxi driver said, uneasily.

"All right. It's got onto the pavement now, anyway. I can stay with it. Might be an idea for me to call the Tower," she said to the elderly man.

"Good idea. I'll keep an eye on it if you want to phone."

So Serena looked up the number and called. At length, she was put through to a man who was, as he put it, on the Ravenmaster's team. Serena was charmed to find that there was a person called the Ravenmaster, so much so that she took a moment to collect her thoughts and explain what was going on.

"Ah," said the man. "That will be Dorothy. I thought her wings were a bit long. She's only just come to us, you see. And now she's been and gone and done it. Where is she? Embankment Gardens! She's a naughty girl! I'll send someone along."

"Do you want me to wait with her? She's hurt," said Serena.

"You could do. That's very kind. I would advise you, madam," – here the man became rather formal "– not to try to pick up the bird. They have a nasty peck and she's not the sweetest tempered I've ever come across."

"Is she microchipped?"

"Her leg band has a tracker."

So Serena sat on a bench in the sunshine, the raven at her feet, waiting anxiously in case the bird tried to hop off. The elderly man had been obliged to go: a dental appointment, he told her apologetically. She did not like the idea of trying to catch the bird if it decided to wander. But the raven seemed docile enough. She hoped an actual Yeoman might turn up, in Beefeater's uniform, but at length, to Serena's relief, a fit young woman with a military haircut and a navy sweatshirt got out of a car, carrying a cage.

"Dearie me!" she said to Dorothy. "What have you been up to, then?" She knelt on the pavement and expertly examined the wing. "I don't think it's broken but you're going straight to the vet." To Serena's admiration, she picked the raven up gently. It clucked once, then subsided into the warden's arms and thence her carrying cage.

"Well done!' said Serena.

"Cheers for keeping an eye on the little bugger! Boss says you can have a free ticket to the Tower. What's your name?"

Serena told her, and gave her phone number to the driver. "Dorothy is an unusual name for a raven," she said.

"Yes, we had a lottery and a member of the public won."

She put the cage in the car, waved, and her driver pulled away. Just as well, Serena thought, for it was starting to spit with rain and the blue river had changed to grey, reflecting the sky. She ducked up Villiers Street, and down into the Tube.

BEE

Bee sat with Nick Wratchall-Haynes in the front seat of Nick's Range Rover, looking out over the land. He had driven down the lane where Luna and Sam had encountered the drove, but it was a Somerset country road, nothing more, and had remained so when he and Bee had got out of the car and walked back. It resolutely refused to become anything else. So they had got back into the 4x4 and were now sitting at the summit of one of the long rolling ridges of land that carried Somerset down to Dorset.

"Now you see it, now you don't," Nick said.

"To be honest I'm a little bit relieved. Luna's experience sounded alarming."

"Yes. You can't muck about with these things. Too dangerous."

"That doesn't seem to have stopped my mother," said Bee, before she could stop herself.

"No. Do you know what Alys has been up to?"

"Not really. Do you?"

"No, not really. Have you asked her?"

"Yes. Cartography, she suggested. Mapping the tracks and the ways. But she's not giving me the whole story and I don't like her links with the Hunt."

"It's a risky game to play."

"So come on, then," Bee said. "How much of this do you own, courtesy of Great Aunt Pamela?"

"Well, you can see my house." He pointed to where a pale Georgian façade was glimpsed between stands of oak. "And the fields to the right and left of Wycholt, and that hill. It's about ten thousand acres altogether so relatively small."

"Riiiiight."

"I know." He did not sound offended. "It's more than enough." He leaned forwards on the steering wheel. "But it's the key to all this, Bee. Land and who owns it."

"People like you?"

"You mean, my class? Robber barons and invaders and thieves made respectable."

"It's not your fault,' Bee said, suddenly uncomfortable.

"No, but it is my responsibility. I think of the Hunt, and those like them. They used to live here once, after the ice. People about whom we know almost nothing."

"The little dark people of the folk tales? The ones who went under the hills and became fairies?"

'Those might have been the Celts or the Picts, although they think now that the original peoples of these islands had black skin, don't they? Black skin and blue eyes. They used to think the Celtic tribes were pushed west into those hills you can just about see now."

Bee could indeed glimpse the Severn Estuary and the faint blue tracery of low Welsh summits beyond: the Brecon Beacons and the Black Mountains. Not really mountains at all: high humpy hills. But people still died on them, when the weather changed and the mists came down.

"Or maybe they weren't. Maybe 'underhill' is a metaphor, for going beyond this land, into others. And who owns those lands now?"

"I don't know. A king, perhaps, sleeping with his knights around him?"

Nick laughed. 'Back to the upper classes."

"I didn't know we had a king. I thought we were an autonomous collective."

Nick obviously knew his Monty Python. "Just because some watery bint gives you a sword… Very apt legend, round here."

"Ladies of the lake, indeed. So your estate manager will chuck people off all that land, will he?"

"There *are* footpaths across the estate."

"And if people stray from the path, will they meet a wolf?"

"'Can I help you?' is usually my opening gambit."

"Implying that they're somehow in trouble."

He was silent for a moment. Then he said, "A lot of this land would have been commonly held, once. Dunmote still has common land, though it's not very big. Hornmoon's a bit more enclosed.

Carved up, parcelled, behind walls and owned. A lot of forest was kept, by the monarchy, in which to hunt. The Royal chases." He grimaced. "Sorry if I'm huntsplaining. You probably know all this."

"And you yourself hunt, of course. Within the Act, I'm sure. Have you considered giving someone else's hunt permission to roam all that?"

He gave her a slanted glance, somehow sorrowful. "Perhaps it was theirs once. Hard to know. I was talking to an environmentalist acquaintance recently, about these new rewilding projects, and she told me that it's essential for diversity to have connecting passages between parcels of land: we haven't got enough of those. Long ago it wouldn't have been an issue, but when the Normans came, the land started to get parcelled up. Although I suppose the Black Death changed things – left room for land to be taken and ownership passed into other hands. This house wasn't built then but the estate was there: Wycholt was rebuilt, replaced an older house after a fire. But no. They don't come onto my property and the house is well protected."

"CCTV? Alarms?"

"And other things. You're welcome, though. Like to see the house?"

"Love to," Bee said. "Because I'm nosy."

A little later, they were standing in front of Wycholt. It was not an enormous stately home, but a small and perfectly formed manor house. Its golden walls caught and held the late sunshine; further gilt was supplied by the winter jasmine that twined up one corner, the yellow flowers shining. Further away, at the foot of a majestic beech, banks of snowdrops shimmered, just starting to go over.

"It's arguably not at its best at this time of year," Nick Wratchall-Haynes said, modestly. "You must see it in June, when the roses are out." He waved a hand at a knot garden, built into a series of small terraced steps.

"It's rather lovely now," Bee said. "You can see the shape and the form of everything. And I always love the winter flowers. Your jonquils are doing well." Double bloomed and with centres the colour of a rich egg yolk, they marched along the south-facing front of the house.

"Shall we go in?"

The doorway was crowned with fan vaulting, but as Nick located his keys, sunlight fell across it and Bee saw initials carved in the old stone.

"Who was V V, Nick?"

"Who – oh, you mean the witch mark. There are several in this house. It's not really a double V – it's an M. For the Virgin."

"To keep out witches, or pen them in? I've seen them in some of the churches round here, now you mention it."

"To keep them out. Otherwise I'm in trouble." He opened the door.

Bee had expected an element of grandeur and she got it, but it was a little faded, verging on shabby, the way that the interior of a manor house should be.

"Peeling paint and dog hair," said its owner.

"You live in it. Not curate it. Where *are* your dogs?"

Nick opened a door, through which Bee caught a glimpse of a large, old fashioned kitchen, and released a torrent of Labradors: two golden and one chocolate.

"Fifi, Bruce and Charlie."

"Hello, hello, hello." Bee allowed herself to be whuffled. "I'm assuming your actual hounds aren't allowed in the house?"

"No, they're working dogs. They have very nice kennels, which I sometimes think are warmer and more comfortable than my actual bedroom, in the stable block. The horses aren't allowed in the house either."

"Do you have staff?"

"Yes. My estate manager, already mentioned, and some people under him, Harris the gardener, and a woman who works as my part-time housekeeper – whom you know. Rachel Stanley, from Hornmoon."

"Oh, yes, of course. I did know that. I was on a committee with Rachel last year. Like her a lot."

"She spoke highly of you, too. Various people associated with the hunt. No butler, though. If I have dinner parties I use a catering company. No Jeeves."

"I see you more as the having a Bunter type," Bee said. "Wimsey, not Billy."

Nick laughed. "That's a bit more flattering. Everyone should have a Bunter. You do need help with places like this. I am doing a bit of renovation and I have more planned – I don't want to turn it into some blingy footballer's type gaff, but Pamela really didn't do anything to the place for years – you should have seen the quote for the roof. I nearly passed out. I am also talking to some architects who specialise in libraries."

"I have some library training," said Bee. "That isn't a hint, by the way."

"No, but I might ask you to come in and cast a professional eye over some of the books, if you'd like to do so. I didn't know that was your background."

"I'm not a career girl. Bits of this, bits of that. But hopefully all useful bits."

The library was beautiful: a long, high-ceilinged room lined with bookshelves. The ceiling was eggshell blue; the floor an ancient parquet.

"It's the floor that needs to go," Nick said, gloomily, kicking at a loose slab. "Come and have a look at the orangery."

This ran along the western side of the house and was, Bee noted but did not say, significantly warmer. Like all glasshouses, it was a suntrap; a curling vine, still with a crimson leaf wisping upon it, snaked along the window frame. A long table filled with potting equipment stood at its centre.

"Someone's been busy," Bee said, looking at the little rows of plug plants. The manor would have an extensive sweet pea collection in a few months' time. Dahlia roots hung from a rack.

"Harris, the gardener."

Bee duly admired a small lemon tree and a number of glossy camellias. As she made her way down the orangery, another tray of shoots, placed on the tiled floor, caught her eye: a dark bed of peat, with a few spires of something that was so white as to be almost luminous. Bee was about to say "What are those?" but something Luna had told her, about odd shoots in the beech mast up in the wood, jogged her memory and she bit her tongue. She did trust Nick Wratchall-Haynes, she told herself, but did she trust him absolutely? She thought the answer to that question should be *no*. She pretended not to notice the shoots, and followed the manor's owner obediently back into the sitting room, where she accepted a cup of tea.

Later, she told Nick that she didn't need a lift back to Mooncote.

"It's less than a mile and I could do with the exercise. Lose some of the Christmas padding."

"You're welcome to have a look round the grounds, if you like. And pop in any time."

"Thank you, I will. But I'll phone first."

"Was that a hint that I, too, shouldn't just drop by unannounced?"

"No, not at all. You're welcome anytime. Although we're not always in, of course."

"Give me your mobile number and I'll text." He grimaced again. "Modern habit."

Bee did so and took her leave. The grey-green front door, with its witch mark above, shut gently behind her and she was alone with the snowdrops and the jasmine. She stood for a moment on the terrace, admiring the view and thinking about the manor and its lovely grounds. A distant racket was raised for a moment – Nick's hounds – then died away. Bee noticed how quiet it was. Mooncote had its moments of stillness, but it was not far from the road, albeit a small country one, and there always seemed to be traffic of some kind: cars, tractors day and night, for in summer the farmers worked late if the weather was fine, motorbikes and the occasional bus.

Here, the manor seemed locked in silence, as though it had its own microclimate of sound. Perhaps this was what was meant by riches, by luxury, thought Bee. You could be sealed off from the twenty-first century, live whatever life you chose, be truly private. Nick was correct; this manor was not big in comparison to some of the great estates and neither were its grounds. She had once read somewhere that a third of Britain was still owned by the upper classes and here was a sliver of proof: how many great estates were there, walled away, sealed off? You thought you knew the countryside, but you did not: you only knew the places in which you were allowed to go. Public thoroughfares and footpaths, cycle tracks and canals, often fragmented and disjointed, like the old ways used by animals for their runs, disrupted by the human world. How many pockets like the manor might there be, hiding in plain sight?

Bee made her way down the drive, the lee of the wall ablaze with daffodils. The gate was ajar; Nick, on driving in, had not fully closed it again, presumably so that Bee could find her way out. She made sure that it snicked shut and, when it did so, an electronic beep sounded from the wall and a small red eye winked at her. She turned to take a last look. The manor was not visible from this angle – can't have the peasants gawping at their betters – and only the curve of the drive could be seen. But Nick had mentioned footpaths. Bee turned from the gate and began to walk along the soggy verge of the road, towards home.

STELLA

Later, Stella tried hard to remember what had actually happened, but it was difficult. The deer spirit seemed to exude her own field of energy, a power which was both heady and alarming. It was hard to notice anything beyond her immediate presence. Stella had witnessed this before, with Anione. Once, during a moment of danger, Ace's girlfriend had assumed what Stella thought must be her true form. She had raised the subject at one point.

"You looked like – well, a goddess, Anione. Is that what you really look like?"

"Sort of. I also really look like this." At the time, Anione had been wearing a mop-like fake fur and sunglasses. "It's a bit like when you're slobbing about at home in your pyjamas, and when you get all dolled up to go out."

This explanation made perfect sense to Stella. However, she doubted whether Noualen possessed the esoteric equivalent of pyjamas. She tried to imagine the deer spirit sitting in a pub in a parka and jeans and failed. From the amused glance that Noualen shot her, Stella also suspected that the spirit had caught this thought and she resolved to be more careful.

Noualen gestured to a stained glass window that Stella had not noticed before. It was a little window, with dots of trees in an expanse of parkland. Spring, Stella thought, for there were bluebells in the grass at the edge of the window, and then the window was gone and the bluebells were at her feet, their strong fragrance drawn upwards by the sun. Stella turned and saw a long bank of hawthorn, all in blossom red and white, running down the slope to a high bank of earth. It looked artificial: a rampart of some kind? In the distance, she could see movement in the oak woodland: a herd of deer, drifting among the blue haze. Beyond, to the north, lay forest, wave upon wave of trees in their springtime leaf.

"This is a lovely place, Noualen! Where are we?"

"St Pancras has changed a little, hasn't it?"

"Okay, *when* are we?"

"Do you see them?" Noualen pointed towards the woodland.

Stella could hear shouts. A group of riders burst out of the woodland, accompanied by a pack of dogs. She heard the note of a horn, haunting on the sunny air, heralding death. The deer sprang away, zig zagging into the trees. At the forefront of the hunt was a big man in a russet cloak on a big horse, a huge bay. He spurred it forwards.

"The king," Noualen said.

"Really? Which one?"

But beside the king, an archer was drawing his bow. He fired and Stella saw one of the deer fall, twitch, lie still.

"Oh!" she gasped. The riders headed into the wood but they were already fading away. A moment later they, the deer and the king were gone.

"Henry," Noualen said. Stella remembered the choleric face she had glimpsed in her vision.

"What, the Eighth? The one who murdered all his wives? Well, most of his wives."

"Yes. This land is Marylebone Park, part of the great forest of Middlesex that you can see running to the north of here. King Henry took this land from the Abbess who owned it and turned it into a hunting chase – you can see that ditch, built to keep out poachers. Before that, part of it was leased to tenant farmers and after the civil strife it returned to such use for a short time until it became a park. But until then, most of this land has always been a hunting ground for lords and kings."

"And how do you feel about that?"

"Why," the deer spirit said, and her green gaze glittered, "I am huntress and hunted, slayer and slain. These are my lands and when I came here first with the tribes, when the ice began to draw north once more, I roamed them as I pleased, as doe and fawn, but with my bow also. All," she said, and Stella thought how cold her face had become. "All, and beyond the narrow sea, where I was called the Pilot, and the great lands of the east, to the steppes and further. All were my territory once, where I and the reindeer herds ran and dreamed and ran again, and I led the Wild Hunt itself before my place was stolen from me and my enemies trapped me here, ensnared me in magic so that when I woke I could no longer remember the way out. I am confined to this old hunting chase, though it is a chase no more."

Stella looked at the greening world before her and thought about it becoming covered over with stone and streets as the centuries wore on. Then she thought about traffic, and taxis.

"You said you wanted a man 'with the knowledge'. You told me that when we first met. What did you mean by that?"

"There is always a man who knows the ways. If I could find him, he could tell me the way out of here: how to break free. Then I could travel the land as I pleased once more. Are you worried about the animals, the woods? About ancient trees being cut down for railway lines and housing estates? I could help. But not in this trap of steel and stone and park railings."

"So just to be absolutely clear, you can't just find a gate and walk out?"

"No. There are gates, but between worlds. There are paths and tracks and droves and leys, but between worlds. I don't have this knowledge any more; that part of my magic is blank, wiped clean. Humans cannot help me; my enemies keep aid from my door. I itch to be free. I am caged."

"And so you need the man with the knowledge," Stella said. "To show you how to unlock the cage."

"And so I need that man."

LUNA

Luna came out of the maternity clinic to find her mother reading a copy of *Hello*.

"Really, this is a pointless publication," Alys murmured. "I haven't heard of half of these people. Who *is* Harry Styles?"

"I think he's a singer," said Luna, vaguely. She had little interest in popular culture, although Sam sometimes put the radio on in the van.

"And this woman?" Alys held up a photo of a smiling blonde with perfect eyebrows.

"I have no idea."

"Enough. Would you like me to buy you lunch, Luna? Somewhere on the way back?"

"Thanks! I'm starving, actually."

Alys laughed. "Having a baby does that to you. Or you lose your appetite completely."

The day was sunlit but chancy. Luna watched as Glastonbury Tor appeared, looming along the Wells road. Alys, who was driving, took the road that led across the top of the town, past the Chalice Well and under the Tor itself; the road by which Sam and Luna had come to Mooncote in the autumn. Content to be a passenger, she looked out over the flat, water-dappled checkerboard of the Levels. The hedges were sprayed white with blackthorn and there were daffodils in the verges, strays from the gardens. Above, St Michael's tower, all that was left of the ruined Medieval church at the Tor's summit, seemed momentarily to wheel and swing, the pendulum of some celestial clock, untethered to the earth. Then they were out on the main road to Pilton, where the rock festival was held every year, leaving the Tor behind.

"Where do you want to have lunch, Luna? There's the Green Lion and the Oak Tree, or we could go into Hornlake and do lunch at the veggie café? It's still early."

Luna was about to say that she did not mind, but then Alys swore and stamped hard on the brake.

"What the hell?"

There was a bus in the road, angled so that it blocked both sides. It was painted in green and pink, and the destination panel had been replaced by a black piece of vinyl decorated with stars. As Luna stared, a man dressed in harlequin rags and a top hat got down from it and ran down the road waving a piece of paper.

"God!" Alys said. "It's Ian Anderson!"

"Who?"

"Lead singer of Jethro Tull? Oh, never mind. You're too young."

"I'm not," Luna said with indignation. "I know who Jethro Tull are – Sam likes them. I don't know their names, though. That's not really him, is it?"

"No, he's about thirty years too young. He looks like Anderson used to look, though. I didn't think anyone dressed like that these days. How funny. I wonder what he wants."

By now, the man had reached them.

"Sorry, we'll move the bus. But take one of these." He shoved the paper in through the window as Alys wound it down.

"What is it?" Luna asked. But the piece of paper was self explanatory. It had a red headline, like a road sign, and it said ROAD PROTEST.

"Oh," Alys said to the man, whose hat was garlanded with red plastic roses. "Is this about the new bypass? I signed a petition."

"Did you? Excellent! You're a star!"

"It was in the Post Office. I made enquiries. What a stupid idea!"

"We're not taking it lying down," the man said. "We're going to fight back. Occupy!"

"I hope you're not going to occupy the festie site. Michael Eavis won't like that."

"Nah, Glasto's sacred space. We're heading for some fields, round here. Farmer's sympathetic, says we can park up. There's a demo planned for Saturday. Maybe we'll see you there?"

"Maybe you will,' said Alys.

The man jogged back to the bus and pulled it into the oncoming lane, so that Alys could get past.

"Good to see someone's on the case about this bypass," Luna said. "There's been an ongoing row about it for ages."

"I only found out about it because of the petition, but apparently it was in the paper at the weekend. I've been away, of course."

"Yes, you missed all the fuss about it. It's been going on for months, but I sort of lost track of what was happening with it. What with – well, other stuff. Glastonbury's getting an addition to the existing bypass to take traffic out of the town centre, which is a good thing, but the planned route really isn't – it's round the back of the Tor and people will need to leave a couple of old farms, and ancient woodland will be affected and so on. I can see why they want one, though," Luna added. "Ginny lives in Bere Road and she says there are lorries thundering past every night."

"They're quarry lorries bound for Hinckley," Alys said.

"I know. Sam's mate Pavel from the pub works at the Hinckley site." Luna liked Pavel, but she did not like the idea of nuclear power. Wind and water, that was the way. It might not be enough, though.

"But the thing is, mum, the new reactor is going to be up long before the new road is built. So according to Gina, there's all sorts of talk about backhanders and bungs to the local MP and so on. We did a couple of road protests before, Sam and I. One of them actually did save a patch of ancient woodland, in Wiltshire, but the local community and the protestors and the farmers and everyone really need to pull together. Otherwise it just descends into squabbling."

"I remember that from CND," Alys said. "And Greenham."

Luna looked at her mother with curiosity. "Were you actually at Greenham, then, Mum? You've never mentioned it." She had a rather hard time imagining Alys, with her languid hippy elegance, hanging out in a yurt with a bunch of anti-nuclear protesting feminists. But then, she had a hard time imagining Alys hanging out in an otherworldly wood with inhuman ancient hunters, too. Best not mention that.

Alys sighed.

"I went on a couple of CND marches, in the eighties. Then my friend Miriam took me to Greenham once. Do you remember Miriam Haskin? Lefty Londoner with a lot of lovely red hair like you?"

"Vaguely," Luna said. "Didn't she have a really loud laugh?"

"Yes. Raucous, like a crow. Chain smoker. Moved up north. She was great. I still get cards from her occasionally. Anyway, yes, she took me to Greenham Common. It was a real badge of feminist honour – but those women were brave, Luna. They faced the American military and those men had guns. And the conditions at Greenham were terrible. The council kept cutting off the nearest water supply or something, trying to drive them out, so everyone stank. I couldn't handle it for more than a week; Miriam stayed and I sloped off home to the bath." She laughed. "Younger me was not like present me, Luna. I've changed since those days. But it was a good experience, all the same. Some of them were bitchy and there was a lot of bickering, but they still managed to hold it together and eventually the airbase packed up and left. The US government said that had been the plan all along."

"Yeah, right."

"It showed me what passive resistance could achieve, I suppose. I've never forgotten it. But you know me, Luna. I was never an activist."

Until now, Luna thought. The words hung unspoken in the air, as they drove slowly home. But for what cause?

STELLA

Next morning, Stella sat on the deck of the *Nitrogen* with her sister, for Serena had come over for supper last night and stayed. Both were bundled up in coats and both held a steaming mug of coffee but the main thing, Stella said, was that they were *outside.*

"It's spring!"

Serena laughed. "Actually, you're not far wrong. Now that the fog's gone…"

"So what are your plans for the day?"

"I should head back home in a bit. I've got to get some things together for the new backer. Paperwork and so on. She's very keen for me to focus on the creative stuff but I want to make sure that I understand the other bits, so I've got a meeting with the accountant this afternoon. But not till four." She took a sip of coffee and pulled a face. "I hate all that stuff. You know what I was like with maths at school."

Stella did. She recalled tears. Not that she herself had been anything to write home about: Bee had been the financial brain of the sisters. Their grandfather, being an astronomer and thus good at mathematics, had done his best.

"Adulting, though, Serena!"

"Yes, big girl pants and all that. Never mind. The accountant's really good – she has a way of explaining things that doesn't make me feel like a complete idiot – and one that's done I can be all virtuous and go and collapse on poor Ward."

"Has he finished filming?"

"Almost. He has some green screen work to do." She paused. "I keep thinking about Brighton. All these bits and pieces. The dead airman. Miranda. The raven. And not just these last few weeks – the winter. I've spent ages on the net looking up stately homes and seeing if any of them have a private chapel, like the house where Cas Pharaoh, well, died. But nothing looks right. I wonder if the house ever existed in our world, if it still does. It's a jigsaw puzzle and nearly all the pieces are missing."

"Well, look where doing some research got *me.* I phoned Luna. She was talking about her map," Stella said. She watched a river police boat chug downstream, the foam of its wake bright in the sunlight. The Thames was busy this morning and Stella liked that; she felt part of it.

"I'm trying to make all sorts of connections but I don't want to end up like a conspiracy theorist. Put two and two together and make seventeen."

"I felt, when I came back to St Paul's in our day, that I'd not really left *London the Book.* As though I was still in the story – but I suppose that's what cities are, aren't they? Stories, along with everything else they are. I've just come to the conclusion that I don't know what's going on half the time and Ace might be able to explain it to me, or he might not."

"At least you have an actual quest, though!" For Stella had related the events in the British Library and after to her sister.

"Yes, a lead! A clue! The game's afoot! The only problem is, I have no idea where to start."

"Want to come to the Tower with me? I'll buy you lunch."

"The *Tower?"*

"Yes. I got freebies for helping them rescue their raven. I thought since I was down this end of the river I might as well take them up on it. I actually have an ulterior motive – they have a Royal Ceremonial Dress Collection exhibition on at the moment and I want to take a look at it, for ideas."

"Your next collection will see them all on the catwalk dressed as Beefeaters?"

"Why not? Vivienne Westwood practically did. And they're insistent about being called 'Yeomen Warders,' apparently, not Beefeaters. But no, I wanted to look at some of Princess Margaret's dresses, in particular. Nineteen fifties sort of thing."

"She was a bit more hip than the Queen, as far as I remember," Stella said.

"Hey, no dissing her Majesty! Country dog breeder style. Knows what she likes and sticks to it."

"I wouldn't dream of it," said Stella. "I shall be trespassing in her Great Park soon enough."

*

In the stark sunlight, Stella could see why it was called the White Tower. The square, turreted fortress still commanded the river, in spite of the high office blocks behind it. They got off the boat near the Water Gate and followed the path around to the entrance. Some of the ceramic poppies from a Remembrance Day display, back in the autumn, were still in place, on loan apparently from the Imperial War Museum, and they spilled down the outer wall of the Tower like the blood that they symbolised. They caught the morning sun and held it in their scarlet cups.

Serena had been sent two e-tickets, it appeared. She checked these in and they passed through the entry gate into the Tower itself, opening out into an inner green.

"I think this is where they beheaded people," Serena said.

"I could do without any time slips right now, put it that way."

"It was bad enough finding a corpse."

"And I see no ravens."

"The ravens, madam, are around the Wakefield Tower today and I shall be feeding them shortly."

Stella turned and was pleased to see an actual Yeoman Warder, in traditional uniform and hat.

"What do they eat?"

The Yeoman Warder rolled his eyes. "Mainly crisps, which they cadge off tourists. What they're supposed to eat, which is what I'll be feeding them in a bit, is a balanced diet of chicks, mice and raw meat, plus some blood soaked biscuits as a special treat if they've been good and I'm feeling generous."

"Ick!" said Stella. "Sorry, resident vegetarian."

"Indeed. Ravens, however, are not."

"We're actually looking for the costume exhibition," Serena said.

"Oh, that's just around the corner. You'll see the sign."

Stella followed Serena obediently around the exhibition. Although not as interested in fashion as her professional sister, and with a strong preference for informal wear, she still liked clothes and felt she had an eye for them. Perhaps she had inherited it from Alys. She looked at the garments belonging to Princess Margaret with awe.

"I mean that… that's just like a meringue. I'm assuming it's her wedding dress. How did she get through the door? How did she fit into a *car?*"

"It's epic, isn't it… and that blue satin thing. That's amazing."

"Oh, come on, Serena, she looks like one of those 1970s conceal-your-loo-roll covers. And what the hell is going on with that fluffy yellow hat?"

But Serena had taken out a little notebook and was making sketches. "It's not the dress or whatever itself. It's the idea behind it." She made a face. "Sorry to be so pretentious."

"That's okay," Stella said. "You know what you're doing. If I tried to make a frock it would have three sleeves."

While Serena was drawing, she wandered around the exhibition, thinking back to the miniatures at the British Library. There were similarities, she thought. Some of the embroidery, so minute, but so perfect in its execution. The rich, deep colours. But although the exhibition had a curious, hushed atmosphere of its own, deep in this thousand year old building, no one came out of the air to stand by Stella's shoulder and assign her a task, nor did any of the headless mannequins come to life and dance her back into the past.

Eventually Serena snapped her notebook shut and said, "Shall we go and find some lunch?"

From the Raven's Café, you could watch the famous birds being fed. But it was a kiosk, with nowhere to sit, and neither Stella nor Serena fancied watching the ravens – all of whom were strutting about the green – choking down mice.

"As if they owned the place," Stella said.

"Well, they do. And if they go, the kingdom shall fall!"

"At least you've done your bit in preventing that from happening. Do you know which one is Dorothy or is she still at the vet's?"

"They all look a bit similar to me," said Serena. "But they very kindly rang me to say that Dorothy is fine if a bit bruised and recuperating in her cage. Look – the Armouries Café. There are seats."

Although it was still early in the year, the Tower was becoming crowded, with groups of tourists thronging in through the gate. Stella and Serena found a spare seat in the café and sat down to eat egg and cress sandwiches. When they had finished, they sat looking out across the sunlit green, Stella saw someone she thought she recognised.

"Shit! There's that man. The one I told you about, who followed me in Camden."

Today he was wearing a long shirt, jeans and the same hat. As they watched, he removed it, rubbed his head, put the cap back and turned. Beneath the cap, the stubble of hair was fire bright. The Fallow sisters stared.

"That man," Serena said, "I'm pretty sure he's also the one who was with Miranda."

LUNA

After the encounter in the lane, Luna found that she was reluctant to go too far from Mooncote. She did not like feeling this way. She had always been independent, intrepid, even. Before her life with Sam she had taken the festival circuit, heading down as far as Portugal with friends doing the summer rave scene, although Luna had not liked the crowds. With her friend Rowan and Rowan's husband Moss, before the arrival of their children, she had travelled up to the Western Isles in Rowan's old camper van and that had been lovely: the memory of those clear seas, the drifts of rain, the islands appearing through the mists, still turned up in occasional dreams. She had always been restless and the road had answered that call. Now she did not feel like going anywhere. It must be pregnancy. She asked her mother, and Alys replied that she did not think it was uncommon.

"You're grounding, my darling. You need a burrow, like a hobbit."

Luna liked the idea of a hobbit hole, but when she found herself reluctant to walk down to the local shop, something was wrong. It was, she recognised, simply fear. *Have a word with yourself, Luna!* So when Bee suggested a walk, she gathered her courage and agreed.

"Where were you thinking of going?"

"Well," Bee said. "Nick rang earlier, and I said I'd take some bulbs over to Wycholt. Narcissi, in exchange for some of his irises. I've got so many in pots. Not that he hasn't got bulbs of his own but these are very pretty when they're fully out."

"So you're on bulb swapping terms now?"

"Hobnobbing with the gentry!" said Bee. "Also, it's an excuse."

Surely Bee wasn't contemplating an affair? Luna chided herself at the thought. But then Bee said, "You know you told me about those shoots you saw in the wood?"

"Yes." Bee had come into the sitting room to find Luna on the floor, surrounded by books about flora, and it had been then that

Luna mentioned the shoots. But the phone had rung and the evening moved on. Now, Bee said, "Nick's got some weird white shoots in his orangery. I've never seen anything like them."

"So in our guise as innocent milkmaids, bearing flowers, we're going to investigate the Lord of the Manor?"

"He did give me a standing invitation," Bee said, somewhat defensively. "And what I thought was, that you and I, rosy-cheeked from the fresh country air and smiling over our milk pails, could sit having tea with Nick if he's in while Dark has a poke about in the orangery. If he's out, we'll all have a poke about."

"Brilliant! Couldn't you just send Dark over there anyway? Since he's invisible. Well, some of the time."

"I did think of that, my dear Watson, but there's a snag: Dark, as a sailor, knows bugger all about plants. You'd think that a country boy from Elizabethan times would do, and I have to say he knows more than the average village teenager these days, not that the bar is high, but he says that although he can tell roses from daffodils, and some of the country remedies like dock leaves and jack in the hedge – which was used to starch ruffs, did you know that? I didn't – he's better with things of the sea than country matters."

"So you're hoping Nick's going to be out, basically?"

"Yes. Dark's my secret weapon of mass investigation but he's only going to be deployed if we can't get into the orangery ourselves."

Changeable, thought Luna, as they set off. She had pulled on Wellingtons and a waterproof, just in case. As they left Mooncote the sun was shining, casting sparkles in the puddles on the road, but a stiff east wind was blowing the clouds along before it, a herding dog, and the light kept snapping on and off as the clouds covered the sun and were driven on again. When they reached the gates of Nick's house, however, it was bright once more and unspeckled by rain. Bee pressed the button and an invisible voice answered. She spoke her name and the gates swung open.

"Wow," Luna said. "It's big enough. I've never actually been inside the grounds of the house, just bits of the estate. Lady P had gone a bit odd by the time I was old enough to appreciate local architecture."

"Yes. When I was here last I kept wondering how much of the English countryside you can't get into and never see."

Luna snorted. "Sam and I could give you a good idea, having been chased off quite a bit of it. Even the bits that aren't private property."

"I'm sorry people are so intolerant."

"So am I but it's not like every travelling person is a saint, either. It's like any community. You get all sorts. Nick doesn't seem to be a bad person, although if you'd spoken to me when I was younger I'd have said we needed a revolution. Actually we still probably do need a revolution. We had one, but it didn't take."

"That was a rebellion against the divine right of kings, not actually a revolution, unless you're thinking of the Peasants' Revolt. Maybe we do need one."

"The peasants are revolting," said Luna. "But I have chilled out a bit. So perhaps we shouldn't have one in which Nick's put up against the wall and shot."

"No, that wouldn't be good. I hope he hasn't bugged the drive."

Luna laughed. "Those daffs are actually microphones."

"I can't help feeling a bit shifty. He gave me free run of the place, pretty much, and here are we planning to break into his orangery."

"I won't need to break in." Luna turned to see Dark, strolling alongside.

"Oh, you *are* here."

"Yes." He smiled. "I think Bee should just ask the huntsman about his garden, though. From what I know, he is to be trusted."

"Maybe I should just do that!" Bee said. "And forget all this cloak and dagger stuff."

But Nick Wratchall-Haynes was not at home, the stablehand who had let them in informed them.

"I've brought him some bulbs," Bee said, displaying the contents of her bag. "He promised me some, too, but it doesn't matter. It can wait. Shall I just pop these in the orangery?" *Well played, Bee!* thought her sister.

"Yes, do you know the way?"

"Round to the left, isn't it? Is the door open?"

The door was.

SERENA

"Are you sure it's the same bloke?" Stella hissed across the café table.

"Yes, positive. It's just something about the way he turned his head. You didn't tell me the chap in Camden had red hair."

"That's because I didn't know. In Camden he was wearing that stupid hat."

"He looked quite dapper when I saw him on the pier. Now he looks a bit of a skater."

"True! At least he's not a hipster. He doesn't have a man bun. The thing is, I wasn't sure if he was actually following me or if I was just being paranoid. But I am sure now."

"Well," said Serena, finishing the last bite of her sandwich and standing up. "If he can follow us – as I have already proved, we can follow *him.*"

Skater Boy, as Serena now thought of him, since it was less alarming than 'Miranda's bestie', crossed the road from the Tower itself and vanished into the nearest Tube station, Tower Hill. Serena and Stella hurried through the barriers.

"Where's he gone?"

"I don't – ah, there. Don't get too close to him. I don't want him to see us."

Skater Boy took the escalator down to the green and yellow sign for the Circle and District line. At a safe distance, Stella and Serena followed, just as a train pulled in.

"Quick!" They leaped aboard.

"Can you see him?"

"Yes. He's in the next carriage. Don't look right now, Stella, keep your face turned. He's sitting down. He's picking up a copy of the Metro… Look now, while he's busy reading."

Stella pressed her face to the edge of the window. "I'll keep an eye on him. Wonder where he's going?"

The Circle Line train took them through the rosary of stations: Monument, Victoria, Green Park and up.

"If he's going all the way round I'll be seriously pissed off," Serena said. She had to remind herself not to whisper: in the separate carriage there was no way that they could be overheard above the clatter and rattle of the tube, but the clandestine nature of their journey was taking its toll on her.

"Yes, I'll have to top up my Oyster card."

"So will I."

But as the train roared into South Kensington, Serena, glancing into the carriage, saw Skater Boy rise, discard the newspaper and exit in the company of a Japanese tour group.

"Wait a moment. Now!"

They joined the end of the crowd and kept his bobbing hat in sight. He took the stairs up and went out into the street.

"Handy for you, Serena," Stella said, with a nudge. "Home turf and all that."

"I don't like the thought of him hanging round my neighbourhood," said Serena.

"Maybe he lives here?"

"Oh, great! And now it's raining." A thin drizzle had started to fall, clouds blocking out the sun.

"It's only a shower," Stella said hopefully, nodding towards the brighter western sky.

They followed Skater Boy as he made his way past the Natural History Museum and into the streets beyond. Cafés, pubs and institutions familiar to Stella and Serena came and went.

"If he lives here," Stella said, "He lives awfully close to you."

"We're nearly at the Lion and Unicorn," said Serena. A horrible suspicion was beginning to take hold of her and she felt queasy and cold. Skater Boy went straight through the arch at the end of the mews and, holding back for a moment, they saw him whisk around the corner, past the pub with its half barrels of daffodils.

"Christ, is he actually going to your house?" Stella said.

"I don't know! I hope not!"

"Is Bella there? No, she must be at school."

"She is at school. Charlie's in the studio, though. I don't like this, Stella. Who is he? No friend of Miranda's can be a good thing – look at the last lot we met."

"First an evil faery, now a man in a stupid hat."

Anxiously, they peered around the corner, but Skater Boy was nowhere to be seen.

"Has he just gone past yours?"

They went quickly down the mews and Serena, gathering her courage, opened the door of the studio.

"Hi, Charlie! Do we have a visitor?" She forced enthusiasm into her voice. The result sounded, to her own ears, slightly deranged.

Charlie looked up from a pattern with a mouthful of pins. "No. Why, are we expecting someone?" she said, having removed the pins. "I thought you were seeing Linda."

"Not till four. Never mind. I thought I saw someone at the door."

"Nope, all quiet," Charlie said.

"I'll leave you to it."

Stella, meanwhile, had jogged down to the end of the mews and back.

"I can't see him. But it's such a warren of little streets round here."

"Maybe he is just visiting someone and it's all a coincidence."

"Serena," her sister said, and pointed. On the tiled step in front of Serena's house was a perfect, damp footprint.

BEE

Breaking and entering was not Bee's style but she felt that, with the permission of the stable hand, this hardly counted. With Dark and Luna, she had made her way round to the side of the house where the orangery basked in the winter sunshine.

"A glass house," her lover said.

"Yes. You've seen them before. We've got one. Well, a greenhouse."

"A small greenhouse," said Luna.

"Yes. Not like this."

"I have seen an orangery in my own day. In Italy, near Naples."

Bee looked at him. "I didn't know you'd been to Italy, Ned! You've never told me that!"

"When I was first at sea. A boy, no more. With a merchant captain."

"How Shakespearean!"

He laughed. "Yes, Illyria. But I did not meet my Juliet. Until later, of course," he added with a small bow. Bee grinned. "It was a lovely country and the orangery was part of a great estate; I remember it was filled with lemon trees and their scent filled the air. Like paradise. Well," a slanted glance, "What paradise is supposed to be like."

"I don't think Nick's orangery is quite so paradisical," Bee said. "But it's very nice. Depending, mind you, on what he's growing in it."

She took the handle of one of the doors and gave it a gentle push. It swung inwards and Bee stepped in.

"So where are these things, then, Bee?"

Bee showed her sister to the seed tray. She felt her skin prickle slightly, as though she was being watched, but when she looked through the windows, across the garden to the dark yew hedge, no one was there. Dark had remained in the doorway.

"Are these like the ones you saw, Luna?"

"Yes. Exactly the same. But these are much bigger."

"They're bigger than they were the other day," Bee said. "A lot taller and stronger."

"What *are* they, though?"

"I don't know, Luna. I've never seen anything like them. Ned? Come and have a look at these."

But Dark did not know either.

"I bet they glow in the dark. They're a bit like those things in the Moomintroll books, do you remember those, Bee?"

"Hattifatteners? Yes, aren't they? Except pointy. And no little hands or eyes."

"Thank God!" said Luna. "They're creepy enough as it is."

"They were a couple of inches long the other day. Now they're six or seven. They're like mushrooms – one minute there's nothing there, then suddenly they're all around."

"Yes, they are. Look, there's a tiny little one just starting to come up." Luna pointed, to a fingernail-sized shoot right at the edge of the seed tray. She and Bee looked at each other in quick surmise.

"We shouldn't," said Bee.

"No. But we're going to." Luna snatched one of the little seed pots, no more than three inches or so. Bending quickly, she scooped the shoot and its surrounding compost into the seed pot, then patted down the compost again with a nearby trowel.

"Quick, take the bulbs out and put it in the bag. It'll go in my pocket."

"I feel terrible!" said Bee.

Luna looked slightly abashed. "I know. I don't like it either. But how else will we know?"

"Dear Nick, we came to bring you some bulbs and then we pinched one of your weird glowy fungal shoots because we couldn't help ourselves. Sorry." Bee took a notepad out of her bag. "I am actually going to drop him a line and put it through the door. But not mentioning this."

"I hope he hasn't bugged the orangery as well as the drive."

"I hope the rest of them don't tell him." Bee looked at the shoots. It could have been her guilty imagination, but they seemed to have grown even more.

"That's a really scary thought."

"If, I mean, if he does realise, somehow, I'll just pretend to be Mad Garden Lady and say oh I didn't think you'd mind, they looked so interesting, I just can't resist a new plant."

"Just tell him the truth," Luna said. "We saw some weird shit in your orangery and we thought we'd check it out some more."

"Now that we're raided the place, I think we should go. I've written him a note – I'll leave the bulbs here and shove the note through the door."

Back at the imposing front of the house, Bee's guilty conscience prompted her to expect the sight of Nick Wratchall-Haynes himself, rocking up in the Range Rover. But the stablehand had returned to the back of the house and the grounds were silent in the sunlight. They went back down the drive and along the road to Mooncote without seeing another soul.

"God!" said Bee, when they were safely inside the kitchen. "I feel like I've robbed a bank."

"You really aren't cut out for a life of crime, are you? What are we going to do with the shoot?"

"I think, since Nick was after all keeping them in the orangery, that we ought to pop it in the greenhouse. I have got some seedlings on the pantry windowsill but I don't really like the idea of keeping it in the house, somehow."

"In case it starts walking about," said Luna, and shivered. "Now *I've* given myself the creeps."

"Greenhouse it is."

"Are we going to repot it?"

"Yes, it was sitting in what looked like ordinary peat compost, so I'll put it in a bigger pot."

"Also, I am obviously going to tell Sam." Luna put the little pot on the table and studied it. The fingernail shoot was, Bee thought, slightly further above the level of the soil, but it had been disturbed. "But are we going to let Mum know?"

Bee considered this. "She doesn't usually go in the greenhouse, although she was talking about her roses the other day and tying up the winter jasmine. She's always been quite into gardening. But she hasn't mentioned actually planting anything although I've got all the seed catalogues. And I expect that's because she doesn't expect to be here when things are due to come up."

"I think you're right." Luna filled the kettle and switched it on. "Dark, when we were in the orangery, did you see anything? Anyone? I mean, like another ghost?"

He nodded. "Yes, a woman in a gown, walking along the hedge. Not from my day, but later. There was a child with her, and a little dog, a spaniel. She was laughing and the child laughed, too."

"Happy ghosts," said Bee.

"Yes, happy ghosts. Nothing felt bleak or wrong. Perhaps in the house it would be a different story – most places have seen violence or death, after all. But it depends if the deaths were peaceful."

"It felt fine to me," Bee said. "It's an eighteenth century house, so it was built after the Civil War. A more peaceful time, at least in England itself. We'd exported a lot of our violence by then."

"Also the huntsman is working magic. So perhaps he has banished ill influence from the place."

"Yes, quite possibly. There are witch marks over the front door, for a start. All right, Luna – let's put the shoot in the greenhouse and keep an eye on it. We'll tell Sam; we won't tell Mum. We have a plan."

Just before she went to bed, Bee pulled on a pair of gardening shoes and went out to the greenhouse. It was lit only by a single dim bulb but it was enough for her to see that the shoot was now a good half inch above the surface of its new abode. Bee contemplated it for a minute, then the thought struck her that she did not really want to watch it grow. She turned off the light, closed the greenhouse door, and went to bed.

STELLA

"Could we get in through the back door?" Stella asked, then answered her own question. "We can't, can we."

"No, we'd have to get over the garden wall. And to do that we'd need to get into the house at the back – that's Marina Adler's house and she might not be in. Also I'd have to explain. Maybe we should just phone the police?"

"He'll have to come out this way, then. Unless he's a professional burglar or something."

"They don't normally use the front door. And how the hell did he open it? If he's in my house," Serena said, "I think I'd rather catch him at it."

"He doesn't look like the kind of person who might carry a knife. I'm sort of thinking Millwall supporter type and he's not like that. He looks a bit too much like a – like a Pink fan."

"Caspar Pharaoh looked exactly like a successful businessman. And look how that turned out!"

"Open the door and leave it open. If we're going to surprise him, I don't think we ought to corner him."

"All right," said Serena, and put the key in the lock as quietly as she could.

Inside, the hallway was quiet. Serena and Stella, mice in pursuit of a rat, crept in and listened. No sound, except for the distant humming of the fridge. Then, upstairs, a board creaked. Stella looked around for a suitable weapon but there was nothing to hand, not even an umbrella. But she had given herself an idea. She went into the kitchen and plucked two Sabatier knives from the rack. She handed one to Serena, expecting resistance, but her sister, mouth tightening, simply took it.

They went up the stairs. Halfway up Serena mouthed something and pointed downwards: Stella remembered the creaky step. She missed it out and soon they were on the landing. The other betraying board sounded again; it was in an upstairs front room, which Serena had turned into a study for Ward. They took position on either side of the door. Stella felt suddenly foolish. What was she going to do, kick it in? But at that point the door opened and Skater Boy came out, rather fast.

Faced with two knife wielding women, he neither fought nor ran. He stopped dead. His mouth fell open. He said,

"Oh my God!"

"Wrong house?" said Stella, archly.

"Okay, look. I know people always say this, but I can explain."

"I think you'd better!" Serena told him. "Who are you? What are you doing in my house?"

"Please don't stab me. That's a lovely pale carpet." He was, distinctly, somewhat camp of speech.

"I don't think you have any right to worry about my carpet when you've just broken into my house! Why shouldn't I just call the police?" Serena demanded, brandishing the carving knife. Skater Boy took a hasty step back.

"You could," he said. "But it wouldn't do much good." He also sounded apologetic.

"And why is that?"

Skater Boy sighed. "This is going to take some time to unpack."

At this point, there was a sound from below. Stella heard the sound of footsteps. A voice called, "Darling? Are you there? Did you know that the front door is wide open?"

"Ward? We're up here, Stella and me. We've got company."

"What do you mean, company?" Ward came rapidly upwards and saw Skater Boy.

"Sorry about this," said Skater Boy, again.

"Good God," Ward said. "Hello, Hob."

Now that Stella had the time to study Hob properly, and he had removed his hat, she could see traces in his face which were not quite human. Angular, like Tam, like Dana, like the Hounds. You wouldn't see it unless you were looking for it. And there was a waxy quality to his skin, although she thought that might be simply to do with fear. She had noticed a very slight tremor to his hands as he reached for his tea. They were now sitting around the kitchen table, for all the world as though Hob had been an old friend, dropping in for a cuppa and a slice of cake. Which Serena had actually given him.

"This is very good cake," he mumbled, around a mouthful of it.

"I'm not entirely sure you deserve it!" his hostess snapped.

"I love lemon cake."

"So." Ward was grappling with this. "Why did you – I mean, what are you *doing* here? How did you get in?"

Hob sighed and finished his cake.

"I have a key."

"What! Where did you get it?"

He sighed again. He looked sheepish but Stella wasn't sure how genuine it was. She didn't trust him. "Miranda gave it to me."

"What!" said Serena, again. "And how did *she* get it?"

"I think she got it from you," Hob said to Ward.

"She most certainly did not! I wouldn't have given her the key to a public toilet!"

"At New Years," said Hob, "you went to a party and Miranda was there. She took the key from your pocket and she, well, she changed something else into it, so that she had two. She put one back and kept the other one."

"You are kidding me! She didn't get close enough to pick my pocket."

"That's what you think."

"Ward," Serena said, "When we were separated, at that party of Cas Pharoah's, do you remember exactly what happened to you, before we met up again?"

"I thought I just hung around in the kitchen eating cheese."

"Uh, I don't think you did, Ward." There was a glint in Hob's eye which Stella didn't like.

"What are you suggesting?"

"I know you didn't fuck her. I'm not saying nothing else happened. I don't actually know the details."

"Sodding hell," said Ward after a pause. "Magically rohypnolled."

Serena put her hand over his. "Whatever happened, it wasn't your fault. It was that bloody woman. I saw you on Brighton pier," she said, accusingly, to Hob. It was his turn to be taken aback.

"What?" he said, in echo of Serena. "When?"

"In 1893."

"I don't – I don't remember." He looked at his plate and for a second Stella felt sorry for him. "Look, I have been to Brighton with Miranda. A long time ago, and when we went – well, we went back through time. I very vaguely remember the pier and some sort of game – she was looking for someone. Was that *you?* But you're not – you are human, aren't you?"

"More or less. I was born properly and all that. But I am sometimes subject to temporal slippages," said Serena, primly, as though it was some condition of which to be ashamed.

"Ah."

"So you have a key to my front door." Serena held out her hand, palm upwards. "I'll have that back now, thank you." Hob reached into his pocket and gave the key to Serena. A moment later something small and gnarled sat her hand. A hawthorn twig.

"It was single use. Apparently."

"Hmmm!" Serena said.

"I really am sorry. Look, Miranda and I have been friends for a long time. But I don't always trust her and I know she gets up to – well, a lot of stuff."

"You've always been decent to me," said Ward, in a slightly gruff Englishmen-do-not-talk-about-their-emotions way, "which is more than I can say for Miranda. I remember that day you disappeared. From the flat."

For a moment Hob looked blank. "Oh. That, yes. I slipped up. Hoped you hadn't noticed. Miranda said she'd sorted it."

"What are you, Hob?" Stella asked. "One of them? The secret people? Like Caspar Pharoah? Like Miranda?"

He gave a snort. "Miranda? She's not like Pharoah. I'd say God rest his soul but he hadn't got one."

"My sister met a person called Hob, back in the winter. He was the brother of – the brother of someone she met. You're not him, are you? Wose kin?"

"Nah, that wasn't me. But in the otherlands it's a really common name. Bit like Dave, I s'pose. Anyway, Miranda – she hangs around the scene hoping to pick up scraps and patches. People hire her to do things. She thinks she's being clever – she can't see they're just using her. She likes to think she's a witch. I worry about her. She's got a bit of magical talent, you might say, but she's malicious, not dangerous. Not really. As for me," he looked downcast, "I don't know. I've never known. My mum was a model, lovely she was. I've seen photos. She died from an overdose when I was a baby and I was brought up by my gran. In Clapham."

"How remarkably unsupernatural," Stella said. "And your dad?"

"I don't know. That's the thing. I don't think he was, you know, mortal. Or not all that mortal, anyway. I've seen stuff all my life, weird stuff, and I can do some shit. Like walk through some walls, not all. Jump about in time, but only sometimes. Miranda's been nicer to me than pretty much anyone else so I stick by her. But I'm not really part of a scene."

"So what were you doing at the Tower? Checking up on us?"

"Yes. I actually followed you from that boat. You looked pretty settled in the Tower so I thought I was sorted." He rolled his eyes. "Obviously not. You followed me. You're not supposed to be able to see me if I don't want you to." There was a touch of petulance in that, but no accusation. "How did you know who I was?" he went on.

"We didn't. I spotted you in Camden the other day. I gave you the slip."

"Oh God!"

"I think, to be perfectly frank, whatever your origins, you need to work on your espionage skills, mate."

"So why did Miranda send you here today? What were you supposed to steal?" Serena was keeping on track.

"Oh," Hob said. "I didn't come to steal anything. I came to leave something. This." And he reached into his pocket once more.

BEE

Next morning, Bee and Luna slipped out on the pretext of dog walking and made their way to the greenhouse. Alys was writing a letter, or so she said; Sam had gone down to check the horses.

"Did you tell him?" Bee asked, when they were out of earshot of the house.

"Yes. He doesn't like it but he said he could see why we'd done it. He's not cross with me. Not," Luna added with some spirit, "that it would matter if he was. But I'd rather we agreed. Also I think he's interested to see what it's going to become although he did say that it might be a good idea to try and fence it off in some way. Magically, he means."

"Can he do that?"

"He's going to talk to Dark," said Luna.

"Maybe he should call his nan?" Bee unlatched the door of the greenhouse.

"I said the same and he's going to do that too."

Once inside, it was obvious that the shoot had grown. It was already more than an inch above the soil, and taking on that shining green-white, like a snowdrop in the sun.

"I can't help thinking it's going to turn into a bloody triffid," Bee said. "Like that film about the dentist."

"Little Shop of Horrors. I think you ought to consider just asking Nick what it is."

"Perhaps I will. I don't think I'd better tell him that we pinched one, though."

"No."

"Luna, did you hear someone calling?" Bee thought she had heard a car door slam, too.

Luna frowned and pushed aside the mesh that protected the greenhouse from the chill. "Yeah, I did." She cried, "Sam? Was that you?"

"Yes!" Sam appeared around the side of the house, dusting off his hands. He was grinning. "Guess who's here?"

And a moment later Ver March, Sam's grandmother, came to join them.

"Well," Ver said, staring down at the shoot. "I can't say that I *do* know what that is, as a matter of fact."

"It's growing really fast," said Bee.

"But some things do, don't they? I mean, you can turn your back on a pot and the next minute it's full of crocuses."

"Toadstools," said Bee.

"Precisely. Well, definitely keep an eye on it."

"Sam thinks we should shut it off, somehow."

"I think so too, but the only trouble is, sometimes by doing that it has a knock on effect and you end up attracting the attention of something else. I'll have a go, though."

"Can we help?" asked Luna.

"No, dear, although you can make me a cup of tea when I've finished. This won't be very dramatic." The old lady closed her eyes, firmly. Bee saw with amusement that she had matched a pair of ancient hiking boots to some bright Scandinavian leggings, just visible beneath her skirts, and a sweater with a Ralph Lauren logo on it. Baba Yaga, Bee thought. Sort of.

"I heard that," Ver March said without opening her eyes. Bee felt herself flush bright red.

"I'm terribly sorry!"

"No, don't be, dear – I take it as a compliment. Now, everyone think of nothing for a moment. I know it's tricky."

After a minute, she opened her eyes.

"All done."

It did feel different in the greenhouse, Bee thought, though she could not put her finger on it.

"Now for that cup of tea," Ver said.

In the kitchen, half an hour later, Alys said to Ver,

"So let me get this straight. *You* are joining this road protest?"

"I am. I've brought my tent." She gestured to a large bundle in the corner of the kitchen. "I've felt a bit cooped up this year and then last week my old friend Janey got in touch and said, how about a bit of troublemaking? Well, it struck me as a worthy cause and I thought it would be a chance to get out and about a bit, so I packed my stuff and down I came. If it had been up in Yorkshire, say, perhaps I wouldn't, but it's a chance to see Sam and the girls, I said to Jane, and what with Luna's baby being well on the way now, an extra pair of hands in this part of the country might not be unwelcome."

"It's lovely to see you!" Luna said. She took Ver's old hand and gripped it.

"Thank you, dear! And a chance to get out in the weather just when the tide's on the change."

"Tide?" asked Bee.

"Yes, the tide of the year. Two of them, one in the spring around the equinox – bit of a way to go before we get to that but it's starting now, you can feel it with the evenings getting lighter and all that – and the other in the autumn. Like a kitchen scales, I always think. But this year they say it's a big one. Remember the Severn Bore? Like that, only magical. Tide's changing and it's time to be on the move."

Later that afternoon, Bee took Ver March down to the protest site. She told Sam, who had offered, that she wanted to get out of the house, clear her head with a short drive. But this was not true. Bee wanted a private word with Ver.

"Is your being here just about the protest and the spring?" she asked, once they were in the Land Rover and on their way. Twilight was not far off, the cold shadows moving in.

"Yes and no. I don't tell lies, it's not my way, but I don't always say what's on my mind either. You're the same, I expect."

"Pretty much."

"The protest's an excuse, although I have been on them before. I don't like the land being threatened, concrete poured over it. It's necessary sometimes, I grant you. But I wanted to keep an eye on Luna and Sam, and I must confess I would like to know what your mother is up to."

"So would I," said Bee, with feeling.

"Jane did ask me to come. I didn't make that up. But when she said where it was, I got that *feeling*. No such thing as coincidence, I always say. So I don't quite know what's behind it – I've told you and Luna what I do know and that's not much – but if the universe gives you a present, well…"

"Not to look a gift horse in the mouth," Bee said.

"Exactly."

The road opened out before them to reveal the hummock of Glastonbury Tor rising from a patchwork of grey, silver and blue.

"I always liked that little hill," said Ver. "I shall be glad to spend a bit more time at its foot."

"Is that where the farm is?"

"I have a map."

Bee pulled into a layby and they studied it. It was drawn on the back of an envelope but she thought she knew where Ver was going.

"Okay. It's down that lane and round. Mind you, you don't realise how much there is of the Tor. It looks so humpy but the back of the hill goes on for ages – I've got lost up there before now."

"I've never been there before, not exactly," Ver said, taking charge of the map, "but I'll do my best."

The road that led to the Tor was lined with hawthorn, more than Bee had seen when she had last driven this way a couple of days before. They found the farm gate without trouble, and got out of the car to discover the air had a softness to it and the light was lingering.

"It'll be down there, I expect," Bee said, pointing to a loose assembly of tents around a central yurt. "I'm surprised the farmer's letting them use his field. They usually don't want the bother. Police and that."

"Glastonbury's pretty alternative, though, and that goes for some of the farming folk. I've met people like that before. Ah, there's Janey!" She waved enthusiastically and a grey haired woman in her sixties came up the track to wrench the gate open.

"Ver! You made it! I'll put the kettle on."

"This is Bee Fallow, my Sam's Luna's sister, who was kind enough to give me a lift. Are you stopping, Bee?"

"No, I'd better get back. Stuff to do. But thank you. And I know where you are. Let me or Sam know if you need a lift anywhere."

"I should think we'll be just fine from now on." Ver hoisted her rucksack onto her shoulders. "Just time to get the tent up before dark."

"Don't get arrested! But we'll bail you out if you do."

Having dropped Ver off, Bee lingered a little on the way home, taking a circuitous route and looking at the lie of the land. There had been lambs in some fields since mid-January, the winter lambs, but now there were more, and Bee watched with delight as a flock of wild swans flew across the road, settling down for the night. With the window slightly down, she could hear the rush and hiss of their wings, like a white river pouring down the sky. They alighted in the water meadows, to pick their way among the snowy little egrets, visitors from Egypt when Bee was a child but permanent residents now. Global warming, she thought, and wondered what changes would be in place by the end of her life. By the time she reached Mooncote, it was fully dark. She went round to the greenhouse first to check on the shoot, but it did not seem to have grown further, somewhat to Bee's relief. She went into the house with dinner on her mind and found her mother and Luna chopping vegetables.

SERENA

The thing that Hob now placed on the table was pallid, and slightly smaller than Serena's thumb.

"Just a doll," Hob said. It was a small, naked child, female, with its hands by its sides and rudimentary feet, more like a little podium than anything else. He stood the figure up: it was not quite steady.

"That looks, what, Victorian? It's china," Serena said.

"I dunno where it comes from. Miranda gave this to me and told me to put it in your house somewhere where it wouldn't be spotted."

"Lovely," said Ward. "What does it do?"

"I don't know."

Serena reached out and picked up the little figure. It was cool and hard in her hand, surprisingly heavy.

"No signs of life," she said.

Ward was looking hard at Hob. "And you are quite sure you don't know what this is supposed to do?"

"No, she didn't tell me. But I should think it's a spy device of some kind."

"Has she heard of tape recorders?" Stella asked.

Hob smirked at that. "She's not exactly a tech whizz kid."

"You're telling me," said Ward. "Miranda could barely manage the TV remote. I'm amazed she's got a mobile phone."

"She keeps losing it."

"Why does this not surprise me? She was like that when I was with her. I bought her a new Nokia and she lost that within a week. She is careless," he said, severely, to Hob. "And you remember, Serena, I also said to you that she was lazy."

"Yeah, that's true, too. To be perfectly honest, Serena, she hates you, but I don't think she's, like, your master nemesis or anything. She was cross with you in the first place because you and Ward got back together, and you'd gone out with him first, and even though she didn't want him, she doesn't like anyone on her patch."

"Effing cheek!" said Ward. "I'm not her bloody territory."

"Yeah, no, but you know what she's like."

"Unfortunately!"

"Anyway, that was then. And also you're pretty and successful. So there was that. And *then* there was the whole thing with Pharoah and I think she might have talked the game up with her mates, because she was all 'ooh, that little fashionista bitch is going to get hers' and then you pulled a blinder and made her look like a dick in front of her friends. Well, she thinks they're her friends." At this, he looked, Serena thought, genuinely unhappy.

"Here am I thinking I'm in some big battle between good and evil and it turns out to be just like school," Serena said.

"She hasn't grown up. Emotionally. Narcissists don't," Ward snapped.

Hob looked even more unhappy. "She's been good to me. Better than most people, anyway."

Serena thought that this might not be saying a great deal. "Will she know, if you don't leave this doll thing here?"

"Haven't a clue."

Serena knew, from the glint in Stella's eye, that she might be about to say something sarcastic, and she felt suddenly sorry for Hob. She thought this might be a mistake, a sudden maternal impulse, but she said,

"Hob, how old are you?" It was difficult to tell. Whether it was his otherworldly origins or something else, Hob's sharp, handsome features had a slightly wizened quality, as though something had aged him before his time. And it wasn't as though they didn't know people walking around Southwark who ought to have died decades ago.

"I'm not hundreds of years old, or anything," Hob said, as if he had read her mind. "I'm twenty six."

"Miranda's thirty two. Allegedly. Assuming she was born at all." Ward looked rather sour.

"She's like my big sister." He looked faintly misty-eyed at this. *Oh dear,* Serena thought.

"Look, we need to make a decision," Stella said. "We can't keep this thing here." She picked up the china figure in turn and weighed it in her palm, frowning. "How would you like a trip south of the river, Hob?"

He looked wary. "To do what?"

"To see a mate of mine, calls himself Ace. Ace Spare."

"Oh," Hob said. "Yes. Miranda mentioned him. Magician. Lives with someone who's not what she seems."

"That's putting it mildly."

"Miranda's scared of her."

"Miranda is right."

"The thing is, I don't know what she'd say if I went running off down there on my own."

"Come on, Hob," said Stella briskly. "You're a big boy. You can make your own decisions, can't you?"

"If she found out…"

"How would she know, if you didn't tell her?"

"Ways and means."

"Well, he doesn't have to go running off to Southwark, does he?" said Ward. "Why don't you phone the Tavern, leave a message, and ask Ace if he can come up here? We can meet him in the Lion and Unicorn while Serena has her meeting with the accountant, or whenever?"

As he said this Serena caught the glance that he shot at the little china figure and because she knew Ward, she knew that he did not want the thing in the house any longer than necessary.

"If Miranda should happen to see you, you can tell her that you ran into us in the pub after planting the doll and cunningly befriended us. Or refriended us, in my case."

"Hmmm," Hob said. But in the end, he agreed.

Serena, though somewhat distracted, went to her business meeting, and applied herself to the figures as best she could. The finances, however, were not as impenetrable as she had feared and her accountant was reassuring.

"All legit. And you won't have to pay tax in the States, by the way. Gail's taking care of all that. I must say, she's great to deal with.

Dots her 'I's and crosses her 'T's. I wish all my clients were like that. So don't worry, Serena, you're in good hands."

Slightly more peaceful of mind, Serena took her leave and walked back to the Lion and Unicorn in the gloaming. She found Stella, Ward and Hob sitting at a corner table in a booth, and at first she thought Ace had not yet shown up, but then a familiar gravelly voice behind her said,

"What're you having, Serena?"

"Oh! White wine, please."

"Big one? Ward said you'd had a meeting with your book-keeper."

"Yes, and she was super-positive, actually, to the extent that it's probably my round."

Ace laughed. "Nah, I'll get these."

"I will have a big one, though. I feel like I've earned it."

"Chardonnay? Sauv blanc? Prosecco?"

"Oh go on, then, Prosecco. I know it's naff but I like it."

"Ace says we need to get rid of the doll," Stella said, when Serena sat down.

"Is that going to make things difficult for you, Hob?" Serena said.

"He thinks he can fix it. Like, if she twigs, I can go and stay with him."

"So are you actually *living* at Miranda's?"

"No, but my landlord's a friend of hers. It could be tricky. But – well. I'm getting a bit sick of being an errand boy, truth be told."

It had the ring of truth but Serena wasn't sure. Ace, at the bar nearby, had obviously heard this conversation, for when he returned with Serena's Prosecco he said, "It can't stay in your house, obviously, and if we leave it with Hob I don't want it getting out and finding its way back to its mistress."

"Could it do that?"

"It's a frozen Charlotte."

"A *what?*"

"Sounds like a pudding," said Stella.

"My assistant's called Charlotte," Serena said. "I don't think she'd like this."

"It comes from some American story about a girl who was so vain she refused to wear a wrap in the winter and so when the sledge got to the dance she was going to, she'd frozen to death. New England, I think. After that it sort of took off and in fact, Stella, you are on the right track – you could buy these dolls in little coffins or bake them into a celebratory pie."

"Jesus!"

"These dear old Victorian customs," said Stella. "Heartwarming."

"Because nothing says *Happy Birthday* like finding a small nude ceramic child in your dinner," said Ward.

"That is seriously creepy, Ace."

"Not half so creepy as what a semi-competent magical practitioner can do with them. Since they're based on a corpse, the original ones – which I believe were made in Germany, by the way – can be, well, not animated exactly although I have known them move. They can see and hear." He fished in a pocket and took out a small bundle of black silk. "Unless hoodwinked. It won't be able to telepathically relay information to our adversary: Miss D would have to actually speak to it in person. So we're assuming the gig was for Hob here to leave it in the house for a week or two, find out stuff, and then retrieve it for debriefing."

"What are we going to do with it – her – now?"

"Bind it and chuck it in the Thames, is my advice. Running water and all that. Binding because it obviously won't drown and I don't want it trundling out onto the foreshore like a fucking gingerbread man and tracking Miranda down to spill the beans."

"Eeuw, no!"

"It's not – it isn't *listening* to this, is it?"

"No, like I just said, not wrapped in black silk in my coat pocket. I could take it home and shove it in a box but you know what my place is like, cats and that all over the place, and I've already got quite enough –" he coughed "let's say *stuff* in drawers. I've forgotten what some of it is; I really ought to declutter or whatever that thing is."

"Swedish death cleaning," said Stella.

"What's that, Stella?"

"Clearing out the house before you die so your relations won't have a load of crap to get rid of." She looked at Ace. "Probably not applicable in your case."

"I should have a spring clean, though, all the same. Anione's been on at me about it. Want to help?"

"Yeah, I'll give you a hand!"

"Sorry to disrupt these domestic arrangements," Hob said, rather plaintively, "But what am I supposed to tell Miranda?"

"Just tell her you did what she told you. You broke into Serena's house and left the dolly. Just *don't* tell her what happened after that."

SIELLA

"So what do you make of Hob?" Stella asked of Ace. She had not wanted to have this conversation on the bus and had therefore waited until they were standing in the middle of London Bridge, looking downriver. The lights played on the black water of the Thames and there was a thin wind blowing from the east, with the bite of the North Sea in its teeth. Ace was holding the frozen Charlotte in his hand, silk wrapped and bound with thread that was the colour of blood.

"Yeah," Ace said. "That's a tricky one. I don't trust the lad, obviously. But I think some of what he said, at least, was true. I don't think everything's rosy between him and Ward's ex, from the sound of it."

"No, it sounded a bit toxic and one sided to me. Like he thinks she's been nicer to him than she actually has? He probably knows deep down he's being used."

"Ward said she's manipulative and hell, we've seen some of her crowd, haven't we? I think young Hob knows more about his origins, by the way, than he's letting on, but why should he tell us anything?"

"Why indeed?" Stella replied.

"Right. Are we going to do this thing?"

Stella nodded.

"Heave ho and over she goes," said Ace. He dropped the black silk bundle off the side of the bridge and they watched in silence as it disappeared into the shadows, with a faint splash. Then there was nothing more.

"Excellent," said Ace. "I am going to the Tavern now, to warm up. You coming?"

"Quick one, but then home. I've got an early start tomorrow."

"Good. I've got something to tell you."

One of the reasons Stella liked the Southwark Tavern was that it never seemed to change: a stable point in a shifting world. Ace's usual seat was unoccupied, though the rest of the bar was crowded, mainly with office workers delaying the moment when they would have to head home.

"Does anyone else actually ever sit at your table?" Stella asked.

"Not when I want it, no." Stella thought he went slightly pink, although in the dim lights of the pub it was difficult to tell. Ace was pale, though, and he seemed more flushed than usual. "Don't tell anyone this, because it's soppy, but it was actually Anione's birthday present to me, some years ago."

"What, a spell to stop anyone from sitting in your seat in the boozer? Ace, that is an epic birthday present!"

"Only when I want it, mind. Not when I'm out and about. I'm not selfish. It doesn't apply to other pubs – I used to spend a lot of time in the White Bear, for instance, and it doesn't hold there."

"And, like, the bar staff have never noticed?"

"That's part of the spell."

"Superb."

"Anyway, moving on," Ace said, "the reason I wanted to talk to you, and definitely not in the presence of young Hob, was that I have been making enquiries. About your deer lady. D-E-E-R not D-E-A-R. And her request."

"Okay!" said Stella. She had confided in Ace regarding what Noualen, dog owning deer goddess, had asked her to do, and now she thought back to their parting.

What happened after the conversation in the hunting chase was hazy. Stella remembered feeling enormously weary. She saw a knoll of grass and collapsed onto it, put her head on her knees for a second. But it must have been a lot longer than that because when she lifted her head again, she was back in the annexe of the British Library, on a bench. A concerned staff member was standing in front of her and the deep light in the exhibition room was caused by the sun sinking down.

"Miss? Are you all right?"

"Visual migraine," lied Stella.

"Oh no! Is there anything I can do?"

"It's going off," said Stella. She stood up. "No, thank you, though. It's just like weird lights and I feel a bit sick." Evie, in fact, was the person who experienced visual migraines occasionally; who knew that it would prove useful? "It doesn't last long. I expect you want to close, don't you? What time is it?"

She had been sitting there, unnoticed, for several hours. Or maybe no time at all.

Now Ace said, "'The Knowledge.' Serena, a while ago, mentioned to me that your sister Luna is making a map and you're also both on the job for London. Exit and entry points round your gaff in Somerset, in the case of Luna."

"Mum had a partial map, as well. And so does Bill."

"I went to see Bill. Haven't seen him for a bit, long overdue. And we chewed the fat on this one, because although I may seem to have about me an air of mystery, know more than I'm telling and all that, I have a confession to make."

"You're actually totally clueless?"

Ace grinned. "You cheeky mare, Stella. I'm not totally clueless but the amount I don't know has definitely long outstripped the amount that I do. I'm a lot more clued up now than I was in my first lifespan, mind you."

"Yes. About that. I know what your date of death is."

"Well, yeah, that. It wasn't going so well. Nineteen fifty six, May it was – I remember that because there was a hawthorn bush in the garden and the May blossom was out, very pretty too. I'd been feeling a bit off colour for some days and I collapsed. Lot of pain, all that. A mate was staying with me at the time, fellow artist, and he got me taken into Stockwell and the doc found a load of other stuff – chest infection, gallstones, anaemia, and what actually carried me off, which was a burst appendix."

"Shit, Ace. About not looking after yourself!"

"I'm amazed I got within months of my seventieth."

"You do not actually look nearly seventy."

"Well, I'm not. Technically I'm well over a hundred by now but I seem very vaguely to remember wanting to be sort of around the late 40s, early 50s mark and that's more or less where I've stayed for some considerable time now. Anyway. I more clearly remember waking up in the hospital and feeling a lot better. Back to normal. *Well, that was a rum go*, I thought, and got out of bed, and found it was dark. I looked out of the window and I could see a very faint star, which after a bit of craning my neck, I worked out was the North Star. Polaris.

Couldn't find a nurse, so I thought, nearest pub, that's the ticket. I could have murdered a pint. Mind you, that's probably what caused a lot of the trouble in the first place, but there you are. I walked out of Stockwell Hospital and then – this is a bit hazy – I started walking. I could not in fact find a boozer, which is odd in itself in London, and I just kept on walking, while the sun came up and went down again and came up again. I crossed the river, I could feel the North Star, even in the day, pulling me on. I saw all sorts of things on that walk, too. Some of them best not remembered. At one point I felt a bit tired and I sat down on a seat in a park. I might have had a nap but when I woke up, there was a woman sitting next to me. Long red hair and a dress with a big New Look skirt. My luck is in, I thought, and as it turned out I was right. "Are you all right?" she said. "Never better!" I replied. "Except I can't seem to find a pub." "Never mind," she said. "I expect things will settle down after the funeral." "What funeral?" I asked and she gave this cackle of laughter and punched me on the arm, as though I'd said something funny. "Why, yours, silly!" she said. "It's in Ilford this afternoon, St Mary's Church." "That's where my dad's buried," I said and she replied "I know it is. They're putting you in next to your old man." I should, Stella, have been completely freaked out by this point but all I could feel was numb, and a sort of relief, and kind of accepting?

"Who are you, then?" I asked and she said, "Why, some used to call me the Path to the North Star, but most people just call me Anione. C'mon. Let's get the formalities over and done with and then we'll go and have a drink." So anyway, I ended up watching my own funeral service and being interred and all that, and a lovely job my friends made of it, too. Once the coffin was in the ground and the first handful of soil chucked into it I felt a snap, like a piece of elastic pinging, and I knew I was free. I said good bye to my friends, not that they could hear me, and walked out of the cemetery and down the road and about until I came to a pub called the Great Spoon, which is named after some Elizabethan actor, and which is now a Wetherspoons, in fact."

"Grim," said Stella.

"They're a plague upon the face of the nation. Anyway, there was my new friend, Anione the Path to the North Star, sitting in it nursing a double port and lemon. We celebrated my demise, I had a bit of money in my pocket, so I spent that with no funny looks whatsoever from the barmaid and then we went home. And there you have it."

"And you've been there – here – ever since."

"Ever since. That house, the one you've been in loads of times, does not technically exist in contemporary reality. It's like Bill's place. I think it was knocked down at some point and replaced by some particularly horrible flats but in my reality it remains, which is just as well as I think someone might object sharing their abode with an alcoholic cat-owning ghost of dubious habits."

Stella reached out and prodded Ace in the arm, quite hard.

"Ow!"

"Sorry. You don't feel like a ghost. But then neither does Ned Dark, although he's sometimes transparent."

"Ned –? Oh, your sister's chap. God, what a long story. Hopefully not too boring."

"No, not in the slightest! I've met Polaris, by the way – she's one of the Behenian stars. Magnet and succory are her attributes, as far as I remember."

"Yes. Anione's not the North Star herself: she's a spirit of the track that leads to it, apparently, and her sister, of completely unlamented memory, is a spirit of something else. This is all really old pre-Roman stuff, apparently, according to Anione. No one remembers her now and she says that's how she likes it: it lets her off the hook. No worshippers asking her for miracles and that so she can put her feet up. I'm wondering if your new mucker Diana the Huntress feels the same, although I think she might have a big Wiccan audience these days."

"So did you have any intimation about an afterlife? My grandfather is dead, but I can still talk to him – he's cagy on the subject and all Ned says is that sometimes he's at Mooncote in our day and sometimes he's in Hornmoon in his. How about you? No pearly gates, choirs of angels?"

"Not unless you count a really long trudge through Plaistow. Which is many people's idea of hell. I've visited other times and other worlds, but not anything resembling an afterlife, and opinion varies. The closest I've come is Bill – he says he has seen a place which fitted the description of paradise, but he's certainly not resident in it now. I told you this by way of a bloody lengthy digression about the Knowledge, didn't I? What was I saying about that… Oh yes. I don't know as much about this city, and its ins and outs, as one might think. I don't have a clear picture of which times intersect with other times, or who's doing what." He took a swig of his pint. "I was worried that you might be thinking ah, at some point soon Ace will tell me what's really going on! How we are the powers of goodness and right, and you, Stella, are the chosen one and there is an enemy behind all this whom we must vanquish! Well, sadly no. I know bits and pieces like you, and Bill knows a lot more, to be fair, but he has the same problem as me and is moreover confined for reasons that I don't quite understand to his patch south of the river. Just as your new friend Noualen seems to be confined to hers."

"I wasn't really expecting you to Tell All, because I think you'd have told me by now. And I don't want to be a chosen anything. I'm less like a chosen one and more like a one who happens to be knocking around at the time. But Ace, if Anione is –" Stella leaned over and mouthed the words "an actual goddess, wouldn't she have more information?"

"You'd think. And she does know quite a lot about some realms. However, as I alluded to earlier, both she and her sister, hopefully now banged up out of time somewhere, weren't so much deities as spirits. Genus loci of the south shore of the Thames, long ago, probably worshipped by about four people. And it seems you can take the girl out of Southwark but you can't take Southwark out of the girl. Funny thing, or perhaps it isn't, when I was in life, as you might say, and making my way as a painter, I had dreams about a red headed woman and sometimes I remembered seeing her around Southwark. I'd go home and think, oh, I saw *her* today. But I knew I didn't know who *she* was. I even did some paintings of her. Seems she'd taken a fancy to a starving artist, and I've always liked cats, with which she has an affinity, and when I'd carked it, she thought, *now's my chance.*"

"I think that's really sweet," Stella said, genuinely touched that he had told her so much.

"I don't want to go all soppy again, though."

"No, down with that kind of thing."

"I really am starting to ramble on. Look, let me get to the point. What taxi drivers have to do, remembering all the streets and nooks and crannies of London, is called the Knowledge, right? Takes about four years, you have to know all of it. I don't know if they still do it or if they just give them a sat nav."

"They still do it," Stella said. "Evie's friend Dave's doing it now – he's in his second year. Has to memorise something called the Blue Book. I think he said it's a certain number of streets – a *large* number – in a radius around Charing Cross."

"Nice to know they still bother. Old school, I approve. So the 'knowledge' that Noualen mentioned to you is like that, but instead of streets and bridges, it's the knowledge of all the entry and exit points to the otherworlds in this city. And there's one person who knows all that, she thinks. Bloody helpful if there was such a person, I must say."

"I think maybe it's one person in every generation or something like that? She said there was 'always a man' which sounds like several men, consecutively, to me rather than one single person. Have you actually ever heard of someone like this, though? Like, in hidden secret London, are there tales of a human Google Maps?"

"Not that I'm aware of but if there was such a bloke, you'd think he'd be really popular. In a bad way. I mean, imagine Miranda getting her hooks into someone like that. So maybe, if he does exist, he's keeping his head down."

"Or maybe he's got the knowledge but he doesn't know he's got it? Maybe he, like, needs to be activated?"

"Maybe."

"Have you spoken to anyone else about this?"

"Yes. I ran it past Anione, and I also mentioned it to Bill. He's been knocking about the city a lot longer than I have and *he* hasn't heard of such a chap, either. But he did confirm the story about St Paul's being built on a temple to Diana – he's heard that as well, although he doesn't personally know anyone who's seen it. Apart, now, from yourself."

"But someone like a human map does exist, unless Noualen's lying. Goddesses do that, one assumes."

"Why would she, though? She's a powerful spirit, from what I hear tell, but she's not a malicious one. Did you think she was lying? Did you think Diana was?"

"No. But you know, Ace, I don't want to end up like Hob – or actually more like Miranda, knocking about the edge of all this and being at the beck and call of random entities just because we've got a bit of odd blood in the family and I happen to be able to see them. On the other hand, I would like a clearer picture of what's going on if I and my sisters are going to keep getting caught up in shit."

"I know you said you've got an early start tomorrow," Ace said, "But can I get you another drink?"

Stella sighed. "Yeah, go on. I think I need one after all this."

"Is it a business meeting, tomorrow? Music gig?"

"No, it's litter picking. Evie's a member of something called Keep Thames Tidy – fat chance of that, she says, but she also thinks we need to do our bit for the environment and she's right – so we're out on the foreshore for a couple of hours tomorrow with a bunch of people clearing up crap. Did you know that there's an island on the Thames up near Teddington made entirely of wet wipes?"

"Jesus, no! That's disgusting."

"Exactly."

BEE

Bee and Luna had woken to frosts for a few days: a white, misty world glittering with sunlight. Despite the chill, they had both welcomed the change in the weather – "kills the germs," said Ver March, whom they had seen twice since her arrival at the protest site. Bee and Luna had gone to visit her, sitting in an old bus which had been converted to a communal café, and looking out over the slopes of the Tor. Bee wanted to keep Ver updated on the development of the shoot, but the frosty weather seemed to have put the brakes on its unnatural growth. It stood up straight in its pot, a strange little soldier, and at night it still emitted a faint but discernible glow. However, for the time being, its upward growth had slowed, rather to Bee's relief: the idea of hosting some supernatural bamboo, breaking through the roof of the greenhouse, had worried her.

On the evening of this last visit to Ver, Bee bundled herself up in a sweater, coat, gloves and a woolly hat and took the dogs down the field for their last walk of the day. It was almost dark, with an iridescent indigo light in the west and a half moon hanging over the hills, Venus in her wake. It was below freezing and Bee walked quickly, listening with pleasure to the church bells toll out the hour, echoing in the frosty air. She took the dogs on a circuit, watching the horses at the bottom of the field as they wandered, lumpen shapes in their winter rugs. Across the valley, Amberley's lights were visible through the trees with the whole ground floor lit up: Caro and Richard must be having visitors, probably some horsy do. She ought to pop over and see how they were getting on, if there had been any more trouble at the yard, and made a mental note to call Caro in the morning. Then she called to the dogs and walked back up the field through the orchard, wondering if Dark might be waiting for her.

He was not, but as she stepped between the still apple trees she saw something white move at the end of the orchard. The spaniels whimpered and pressed close. What was it, thought Bee, a ghost?

The glimpse she had got had been tall and she'd had an impression of skirts, somehow. There it was again, just a flicker.

"Someone's here," a voice said, and Bee jumped.

"Ned! Don't creep up on me like that!" She was getting more nervy about surprises.

"Sorry, I thought you'd seen me."

"Ned, who is that?"

"I don't know." He was peering towards the end of the orchard. "I couldn't see them clearly."

"Was it one of the stars, perhaps?"

"Maybe. But the dogs don't like it."

"You're supposed to protect me!" Bee said to Hardy and Nelson, who were hiding behind her Wellingtons. "Fat lot of use you are! Oh well. It's gone now."

With Dark, she went back into the kitchen to find a message on the answerphone.

"Bee? Nick here. Harris says he's got some miniature irises for you, if you'd like them. And thanks so much for the bulbs – sorry I haven't been in touch. I've been in London, just got back."

"How kind of him," Alys said. "Sorry I didn't pick up the phone. I was in the bath."

"It's hardly urgent."

"Caro rang me earlier, by the way."

"Amberley's all lit up tonight. Big do."

"Yes, they're having a party – the reason we weren't invited is that Caro and Richard decided to throw a buffet and drinks bash for all the people they owe invitations to but can't stand. She was phoning from the downstairs loo. Said she'd escaped for a couple of minutes and wanted to bitch about Arabella Beaufort, who is apparently being a perfect cow."

"Oh dear!"

"Kept asking what the wine was and then, when told, remarking "Oh" in that sort of flat voice people use when they're being disparaging. Anyway, eventually Caro said to her that it was free wine, and that shut her up. She – Caro, not Arabella – has asked us to dinner tomorrow night so that, I quote, 'I can talk to some sane people'."

"Great minds," said Bee. "I was thinking of giving her a ring."

"At seven. You and me, although she invited Luna and Sam as well, but apparently they're taking Ver out to the Green Lion."

"Lovely!"

And it would be, Bee thought. She might even dress up.

But first, in the morning, she walked up the lane to Wycholt. Overnight the frosts had gone, the rain clouds had not yet rolled in, and Bee found herself walking in a softer sunshine than she had seen for some time. The hedges were full of blackthorn and there were hazel catkins stirring in the breeze. Bee walked the length of the manor drive, once more admiring Nick's daffodils. He met her at the door, also Wellington clad.

"Morning. Lovely day!"

"Isn't it?" Bee said. "Really feels like spring."

"Ne'er cast a clout, though."

"Trust me, I won't be casting clouts till mid-July."

"I was out seeing to the dogs. Want to come and pick up your irises? Harris has put them in a pot – he says he doesn't need it back but I hope it's not too heavy. And you can see what he's done with your bulbs, too. Would you like some coffee?"

Bee said she would. She could detect nothing untoward in his manner and she had just about stopped feeling guilty about her theft. If he found out, though... Well, she could come clean then, confess all, throw herself on the Lord of the Manor's mercy. She told herself sternly to stop LARPing the eighteenth century; she was not an errant servant girl. Nick ducked into the house to have a word with an unseen person, presumably she who was to make the coffee. This turned out to be correct, for a moment later Rachel Stanley appeared, red cheeked and wiping her hands on a dish towel. Apart from the cheeks, Rachel was rather glamorous, with her dark glossy hair pulled up in a knot.

"Bee, hi! Nick said you'd be turning up."

"The great British bulb swap," said Bee.

"Oh, but isn't it nice to see the year moving on a bit! After those floods… well, winter won't be over yet but it's on the way. Mind you, I've seen snow in May up on the Mendips."

"Two steps forward, one step back."

"Milk and no sugar?"

"You've got a good memory!"

"A lifetime on committees. Go on, I'll bring it out to you."

"We'll be in the sitting room," said Nick.

Bee followed Nick around to the conservatory, a route with which she was becoming familiar. Her bulbs sat fatly in a series of blue and white Wedgewood bowls, ready to adorn the house. They were already starting to shoot. She cast a quick glance across the conservatory. The tray with the shoots had been removed and there was no sign of them elsewhere. Bee was immediately consumed with curiosity as to what Nick had done with them.

"You're doing well," she said, as casually as she could manage. "I see Harris has been planting things out already."

"I expect so, yes."

"I've put a few things in the ground," Bee persevered.

"You know what gardeners are like, you're one yourself. Always something on the go. Here you are, have some of these." He handed her a handsome terracotta pot full of irises

"I ought to have a word with him and see how far ahead he is."

"He's a man of strong opinions, is Harris. Brace yourself!"

And with that, he headed for the house; Bee had no option but to follow.

She left after coffee, having promised to make lunch for Luna. As she headed for the door, she said, 'Thanks for the coffee, Nick, and the irises and say thank you to Mr Harris, too. I'll see you when I see you, then."

"Which will be this evening! I've just remembered. Caro's in-recovery dinner party."

"Oh, are you coming to that? Good! Mum and I are going. As you say, in-recovery."

"I spoke to Richard. He told me what last night's bash was about – he actually invited me to it, not quite sure what *that* says, but then confessed and said I'd probably prefer tonight."

Bee grinned. "Depends how many people round here you've learned to hate."

STELLA

"If my alarm doesn't go off," Stella had said to Evie, "make sure you wake me up when you get up. I'll need coffee before this litter picking business."

"Gotcha. I'll bang on your door if I don't hear you moving around. I might even *bring* you some coffee."

"Excellent," said Stella, and retired to bed. It seemed that her alarm had, after all, failed her, because she was woken by a soft knock. Then she realised that it was still dark. She got up and padded to the door.

"Stella? It's me. Keep as quiet as you can."

The door opened to reveal Evie in a set of fleecy pyjamas.

"Everything okay?" mouthed Stella.

"No. Someone's prowling round the boat."

"Rumpole?"

"No, he's been on my bed."

Stella was not unduly surprised. This had happened a couple of times before; mainly, the police had said, villains creeping about to see if there was anything loose on the dock or the deck. But both Evie and Stella thought they could not be too careful. Given recent activity of a supernatural nature, Evie had not only undertaken some 'precautions' herself, but had called Ace in to do so as well. Stella was not sure exactly what he had done, but he mentioned something about 'tripwires' and Stella assumed that these were of a magical nature. All the same, she was glad to see Evie picking up the boathook from its place beside the couch as they made their stealthy way to the cabin portholes and looked out.

Nothing. Canary Wharf glittered up the Thames. Across the river, the lights glinted on the opposite shore and a tug was making its early morning way along. The steady chug of the engine and distant sirens were the only sounds that Stella could hear. But then there was a thud on the roof of the cabin and the air jangled and crackled with energy. Stella jumped. Couldn't be the cat, because that wouldn't set off the tripwires, and Evie had said he was inside.

Evie put her finger to her lips. She moved cautiously to the door, breathed 'one… two… three' and flung the door open. They ran out onto the deck. The sides of the *Nitrogen* were awash with blue light, hissing and spitting. Ace's tripwires.

Something shot towards Stella's face. There was a ginger blur as Rumpole raced across the deck, also spitting. Stella threw herself to one side and landed on the boards as a huge gull hurtled over the railing and downriver, shrieking.

"Fuck!" shouted Stella.

"Are you all right?" Evie hauled her to her feet. "Jesus. Those birds are right bastards. The number of times I've had rubbish bags rifled…"

"Oh." Stella sat down on the seat. "Yes, I'm fine. Just a shock. They're horrendous. When I was a kid a gull in Mousehole snatched an ice cream cone out of my hand."

"They're total pirates. Anyway. No harm done but I think Ace's wards might be a bit oversensitive. Rumpole certainly is." The cat was now washing, in a self-righteous manner.

Stella nodded. "I think you're right. Well done, Rumpuss! Extra Dreamies for you… Given the number of crows and gulls around here – and look over there."

There was a rat scuttling along the wharf. It disappeared behind a pallet.

"You're never more than twelve feet away from them, apparently," Evie said. "I've never seen one on the deck, to be fair. Mind you, Rumpole was a great ratter in his day; bit old for it now. Maybe they don't like magic."

"Probably not enough cheese on board."

"Say it isn't so. Anyway, I'm going back to bed. Still want me to wake you if your alarm doesn't go off?"

"Cheers. And let's hope the rest of the night's quiet."

Later, Stella straightened up and tried to work the kinks out of her back. "Ow. I thought I was fitter than this."

"It's bending that does it. You're not used to it. Neither am I."

Stella peered into the plastic sack. It was full of all manner of stuff: bottles, also of plastic, a disgusting sodden mass which she did not want to investigate too closely, crisp packets, a lot of iron nails and squashed soft drink cans. The foreshore also smelled: mud and a slight reek of chemicals. She was glad of the strong easterly that blew down from the river mouth.

They had also found a statue of Ganesh. The gilt had worn off but Stella had greeted his small elephantine face peering out of the mud with delight and surprise.

Evie was less astonished.

"Most of the religious stuff that gets washed up on the Thames is Hindu these days. Someone will have chucked him in for luck or as an offering. They do it with the Ganges."

"I couldn't help wondering – we've got all this supernatural stuff going on, and it's local, but presumably people from other ethnic backgrounds must connect with it, too?"

"Yeah, I gather they do, but they've got other things happening as well. After all, London's been a melting pot for centuries – you had the Romans, obviously, then a whole bunch of other people and they've all brought their gods and that with them, including Lord Ganesh here. And djinns, and lwa and all sorts. You won't necessarily run into it but I've got a mate from Antigua who can, well, see stuff, bit like you and me, and he says it never stops, you wouldn't believe the half of it. And the imam from the mosque up the road's had a quiet word now and again, too."

"Makes sense." Stella hoped that, in time, no litter picker or mudlark would be fishing the frozen Charlotte out of the foreshore.

After some debate, they placed Ganesh carefully on a projecting brick in the river wall where he sat, overseeing the proceedings.

"Make sure you wash your hands after this, by the way. I'm sure you would anyway. You can pick up some nasty bugs from the Thames, even if it is cleaner these days." Evie nodded towards a row of rotten pilings, where a cormorant sat, hunched and black, and gingerly picked up a lump of something. "What the hell is this?"

"I think it used to be a hat."

"The things you find," Evie said. "It's why mudlarking is a thing. People have written books about it. I've found false teeth before now, and a colostomy bag, and the amount of stuff that turns up from Roman and Medieval times is unbelievable."

No wonder it seemed so easy to slip from time to time along the river, Stella thought. All the city's history was contained within it; perhaps it cast up vignettes from past times, just as it did buttons and plastic bottles and cans, and what Serena and she had seen was nothing more than temporal flotsam. She sighed at the thought, picked up a small plastic float, and put it into the bag.

"It does make you wonder what's swimming about in there," she said.

"I told you when you moved onto the *Nitrogen* – just don't fall in!"

"Too right." Evie had given her a health and safety lecture on her first evening aboard: *"the tides are strong. Even if you're a good swimmer, there are eddies and undertows, it's full of sewage, you might get swept into the pillar of a bridge and it's often freezing cold – you can go into shock."*

"Not worth testing!" Stella had said.

"If you want to swim, there are plenty of public pools."

"Hang on," Evie said, interrupting her memories. "Isn't that your friend Ace?"

Stella looked. The figure trudging along the foreshore was unmistakable. "Yep. I did mention it to him. Maybe he's come to help."

But Ace had come with a message.

One needed to be a little careful about water conservation on the boat but Stella, accustomed to festival sites, was used to finding hacks around full-body washing. After the muddy morning, however, it was essential and once done, she dressed warmly in a sweatshirt and fleece, with a parka over it. Life on the river, even at the edges of it, was colder than life on land. She had refused, for reasons of common civility, to speak to Ace before having a shower and she now went back on deck to find him sitting chatting to Evie over a beer and making a fuss of Rumpole.

"I hope you feel virtuous, Stella, after your morning of civic duty."

"I certainly do. Also cleaner."

"Yes. You did stink a bit."

"Thank you, Ace. You should see the shit we picked up."

"I did. Also I've lived near this river for, cough, a long enough time. It used to be much worse. Anyway, I didn't come all the way here to cheer on your community spirit, fine though it is. I've had a message."

"Who from?"

"It actually came via Bill Blake this morning. I think the person knows where you live but sent it to Bill to demonstrate trustworthiness. It's from someone called Davy Dearly."

"Never heard of him."

"Neither has Bill. Evie?"

Evie was frowning. "I don't know Davy Dearly in the sense that we've met, and I've never heard of him in particular, but I know of the Dearly family."

"Are they watermen, too?"

"A lot of them were but back in the day some of them were toshers. You know what those are?"

"Sewer men," said Ace.

"That's the one. Horrible job, worse than mudlarking, although they considered themselves a cut above, since they scavenged for valuables and the larks just went for bits of coal and that. Anyway, one of the Dearly boys is said to have met a beautiful woman in the local pub one night, like you do, and had a fling with her."

"Lucky him," Ace said. "This is ringing a faint bell. You'd think it might be a bit difficult to meet girls, in that profession."

"I think people were less fussy then although I have to say, even after this morning, a strong whiff of the drains would put me off a chap, but perhaps I'm just picky. Anyway, in due course she brought him a baby to look after but she didn't exactly settle down with him – kind of a reversal of what usually happens. Also, she wasn't exactly a woman."

"Blimey, what was she, then?" Stella asked.

"So even out here," Evie said, "you never know what's listening. I'm going to leave you to find that out from this Davy and it might not even be true."

"All right," Stella said, intrigued. "But there's no one in earshot."

From the deck, she could see the nearest bunch of litter pickers, some distance away along the foreshore, gathered around something one of them had found.

"That's what I mean. And after last night. I was telling Ace about that."

"Riiiight… I won't press you," said Stella.

"Dearly says he wants to meet up, in the Prospect of Whitby. Tonight if possible – I got the impression it was a bit urgent. Since he made the effort to track down Bill…"

"The Prospect is a fine old pub, anyway," Evie said. "You'll like it."

"Is that the one on the river? Wapping?"

"Yes. You could row to it from here, were you of a mind to do so, but otherwise I'd suggest the bus."

"I could do with a night out after this." Stella was wearing gloves but her hands were still chilly and her face felt pinched. "Even if I've just had one."

"Me too. And I'm having one myself in reward for my virtue and good citizenship. I shall be in the Rochester with the lads, if you get back early. Ace, are you going with her?"

"Be good if you did," said Stella.

"I'll come. It is indeed a nice old boozer and it's a long time since I set foot in it. I'm got a few things to do, though, so I'll head off in a bit, and see you later at the pub."

BEE

Bee had already decided what to wear to the dinner party and stuck to it: a wine red woollen dress, a striped pashmina and a pair of strappy, rather 1940s shoes.

"You look very nice," Alys said, herself resplendent in an ice blue Indian embroidered coat.

"Thank you. So do you – I love that coat. I also particularly admire your optimism in wearing white trousers."

"I'll almost certainly drop something on them but that's what the dry cleaners are for. And we are to be chauffeured, you tell me?"

"Well, if you count Harris as a chauffeur, yes. When I was leaving Wycholt earlier, Nick very kindly offered to pick us up. Harris is the gardener but he doubles up."

"You'd think Nick would employ more staff. I made some discreet enquiries. He's really rather wealthy. Lady Pamela must have stashed it all under the bed. Not that one can blame her for that."

"He still has property in Cumbria but he told me the money comes from wool originally. His father was Sir Someone; I think he's the second son. He's Dr Wratchall-Haynes but it's not medical. I think he studied history. And he has a large investment portfolio. I only know this because I googled him and there was an interview with him in The Field."

"But not even a live-in housekeeper and I'm sure someone round here could do with the work even if Rachel actually wants a life."

"Maybe he likes the simple approach," Bee said. It had occurred to her some while ago that perhaps the reason the hunt master did not have live-in staff was because he had something to hide. Harris resided in a cottage on the edges of the estate and the other staff, like Rachel, lived in Hornmoon. She could hear a car drawing up now, the distinctive purr of an expensive engine. "I think that's our lift."

"This really is terribly kind of you," Alys said to Nick, who was in the front seat beside Harris – the poor man was barely tall enough to see over the wheel, Bee thought. He was hunched over it with a set expression; Bee did not like to ask if he had actually driven the Range Rover before. Alys swung, agile, into the high back seat and rearranged her sparkling coat. "We could easily have called a taxi."

"Not a problem. It's not a very nice night and we'd be going past Mooncote anyway. This way, everyone can have a drink."

"Except poor Mr Harris!"

"I don't drink, madam," the gardener said, somewhat morosely. "Doesn't agree with me, never has. And I'm being paid so I shall have a nice cup of tea with my feet up at home in front of *Call of Duty* and wait for the phone to ring."

"Did you remember the wine?" Alys asked Bee.

"It's in that bag on the floor."

"Thank God for that."

Amberley was less illuminated than upon the previous evening, but still welcoming. Bee and Alys made a dash for the house under a squall of rain as the Range Rover wheeled away.

"I think your gardener likes driving that monster," Alys said to Nick.

"He loves it. Hello, Caro. You look lovely."

Caro swept into the hall, elegant in dark blue cashmere. Compliments were exchanged.

"We come bearing gifts," Bee said, proffering the wine bag.

"Oooh, lovely, and truffles!"

"Bee feels duty bound to tell you that Luna foraged these in the village shop, and they were Christmas truffles, which is why they've got a picture of Santa on them."

"They were half price," Bee said. "I should have rebranded them."

"I know. I snaffled some myself and put them out on a tray, and I wasn't going to tell you they were half price either, but now I have. Come in. Richard's pouring sherry. We are on a mission to get sloshed tonight as we were very abstemious and restrained last night, although I now think we should just have drunk as much as possible because coping with Arabella Beaufort and Alexandra Houghton-Smith *and* that terrible man Piers Simpson who's supposed to be a theatre director but who can't string two words together and leers down one's cleavage..."

They followed her into Amberley's cavernous drawing room, which still bore traces of its Arts and Crafts beginnings. Alys caught Bee's eye and mouthed, "Back on form."

Bee smiled. She had at times wondered whether Caro Amberley would survive the winter, given what had happened, but here she was, and yes, back to normal. Bee suspected she had a few more grey hairs but you would never know. Caro had the money for the pricier end of hairdressing and her hair was now as glossy as the coat of one of her husband's thoroughbreds. As they came in, Ben rose from an armchair. With a shorter haircut of his own he looked less like a rock star and more like a scion of the gentry.

"Hey, nice to see you!"

"Hello, Ben. How are you?"

"Not too bad, thanks."

"Over his illness, thank God," Richard said, slapping his son on the shoulder, slightly too heartily. "All these post viral conditions can really take it out of you. Sherry, Bee?"

"Love some, thanks." Whatever had afflicted Ben Amberley and Caro was not post-viral, Bee thought, and for a fraction of a second she caught his eye.

"But you're quite well now, Ben?" Alys asked.

"Yes, and playing with my new sound deck. Really quite exciting. Like to see it?"

"He's obsessed," Caro said, and laughed. "All those dials – it looks like something from the Starship Enterprise."

"I'd love to take a look, actually," Nick Wratchall-Haynes said. "I was quite into music back in the day although I must admit, if I picked up a guitar now I suspect Eric Clapton would be spinning in his grave..."

"If he were dead," said Alys. "What sort of music did you like, Nick?"

Nick hesitated. "New Romantics, actually. I rather liked Adam Ant."

"Oh, totally! Stand and Deliver!"

"Although at one point I bought a black leather jacket and pretended to be a punk. My father was horrified. Before your day, Bee. Probably just as well."

Bee and Alys followed the two men into the hallway and up the stairs. Once on the landing, Ben showed them into a side room, now a study. An impressively large mixing deck sat at one end.

"Pity Stella's not here," Bee said.

"It's amazing, but I didn't really want to show it off. I wanted to talk to you – all three of you. I can't talk to Mother or Dad. Dad's pretending Mum and I had some sort of flu over Christmas and I went missing because I was admitted to hospital somewhere. Mum knows what happened but she won't talk about it."

"I think it's just freaked them out too much," Alys said. She leaned against a couch and folded her arms. "You can't blame them but I think, Ben, that you might just have to accept the story your family is telling themselves and not expect miracles."

"She's right," Nick said. "It's too weird, and I would say that it's too out of their experience, but actually I'm not sure that it is. You know there are rumours about your family?"

"That's what Ward said." Bee sat down on the couch. "But he doesn't know what they are."

"Neither do I. Ward did tell me about that recently, but no one else has ever said anything to me."

"You said you can't talk to your mum and dad. Have you spoken to your sister?"

"*Laura*? You're joking, she's as normal as they come. Obsessed with horses. She's never even mentioned seeing a ghost or anything. She glazes over if anyone starts talking about religion, let alone the supernatural. Last summer I'd have said all this was nuts. But now I don't know. And I keep thinking that perhaps I just started going a bit crazy. I can't remember half of it."

"You remember the maze?"

"Sort of. But you know how when you have a dream and it seems really vivid at the time, but then you wake and you kind of snatch at the dream but it whisks away and there are only bits left? It's been like that. I'm trying to write a song about it."

"Well," Alys said, after a pause. "I have a glass of Richard's excellent sherry waiting downstairs and I suggest we get back to it rather than discuss this here. Ben, whatever happened between Serena and yourself, you're still very welcome to come over to Mooncote if you need to talk to someone."

"Or Wycholt," Nick said.

"Thank you. I really appreciate it. I'm going to stay here for a bit, anyway. The band are coming down next week, having just about forgiven me. Seelie knows someone with a recording studio near Glastonbury – we're going to work on another album. I can't face going back to London yet. I'm going to rent out my place in Camden."

"Sounds like a plan," Bee said, encouragingly. They filed back onto the landing and as they did so, from the corner of her eye, Bee saw a door swing shut. Then it opened again and Ben's sister Laura, ethereal in white, appeared. Bee knew that Laura was not in fact ethereal: she was a strong, athletic girl, like most professional riders, but tonight, with her long blonde hair loose, she looked almost shadowy.

"Hi! Sorry, have you been here long? I'm running late, just been putting on my face."

"Ben's been showing off his music kit. We haven't even had drinks yet," Bee said.

"Thank God for that."

But Bee could not help wondering if Laura had been listening.

Caro had made an Italian roast chicken dish, followed by sticky toffee pudding. Bee had decided that this was no time of the year to think about dieting; the rainy dark beyond the windows made her instinctively want to seek warmth, comfort and good food. Ben, Richard and Alys engaged in a long conversation about music festivals; Ben's band would be appearing at Glastonbury this year.

"Assuming," Richard said, "that anyone can get onto Worthy Farm in the first place."

"Oh?" Alys asked. "Why, are they expecting problems?"

"I keep my ear to the ground. I suppose you know there's a road protest camp near there?"

Before he could say anything truly tactless, Bee said, "Yes. Sam's gran is part of it." Then she wondered if she'd been the tactless one: Sam was, after all, currently in Richard's employ and she didn't want to make things difficult for him. Alys shot her an unreadable look. But Richard said,

"I know – he told me. That's why I assumed you knew."

"Is it a problem for you?" Alys asked.

"Not really, it's a free country. They can protest if they want to. I have a bit of sympathy, actually – I'm no tree hugger but I don't like seeing ancient woodland cut down and some of these companies aren't as legit as they'd like to pretend. I've known one or two cases where some development clearly went through as a backhander to some local councillor."

"Someone told me they're constantly having to fend off attempts to put housing on the water meadows," Nick said.

"Yes, that's true, and bloody stupid, as well. Look at places like Tewkesbury – flooded since Medieval times and there's not a lot you can do about it except not build on it. They're called water meadows for a reason; the clue's in the name."

"So, about the festival," Alys prompted. "Why would the road protest cause problems?"

"There's been a suggestion that they might picket the site. Raise publicity."

"Well, yes, but bad publicity, surely?" Bee helped herself to more pudding. "All it would really achieve is to piss a lot of people off who'd otherwise be sympathetic."

"When I spoke to Sam, he said the problem is – and he wasn't the one who told me about the picket, by the way – that a number of the people involved in this come from Extinction Reaction up at Stroud, and they're not old hands at activism. Nice lefty middle class people who've just woken up to the fact that there's a cause for which to fight. So they're gung ho about getting their message out but they're trying to reinvent the wheel and they don't know what works and what doesn't."

"Are they the bunch who glue themselves to trains?" Nick asked.

"That's the one. Bloody nuisance. I had to wait for forty five minutes at South Ken freezing my backside off while they prised someone off a Tube carriage."

"The thing is, though, we're going to have to do something about the climate," Bee said. "Whatever you think the cause is, the planet's warming up. I see it in the garden – these swings of weather, and things coming out way before they're due."

She hoped that Nick might be tempted into mentioning his shoots, but instead he said,

"You're right. Although it's been a bit late this year… And I don't think supergluing oneself to rolling stock is really the answer."

"Anyway," Richard said, "We'll see how disruptive the camp turns out to be. I'm not taking it out on Sam, though. He says his gran's sensible enough and maybe they need older and wiser heads around."

"Old ladies behaving badly," said Caro, and laughed.

"How can one not approve?" And Alys reached for the wine. "Maybe Harris should come along, Nick – might liven him up a bit."

"Harris reminds me of someone," Bee mused. "Who is it? I'm terrible with faces."

"When I saw him behind the wheel this evening I thought, God, it's Sir Ian McKellen," Alys said.

"You're right!"

Nick laughed. "I've thought that myself. Separated at birth!"

Richard joined in. "Ever seen them in the same room together, Nick? Here, have another glass since you're not driving."

Nick phoned Harris to collect them just before midnight. Laura had already gone upstairs, pleading tiredness, and Ben told Bee that he intended to spend some quality time with his music deck, being a night owl. Outside, the rain had passed and it was very still and starlit; Bee looked up and there was Orion, striding high in the southern sky with the blue fire of Sirius at his heels. There was a small, hard moon, bitterly white. Despite the majesty of the sky, she was grateful to clamber into the relative warmth of the Range Rover and be driven home. But as the 4x4 pulled out of the drive between Amberley's imposing gateposts, Nick said suddenly,

"Stop the car!"

Harris slammed his foot on the brakes, sending Bee slightly forwards.

"Sorry! I saw someone."

"Where?"

Nick and Alys were getting out of the car. Bee scrambled down too.

"Over in the field. Wait here."

Alys and Bee ignored this instruction and followed him into the lane. There was a stile, Bee knew: she had come this way in the winter, searching for a missing Caro. Then, the fields had been flooded, but this evening, they were ploughed and empty.

"Damn! I'm sure I saw someone, running along that hedge. They hopped over the stile."

Alys swung her leg over the slats. "I'll take a look."

"All right. Mind your trousers."

Nick and Bee waited.

"I'll feel like a right idiot if I'm wrong," the hunt master said.

"Well, let's hope you *are* wrong. Could it have been someone poaching bunnies, maybe?"

"Possibly."

Bee looked up and down the lane. It was very quiet; the stars still prickled above.

She turned to the hedge: there was a horned face looking out of it, grinning. Bee gave a yelp. She saw yellow slitted eyes and, confused, she thought "it's a goat!" but it was not a goat, the face was human, and malign. And then not there.

"Bee! Are you all right?" Nick grasped her arm.

"I saw a face!" She told him.

"Christ," the hunt master said. He went to the stile and leaned over it. "Alys! Get back here."

Within moments, Alys was in the road, dusting herself off. Only her mother, Bee thought, could run around a ploughed field in white trousers in the middle of the night and remain apparently unstained. "There's no one there that I can see," she said. "Did you hear a shout?"

"That was me," Bee said. "I saw something – a face. A man, sort of, looking at me out of the hedge. He had yellow eyes. Like a goat's eyes."

"God, how scary. I've never seen anyone like that," Alys said.

"Neither have I and I hope I don't again."

"I think I ought to give Richard the heads-up," Nick said. "I won't give him full details but he does need to know that someone's prowling around."

"He's got CCTV, apparently."

"Yes. I doubt the owner of your face will show up on it, though."

Bee thought he was right. They waited by the car while Nick went back up to the house, and, shortly, returned.

"I've spoken to Laura."

"I thought she'd gone to bed?"

"Well, she answered the door. She says thanks and she'll go and check the stables."

"I don't think she should go on her own," Bee said.

"No, she said she was going to get one of the lads in the block out of bed."

"I always think of them sleeping in the straw," Alys said. "I know they don't, obviously."

"No, you're at least a hundred years out of date." Nick got back into the car. "Richard and I have spoken about this previously – his security's very good."

"Depends who they are," Bee said. She did not want to mention the face in front of Harris, who had now set the 4x4 in gear and was pulling into the lane.

"Well, quite."

Nothing more was said until they reached Mooncote; Nick waited until they were safely in the house and then Bee heard the big car pull away.

STELLA

The evenings were drawing out and there was still a faint stain of light in the west when Stella set out from the *Nitrogen*, but by the time the bus had trundled through Limehouse, it had gone. Stella checked the location of the pub on her phone and got off the bus. The area had been substantially gentrified in recent decades: there were more hipsters here than you could shake a stick at, but the old skeletons of dockland warehouses remained and it was still not an area that Stella was totally happy about wandering around after dark. Perhaps she should have got an uber... but never mind, the Prospect of Whitby was not too far away. Stella marched onward.

As she turned the corner, she wondered if her earlier thought about gentrification had been wrong. This street still retained the old Victorian warehouses, and several of them had substantial hooks attached to their eaves to haul cargo up to the attics. The air smelled strongly of the river, making Stella ask herself whether she should have bothered with a shower. Then something scuttled off to her left and she glanced round to see a large rat whisk into the shadows. Well, Evie had mentioned the twelve feet thing earlier. Stella didn't mind rats: she thought they were cute, though this one was big, similar to the rat she had glimpsed on the dock last night. It could almost be the same rat... Feral city vermin, though, perhaps best avoided and no doubt the rat felt the same about her. She walked on, feeling nonetheless that something was watching her. She whipped round. The rat was sitting upright on a nearby wall, cleaning its whiskers.

"Hi, rat," said Stella, feeling foolish. "You're a bold one, aren't you?"

The rat dropped to all fours and ran the length of the wall, keeping pace with Stella, who was more amused than alarmed. Pity about the street, however: this was obviously one of those corners of the city which did not attract the maintenance it should, and she felt sorry for the landlord of the Prospect of Whitby, trying to keep a pub going in this run down section of Wapping. She had passed a substantial Georgian church and a park – that had looked all right, with children's swings and neatly kept flowerbeds – but this side of the Shadwell basin didn't seem to be developed at all... Funny, most of Docklands had been redeveloped by now.

She looked up. There was a triad of stars overhead and she could make out the long cross of the swan, Cygnus, following the length of the street. Normally you couldn't see many stars over the city at all: the light pollution blotted them out. But Cygnus was clearly shining, with Deneb blazing at its head.

Then Stella heard hoofbeats, and more than that: a trundling sound which after a moment, she identified as a carriage, and she thought *oh no.* The hansom cab came round the corner of the street at a quick clip, the coachman urging the horses on. Stella shrank back into the shadows. The windows of the carriage were blacked but for a second she thought she saw a face peering out. Then the cab was gone down the street which, Stella now realised with dismay, didn't just look Victorian.

It was.

"Shit," said Stella aloud. She hesitated for a moment, thinking. If she tried to retrace her steps, there was no guarantee that she would find the twenty first century waiting for her. All the jokes she had ever made about Holmes and Watson now returned to haunt her. And yet – hey, she'd already been to the ancient Roman city. It would be interesting, wouldn't it, to see what Victorian London was really like? Hadn't Holmes and Watson in fact come here, when Limehouse was a no-go area of opium dens?

You dickhead, Stella. Sherlock Holmes did not actually exist.

Limehouse did, though. After a moment's indecision, Stella decided to head for the pub anyway. She set off down the road again, grateful that she had worn Converse as usual and not taken it into her head to dress up. The cobbles were slippery in the misty air – was this an actual pea souper? Stella thought – and difficult to walk upon. At least she wasn't hobbled by Victorian skirts. At this she looked down in consternation but saw her own jeans clad legs as usual.

The rat was still keeping pace. She could see it running along the opposite side of the road. The tang of the river was stronger now, along with the drains – old London town really *smelled*, Stella realised – and as she turned a corner and found herself looking out over a stretch of the Thames itself, the creak of masts was audible, too. There was a lot of shipping clustered not far from the shore, and distant shouts from a wharf. She could see the pub now, a little building hunched between the big warehouses, a single lamp hanging from its wall. But without the many lights of the modern city, the river path was dark and took her past the hulk of a warehouse. Stella took a deep breath – *not far! You can see the pub!* – and marched on. But as she passed the first shadowy doorway, someone stepped out behind her.

Stella swung round, ready to fend off her assailant and, if she could, make a run for it.

"Steady on, Stella. It's only me."

Stella nearly collapsed onto her pursuer in relief.

"Ace! God! You gave me such a fright."

"Sorry! I can't bloody see anything. I got halfway down the road and then thought, hang on a minute, something's not right. I checked that the pub was still there – should have been, it was built in fifteen hundred or whatever – and it was, so I thought I'd better wait for you. I'm glad you made it. I had a nasty feeling I might be a hundred and thirty years too early."

"When are we?"

"I don't actually know. I saw a hansom cab a few minutes ago – it dropped someone off at the pub – so I suppose, late nineteenth century."

"I saw it too. I keep thinking of Sherlock Holmes." Then something occurred to her.

"Ace, when were you actually born?"

"1886."

"So somewhere there's a nine year old or whatever you running about?"

"Not in bloody Wapping there isn't. Shall we give the pub a go? I'm hoping the money's translated."

"You said you hadn't actually met Davy Dearly?"

"No, I've no idea what he looks like, either. Or if the poor bloke's sitting in a pub decades from now, wondering where we are."

"I'll have to pretend to be a boy," said Stella. "A strangely dressed boy." Ace, in an overcoat, could have been anywhen as long as one wasn't an expert on male fashion.

"Keep your hood up and adopt a gruff voice. Or let me do the talking. We'll say you came off a ship. From the Arctic. That parka is slightly Inuit-like."

"Won't explain the sneakers, though."

"We'll say they're native footwear, if anyone's rude enough to ask. This strikes me as the sort of pub in which people mind their own business."

"Let's hope so," Stella said.

The Prospect, inspected more closely, was a substantial three storey building with small leaded windows, through which a dim light was visible. Ace pushed open a creaking door and they stepped down onto flagstones. The place was low beamed and with the characteristic smell of old pubs which, Stella was interested to see, had not greatly changed apart from the pipe smoke and a stuffily unfamiliar odour which, after a moment, she identified as gaslighting. Dim globes hung from the walls. The pub was divided into small partitions and she could see faces looking up at them. They were, however, greeted affably enough by a couple of customers, old salts if ever she saw them, thought Stella, and the landlord: a middle aged man in sidewhiskers and an apron, engaged in polishing a pewter tankard.

"Good evening, gentlemen."

"Good evening."

"And what can I get for you?"

"A couple of pints, please. Wait. Let me see if I've got any actual money."

"That's quite all right, sir," the landlord said. "I'm thinking you'll be Davy Dearly's guests this evening?"

"Oh, thank G – yes. We are."

"Standing tab, then, although I expect a round from you in the fullness of time won't come amiss. In the back."

Ace and Stella followed his instructions and followed the bar around to a smaller back room. This had windows overlooking the river and was empty apart from a long table at which a woman sat, in a high necked blouse and ankle length skirts. She was, however, peering into a mobile phone.

"Er, hello?" said Ace. The woman looked up. Young, maybe in her twenties, Stella estimated, with light brown hair caught up in a bun. When she met Stella's gaze, Stella saw in the light from the gaslamp that her eyes were different colours: one grey and one a bright and vivid blue.

"Evening! Ace Spare? And Stella Fallow? I've Davy Dearly. Davina, before you ask, let's get that out the way. Named after my dad. Thank God he wasn't called Nigel, eh? Could've been worse."

"Good to meet you," said Ace. "I must say, I'm a bit relieved to find you here."

"We did say seven, didn't we?" In the depths of the Prospect, a grandfather clock chimed the hour. "Oh, sorry – you mean the slip in time. That was me, I'm afraid. Don't quite trust the present day and age for important meetings at the moment. Can't always pull it off but, well, here we are."

"We weren't sure if you'd be here," Stella said.

"Do sit down. I see you've got drinks. The beer is quite good in here if you're a CAMRA type although I expect twenty first century health and safety would have a fit. Never done me any harm, mind you."

"Do you come here, um, often?"

"In my day and this day, yes I do. A foot in both worlds, you might say." Her accent was pure Hackney. "I know it's a bit unnerving, slipping through time, you might say."

"I didn't in fact have any problems getting here. The scariest thing I saw was *him,*" Stella said.

"I know. I was keeping an eye on you, just in case. I know what it's like being a woman on your own at night at the best of times and this isn't one of those."

"Did you? You were very subtle about it. Secret agent level! All I saw was a great big rat." Then she caught Davy's sidelong look. It was beady. "Oh!" said Stella.

"Yeah. I'll give you a clue. Mammal, three letters, starts with 'R'."

"After I talked to Bill, and then you, Stella," Ace said, "And I got back to Southwark, Anione – that's my other half, Davy – remembered where she'd heard the name 'Dearly' before."

"Evie, my shipmate, knows who you are."

"Ah. She would do. I know about her, too. Live on the *Nitrogen,* do you? Nice old tub."

"She said there was something, well –" Stella stopped.

"Funny about me?"

"About your family. A legend, that your ancestor met a woman in a pub but she wasn't a woman."

"That's right." Davy seemed pleased rather than offended. "It's not a legend, though. It's the truth. My grand-dad – it was his grand-dad as had the encounter and it was in this very pub."

"I love a local boozer," said Ace.

"So do I. Dearlys have been coming here for generations."

"Evie said your family are toshers," Stella said. "Or were."

"Yes. Not all of them. Big family. Some were watermen, like my dad, or lightermen, like his dad. Some of them run markets. I myself went to uni and I am in fact a data analyst when I'm at home. People expect me to run a blimmin' jellied eel shop but this is my home town, this is how I speak, and I don't see why I should be any different. I work for Enrow and Wilson in Shoreditch, if you ever need to find me at work. Also analysing data for marketing companies isn't a million miles away from toshing and mudlarking – it's all about looking for patterns and nuggets of valuables, except it's information, not lost watches and that."

"When we came in," Ace said, "I'm curious. Your mobile doesn't work in here, does it?"

"Not now, no, I can't get a signal – hasn't been invented yet. I was playing Jelly Jewels while the battery lasted."

"Oh, okay."

"Anyway, your great great something grandma," Stella said, "was, uh, a rat?"

"Sort of a human rat hybrid, actually. Don't ask. Long story. I don't actually know the ins and outs of it. She was mostly human but she had claws and apparently, in the throes of passion, she bit great Grand-dad in the neck to mark him so that the rats in the sewers would leave him alone. Because she wasn't just any old rat but – taah dah! – the Queen of the Rats. I like that because I'm secretly a bit of a monarchist and it makes me feel posh. Anyway, having had it away with her, he went back to his girlfriend and Queenie took amiss to that, had a bit of a Fatal Attraction moment, and whacked a curse on him."

"Oh dear!"

"In every generation one of us has a blue and grey eye – a land eye and a river eye – and the ability to turn ourselves into a rat. You can Google all this. Sometimes people do, so I'm quite open about it – obviously, I make a joke of it, though, I don't tell 'em it's real. It's a running gag in the office. One of my bosses bought me a plushy rat. It sits on my desk. It's called Roland."

Ace said, "Stella's family has a bit of that going on. Hares and that."

"Oh, really?" Davy's eyes grew bright and she clasped Stella's wrist briefly. "It's so nice to meet someone who gets it! What was it – family curse?"

"We've no idea."

"That's so annoying!"

"It's mainly my sister Serena but my other sisters, Luna and Bee, have had it as well. Wrens and bees in their case. I seem to be the odd one out." And as she said it, Stella realised that this sounded a little sad. "I don't mind," she added, bravely.

"I am here to tell you that it can be a right old pain in the arse. Anyway. Bill Blake said something about the Knowledge. Like a black cab driver, only for all the ins and outs of the city?"

"Well, so I was told. I think." Stella recapped recent events, as succinctly as she could: the time slips in London and Noualen's instructions, the intrusions of the otherworld and Stella's own experiences at New Year on the old Maunsell forts at the mouth of the Thames. Even concisely, this all took some time and Davy dispatched Ace to the bar for another round.

When Stella had finished, Davy was silent, her bright uneven gaze downcast. Then she said, "It would certainly be bloody useful if there was a comprehensive map of the city. Look, I know quite a bit myself. I've got a map of my own but it's in here." She tapped her head. "And with me, it's little ways – like rat tunnels through time and place. I know about six or seven points along the river – mainly the wharves and one sewer exit – but there's also a place up near Richmond. And three or four more in town. I've never written it down just in case it gets into the wrong hands. Or the wrong paws."

"Like who?" Stella asked, intrigued.

"Like Mr P of your late acquaintance, for instance. There are some nasty people about."

Davy wouldn't have any reason to trust herself and Ace, it occurred to Stella. She said so.

"I know Bill, though, and everyone whom I trust, trusts him. He's absolutely kosher. Your shipmate, Evie – she's got a good reputation as far as I can tell, too. I made some enquiries when I knew I'd be meeting you. But she's one of the old river families – there are a lot of clans, watermen, bargees, lightermen, toshers, mudlarks, and not just the water, either – some of the remnants of the other old Medieval guilds, too, plus the pearly lot. It's all families and they know stuff, but they all know different stuff as far as I can make out and they guard what they know quite jealously. I have to say, Stella, because it's all families it's like a fucking Eastenders Christmas special half the time. *He* won't speak to *her* because of something her grandma said to his grand-dad in 1873 and *they're* not talking to *him* due to a falling out over some buttons. Or something equally trivial."

"This does not surprise me," Stella said. "Evie's said more or less the same. Her family were lightermen as well. And bargees."

"I know. Different lot to mine but we're probably related somewhere. As I said, though, quite a few managed to fall out with each other and I think her lot are mainly from Essex, Canvey Island and that."

"Evie also says she talks to the local imam about this."

"Yeah, that's another thing. People from different ethnic groups all have their own magic going on – I've got some contacts who trust me enough to talk about it but a lot won't. Why would they? Look at the Windrush scandal and all that – the last thing you'd want to do is confide in a load of white people. *And* class. My dad's voted Labour all his life – he's not going to go cap in hand to the toffs if he's got a problem, but I know for a fact that the aristocracy are involved in quite a bit of this stuff."

"So do I," said Stella, thinking about Nick Wratchall-Haynes.

"Right up to the Royals, apparently – maybe not the current lot, but certainly in the past. If everyone banded together it might make a lot of difference, but then there's the question, band together against *what?* Or who? It's all individuals and small groups, not one big foe. Having said that, there was that episode in Brixton last year where a whole bunch of people did actually team up and got something done. Did you know about that? Long story."

"No, I didn't. We've come across the Hunt," Stella said.

"They're quite nasty but that's a countryside thing. That's another division, by the way. Rural versus urban. The Hunt don't come into the city."

"Could they?"

"Probably, if they wanted to. I've never heard of anyone who had all the answers, cartography wise, but I'll tell you what, Stella my girl, this has caught my interest and I'm willing to give you a hand with whatever you want to know. I think it would be a good thing."

"Would it be to your advantage?" Ace asked.

Davy Dearly snickered. "I'm a rat's grand-daughter, mate. I don't do anything unless it's to my advantage. However, I'm also human and, to be honest, I do think out of a purely altruistic sense, this is worth pursuing. I've always said – and I've fallen out with some of my family about this – that we can't just keep all this stuff to ourselves. I don't mean sharing it with the wider world because that's a good way to get a visit from some nice people with a funny corset and a white van – although these days people seem to get away with believing fricking *anything* – but I think more co-operation not less is the way forwards. I mean, look at the upper classes and politicians. Can't stand each other half the time but they'll still muck in together when they have to. We need a union."

Ace snorted. "I can see *that* working."

"Yeah, you're right. Well, a girl can dream. Also, Stella, I wanted to talk to you about last night."

"So that *was* you on the dock!"

"Yeah, that was me. I didn't come onto the *Nitrogen* because polite, also magic, also mainly because of your whopping great ginger mog. Anyway. Someone's been making waves recently. Asking questions about you. And about your sister, Serena. I was down your way last night and a ship was coming in – I don't mean a modern ship, either. An old one. No flags or navigation lights. So I thought I'd hang about and see what I could see. No one pays any attention to rats – we're all over the place and thus invisible. Anyway, it didn't pull into shore – it went on down the river towards London Bridge – but someone got off it all the same. A great big herring gull."

"We disturbed a gull on the roof of the cabin," Stella said. "It flew right at me, and it set your tripwires off, Ace."

"That's because it wasn't a gull," Davy said. "I watched it: it flew from the mast of the ship and landed on the roof of the *Nitrogen.* And then it turned into a woman."

"Did it, indeed?"

"Dark hair, as far as I could see, which wasn't much. A long coat. Then you two came barrelling out of the cabin and I must say, tell your friend Evie that I greatly admire a woman who carries a boathook. Well played. I saw you duck and trip, and the cat go for it, and the gull went off down the river screeching its head off."

"We wondered why it had activated the wards. Ace, if she had dark hair, I bet that woman was Miranda."

"Miranda?" Davy said. "I've heard that name a couple of times and not in a good way."

"She used to go out with my sister's boyfriend. Ward Garner?"

"What, *the* Ward Garner? Seriously? Total fangirl moment here – I loved him in *Death Grip.*"

"I'll tell him. He's an old friend of the family. Anyway. Miranda is *the* Miranda Dean."

"The actress? No way! That's a shame, actually. I liked her, too."

"Unfortunately she's actually quite good," Stella agreed. "But she's got it in for Serena and we've had a few problems." She filled Davy in. When she had finished, Davy thought for a moment. Then she said, "So, look, Stella, how about joining forces a bit? I'll share what I know with you, and you can share what you know with me if you're willing. If you trust me."

Stella found that she did. Until there was evidence to the contrary, anyway. "I'll talk to Serena, too."

"We'll meet again. Here, maybe. I know the street down here looks a bit dodgy but I can meet you, now we know each other, and bring you in."

"I'll tell my sister to get her crinoline out."

"She'd actually be a bit late for the crinoline per se. Tell her to get a bustle. But a small one. Big ones are not in fashion anymore."

"Thank God for that."

"Or just dress normally. No one would blink in here if you strolled in stark naked, trust me."

"I do in fact possess an ankle length skirt."

"Knock yourself out, Stella!"

Outside, the mist had congealed into drizzle. Davy Dearly unfurled a large black umbrella.

"It's my Mary Poppins look. Want me to call you a cab?"

"I've always wanted a ride in a hansom," Stella said.

"Unfortunately now's not your chance," Davy replied, as a BMW shot past along the modern road. "However, black cabs are available these days." She stepped off the edge of the pavement and waved one down. "Here, you can take this one; I'll catch the next. Nice to meet you both. See you soon."

"Good night, Davy!"

"Where now?" Ace asked, as they clambered aboard.

"Evie's in the Rochester with some mates, said we'd be welcome to join her for last orders. Although it's not actually that late." She leaned over to the driver and gave him instructions. "He can take you on to Southwark if you want."

"Nah, I'll stop off with you, if that's all right. What did you think of Ratty, then?"

Stella laughed. "Does that make me Mole?"

"I am glad to see that a young whelp such as yourself is conversant with the classics of children's literature," said Ace. "I thought it might be all Ninja Mutant Turtles with someone of your age."

"We did it in school. *Wind in the Willows*, I mean, not mutant turtles. But actually my grandfather read it to us as well. I loved, loved, *loved* the bit with the baby otter and Pan. Oh my God, how adorable was that."

"Pan was a big thing with Bohemian Edwardians back in the day. Odd one for the Brits, but shows what happens when you repress sex, I suppose. I've drawn loads of satyrs. Hang on, though, if you're Mole, what does that make me? I'm not being bloody Mr Toad. I don't even own a car."

"No, you're badger, of course! Grumpy, hard drinking, anti-social…"

"Oi!"

"But anyway, Ratty – I liked her. I got a good vibe. Even if she is, well…"

"Vermin. I'm inclined to agree. I'll give her a chance, anyway. I'm not very up for trusting someone I've only just met, but I quite took to that young lady, I must say. Although you gave *me* a chance, you trusted me from the off. Or were polite enough not to tell me if you didn't."

"Yeah, and look how that turned out, Mr Badger. Oh, there's the Rochester. Let's hope it stays twenty first century this time."

LUNA

Like Bee, Luna went every day to check on the shoot in the greenhouse, sometimes twice. Even when the frosts came and it seemed to go into suspension, Luna still checked, and she and Bee had a little conference about it each day. She did not trust the shoot. And Ver wanted regular bulletins, too. Just in case.

Luna had also not forgotten about the shoots in the wood. She had a plan in mind, but she needed back-up. Bee was one of her choices, but the other was currently immured on a road protest site. So Luna waited until Sam was at Amberley, and then, after lunch, she commandeered Bee and suggested they drive to Glastonbury to collect Ver.

"Hopefully she's there and hasn't had a lift into town or something."

But as the car bumped down the muddy track to the gate, there was Ver March, perched on a stile as though she'd known they were coming. Perhaps she had.

"Fancy an afternoon out?"

"Just as I was starting to get cabin fever!" Ver said, indicating, with a sweeping gesture, some two hundred acres. "Where are we going?"

Once in the car, Luna told her.

"Good idea. Best keep an eye on these things, if you can. Ooh, look, Luna! Lambs!"

"Good thing we didn't bring the dogs," Bee said. "They'd be barking their heads off."

"Moth wouldn't," said Luna, indignant. "He's a good dog. Sam took him to work today," she added, to Ver.

"He's a lovely dog, your Moth. I remember him as a pup."

Bee was driving back, so Luna could concentrate on something other than the road and she smiled at the little things bouncing about in the field, though a bit sad to think about their eventual destination. But for now they were happy in the thin sunshine. Bee took a different route back, up the road where the hollow way had appeared, and parked in a layby near the wood.

"Oh," Luna said, when she got out of the car. "*That's* new."

There was a fence of stripped pine posts, looking shiny and somehow unnatural, marching along the edge of the wood, with sharp barbed wire strung between them, and a sign that read *keep out.*

Ver and Luna looked at one another.

"I hope that's not going to stop you, young lady," said Ver.

"It certainly won't," Luna replied and, over her sister's murmured protest, she took off her thick jacket, laid it on top of the wire, and swung her leg over. This sort of thing was getting a little more tricky but she managed not to fall flat on her face in the beech mast.

"Nice one," said Ver.

Luna expected a little more protest from Bee, who had never really approved of this kind of thing, but her sister's mouth was set in a tight line and Luna did not think that her annoyance was directed at her companions.

"Hmmmm," was all Bee said. She followed Luna into the wood.

Luna took a last look over her shoulder. Through the beech trees she could see the high bright line of the sky, scudding with clouds. Then one, in the arms of the west wind, blotted out the sun. The wood was plunged into a cold shade and the wind, rising, roared in the branches. For a moment, Luna felt as though she were on the deck of a ship: ahead, the land seemed to plunge, vertiginous. Then it righted itself. Luna blinked, grateful to find that she was still where she had been and not snatched into some other realm. Bee and Ver were waiting for her patiently.

"Are you all right?" Bee asked.

"Yes. Felt a bit faint for a second."

"That could be the baby," said Ver. "When I was expecting I used to pass out for a hobby. Blood pressure."

"Tell us if it happens again," Bee told her.

"Now, where did you find these shoots, Luna?" Ver scuffed the beech mast with her boot, forming a small rampart on the woodland floor.

"Over there." She led the others to the place where she and Sam had found the shoots. But there was no longer anything there.

"Are you sure it was here?"

"Yes. It was just by these big beech roots." Part of the earth had fallen away, making a bank. The roots of the beech cascaded down it, serpent thick, stony hard. Below, the ground was disturbed; the mast scraped away and the earth rumpled.

"That looks like badger's been at it," Ver said. She sniffed. "Can't smell him, though."

"They were definitely here," Luna insisted.

"Yes, I believe you, don't worry. But they're not here now. By the way, if you hear a creak, watch out. Beeches have a nasty habit of shedding a limb, all of a sudden." Ver knelt and ran a hand over the disrupted soil.

"Wait a mo. What's this?"

She had uncovered something pallid and faintly shining. It lay on the dark soil in a little spiral. Ver picked it up and it came free to hang limply from her palm. It was attached to something, which came free.

"What's that?" Bee asked, peering over Ver's shoulder.

"Its seed, I think. When you repotted your one, did you see one of these attached to it?"

"No, but I didn't want to mess about with it too much – it was fragile. I just turned it out with the rootball and put it in a bigger pot. Although come to think of it, there wasn't much of a rootball – a few filaments but it was mostly soil."

"That doesn't look like a seed," Luna said. There was something about the shoot which repelled her: its pallor was maggot-white. She half expected it to squirm; it was more like a fleshy worm than a stalk. And it smelled putrid. "It looks more like a – like a tooth."

"It's dead, whatever it is," Ver said. The shoot was decaying before their eyes, turning to slime. Ver hastily brushed it off her hand and it fell to the earth and became no more than a slightly oily sheen, soon gone. The seed remained, hard in her palm, the colour of old ivory. "It does look a lot like a tooth, I must say. Not a very sharp one, though."

"What are we going to do with it?" Bee asked.

"I'm going to wrap it up and take it with us." Ver's head went up. "What was that?"

"A car."

Luna could hear it slowing and stopping.

"Over here," Ver said. They took refuge behind a big stand of beech, hiding them from the track. Luna could hear footsteps; whoever it was had no concern, it seemed, about being heard. She risked a quick look around the trunk and saw Nick Wratchall-Haynes' estate manager striding down the track, clad in Barbour and flat cap with a cocked shotgun over his shoulder. He did not pause at the place where the shoots had been, but carried on, looking neither right nor left. Luna held her breath. Bee and Ver were very still. It occurred to Luna that they must have left footprints, but perhaps the beechmast had protected them from that. The man walked to the edge of the wood and was gone.

"He'll have seen the car!" Bee said.

"But no proof that we went into the wood. For all he knows, we went for a walk down the road."

"Unless he catches us," said Luna.

As quickly as they could, they went back through the trees and climbed over the barbed wire. Bee fumbled for the car keys. The gamekeeper's Land Rover was parked higher up the road, tucked against the verge.

'If he's taken the number plate, it wouldn't be too difficult to find out whose car it is," Luna said, as Bee pulled away.

"I don't know what freedom of information has to say about that. I don't think the DVLA are allowed to tell you, but all he'd have to do is ask in the post office what you drive and he'll know because Gina will tell him."

"Maybe he wasn't even looking for us," Ver said. "He didn't seem to be doing a very good job of searching for intruders. More like a man on a mission."

"He had a shotgun," Luna said.

"Well, they all carry those. I don't find it terribly sinister, to be honest."

"And he has no proof that we were even in there," said Bee. "Anyway, home again, home again. Cup of tea, Ver? And then I'll run you back."

But before she left, Ver suggested an experiment, which prompted Bee to go into her grandfather's old study and ransack a drawer.

"This is the OS map of the area. It's the most detailed one I've got."

"That will do fine, lovey. Now. I'll need a piece of red cotton, embroidery thread, whatever you've got."

Bee fetched her sewing basket into the kitchen and rummaged in it, producing a skein of scarlet silk.

"Will this do?"

"Perfect!"

Luna watched as, with care, Ver tied the silk to the tooth.

"Bit slippery, but this should do. Now, if you can spread the map so that Hornmoon is roughly at the centre."

Luna, loving maps as she did, took pleasure in finding the small square that was Mooncote among the contours of the OS plan. She traced how the lines rose and fell. Across the map were faint pencil lines, joining spire to spire, beacon hill to standing stone.

"Someone's been working out their leylines," Ver said. "The old straight track! I love a bit of Lethbridge."

"Yes, that was me and Luna," Bee told her. "We spent an evening doing it. The trouble is, this country is so small and there are so many ancient sites that it's easy to find links between anything, really. All you have to do is stick a ruler on the map and bingo, leylines."

"Discernment is always important, I say," said Ver, tying a final knot. "It's very tricky. Some say as how churches are built on older pagan sites but I got Sam to look it up on the internet and it's not often so, it told me, though St Paul's is supposed to sit on a Roman temple. But a lot of them are old, so they're a good bet and so are standing stones and natural features. I'd say if you've got four things in a line in a short distance, you're doing a good job. Now. Everyone close their eyes for a moment and think of where we are. Root yourself, then open your eyes."

When they had done as she asked, Ver held her home made pendulum over the map. "My hands aren't as steady as they used to be but – ah!" The tooth, on its scarlet thread, had started to swing, describing a wide circle in the middle of the map. Luna, almost hypnotised, watched it sweep past. Outside, there was a sudden flare of sunlight, chased by shadow as the sun went behind a cloud. In that winking moment, the thread came untied and the tooth fell, tumbling, to rest on the map. When it hit the paper, it crumbled apart into dust. Everyone leaned forwards to see where it had landed.

Not far from Mooncote and the church, on a little oblong, contained within an irregular outline. Wycholt Manor, home of Nick Wratchall-Haynes.

STELLA

Stella woke late and spent the morning tidying up. This was an issue with life on a boat, she had realised: she now had a more comprehensive idea of what 'shipshape' meant. She gave an accusatory Rumpole what was without doubt his second breakfast and went on deck in time to see a bright red van pulling up at the end of the wharf. "Postman's here," said Evie, and went to meet him. Stella watched as he handed over a brown package and some letters.

"It's for you, Stella!"

"Ooh!"

"Did you order something from Amazon?"

"No." Stella was inspecting the packaging. "It's from Bee. She said she was sending something but that was ages ago – look at this postmark."

"Bloody hopeless," Evie agreed. "It's probably been sitting in a sorting office somewhere."

Stella found some scissors and cut the package carefully open. Inside, was another parcel and a note.

Hi Stella, we found this when we were clearing out – it's got your name on it and we thought you'd better have it. Lots of love Bee. xxx

Evie guffawed. "Maybe it'll be like one of those Russian dolls."

"Yes, more and more wrappings and inside will be like an acorn or something."

"Do you know what it is?"

"Haven't a clue." Stella slit the second package open.

It was filled with fawn fur. It stirred in the light wind from the river.

"It looks like one of those stole things that go round your neck." Stella grimaced. "I hate those. Creepy. Not because it's a dead animal, but because someone killed a beautiful creature, just for show."

"I know what you mean. With the snout and feet dangling… It looks too big for a stole. I suppose furs do pack flat."

Stella pulled the fur free, and it turned out to be both footless and snoutless. It was wider than a stole.

"More like a wrap," said Evie. "I have to say, it's lovely fur."

"I don't think it's mink," Stella said, after a pause.

"No. The texture's wrong."

Stella, along with her sisters, had suffered a bad experience with mink, back in the autumn. But this fur was shorter and did not have the glossy, expensive sheen of farmed mink. Its backing was either skin or some fabric akin to suede. Stella held the garment up: it was perhaps the length of her arm.

"I think I ought to get rid of it but I don't want to just chuck it, somehow."

"You could wear it to your Windsor gig. Keep out the chill. When's that again?"

"Saturday. But the fur, maybe not. It might look a bit weird standing behind a mixing desk wrapped in a fur stole like someone's grandma, even if they are aristos."

"Find someone with a brazier along the shore, maybe."

"Well, that might be a bit weird as well – *hi, you don't know me, but I've got this dead animal skin I'd like to get rid of.*"

"I suppose we could just let the river take it – after all, everyone else does."

"True. But it's a bit too much like littering and after we spent all that time cleaning up the foreshore..."

"I know!" Evie said. "Brainwave! My friend Jas has a vintage store off the back of Tottenham Court Road. If you're going into town at some point, you could take it in – I'm sure she'd give you something for it but if you don't like that idea you could just give it to her. She sells furs; she showed me this amazing mink hat once. Then you're not being wasteful, it's like recycling."

"Excellent suggestion!" Stella said, relieved. "I'll do that, then." She stashed the fur carefully in her backpack and forgot about it. She wanted to call Ace.

"Ace? Hey. Just checking that you're still up for a trip to Windsor. Davy's coming too. I hope you don't mind me asking her – I thought the more the merrier."

"It's your gig," said a voice that echoed in the depths of the Southwark Tavern. "Also, if something kicks off, it'll give us a chance to see what she's made of. What time it is again?"

"The gig itself starts at seven but I'm planning to go along earlier. I've been invited to the afternoon do – they've basically got food and a marquee and that sort of thing."

"Bouncy castle?"

"Somehow I can't see the Queen allowing a rival castle on the property, even a bouncy one. Anyway, I ran it past Les and Lady Georgina and said you and Davy are my roadies. Quite how we explain that when I'm not bringing any equipment with me, I'm not sure."

"I'm very plausible," said Ace.

BEE

Luna took Ver back to the campsite and after they had gone Bee spent some time poring over the map, playing with the ruler, making ley lines.

"What is that?" Ned Dark said, shadowy in the corner of the room. Bee looked up.

"Oh! I didn't realise you'd come in, Ned." She prodded the remnants of the tooth with the ruler, edging the off the paper. Then she folded the OS map and picked up the remains with the kitchen tongs, transferring them to a plastic takeaway tray.

"A seed. From one of the shoots. We went up to the wood today, but the estate manager scared us off. I don't mean we had words – he didn't see us. But all the shoots Luna saw had gone, there was just one, and it died. It left this." She looked at him. "It fell apart when we did some divining with it."

"What are you going to do?"

All at once Bee made up her mind.

"I'm going to speak to Nick. I should have done it before."

"Do you want me to come with you?"

"No. I think I should go alone. Although if you want to, maybe, wait outside the manor until I come out, that might not be a bad thing."

"Then I shall do that."

Bee found the hunt master, appropriately enough, in the company of a horse. It was the big chestnut that he usually rode and it was standing patiently in the yard behind the manor while a young farrier removed a loose shoe.

"He kicked it off up the road," Nick said. "I was lucky Jim could come out – they're like bloody supermodels these days, farriers, won't get out of bed unless you make it worth their while."

Bending over the hoof, tucked onto its iron stand, Jim grinned.

"Bet it's harder work than the catwalk," said Bee.

"Who does your two? The piebalds?"

"Sam does. I don't know whether he's actually allowed, these days – I think the legislation changed a while ago. But they're not shod at the moment."

"He's all right," said Jim, rather indistinctly; the chestnut had become restless. "As long as he's not shoeing them – you need the qualification. But he can rasp their feet without that."

Nick nodded at her. "There you are. Straight from the farrier's mouth. Right, Jim, I'll leave you to it – Andy can pop him back in his stable."

"Cheers, sir."

"Tea?"

"Yes. Thank you." She followed him into the house, noting again the silence, interrupted only by the ticking of the grandfather clock. Rachel was evidently not there as Nick was obliged to make the tea himself, which he did without demur, leaving Bee in the drawing room. She was admiring a set of architectural drawings of Regency Bath when he returned.

"There you are. We've run out of cake. Shoddy service."

"I do not deserve cake," Bee said, sounding to her own ears rather more dramatic than she had intended. "I'm afraid I pinched a plant from you the other day."

"Oh, that's quite all right. You're welcome to take what you want, as long as it's not great sheaves of irises but you wouldn't do that anyway."

"Well, it was one of those shoots in your orangery. Also, I have a further confession to make. We trespassed on your property this afternoon."

"The wood up on the ridge? Yes, Mike said he'd seen your car. Really, no one's worried about you or Luna or anyone from Mooncote – I had that fence put up to keep random walkers out and I don't care if hikers traipse through it, in fact. In normal circumstances, anyway. I actually put it up for their protection."

Their eyes met.

"What *are* those shoots?" Bee asked.

After a moment, Nick said, "I don't know. Well. All right. That's not quite true. I have some idea."

"We found a stray one in the wood that died. It just sort of, faded away before our eyes. It left this thing, like a seed. Actually, more like a tooth."

"I thought *all* the ones in the wood were dead."

"What killed them? Do you know?"

"They did."

"Sorry?"

"They grow to a certain point and then they turn on each other. I watched them do it, in the orangery, one night when the light of the full moon fell on them. They twisted round each other like vines and strangled each other until only one was left. Took about eight minutes – I timed it, being anally retentive."

"Plants don't do that," said Bee, shaken.

"They're not plants."

"What are they, then?"

"People."

"Shit," Bee said. "Sorry. I *thought* it looked like a tooth."

"Do you remember the story of Cadmus, in the Greek legends? Despite a classical education at a reputable public school, I can't remember who wrote it – I think it was Homer. Cadmus kills a dragon and Athena tells him to sow the dragon's teeth on the plain. He does and they grow into fully armed warriors. He chucks a jewel in the middle of them and they all fight until only a handful are left."

"And that's a *dragon's* tooth?"

"No, I don't think dragons are actually real. Although you never know." Nick took a sip of his tea. "It's a hunter's tooth."

"What, like the hunt in the – the otherworld, or wherever it is? One of *those* hunters? Like the Lily White Boys?"

"Yes, although not the Lily White Boys themselves, as far as I can gather. Some of the Hounds were once men. You'll see others with them, however, and some of those will have come from sown teeth."

"Oh, Christ! And I've got one growing in the greenhouse!"

"Not all of them become hunters. And not all of the hunters grow from teeth."

"What do some of them become, then?"

"They become people, girls, but I don't know what happens to them or where they go."

"And this takes place every spring? How many teeth do they *have*?" Bee had an image of a member of the Hunt in a dentist's waiting room, perusing old copies of *Country Life*.

"No, it's not every spring. I don't know how often it is exactly but it's not even every ten years. Maybe more like every hundred. This spring is unusual, I gather. I don't know if their teeth drop out or if they use ones from a dead huntsman or what. I just know what I was told and that was a long time ago – I've never seen the shoots before this year."

"You said the ones you had all killed each other, except one. Where is it?"

Nick grimaced. "Yeah, my eldritch botanical experiment has not ended well. It died too. I took it out of the orangery after it had dispatched all of its siblings – I didn't know, until that happened, what those shoots were. As I said, someone told me about them ages ago but I didn't immediately make the connection. I put it in the shed, warded, but in the morning it had collapsed and then it faded away, as did the tooth."

"Ver did the same. Except ours has survived."

"I went up to the wood with the full intention of dispatching the rest of them – having worked out what they must be, I asked… a friend, and they said that a knife made out of meteorite iron will kill them."

"Which you just happened to have lying around? In the kitchen drawer?"

"I do have one, yes. I don't keep it in the kitchen drawer, though. I took it up there but I was too late – they'd already fought it out. I couldn't find any survivors. But it seems that you did."

"Yes, and it died, the one we found in the wood. Nick, the one I pinched from you is still in the greenhouse. I don't like the idea of killing it but I think we'd better do so."

"Yes, I think we had. I'll get the knife and run you back to Mooncote."

"All right. And Nick – sorry. We had no business just taking it like that."

"You weren't to know. I'm not cross, just a bit concerned."

When they reached the house, Nick, carrying the blade in a bag of black silk, and Bee made their way straight to the back of the greenhouse.

But the shoot was no longer there.

STELLA

On Saturday Stella and Davy Dearly met Ace at Paddington Station. He was sitting on the plinth of the statue of the famous bear, beneath the station clock. Paddington Bear wore a hat, Ace did not, but Stella felt that there was some resemblance between them all the same. Kindred spirits, perhaps. She decided not to say so.

"Afternoon," Ace said. It was four o'clock. "Everything all right? No problems?"

"No, we're good. Any sign of the train?"

Ace jerked his head at the departures board. "Not yet. I think it's in, though – platform two. They're cleaning it."

A minute later the board refreshed itself. It was indeed the second platform; the Reading train. They would need to change for Windsor but it was not a lengthy trip.

"Barely time to sit down," said Davy, as west London shot by.

"It's usually half an hour to Reading. Slough is before that."

"It's good to get out of the capital," Ace remarked. "I ought to do it more often. Last time was that trip with you, Stella. Gives one new horizons. I get too set in my ways, me."

"Same here," said Davy. "It's why I go into the office."

"I hope it's not going to bloody rain," said Stella. The sky looked ominously overcast, but by the time they got off at Slough, it had begun to clear and promised to be a mild evening.

"God, I'd forgotten what a dump this is," Ace said. "Betjeman was right – 'come friendly bombs and fall on Slough.'"

"Don't be so mean," Davy said, amused. "I'm sure plenty of people like it."

"There's the Windsor and Eton train," Stella pointed out. They were just in time and there were no seats: a large tour group had taken them all.

"It's not far, though, is it?" Davy said.

"Literally ten minutes."

The train pulled into Windsor and Stella and her companions were squeezed out of the carriage like toothpaste.

"You know," Stella said, "It's a good thing I don't have any actual equipment with me."

"You'd need a van," Ace said. "Old school. Your birthday girl must know we've not come along to hump amps."

"I don't think she cares. She's a real party girl with a generous spirit. Serena and Ward are coming as well, by the way, because she'd ordered a dress from Serena. Oh, I think that's our ride."

Georgina's brother had come to pick them up in a Range Rover. Jasper was a handsome young man, with wavy dark hair and not much chin. He was delighted to see them, really delighted, and he was of the sort whom Stella mentally characterised as Tim Nice But Dim, an actual chinless wonder. She had met his ilk before and set out to charm him. This was not hard, since Jasper was rather Labrador-like. Stella, alongside her in the back seat, could see that Davy was biting her lip as he chattered away. They swung through Windsor under the massive lee of the castle and out.

"So – Windsor Great Park's not actually *in* Windsor, then? Or is that a stupid thing to say?" Stella asked as they left the town and its towering monument behind and headed out on the main road south.

Jasper was quick to reassure her. "No, no, no, no. It's massive, but the entrance where we're going is about five miles from the actual town. You'll see the castle again from it. If you'd not been here before, you wouldn't know that, though."

"I've been to Windsor once," said Stella. "On a school trip. Her Majesty was not at home."

"She is now, though. Did you see the flag?"

Stella had not.

"The Easter Court," said Jasper. "The flag flies when she's here. She's usually here from March to April."

"We should have popped in and paid our respects as loyal subjects," said Ace.

"I have a lot of time for her Maj, I must say. Game old bird."

This amused Jasper greatly and it was some minutes before he stopped laughing.

"She's not coming to the party," he managed to say.

"I think that's a terrible shame," Stella said. "I could get her on the karaoke."

The entrance to the park was now looming ahead. Jasper drove straight through the gates and up a long avenue of trees. Stella could indeed see the towers of the castle; they had come around the park in a curve. She could also see a herd of deer, drifting among the oaks.

"This is really lovely," said Davy.

"Old George is awfully chuffed that you're doing her party," Jasper said, suddenly shy.

"A pleasure!"

Stella meant it, too, although the phrase 'two birds with one stone' resonated inside her mind. She was interested to see what the Great Park might come up with. Jasper pulled the Range Rover up in front of an enormous marquee, not far from a pavilion.

"That's the Polo Club," Jasper explained. "Belongs to the Guards – George's boyfriend sorted it, since he's in 'em. I expect you'll want to check your sound equipment?"

"Yes. That's what these guys are for."

"Lead me to it," Ace said. "I want to have a look at the – the thing."

"Technical term," Stella said.

The gear that Stella had requested had been set up on a small stage at the far end of the marquee. All was in place and as it should be. Stella derived a certain amount of private amusement at Ace trying to appear as though he knew what he was doing. But no one was really paying attention. Just as they were finishing up Georgina Hammond bounced up, a blonde with a bony English face, stunning in a Serena creation featuring chiffon and embroidered spring flowers.

"Oh wow!" Stella said to her, as they air kissed. "You look amazing. I got you a birthday present." She fished in her bag and produced a small box and a card.

"Thank you so much! That is so kind! Is everything all right?"

"Everything's fine."

"So you are totally welcome to just enjoy the party, and have some food, and then are we good to start at seven?"

"We're great."

Stella thought an early supper might be a good plan, and after that, taking a look at the lie of the land and seeing what might show up. It was now well after five and the sun was low. Above the park the sky was criss-crossed with contrails from nearby Heathrow, but the sound of the traffic was muted. London felt very far away.

"It's like one of those Shakespeare plays," Davy said, munching a cheese *vol au vent*. "A woodland scene."

"Arcadia," said Ace.

"I loved that herd of deer when we drove in. Richmond has deer, as well."

"A lot of the old parks do. So does your friend Noualen's influence not extend out here, then, Stella?"

"No, I don't think so, that's why she's sent me out and about. But I was coming here anyway – the Huntress knew that. I think someone's pulling strings… Noualen is snared in the city."

"You mentioned that. Might be another reason," Ace said.

"Which is?"

"This isn't her patch anyway. It's Herne's."

"Yes, that had crossed my mind. Like I said, I can't help thinking that the location of this gig wasn't accidental."

"They booked you quite late, didn't they?"

"Yes." Stella remembered Lez saying, "It's not like she didn't know she was going to be twenty one." She found it difficult to envisage Lez as an agent of darkness – but perhaps she wasn't. Perhaps she was an agent of Noualen, instead, or the Huntress Diana, or maybe all of them were subject to forces beyond their control? She would not put it past *London the Book* itself to have some active role in the whole affair. Stella added, "You know I am assuming I *met* Herne? In Somerset?"

"You met some kind of ancient deer spirit, for sure. But Herne himself is quite recent. Shakespeare took the story of a fourteenth century hunter and tweaked it a bit. Originally he was just a ghost."

"So how come he's now an antlered mega-nature spirit?"

"A writer of Victorian pot boilers tweaked it some more – Harrison Ainsworth, in a book called, with great originality, *Windsor Castle*. I have read it, but years ago. It's not bad, actually. I seem to remember he makes Herne a hunter who serves Richard II and dies. Then he becomes a ghost. Wiccans took all this up in the 50s and turned him into an antlered god based on Cernunnos, but his origins are a bit iffy as well. He's supposed to lead the Wild Hunt but he doesn't seem to be doing that right now."

"Noualen said she used to be in charge of it."

"There's a painting of her doing so, alongside Odin, you'll be pleased to know. Whether Herne actually is some old forest spirit and someone had a revelation or something, I'm not sure. He's another one who is supposed, like King Arthur, to turn up in the country's greatest hour of need."

"You'd think he'd have rocked up before now, in that case. Ditto King A."

"Maybe he did and was not visible to general view," said Ace whom, Stella suddenly thought, would have been around during the Blitz. For instance.

"I hope he doesn't mind me tramping round his hunting park, whatever he is." It was a complication that Stella did not think she needed, and it wasn't the first time the thought had occurred to her, either. She thrust Herne firmly out of her thoughts, just in case the thought might escape and be overheard. The memory of that antlered shape rushing at her at Mooncote was still fresh in her mind.

Having worked their way through the buffet, Stella, Davy and Ace worked out a brief plan of action: have a wander about and see what there was to be seen. Prior to their visit, Davy and Stella had done some thorough googling of the Great Park and they thought they had an idea of the lie of the land. The park was huge, but Georgina's marquee was not too far from the site of a grotto.

"It's actually on the lake. Near the cascade, but didn't the website say it was shut?"

"Yes, too unsafe. Isn't there a folly in here as well?" Stella said.

"A chunk of Roman temple. They brought it from Libya. God knows what's lurking in *there.*"

One thing at a time, thought Stella. "Grotto first."

They walked down towards the lake. An unlikely vision rose before them.

"Tell me that's not an actual totem pole," Davy said.

"I think it is, though. Wonder where they nicked that from?"

"I bet it's Victorian. Going around the world, stealing everyone else's shit."

"It doesn't look right in the middle of English parkland."

They skirted the totem pole. Stella heard the cascade before she saw it: an artificial waterfall on the other side of the lake, rushing in a picturesque manner into the calm waters. She could hear traffic as well; the cascade was adjacent to the road.

"Not very peaceful."

But it was shaded by trees. Trying to look unobtrusive, Stella and Ace climbed up the small slope at the back of the cascade. The grotto was visible: a pile of overgrown stones.

"This is not promising," said Ace.

"Not in our day and age, anyway."

They poked about for a bit, but the grotto was unforthcoming.

"Worth coming back after dark," Ace said. "What time do you finish your gig, Stella?"

"I'm on from seven till ten. After that, young Jasper wants to try his hand at DJing and so we can slope off between then and midnight, when we have to get out of the park. Noise regs or something. I expect Her Majesty doesn't want to be disturbed. So Jasper says he'll collect us from the Polo Club around a quarter to twelve. That gives us a couple of hours to have a look round the park and do some scouting."

"Sounds like a plan," said Ace.

They went slowly back to the marquee. As the Polo Club came into view, so did Serena, getting elegantly out of a cab. Ward was holding the door open for her. Stella ran across.

"Hi! You made it. Davy, meet my sister Serena and her partner, Ward."

"Massive fan of yours," said Davy, gruffly.

"Thank you so much – that is lovely of you to say so. How are you getting on?" Ward asked Stella.

"Fine. More or less. We have a plan." Stella explained. "Not that I expect you to join us in those shoes."

"I've brought a pair of trainers in case." Serena held up a bag.

"We'll see what happens," said Ace. "It might be best if you stay here – we're going to hive off later after the gig."

"Just let me know what you'd like me to do," said Serena.

"Have fun and keep an eye open for anything untoward."

"Much as usual, then!"

Stella procured a large bottle of mineral water and went to sit in the marquee to run through her playlist and get her head together. This should be straightforward, but one never knew… The environs of a polo club were not the most likely place for supernatural untowardness, but Stella was rapidly learning not to trust appearances: look what had happened out at the Maunsell Forts, for example. She still did not know what to make of that curious wartime episode, the sirens, the searchlights…

She looked up from her list and there on the other side of the marquee was an old woman in black, staring at her. Stella gasped, the clouds shifted, a shaft of early evening sunlight fell through the opening of the marquee and the woman was gone into golden. Stella sat slowly back down; her heart was thumping.

Outside, the marquee was edged with large portable burners, made to resemble actual torches. They would need them, Stella thought: the spring air was chilly. Gradually, people were starting to file into the marquee, bringing drinks and plates of food with them. Stella vacated her table and went to sit behind the mixing deck. Nearly kick off time. Things went quickly after that: Georgina came to speak to her, she ran through the equipment with Jasper (who, despite vacuous appearances, seemed reasonably capable – he had done it before, he said, "In Ibiza," which was perhaps not so promising), and then the dusk was falling fast and Stella was on.

Ace had installed himself at the back of the marquee, behind Stella, with a beer, and she saw Davy Dearly moving around as well.

Serena came in and danced, with Ward; she looked as though she was enjoying herself. This being a twenty first birthday party, the crowd was young and accustomed to having a good time: high energy, Stella noted automatically. But there were a few tweedy parents floating about as well. No Bullingdon Club-type antics would be permitted under those watchful eyes, Stella thought. Just as well. She could cope with the odd flung bread roll, but not with the equipment being trashed, for example. Unlikely to be a problem but you never knew. She voiced this thought to Davy in the interval, wiping herself down with a towel. The marquee was stiflingly warm by now.

"Yeah," Davy said. "I know what you mean. Quite a few Hooray Henrys in with this lot but they're well behaved enough, I must say."

"You can't always expect it with the upper classes. I did a May Ball once at one of the Oxford colleges. I saw things I hope never to see again."

"If they came from Hackney and weren't white you'd never hear the end of it," said Davy, adding darkly, "Look at David Cameron and that pig."

"Yeah, right. Pass the brain bleach! Thanks for the towel."

"No worries. Do you need more water or are you all right?"

"I've got plenty. Right, let's get on with it."

For Stella, time spent at the deck was no time at all. It passed so quickly that she was quite surprised to find a flushed but still bouncy Georgina coming onto the mike stand to thank her profusely, announce a short break, and that the next set would be headed up by her brother "but I don't think he'll do such a great job."

"He totally will," said Stella.

"That was so fabulous! Thank you so much!"

"Thank you for having me," said Stella, like a child at a birthday party.

"Go and have something to drink – I don't suppose you have yet, have you?"

"No, I lay off the booze when I'm working. I've had water but I will, in fact, go and have some champagne now and raise a toast to your birthday. Have you seen my sister?"

"She was sitting outside on the grass – oh my God, she brought *Ward Garner*. I'm so psyched, I can't tell you… I asked him about his new film. He's given me tickets to his next play as a birthday present, imagine, so kind!" Georgina pressed a hand to her heart.

"That's really sweet of him," said Stella, thinking: *nice one, Ward.*

Serena, when located, said that it was just too hot in the marquee.

"Are you going to take a look around now?"

"Yes. You and Ward stay here, keep a look out."

"Nothing's happened so far."

"It has, actually. I saw what I think might be one of the Searchers. An old woman, in black, like the one you said you saw when you rescued the raven?"

"Oh my God! Where?"

"In the marquee, before the gig. I don't know if it's a good thing or a bad thing."

"Just take it easy," Ace said. "Okay, Stella, let's get going."

BEE

Bee was just about to close the velvet bedroom curtains against the fall of dusk when she glimpsed movement in the garden. The days were noticeably longer now, with a haze over the sky and the last lemon light only just fading in the west. It was shadowy in the garden, but Bee was just in time to see something white flitting along the hedge. Too tall for a lamb. A person. Mr Goat Face?

Right, thought Bee, angrily. She raced down the stairs, flung open the French windows in the dining room and was out into the slightly damp evening air. Where had it gone? Then she glimpsed it again, moving quickly through the orchard.

Bee followed. The air smelled fresh and flowery: hyacinths? They were coming out now and releasing their fragrance into the twilight, but it wasn't quite the same scent. As though a woman had dashed from a room and left the lingering betrayal of her presence behind. Bee pursued, into the orchard.

She thought she had lost the thing, whatever it was. Breathless, she reached the end of the orchard. Had it gone through the hedge? She peered through the hawthorn branches, trying to see into the field, but it had grown too dark in the handful of minutes that she had spent in the chase. She could not see anything in the field – no, wait, there was something white there. Then it gave a peevish cry and Bee realised it was just one of the old ewes.

She gave a last huff of breath and straightened up. Damn. She would just have to go back to the house. She turned and the thing was standing behind her.

Bee gave a faint shriek. It was not the goat faced man. It looked like a girl, young, with white hair streaming down its back and the loose shift that it wore. Legs and feet bare, arms behind its back. It was smiling. Its eyes flared a pale sea-green, like water in moonlight. Bee knew, though she could not have said how, that it was no girl, nothing human at all, just the shape it had assumed.

"Please," she whispered, and the thing smiled. Its small teeth were sharp. It cocked its head on one side, like a dog trying to understand, and then without any warning it flared up, bright as naptha, a brilliant white-green column of fire that made Bee cry out again and throw her arm over her eyes. When she lowered it again, her vision danced with green and white flames.

"Bee!"

Dark was suddenly there. She leaned against him, gasping.

"Ned. Sorry. Had a bit of a fright."

"I saw it."

"What *was* it?"

"I think," Dark said, holding her tight, "that now we know what became of the shoot."

They went back into the house. Bee felt embarrassed about being feeble. She said as much to Luna, whom she found sitting in the kitchen, poring over the map on the table once more.

"You're not feeble!" her sister said. "It sounds scary as hell."

"It scared me," Dark confessed.

"See? It frightened him and he's dead."

Dark shivered. "That does not mean that you are safe."

"Great," Bee said. "Something else to look forward to!"

"So what's happened to the shoot?" Luna asked. "It's – what, grown into a person?"

"A spirit, I think."

"If they'd all grown, then, would they all be like that? There were several of them in the wood and there were about the same in the greenhouse, too."

"Nick said some would have been male. Oh God," said Bee. "I'd better warn him it's on the loose."

"Assuming he doesn't already know. I want to speak to Ver, too."

"I'll call Nick now," Bee said. "And then we can go over to the protest site, if you like. It's only just dark."

"Okay."

With Dark and Luna on either side, Bee rang Nick Wratchall-Haynes, but there was no answer. Eventually the answering machine kicked in and she was able to leave a message.

"Nick? It's Bee. Can you call me? On my mobile? It's quite urgent. Something's just happened. Thanks."

She hung up.

"All right, Luna. Let's get going. Ned, I'll see you later."

"I'll be here."

Bee collected her car keys, changed her shoes and put her coat on. By the time she had done this Luna, similarly wrapped up, was waiting by the back door.

"Ready? Great."

She opened the door. The goat-faced man stood on the step; a Hound behind him. Bee saw the long white face and flashing eyes. The Hound wore rusty chainmail and stank of blood and fear. She tried to pull the door shut but the goat-faced man, still grinning, wrenched it out of her grasp and gripped her by the wrist, pulling her forwards, out of the house and into the yard.

Then the Hound's long arm was around her waist and he plucked Bee off her feet with ease. He rolled her over like a bolster so that Bee, shouting and pounding him with her fists, was facing the ground. The yard was suddenly full of people. Bee glimpsed Nick Wratchall-Haynes running up the drive, followed by Sam and she could hear Luna shouting from the house. Then Dark was there, a rapier in his hand. He darted forward in a long fencing step and struck the Hound in the shoulder. There came a stab of light, a bright spurt of blood and the Hound, hissing, dropped Bee onto the cobbles. Shielding her face, she tried to roll away but the goat-faced man was standing over her. She saw a flicker in his hand, he was holding a bone knife, wicked as a dragon's tooth, straight as an arrow's flight. As she tried to scramble backwards, he brought it down.

SERENA

Serena was enjoying herself. The last proper party she had attended had been on New Year's Eve and that had been a bit – odd. Since then she had been to several drinks dos, a friend's wedding, Milan, and a number of dinner parties, but not something like this where she could just sit on the grass and drink free champagne and laugh. Admittedly, it wasn't warm and she was wrapped in a pashmina and an evening coat, but she was British, she could handle it. And Ward had found them a place near one of the outdoor burners; in its proximity, sitting out was really quite pleasant. She kept her promise to Stella, who had not yet returned, by keeping an eye on the scene: not too much champagne, therefore.

"What the hell is he playing now?" Ward asked. The sounds from the marquee had grown cacophonous. "God, I sound like my father."

"It's young people's music, Ward."

"I thought I *was* a young person!"

"Not as young as Jasper will probably always be."

"He won't be young for much longer. Sloanes go over fast, like annual plants. Give him another couple of years and he'll be wearing scarlet trousers at a point to point and manhandling a couple of snotty nosed kids with ponies into a loose box with a woman named Annabel."

Serena had to admit that Ward might be right.

"I thought Sloane Rangers had all died out when Lloyds collapsed," she said.

"They will never die. They will always be with us, like taxes and the poor."

"Well, it's nice for Jasper to enjoy himself while he can," Serena replied.

A group of people, laughing uproariously, had come out of the marquee.

"Let's throw old Rupert in the lake!" bellowed one.

"Oh, here we go," said Ward. "See? Not extinct at all. They've probably all been hurling buns at each other."

But Serena was not listening. At the back of the small crowd, she had seen a figure that she recognised, slipping around the side of the marquee.

"Ward, that was Miranda!"

"What? Where?"

"She's just gone round the back of the tent." Serena rose, drained her champagne, and slipped off her heels, exchanging them for her trainers. "Come on."

By the time they got to the other side of the marquee, Miranda was nowhere to be seen.

"Are you sure it was her?"

"Yes, one hundred percent."

"Told you we couldn't trust her."

"Well, no, Ward," Serena remarked with some tartness. "We knew *that.*"

"I wonder if she's brought Hob with her. Serena, look! There she is!"

Miranda wore a dark blue dress, knee length. She was hard to spot in the twilight park, but Serena saw her running down the edge of the trees towards the lake. They followed, but by the time they reached the lake she had vanished. Serena cursed. She could really do without Miranda now.

Since there were lamps around the lake it seemed reasonable to assume that Miranda had seen them, but they looked around anyway. The place felt ominous to Serena; she wanted to go back to the party rather than hunt for an enemy in this dark patch of woodland. But they found no trace of Miranda, the grotto was still firmly sealed off, and when Ward suggested returning to the Polo Club, Serena gratefully agreed. She was even more thankful to find that the Polo Club was still there, music belting out of it and Rupert apparently unhurled into the lake.

"I think more champagne is in order," Ward said.

"Good idea!" But as she turned to follow him to the bar, someone stepped from behind the burner.

"Serena!"

"Oh!" Serena said. Ward turned. Hob grasped her by the arm.

"I've been looking for you. Miranda's here." He was wearing the clothes in which Serena had last seen him.

"We know. Did you come with her?"

"No, she doesn't know I'm here."

"How did she know about the party?" Ward demanded.

"I've no idea. I followed her."

"We saw her going down to the lake but we lost her."

"I don't know if she has a plan. Hard to tell, with Miranda. Will you come and look for her, with me?"

Serena was not sure. A trap? But Ward would be with her.

"Let's all go and look, then," she said reluctantly.

As they followed the path to the lake Serena became aware that the music was no longer to be heard. The park seemed very dark, and silent.

"Ward?"

"You all right?"

"I'm not sure. I think we might have slipped again."

"We have," said Hob.

Off to her left, Serena saw a sudden rush of movement and she clutched Ward's arm, only to see a herd of the little deer, racing away. The moon came out from behind a cloud, turning the park to silver and black. Beside her, she felt Hob shiver. She took his arm, too, but this time to give reassurance.

There was a huge tree up ahead, on a small knoll not far from the water. Serena could see someone standing beneath it, motionless and in shadow. The moon had gone again.

"Ward? What kind of tree is that?"

"Don't ask me – you know what I'm like! I can just about tell a pine from a palm."

Serena waited for a moment until the clouds raced away and she could see the tree more clearly. The wide, sprawling branches suggested horse chestnut. Not an oak, then, not Herne's oak. But something about the unmoving figure made her heart beat fast and hard. She swallowed.

"Let's go on."

Through the trees, the grotto gaped open, the rocks piling up behind it in artistic disarray. It had been the fashion then, eighteenth and nineteenth centuries, to build follies and grottos: whimsical and eccentric. But now, in the chancy light of the moon, the grotto looked simply sinister.

Ward said, suddenly, "I can see her!"

"Where?" Serena whispered.

"Don't move! Down there, by the side of the rocks. Do you see?"

Now that he had pointed her out, Serena did. She could just make out the wan oval of Miranda's face, very low; she must be crouching down. An owl cried out and Miranda looked up. From behind Serena, a voice whispered, "Serena? It's Stella's friend, Davy. Can you see her?"

"Yes," Serena whispered back. "We followed her. Is Stella with you?"

"No, I've lost her. Do you know where she's headed?"

"No." But at that point, Miranda rose, cat-swift, and ran for the grotto.

LUNA

Luna screamed as the Hound struck at her sister, but the air shivered gold and Bee wasn't there. Instead, a humming swarm rose into the air, the bone knife plunging harmlessly through and shattering on the cobbles. The goat-faced man swore in a language that Luna did not understand and spun around to find Dark behind him. The swarm buzzed angrily: Luna didn't know how this particular transformation worked but she was willing to bet that Bee was really pissed off. The bees whirled up, forming a cloud, a comma like the murmurations of starlings around the ash trees every night, and Luna felt the air grow heavy and hot. There was a click at the edge of the world; somewhere, a door was opening and the bees were moving towards it, taking the Hound with them, stumbling him through the golden air. The yellow-eyed man whirled around and ran after the Hound. The door had unlocked something in Luna, too. She felt herself shrinking, compacting down into wren, and as the door swung fully open she was flying quickly after them. She heard the men shout her name and Bee's name, but it was too late.

A dazzle of light and Luna, still wren, was back in the world she had visited in December. Spring was coming here, too. The hawthorn brakes were touched with green, the colour of cold sunset, and windflowers were starting to come up through the leafmould. Somewhere not far away she could smell rampions, the strong scent of wild garlic. The wood felt milder, a gentler place – but there was the Hound, striding down a slope into a dell. The goat-faced man was nowhere to be seen. The flicker, again, and the Hound was a great white dog with a bloody shoulder. He whined, pawed, tongued, but could not reach the shoulder over the spikes of his collar and Luna, knowing the truth of him but loving all animals, felt a sharp pang of pity. If she had been in human form, and not clinging to a long spine of briar, she might even have gone to help, but at that moment she heard a rustle behind her and a hand closed around her little form.

Luna squeaked in alarm but she was held too tightly to struggle.

"Hush," a voice said, and released her. Luna fell away, changing, crouching, and found herself in the leafmould at the feet of Kit Coral.

He waited until she stood, then nodded towards the dell. The Hound, in human form once more, was moving away and almost out of sight. Luna heard Kit exhale a sigh of relief.

"He's gone, good, and so is Aiken Drum. Are you well, jenny wren?"

"I think so. He tried to snatch my sister. From our house." She looked in the direction of the Hound but no bees hummed in the bramble thickets, or in the tangled masses of the oaks.

"Where is your sister now?"

"Did you see any bees a moment ago?"

"No." Then Kit's head cocked. "Wait. What's that?"

A short distance away, a log was moving. Luna stared at it for a second before she realised that it was crawling with insects. A second later Bee stood there, dusting herself off.

"Bloody hell!" she snapped.

"Are you okay?"

"I'm really quite cross."

Kit Coral grinned at her. "No prizes for guessing who you are. That's an unusual gift. Don't see that very often."

"I suppose wrens are normal, then?" said Luna. He included her in the grin.

"Ten a penny. Well, birds, anyway."

"To be fair, Luna, we do know other people who can turn themselves into birds. And you might be?" she added.

"Kit Coral, at your service, ma'am. I shall take care to keep on the right side of you, too, so don't worry. I mean you no harm and I prefer honey to the sting."

"That Hound got plenty of those," Bee snapped.

"Why did he attack you? What did he want?"

"I really don't know."

"To cross into the world of men, to snatch a mortal woman? It has happened, but in these modern times it's rare. You must have done something to greatly anger him, or to make him very afraid."

"I have no idea what," Bee told him. "His friend? I've seen him before. But I'll be careful from now on, you can be sure of that."

"Kit, do you know the way home?" Luna asked. "Our friends will be worried."

"I know the way. The short way, or the long?"

"Short's better."

He laughed. "I thought you might say that. The longer way's more scenic, though."

"Do you happen to have a map?" Bee asked.

"No, it's all in my head. I'll show you the shorter way, and then if you choose and if you can, you can return here and take the longer path. But if you do come back, I'd do it as bird and bee if I were you. Neither path is very safe."

"Can I mark the path?" Luna asked. "I have some thread in my pocket."

"Not unless you want something to follow you home." He tapped his capped scalp. "Keep it in here, Jenny Wren."

"All right, I will."

And they began to walk.

"Uphill and down dale," said Bee in an undertone, a little while later. Kit Coral's stride was brisk, and he followed no discernible track. Several times they had to push through tangles of briar and once a thicket of holly. Both Bee and Luna became slightly scratched and breathless. Luna did not dare say so to Bee, but it crossed her mind that they were being led on a wild goose chase: she knew too little about Kit Coral to trust him entirely. In addition, Kit kept stopping and listening for something unknown, with his head on one side. Once, Luna heard a distant shout, abruptly cut off, and once, far down a steep hillside, she glimpsed a man, running. He wore long, spurred boots and a helmet and his collar was white. He carried a spear, or perhaps a pike: Luna did not know a great deal about weapons.

"Civil War?" Bee wondered aloud but then he blinked out of sight. Luna did not like to think what might have been chasing him and she found herself looking over her shoulder, to the extent that she stumbled and almost fell.

"Careful," Bee murmured, steadying her. "The last thing you want is a ricked ankle. Are you taking notes?"

"Yes. That big beech with the hanging branch is one, and that slight rise."

Bee nodded. "I'm doing the same. I wish I had my phone – it must have fallen out in the yard. Or even pencil and paper."

Luna did, too. The trees were starting to thin, the light growing stronger. They were at the edge of the woods now, coming out onto a long bare slope of grass. Luna could not see the sun, but it felt like early evening. Then there was a clatter of wings overhead, making her jump: wood pigeons, hurtling home to roost for the night. The sky was stained with faint rose. Kit Coral pointed.

"Down there. I won't come with you. Do you see that stile, at the edge of the wood? Take it and don't look back. You'll be home in a twinkling."

Rather uneasily, Luna and Bee did as they were instructed. Luna stole a quick glance behind her, since they were not yet at the stile. There was no one at the edge of the woods but she felt as though they were being watched, all the same. And it had not really felt that late, but by the time they had covered the short distance to the stile the dusk was a blue bloom across the sky and a star hung in the east: Venus, coming to greet them. Looking up, Luna was not surprised to see the three stars of the Spring Triangle overhead, fainter than the planet but not far behind.

"You first," Bee said, for they had reached the stile. Luna clambered over and blinked into full darkness. She turned and held out a hand to Bee, who hopped down.

"I can hear something." They listened. Powerful lights shone in the distance, a tractor rumbling up the lane. There was tarmac beneath Luna's boots.

"Thank God," said Bee. "I hope we haven't been away for days."

"It's been all right before." Not that this was any guarantee.

"Fingers crossed," Bee said, and they walked quickly down the lane to where it met the main Mooncote road.

STELLA

Stella looked around in frustration. Ace and Davy had been right behind her – and then they weren't. She called, softly, but there was no response. She searched quickly: no one was there. Stella fought down a rising impulse to panic and took stock of her surroundings. She was standing on a slight hill, able to see right down the park towards the castle. Windsor Castle itself was still there, but no lights showed in its turrets and the stars were bright above. Stella glanced away, glanced back. The castle had gone – no, there it was again, looming unlit over the park.

"You're big enough," Stella said to it, accusingly. "Don't disappear." She could hear something, a drumming sound, and turned to see the deer running up to meet her. They were, appropriately enough, fallow deer: small and neat, with red spotted hides. She had enough time to note that none had antlers but then they were upon her and around. Stella stumbled at the glancing impact of their bodies but they swept her up and away. She was running with the herd, far faster than she could run in the everyday world, legs pumping, heart racing, but there was no strain; she was able to keep up. Down the slope and away, up a long chase that led straight to the castle. But they did not go to it. The herd swerved, carrying Stella with them, and veered off into the trees.

This was oak parkland, now. Stella ducked under the occasional low branch but the herd took her out into an open glade. In the middle of one stood an old tree, a half hollow oak. Stella was left standing beneath it, abruptly, as the herd left her behind and vanished into the trees. Fearfully, she looked up into the twisting branches. Only a star, bright Spica. It gave her heart. The glade was silent. Stella looked to see if she could see the castle. One of the big towers, still dark, rose above the trees but it was a long way away; she was, she realised, on the slope of a hill. Stella turned and there was a body hanging from the oak.

Stella stared. She had seen dead people before, but there was something both pathetic and repulsive about this motionless form, the head wrenched to one side, the booted feet pointed and dangling. An owl shrieked out; Stella looked away then back and the figure had gone. Instead, he was standing in front of her. He wore a cap and a short cloak; his eyes were dark and sad. A bow was slung over his shoulder. As with Ned Dark, the oaks could be seen through his form.

The wind rose, hissing through the oaks and stirring Stella's hair. She shivered. The ghost reached out.

"Take it," the tree said. It had a quavering voice, the voice of an elderly, uncertain person. "Take."

Stella held out her hand and the ghost dropped something into it. Then the wind caught him and blew him away in tatters; the oak stood blasted in the glade. Its spring buds were gone and it was nothing but dead wood, quite silent. Stella looked at her gift: a little antler prong, which she dropped into the side pocket of her back pack.

The distant castle was suddenly ablaze with lights and then floodlighting switched on, turning the castle walls to a livid lightning blue white. Stella could take a hint. She went to the edge of the glade and saw that a long track ran from the hill to the castle. There was now a statue on the hill: a man on horseback. A king? She looked back; the oak had disappeared. Stella gave a nod to the statue and started walking.

SERENA

The grotto rose before her, its entrance too mouth-like for Serena's comfort.

She took her phone from her pocket. There was no signal, but she had plenty of battery and the torch app still worked.

"Don't go in," Ward said. "Leave her."

Serena thought he was right but she still wanted to see. Hesitation warred with annoyance and curiosity.

"Come with me. Just a little way."

With the aid of her phone's faint light, she could see that the entrance to the grotto was spiralled with shells, set into the wall. One big conch was at eye level and looking at the patterns made by much smaller shells, whelks and mussels and little scallops, Serena had the odd, compelling sense that the wall held a message; that if she could only decipher it, it would shout at her what she needed to know. She reached out and touched the shells and found as she did so that she could hear a distant hush and roar, like the sound of the sea, as though she held the big conch to her ear. She paused for a second, not liking to think of Miranda lurking in the darkness. She nodded to the others, mouthed, 'Back.'

Outside it was still dark but Serena could not hear the music and laughter from the party.

"Damn!"

"Not worth risking a trap, Serena."

"No, you're right." She hesitated. "Where's Davy?"

The young woman was nowhere to be seen.

"I don't know where she went," said Hob.

"Did she go into the grotto?" Then something skittered out of the bushes. Serena gave a yelp. "A rat!"

"Less of that," Davy said, standing suddenly up. "There's a lot of prejudice."

"Sorry!"

"There's a door at the back of the grotto; I followed her, she went through it and doubled back. She's heading for the cascade."

They followed the path, which was narrower than Serena remembered it. Perhaps the park had been landscaped… The trees grew more thickly here and there was a sharp, green smell. What, Serena wondered, were they actually going to do if they caught up with Miranda? Chastise her? Try to reason with her? Take her prisoner? None of these options seemed very realistic. Perhaps it was time to simply go back to the Polo Club. If they could find it.

There was something in the trees: a light. It was blue and dim, like marshfire.

"What's that?" Stella whispered.

"Don't know. Can you see her?"

"No." The light bobbed further into the trees. Serena didn't fancy the idea of following that, any more than she had liked the notion of going deeper into the grotto.

"Let's keep to the path," she said. They ignored the light and kept going. She could hear the rush of water now, and that had not been audible before. Above it, there was a distant thudding bass and the sky glowed orange dark. Welcome back to the 21st century, thought Serena. The track brought her out by a rocky incline, water thundering down it in an ornamental cascade. Sudden movement caught her eye, she turned to see Miranda. Serena didn't have time to react. Miranda threw something – dust? A powder? – and Serena reflexively ducked. She felt the air sizzle and spark, blinked, but it had missed her, whatever it was. Her sight was unaffected.

"Serena!" Ward shouted.

Hob shot past her. He pushed Miranda and she fell, down towards the cascade. She gave a shriek of fury, the air shivered and a gull shot up over the rushing water. It turned with a falcon's fast grace – Serena had forgotten what strong flyers they were – and, screaming, it flew over the lake and back towards the castle. But now Hob was nowhere to be seen.

LUNA

Luna had errands to run that day, so had taken Sam to Amberley in the morning and was due to collect him at four. Now that they had all the vehicles back from the garage, getting around was a lot easier, although Luna wondered how long it would be before she couldn't fit behind the steering wheel. She set off from Shepton with a boot full of Bee's shopping, some herbs from the garden centre, and pulled into Amberley's drive on time with a pleasant sense of achievement.

"Hello, Luna!" Laura was waving from the door of the stables, her long blonde hair caught up in a scrunchie. Her jeans betrayed her recent occupation: mucking out. "Sam's gone up to the top paddock to see to some loose fencing but he'll be back in a minute."

"I'm not in a rush," Luna said. "How are you? Sam told me Cloudy's going to be running at Cheltenham." As a believer in animal rights, she didn't much care for that, but she knew how well the Amberleys treated their stock.

"Yes. It's an amateur race but we think she's up to it." A nervous expression crossed Laura's face. "Hope so, anyway."

"Good luck! Oh, there's Sam."

Sam was coming through the gate which led to the fields, holding a tool bag.

"Ready, Luna? Did you get everything done?"

Luna was just about to reply when there were shouts of dismay from beyond the stables.

"What's that?" Luna asked.

Sam didn't hesitate. He whipped round and started running, with Laura behind. Luna followed more slowly, a result of pregnancy, but when she got through the gate she saw a man struggling with the bridle of a bay mare. The horse's head was tossing, her eyes wide and frightened.

"Leave her alone!" Sam shouted. The man turned. Luna saw a dirty, unshaven face above a kind of tunic and trews; a long liripipe hood dangled over one shoulder. He drew a knife – no, a dagger –

from his belt and struck at Sam, who dodged. A stablehand – the one who had shouted, thought Luna – was running down the slope.

Luna looked quickly around her, found a stone and flung it at the man, hoping she wouldn't hit the horse. But the stone struck the thief on the arm and he dropped the dagger. She heard him curse and then his gaze went to something behind Luna. She looked over her shoulder and saw a Hound standing in the yard. He was in dog form, huge and white coated. Muscles bunched as he sprang. Luna threw herself against the gate as he passed; she slipped and fell into a patch of grass, narrowly missing the side of the stone horse trough. When, momentarily breathless, she looked up, she saw that the bay mare was cantering along the fence. In a grey streak Cloud Chaser ran down the field and reared up over the Hound. Sam was grappling with the thief and the stable hand had reached them by now and snatched up the dagger. The Hound flickered from dog to man and back again and Cloudy lashed out, bringing her hoof down on the Hound's skull. He fell, lay motionless for a second, then was gone, along with the man in the liripipe hood.

"Luna was very brave," Laura said. They were sitting around the dining table at Amberley, waiting for the police. "She threw a stone at the thief."

"Then I fell over," said Luna. "Which was a bit rubbish, really."

"You're pregnant," Caro said. She put a tray of tea on the table. "You ought to be looking after yourself, not tackling horse thieves."

"Laura was brave, too," Luna said. "She was first in the field, with Sam."

"I should have tackled him," Laura said. "But I was worried about Shelty – the man grabbed her bridle, she's such a nervous individual…"

"Your mare was bravest," Sam said. "I've never seen a horse go for a – a man like that."

Jack, the stablehand, said, "I have once, in Newmarket. Mind you, that horse was a right bastard."

"So did any of you recognise this man?" Caro asked.

"No, dirty type he was. Traveller, I expect." Then Jack realised what he had said.

"Sorry, mate, I didn't mean –"

"No worries," said Sam. "I'll know him again if I see him."

"He had a big dog with him, too, like a mastiff, but I don't know – did they run off, then, when the mare went for him? I had my back to him."

"Must've done," said Sam.

"I didn't see either but I think he must have run back through the yard and into the lane," Laura said. "I was more concerned about Luna and Cloudy at that point. I got madam straight into her stable while Jack dealt with Shelty."

"Nasty business," said the stablehand. "I've a mind to sit up tonight with the shotgun."

"Oh God, please don't shoot anyone, Jack! We've got enough problems as it is."

"I won't do that, Mrs A. But I'd like to give him a fright if he shows his face around here again."

"Let's hope he doesn't," Luna said. She was thinking about the Hound, struck down. She would ask Sam later, but she thought she had recognised him: one of the Hounds in green, the ones who had run behind the drove. The Lily White boys. Won't be telling *that* part to the police, thought Luna.

STELLA

To Stella's relief, it was not yet midnight. The birthday party was still going on; she could hear it before she saw it. As she made her way through the trees, there was a rustle in the grass and a rat stepped into her path. A moment later, Davy Dearly stood before her.

"Stella! Thank God for that." They clasped hands briefly.

"I'm really sorry. I thought you were behind me and then you weren't."

"You just – vanished. Ace went back to the totem pole area to look for you and I've been scouting around here ever since."

"I've been gone a lot longer than the clock says. But hours, not days. Is everyone else all right?"

"Yes, except there was a bit of a scene with Miranda."

"You'd better tell me," Stella said. So Davy did so, as they walked back to the marquee. Serena, Ward and Ace were waiting anxiously on the lawn.

At this point Jasper appeared, still cheerful and, since he was designated driver, not the worse for wear, which Stella feared could not be said of other party goers. Ace and Davy and Stella herself were loaded into the Range Rover, and Jasper said he could fit in Serena and Ward, too: "You'll just have to squash up in the back." He chattered about music and Ibiza all the way back to the station, thus relieving Stella of the responsibility of making small talk. Once at Paddington, she went back with Serena and Ward, this being closer than the *Nitrogen*. The prong weighed very little, but she was conscious of it in her backpack all the way home.

When she was finally alone in Serena's spare room, Stella unzipped the pocket and took out the prong. It lay in her hand for a moment, but then it changed: Stella was holding a little horn key.

"Oh!" she said. The fragment of antler was back. Stella stared accusingly but it did not change again. She put it carefully back into the backpack and went to bed.

SERENA

Stella slept until lunchtime and, on the grounds that she had just been handsomely paid, bought her sister Sunday lunch in the Lion and Unicorn before returning to the boat. Aside from this, since Ward wanted to learn some lines, Serena had spent a quiet day in the studio, did a lot of work, and went back into the house at six to open some wine and put a casserole in the oven. Bella was upstairs, doing her homework, and Ward was still in his study. But she was vaguely expecting an Amazon delivery at some point soon, so when the doorbell rang she hurried to the door and flung it open.

Hob stood on the step, looking bedraggled and unshaven.

"Oh!" Serena said. "It's you."

"Don't sound so pleased."

"Sorry! I wasn't expecting to see you."

"Can I come in?"

He looked so woebegone that Stella had a momentary lapse into the maternal and said, "Oh, all right. No tricks, though."

"I promise."

In the kitchen, Serena looked at him more closely.

"When did you last eat? And, not to put too fine a point upon it, when did you last wash?"

"Sorry," Hob said. "Do I smell?"

"Sort of, yes, quite frankly." Serena could not actually tell what he *did* smell of: it wasn't human body odour, but it wasn't good.

"I last ate – something. I can't remember." He blinked.

"You'd better have –" Serena hesitated. "Some toast. Do you eat bread? I know you eat cake. There's a casserole in the oven but it won't be ready yet."

"Toast would be fantastic. Or just bread and butter. Or just anything, actually."

"I'll make you some toast," Serena said, hoping Ward would soon reappear. Then she heard him coming down the stairs. She jumped up.

"Ward! We have a visitor."

"Oh," Ward said, unenthusiastically. "It's you."

"Look, I can understand that you might not be very pleased to see me right now, but I don't have anywhere else to go."

"And that's our problem, is it? What about Miranda?"

"I didn't see her after the park. She – left, suddenly."

"And you expect us to believe that you've not seen her since?"

"I haven't but she's got me chucked out of my place. When I got back, which was about six o clock this morning, all my stuff was in the street and half of it had been nicked. It's in a neighbour's garage now – there wasn't that much but they felt sorry for me. The landlord's not terribly popular."

"You can't stay here!"

Serena, more sympathetic even though she thought this was a bad idea, was about to say, "Oh Ward…" but told herself to shut up instead. Did she really want Miranda's creature in the house, a spy in the dark? The answer had to be no.

"Do you have any money?"

"A bit. Not enough for a deposit on another flat."

"And you can't nip back into the past? Find a hovel?"

"I don't want to live in the past! There's all sorts. Rickets, diptheria, press gangs…"

"Eat your toast," Serena said, and did what she had become accustomed to doing in times of crisis: she phoned the Southwark Tavern.

"Send him down here," Ace said, once she'd explained. "I want to talk to him anyway about what happened at Windsor. I don't trust the little shit but he'll be safe enough with us or Bill, either way. I might actually insist on taking him round to see Bill."

"That would be awesome," Serena said, relieved. "Sorry to make him your problem, though."

"He can't stay with you – Ward's quite right. We don't know what his capacities really are, I suspect he's lying through his teeth half the time and we don't know where his mistress Miss Miranda Gull has got to. If she turns up here or at Bill's, she'll find a few nasty surprises waiting for her, which won't be the case at your place. So put him on the bus and tell him to come in here."

Hob blinked nervously when Serena gave him these instructions, but after a minute's thought, when it presumably became apparent to him that he didn't have much of a choice, he said, "All right. I'll do as he says." When he had finished his toast, Ward walked him to the bus stop. The rest of the evening was quiet in comparison. Ace rang Serena back, around seven thirty, to let her know that Hob had arrived safely and was now ensconced on the sofa. Serena rang Stella and brought her up to speed.

"Hey," Stella said, tinnily from the barge. "That's *my* sofa. *I* sleep on that when I stay at Ace's place."

"Perhaps Anione will have it magically fumigated," Serena said.

"Did you ask about Miranda?"

"Yes. He says he hasn't seen her. Anyway, I'm sure Ace will keep an eye on Hob."

"I'll ring him tomorrow. I might even go down there."

"Glad to hear it. Speak soon," Serena said, as the oven pinged at her. "Dinner's ready."

An early night was definitely required. Ward went upstairs for a bath, and Serena went round to the studio to lock up and check that she had set the alarm. She went inside, flicking on the lights, and looked with satisfaction at the new collection, at the soft watercolour blues and greys, aqua and umber and ochres. Charlie had said that she thought this was the best collection yet and secretly Serena agreed, although she was a little afraid to think this, partly because it felt as though it might be courting bad luck and partly because she had to try to detach, a bit, in case anything happened to this collection, too.

But Caspar Pharoah was dead and Anione's sister was – what? Out of time and not coming back soon, according to Anione herself. When her previous collection had been trashed, back in the winter, Serena had wondered if Miranda had been the culprit, but Ward had said she was too lazy to bother with such an effort. Now, Serena wondered if that was really the case, even if the actress had not been the immediate agent of the previous destruction. Miranda seemed quite active, in this time and others, and she had it in for Serena.

"You stay safe," she said, reprovingly, to the silent racks of clothes. Then something moved. Serena gave a little shriek and grabbed the nearest rail.

"Who's that? Who's there?"

She half expected to see the watchful demon, Blake's creature. She could see someone now, standing in the corner of the studio.

"Who is it?" Serena whispered, but suddenly the fear left her altogether, as though someone had reached out and plucked it away. Featherlight, she stepped forward and saw a man, lit faintly, as though from below.

"I saw you on the shore," she said. "You were dead."

It was the young airman, clad in his blue uniform, whom she had seen on the shingle in Brighton. He was young, Serena thought, twenty five or so, but there was a sombre cast to his face which made him look older.

"Why have you come back? Why are you here?"

But he said nothing, only stared. He was very insubstantial.

"Serena, are you all right?" It was Ward, swathed in a dressing gown. "I came downstairs and you'd gone."

"Yes, fine. I was just –" she looked back but there was no one there. "I'll tell you in a minute," she said, and locked the door behind her.

Part Two

Selling England By The Pound

BEE

Bee sat and watched the sunlight glinting from her glass of champagne, surrounded by sixty thousand of her closest friends. Well, people, anyway. Ahead, through the immense plate glass windows, she could see a green bowl of valley, with the scarp of the Cotswolds beyond. The yellow limestone of the upper hills was similarly sunlit: this was a fine March day and as they had driven in, the streets of Cheltenham had been lined with daffodils.

A day at the races. It would be nice for Caro to have a friend along, Richard had said when issuing the invitation, although Bee thought this was ridiculous: Caro had dozens of friends and she was now zipping about the Owners and Trainers Bar, greeting them. He had also said that Bee herself could probably do with a break, which was true, although having booked a family holiday in Cornwall for the summer, she felt that she would not do too badly this year. Visits to the otherworlds did not count as a 'break.'

Bee also now felt significantly underdressed, for this was Ladies' Day and there were an astonishing variety of elegant tweed suits, feathered hats, sparkling fascinators and, in more regrettable instances, rows of perma-tanned orange legs beneath pelmet skirts. Bee did not like disparaging other women and she would not have criticised this on the basis of taste, but she had winced a bit because the spring wind was sharp and those legs were unstockinged and rapidly becoming goose-pimpled.

"They think it's Ascot," said Caro, after they had held the door open for a couple of shivering girls.

"Which is when, remind me?"

"June."

"Ah."

Bee may not have been as glamorous as some of the women here, but in knee length boots, a brown polo neck sweater and a stout tweed skirt of her own, she certainly felt warmer. The bar was well heated, but outside was a different matter. Idly, she listened to conversations about the going, the form, the results of yesterday's Champion Hurdle, the various merits of the Ditcheat string. Bee pricked up her ears at this because this was the closest trainer to Mooncote, just a few villages away, and she often saw the owner of the yard, stout and jacketed, or in local pubs as his handsome horses paraded through the streets on their morning or afternoon ride out. Sam had said that there had been someone snooping about that yard, too. But her eavesdropping was interrupted.

"Bee! Hi!"

She had known Nick Wratchall-Haynes was coming to the races, as he had dropped in at Mooncote at the weekend. She smiled, saying, "You're in your natural habitat." For he was wearing a three-piece suit and a trilby. His shoes shone like chestnuts.

"Like a duck-billed platypus."

"Well, not *quite* like a duck billed platypus."

"I always think of them in connection with natural habitats. I blame David Attenborough. Did you have a good run up the M5?"

"Yes, it behaved itself, even round Bristol. Did you?"

He nodded. "I'm staying at a nice boutique hotel near Tewkesbury – I think I mentioned that on Saturday, didn't I? Came up on Monday night to catch up with some friends. Only just got rid of the hangover. Is your sister with you?"

"No, she doesn't really approve of horse racing, if you mean Luna. Stella doesn't either; Serena likes it for the hats. But they're both in London. Ned isn't here. As far as I know!"

"Fair enough."

"Sam's here, though, to give Laura and the team a hand with Cloud Chaser."

"And she's fine, is she? I mean the mare."

"Yes, in good form, apparently. None the worse for her adventure although Laura said they've been keeping a very close eye on her. It's not a Grade One race, mind – it's one of the amateur ones later, with Jason Prior on board. Laura's not riding Cloudy herself. Richard has got a couple of horses in other races. I hope for his sake they do well."

She chatted to Nick until a similarly tweed-suited man clutching a race card came and claimed him, and then she herself was snared, by Caro Amberley.

"Come and have lunch! We're booked in. Might as well get the afternoon off to a civilised start."

"Is Laura coming to lunch?" Bee asked, as they made their way to one of the on-track restaurants.

"No, she's always nervous when Cloudy's running. She said she was going to sit in one of the stands on her own for a bit. Well, as far as you can be on your own in this throng."

Bee enjoyed her prawns and smoked salmon; poor Laura was missing out, she thought, and resolved to have a word with her later, although she thought Caro would probably make sure that her daughter got something to eat. Mustn't fuss, Bee told herself sternly, and devoted her attention to her lunch and the promenade of hats and skirts and dresses that were going to and fro past the wide windows of the pavilion. She turned down more alcohol, however, feeling that she needed to concentrate on the afternoon's events.

And they were exciting. One of Richard's horses came second in the 13.20, the first race of the day: a thrill for the owner, who had not expected to be placed at all.

"Good prize money, too," Caro said in an undertone to Bee, "though it *is* the Festival."

"I'm always a bit horrified by how much money exchanges hands at these things," Bee confessed.

"It mainly goes to the bookies," Caro said, cynically. "Although an Irish chap won £250,000 this week."

"Yes, I saw that in the paper today. That's really life changing, isn't it? Good for him."

"Are you going to be betting, Bee?"

"I have already had a flutter, thank you," Bee said. "I put it on Richard's horse just to be loyal and now he owes me a fiver."

Caro laughed. "Hot tip for Mondegreen in the 14.05."

"I'll trust you. Thousands wouldn't."

Feeling pleasantly wined and lunched, Bee followed Caro to Richard's box and watched the first two races from there.

Mondegreen came in sixth, losing Bee another fiver. It did give an edge of excitement to the race, although Bee privately decided that Paddy Power and their ilk could do without her custom for the rest of the afternoon. The sun was still high and the air held a definite warmth, so much so that when it finally came to the race in which Cloudy was running, Bee grew restless in the box and decided to go down onto the track, to mingle with the crowd. She made her way to the paddock and watched the horses being paraded round the ring, admiring their long stride and delicate heads, the shining coats brushed to gleaming and stencilled with stars. Cloud Chaser would have been easy to pick out even if Bee had not known the horse: she was the only grey running in this race. Bee looked for Laura, but could not spot her amid the throng of owners and trainers mingling on the lawn. Then the bell rang for mounting up and she saw young Jason Prior clad in Richard's owner's colours, crimson and cream, spring up onto the mare's back. Her ears were pricked forwards: she looked ready to run.

As the horses made their way down the shute to the track itself, Bee slipped in through a set of double doors, heading for the area where the bookies had their kiosks, and found herself on the members' lawn instead. She felt rather guilty about this – her pass did not entitle her to step out onto the hallowed turf, but the stewards must have been distracted, for Bee was through before she knew it. Oh well. It was a little less crowded here and she might as well enjoy the view. She wove between a sea of tweed and established herself firmly by the winning post, feeling in the thick of it and enjoying the site of the horses galloping back down the track to the start. As well as being the only grey, Cloudy was also the only mare. All the more reason to want her to win, Bee thought, and looked again, in vain, for Laura.

"And they're off!" The commentator's voice rang out across the track, drowned out by a cheer. Bee glanced back to see the thousands of people thronging the stands. She hoped Cloudy won, but as long as they all came home safely... The horses themselves were almost invisible from this distance. She could only tell where they were from the distant vehicles – vets and cameramen – which followed the horses round the track, but there were enormous screens which displayed the race. The commentator had settled into his own stride now.

"Serengeti in the blue stripes, still the front marker, Sizing Hundred in second on the outside… Jaystorm's being pulled up but they're coming round into the home straight now… Cloud Chaser in fourth, just starting to be asked along…"

"Hi," said a familiar voice, and Bee turned to find Nick standing behind her. "Thought I saw you."

"I fancied being down on the track," Bee said. "I know I shouldn't be in the Member's bit. I didn't mean to sneak in."

"Don't worry, I won't rat on you. And same here. Nothing like the winning post. Cloudy's doing all right – she might just pull this off if young Jason doesn't balls it up."

"I thought Laura might be down here," said Bee.

"I saw her just after lunch. Said she was having a nervous breakdown but would be fine."

"Oh, poor Laura! I know how much they worry about their horses at Amberley."

"And third from last now. Cloud Chaser nudging into second, just being taken off the bridle. Serengeti falling a little behind, Sizing Hundred now in first place… Cloud Chaser a length behind – and they're over the final hurdle. Serengeti just clipped it slightly there but they're coming up the hill…"

That long last rise to home and the grey was up with the leading horse. Bee felt her heart leap inside her; she gave a small strangled cry. Around her, the crowd were now shouting: "Come on, Sizing, come on, my son!"

But Cloud Chaser, with Jason Prior aboard, was fast behind Sizing Hundred, and then more than behind, alongside, and then ahead, and then she flashed past Bee and the winning post as the commentator yelled "And it's number seven, Cloud Chaser, wins the Amateur Brideway Hunter's Chase!"

"Yes!" Bee heard herself yell, like Eliza Doolittle. "Yes!" She threw her arms around Nick Wratchall-Haynes, who after a startled moment, hugged her back.

Then, at the top of the track, the shouts turned to a murmur of consternation. Something was wrong. Bee saw men running across the course, holding the big green screens which curtained off an injured horse from the sight of the public. She caught sight of a 4x4, labelled VET, turning fast onto the track.

"Shit," Wratchall-Haynes said. "Shit, she's gone down."

"What? Why?"

"I don't know." He was craning to see. "Maybe heart? It does happen."

"Oh no, Laura will be –" Bee started to say, but her thoughts were cascading in on her.

Laura, who was neither riding, nor at the winning post, or anywhere in sight, to watch her precious mare sweep by.

Cloudy, glimpsed in the fields late at night, at Christmas and beyond, not tucked up in her stable but all on her own and running free, as no prize racehorse should be allowed to do.

Nick, laughing with Alys over the table at the dinner party about the old gardener Harris, saying, "Well, you've never seen him and Ian McKellen together, have you? Separated at birth."

Ben, remarking that his sister was obsessed with horses and didn't like talking about anything supernatural.

Ward, saying "There's definitely something odd about my family, but I just don't know what it is."

And a man with a goat's yellow eyes, sneaking around Amberley. Looking for what? Just a horse?

Before she knew it, Bee's hands were gripping the rail. She threw herself over, tumbled painfully to the ground, stumbled up and was running up the chute towards the green screens as fast as she could. Shouts followed her.

"Hey, you can't do that! Lady, what are you doing?"

"Bee! Bee, you're not allowed up there!"

But Bee ignored them all. It was not far to the top of the racetrack. She passed Jason Prior, white faced and tearful. A steward, gaping in astonishment, stepped into her path.

"Madam, you can't –!"

Bee shouted "I'm the owner!" and shoved him out of her way. She tore the edge of the nearest screen out of the hands of an equally astounded assistant and was into the makeshift tent just as a burly middle aged man in high viz over his tweed jacket was saying "She's broken that leg going down. I've spoken to the owner. I'm going to have to - "

Bee had seen the device in his hand before, on a farmer's kitchen table. It had a round, bulbous nose and she knew what it was: a bolt gun.

"Stop!" Bee shouted at the top of her voice. "Stop right now!"

To her surprise, it worked.

Everything stopped.

STELLA

Stella was sitting out on the deck with a beer when Ace called her.

"How's it going?"

"Good, thanks. I rang you for two reasons: one is that Anione and I have moved young Lochinvar to Bill's place."

"Southwark too hot to hold him, eh?"

"Thing is, I don't mind guests but as the old saying goes, they are like fish – they stink after a few days. He's very eager to please, does the washing up more than I do, but let's say that there are a few things in the house that I don't want him poking his nose into and he asks a lot of questions, about magic and that. I think he's a bit of an aspiring magician and I don't really want an apprentice. Bill, on the other hand, really is full of the milk of human kindness despite his grumpy appearance, although you'd think he'd have grown out of that sort of thing by now, and if he thinks your boy is suitable material, he might not only teach him something but also put him back on the straight and narrow, assuming he's ever been on it in the first place. With a more normal sort of guest, I might balk at bunging him back in the 1700s, but Hob's used to that sort of thing."

"Okay, sounds good," Stella said. "I'm sure he'll be safe there, as long as *Bill's* safe from *him*."

"Oh, don't worry about that. Blake's a wily old bird."

Stella had no doubt that this was true. He hung up and she returned to her contemplation of the river. There was still a bite to the air but the spring had treated the city that day to a flawless blue sky and Stella and Evie intended to make the most of it. Evie herself now appeared with a plate of falafel, hummus and flatbread.

"Supper!"

"Cheers. Want a beer?"

"Cheers. Oh, someone's coming down the dock." Evie peered into the distance.

"That's Davy Dearly," Stella said.

"I'll open another beer, then. And make sure the cat's inside."

"Welcome on board!" Stella called.

"Evening," Davy said, stepping onto the deck. Ace's wards did not react, Stella noticed, perhaps because Davy had been invited. Or was that just vampires? "Hope you don't mind me showing up without warning."

"Not at all. Good to see you."

"How are you?"

"Fine. You okay?"

"Also fine." Davy sat down on the bench and accepted a bottle of Ghost Ship. "I didn't have you down for a real ale type, despite our excursion to the Prospect of Whitby."

"Friend of Evie's left them after a party last week. Free beer. Might as well drink it."

"Indeed. I popped over because I have a job for you. A mission, should you choose to accept it."

"Exciting! Another trip to the past?"

"No," Davy said. "A trip up the river."

BEE

Everything was suspended. Bee had time to take a big painful rasping breath, step back, look around the shaded green tent: the motionless stewards, the vet with the bolt gun, the heaving, wounded horse. Then there was a flutter behind her and Nick Wratchall-Haynes hurtled in through the side of the screen.

"Bee, what the actual hell?"

"It's Laura," Bee wheezed. "It's Laura!" and the girl's name broke the spell. The grey mare shimmered and was gone. Laura Amberley, as Bee had last seen her in jods, boots and hacking jacket, was sitting upright, clutching her leg and swearing. When she saw Bee, she burst into tears.

"Oh God! no one's supposed to know!"

"Shush," Nick said. "It's all right. We'll sort it out."

"Fucking hell, my leg. Fuck!"

"I know. Come on, we need to get you to A&E."

He put an arm round Laura and with Bee, got her onto her feet.

"Can you manage? You'll have to hop."

"I think so."

As soon as they went through the screens, time speeded up. Bee blinked. Nick helped Laura away up the course. The stewards were taking the screens down. The vet was saying to a racecourse official, "Thought we were going to have her put down but it's all right, the horse ambulance is getting her in. You can tell the crowd she's going to be okay – not nice to see a death at the winning post and thank God we haven't."

No one seemed to see Bee. It was as though events had rearranged themselves around her. Had Laura done this herself, or Nick, or some other agency, unknown to them all? Still feeling winded, she walked slowly around the top of the track, past the milling jockeys and their mounts, and back onto the concourse. On the roadway which led past the big indoors centre, aptly named the Centaur, a red coated official in a vehicle like a golf cart pulled up. Nick sat within, with a white-faced Laura by his side.

"Come on, Bee. Hop in."

As they pulled away towards the members car park, Bee heard the commentator say, "Richard Amberley is asked to go to the stewards' room, this is an urgent announcement for Richard Amberley…"

Laura Amberley said, "You know, I was actually stupid enough to think I could get away with it."

Her leg was encased in a brace, from knee to ankle. "A nice clean break," the doctor on duty had remarked. "How did you do it, again?"

"I came off a horse."

Now, they were sitting in Nick's Range Rover, in the car park of Cheltenham Hospital. The most remarkable thing of all, Bee thought was that Laura had been seen so quickly. She laughed and said, "And you would have got away with it, too, if it hadn't been for those meddling kids!"

"Meddling middle aged people," said Nick.

"You saved my life. He was going to shoot me."

"So, just for the sake of argument, Laura, if he had – would you have turned back into a woman again?"

"I don't know. God, how horrendous for the poor vet. Bad enough thinking you've done the most difficult part of your job and put down an injured mare and then find the trainer's daughter lying there with her brains all over the floor. I *knew* we shouldn't have entered her."

By now, Nick Wratchall-Haynes was rather pale himself.

"That does not bear thinking about," he said. "So how long have you known, Laura? This must have been with you all your life."

"Not when I was very young. I was just horse crazy like a lot of little girls – I wanted to be a horse, I galloped everywhere. When I got into my teens, though, suddenly, I *was* a horse. Once or twice, up on the hills. Thank God, not like in the middle of Pony Club or something – that would have given all those mums a shock. I could control it somehow – I don't know. It's always been weird."

"And you've never told anyone, obviously?"

"I've never told anyone but a couple of years ago I spoke on the phone to a wonderful woman in Oxford who does shamanic consultations and knows about animal totems. I didn't tell her I was a horse – I didn't want her to think I was nuts – but I did say that when I was a kid, I wished I was one and she said she thought that was perfectly normal and a lot of little girls were part time horses. So that made me feel a bit better."

"And Richard and Caro have never noticed?" Bee said.

"My parents must have sort of known that the mare and I are the same person – surely – but they have memories of me riding Cloudy. Of her coming to us from some man my father met at some equestrian event. But there are no photos of me on her back – how could there be? I'm sure if you asked my mother, though, she'd say there were plenty."

"And do you think this is – genetic? Or a spell that's affected your family for a long time?"

"I don't see how this could be a genetic thing. It's not very scientific, is it? So it has to be magic."

"Ward thinks something's up with your family," Bee said.

"Ward is right! We don't talk about it. It's like what happened to Ben. We just have this convenient fiction that he was ill at Christmas, but that's not what happened at all, is it? Sometimes I think even Ben thinks that, now. It's either that we're all like Cleopatra Queen of Denial or we actually can't discuss it. Something's not allowing us. So we end up fictionalising it." She took a gulp of her cooling hospital-dispenser tea. "Fake news! Oh, I had such a silly dream – that sort of thing."

"You do know you're not the only one who can turn into an animal?" Bee said. "Actually, rather a lot of people seem to do so."

"I – I sort of guessed something was up. Those people in the autumn, Tam and Dana, brought matters to a head around us all, I felt. Triggered something, somehow."

"It'll be interesting to see what your parents have to say about your leg."

"Especially since they'll be going home with an empty horsebox," said Bee.

"I drove it myself on my own. Jason went up with Susie and Sam and Dad obviously brought you and Mum."

"But you're not going to be able to drive it back," Nick said. "Not with that leg."

"I'll ask Sam to do it. Tell everyone else Cloudy's at the vet's up here and I'm staying with her."

"How are you going to explain the boot?"

"Oh God, I don't know. Tell them I fell over in the car park?"

"Look, phone your parents and tell the staff that you're staying with the 'horse'. I'll drive you back to Amberley after the Gold Cup – you can come back to the hotel with me tonight. I'll sleep in the car if they don't have a spare room, but I know some of the Irish stable staff who were there this morning are heading home tonight so we might be lucky." He hesitated. "I don't actually think I've had a more memorable day at the races."

"Also, Laura, you bloody won!"

"Yes!" Laura looked a bit more cheerful. "I did, didn't I? I was actually placed! Oh my God, I am a Cheltenham winner!"

"Your dad will be pleased. That's some serious prize money."

"So what actually happened, Laura? Why did you go down?"

"I saw something. A man with horns like a ram. He was wearing a mask, but his face – it wasn't really a human face. He threw something into the air. Then the next thing I knew, I'd chucked poor old Jason off and down I went. I couldn't breathe. I felt my hind leg buckle. Then the screens came up and I tried to change back but I was stuck. I heard you, Bee."

"Thank God Bee realised. I couldn't believe it when she vaulted the barrier."

"Neither could I. I'm not exactly a champion hurdler. I don't think I've run so fast in years. They ought to give *me* some prize money! And you know, Nick, I thought I might change, too. I could feel it around the edges, if that makes any sense. Like a sort of shimmering. But I stayed human."

"What?" Laura said.

"Yeah, I didn't suddenly shapeshift into a swarm of bees, as has happened before."

"Oh my God."

"We can all do it. Don't think you're special!" Bee said. She patted Laura on the arm. "I'm joking." She explained, about her sisters, about hares and bees and wrens. Laura said, "I didn't know," and burst into tears again. "I've felt really alone," she added, between sobs.

"Now I feel terrible," Bee said.

"Oh come on, Bee. Laura, it's not the sort of thing you can discuss in the village post office over the sweet rack."

"I'm not blaming you, Bee! I'm just really grateful it's not just me!"

"Dinner parties will be interesting, from now on."

"Nick, shut up."

"I'm just wondering who else. It can't be *that* common. Do you know if you're related?"

"We probably are. The Fallows and the Amberleys and so on have been in the area for a while and you know what the county's like. Inbred until recently, basically, like most rural areas."

"Yes, the advent of the bicycle was said to work wonders for genetic diversity."

Laura laughed, choked, and blew her nose. "Sorry. Thank you. Both of you. You've been absolute stars."

"By the way, Laura, that Irish stablehand? The one who got his leg broken and left? I assume *you* actually kicked him?"

"Yes. He groped my arse. As a human. So as a horse, I thought I'd teach him a lesson."

By the time they got back to the track, the racing was over for the day. Bee had texted Caro to explain ("went with Laura to the vet's") but in fact she did not have too much in the way of difficult explaining to do. Richard accepted her account of events, accepted that the mare was at the vet's and Laura staying with her – surely, Bee thought, he would ask questions when no enormous bill arrived? It was as though Caro and Richard had entered a fog when anything to do with the horse was mentioned, and it made her look back on the winter in a different light, at Richard's insistence that his wife had gone down with some post-viral illness. Then, Caro seemed to have broken through that haze, but now they were both enmeshed within it and Bee was the clear-seeing outsider. All in all, though, she was thankful not to face the necessity of labyrinthine and unlikely explanations.

But she couldn't help wondering what *she* might not be seeing, all the same.

When they got back, Richard dropped her off at the end of Mooncote's drive. It was nearly dusk, and Bee did not linger: if there were any eldritch plant children lurking in the shrubbery, she did not want to see them. The lights were on in the kitchen and Luna was making a lasagne. To Bee's delight, Ver March was sitting at the kitchen table.

"Oh, hi, Bee – you're back! Look who's here."

"Is Mum around?"

"No, she went up to Bath today to meet her friend Lucy. Sam phoned me, though, a while ago – he was bringing the horsebox back. He said poor Cloudy had an accident?"

"In a manner of speaking," Bee said, sitting down and accepting the glass which Ver thrust towards her. She told them what had happened.

"Well, well, well," Ver said, when she had finished. "That explains your horse thieves. What they wanted her for, though, is anyone's guess. Whoever it was can't have expected to steal her away from the races, surely, not with all those people there?"

"I wondered if it was revenge," Bee said. "For escaping, last time. For taking down the Hound. She saw the man whom Kit called Aiken Drum. The one with goat's eyes."

"Where's Laura now, then?"

"In Gloucestershire, with Nick. He's bringing her home on Friday – basically I think they both want to watch the Gold Cup and nothing's going to get in the way of that – and I don't know what they're going to do about a horse which doesn't exist. Except she sort of does."

"Sam and Nick between them can figure that out."

"It was as though Caro and Richard were in a kind of dream."

"These things have a way of protecting themselves," Ver remarked. "And also people are very good at protecting their own sanity – they rationalise what they see but don't understand, a lot of the time. I've seen it happen over and over. The weird memory runs out of them like water down a windowpane."

Bee suddenly found that she was extremely shaky. She downed her wine.

"Sorry. Reaction."

"Have some lasagne," Luna said. "And a glass of water."

"And an early night," Bee added.

She was true to her word. After supper, she had a quick, hot bath and sought her bed. Dark was not here tonight, and Bee was half relieved, half sorry. She could not wait to tell him… but on the other hand, she was exhausted. She went to sleep almost at once, but later, in the night, she woke. Without knowing what was drawing her, she got out of bed. Three in the morning, said the little alarm clock, the deepest part of the tide of night. Bee shoved her feet into her slippers and went along the landing to the spare bedroom. She could hear the faint creak before she reached the door of the spare room, but there it was: the old rocking horse, up and down, up and down, rocking to and fro in a shaft of moonlight.

"What are you doing?" Bee asked, though she was not sure if she had spoken aloud. Otherwise, the room was quiet: the light falling softly on the floorboards and the blue tiles around the fireplace. The mirror, in which Bee sometimes glimpsed the Behenian spirits, reflected only the room. But stars were caught in the rocking horse's mane, tiny sparkling points of light, and for a moment Bee looked down on the room and the house and the fields beyond from a bee's flight. The great pathway of the ley was gleaming, the landscape lit. Wycholt glowed gold, the sun to Mooncote's pale, and so did the parkland further off to the east: Stourhead, over the county border in Wiltshire. The lych path flared with its green corpse light and Bee could see the drove, heading off into darkness. To and fro, to and fro. She woke again at first light, with Dark's arm around her.

LUNA

"Drove the horsebox out in the morning, parked it at Nick's place, drove it back later and there, bingo, was the horse, safe and sound, back at home," Sam said.

"Did they not say, oooh, Laura will be so excited, where is she?"

"No, I think they thought she was there."

"Weird," Luna said.

"Laura does all the grooming and everything, but I think when Cloudy's supposed to be in her stable, everyone else at the yard actually does see something. I mean, I've *thought* I've seen her. I'm sure I have, in fact. But I think now it's just something putting ideas in my head."

"Doesn't it make you wonder what's real and what's not?"

"I wonder that anyway."

"Fair play," said Luna, who felt that this was an unassailable argument given recent events. Perhaps it did not do to think too hard about this kind of thing – but she could not help but question the dynamics.

"Laura is also healing far more quickly than she should. That boot was off by the time she came back down from Cheltenham with Nick."

"I hope that's a thing with animal people! Fingers crossed it applies to wrens."

But she did not have too much time to dwell on Laura and her newly-revealed equine nature. The road protest was kicking off in earnest later that day, according to Ver.

Luna had said that she would go down and take a look. In doing this, she felt torn between her sister, Sam and his gran. Sam was working that day and Luna felt she ought to look after Ver, just in case trouble started, but both Bee and Sam thought she ought not to go.

"I don't want to be all patriarchal," Sam said.

"I do," said Bee. "Matriarchal, anyway. I'm worried about you."

"You don't have to worry. I'll be all right."

"You want to ask Ver about the Battle of the Beanfield," Sam said. "Stonehenge, 1985. Pregnant women dragged screaming by the hair, by the police."

"To be fair, I think it was only one pregnant woman, Sam. But I agree. One's too many!"

"I don't trust the police," Luna said, "But it's all very well trying to stay safe when the otherworld comes looking for you. Perhaps I can wren it. If Laura can choose when she changes, I bet I can, too. I just have to learn how."

"I'll drive you," said a voice from the door.

"Mother!"

"Bee, if she wants to go, I think she should. But on condition that she stays in the car until we see the lie of the land."

Luna thought that Alys might be rather keen to go, too. For reasons of her own, or simple curiosity? But she knew a bargain when she heard one. "All right! Thanks, Mum."

"Text Ver and tell her we're on our way."

"Text me if she gets arrested," Sam said.

"I bet your gran's too canny to get arrested," Alys said.

"You might be right. She never has been, not as far as I know. But I wouldn't put it past her to do it just for a new experience. That's all we need."

Luna agreed. All the more reason to keep an eye on Ver.

Thus Luna and Alys, sensibly dressed and with flat shoes in case they had to move quickly on rough ground, drove to the camp and parked up. The place seemed deserted, but as Luna got out of the car a very young woman in her teens, came up holding a baby and smiling.

"They've all gone down to the road. You're Ver's grand-daughter, aren't you?"

"Her grandson's my partner, actually, but I'm happy to claim her as my nan!"

"She's so great. I love her. I didn't go coz of this one but that's okay, I can tell people where they are." She pointed with a brightly mittened hand. "See the track? Keep going and you'll come to a lane, then turn left and it's down the road."

"Thank you," Luna said and they set off, over old pasture starred with celandines. There were dandelions starting to come out now, drawn by the warmth of the sun, and Luna reflected that it would soon be time to make dandelion wine, and to see if any coltsfoot was to be found in the hedges, to be made into remedies for coughs.

She could hear the protest before she saw it. There was drumming and some kind of chant, which came to them faintly across the mild air. Someone whooped.

"Sounds like they're having a good time," Alys said.

"It sounds – happy," Luna agreed.

"We needn't stay long – you just tell me if you want to go. I'm sure Ver can look after herself, and maybe we can talk her into coming to supper."

"That would be good."

Luna had not had a chance to check with Bee if she had told Alys about Laura. So she did not mention it, just in case. Alys had shown no signs of having overheard Luna's remarks about Laura and her control over changing her form, but that constraint was still there between them. And where had Alys been when Bee was attacked in the yard? She did not know of any man with the yellow eyes of a goat, or with the horns of a ram, or so she claimed.

Moreover, Luna wanted to talk to Ver first. *Now's your chance!* she thought, for there was Ver herself, perched on an ancient tractor and waving.

"Like your new motor!" Alys called up. Ver looked very small, high on the bucket seat behind the driver, a young man in a spotted scarf like Pigling Bland.

"I'm not driving it," Ver said. "Just along for the ride. Hang on, I'll get down." And she did so, in a flurry of skirts. "So," she said, once she was on solid ground. "They're planning on a blockade. The first earth moving equipment's due in tomorrow morning – people will be lying down in front of it. The rest of us will be chained to the tractors. This afternoon's just for show, but we will be having a go-slow along the main road, should you care to join us?"

"Luna, are you up for a walk? A slow one."

Luna nodded. "I can manage that for a couple of miles."

"It will be a pleasure to have you along. We're going east, anyway, so you'll practically be back at the lane going down to the campsite before you know it."

Luna looked down from the high ridge of land. They were on the slopes of the Tor, still: the long rolling skirts of the hill, and she could see west towards the estuary. The hedges were greening with hawthorn. She looked up into the mild, bright sky and thought that this was a good day to be out on the land. She had missed this, early in the year, despite her adventures. But those had been in the winter world, when the land had drawn in on itself, bud cramped in the twig and the sky lowering.

A sound interrupted her trance. It was sonorous and booming, atavistic as a bittern's cry. Luna looked along the road and saw a man, bare chested and spiralled with blue, blowing a long battle horn. For a second she wondered if he'd come from the otherworld but then she realised that he was wearing a plaid shirt tied around his waist and stout boots.

"Hiya, Mac!" someone cried.

The man waved, raised the horn, and blew again.

"I think they used those against the Romans," Alys said.

Luna could see why. The sound made her shiver. She wanted to run over to the man and say: *don't. You'll attract too much attention.* She wondered why the thought had come to her and told herself that it was silly, but perhaps it was not. The tractor on which Ver had been perched was pulling ahead, the crowd parting like the Red Sea. There was a creak of gears and it reversed, turned and stopped, blocking the road. The engine was switched off and the tractor shuddered into silence.

"Well," said Alys, "no one's going to get past *that.*"

Luna went to sit down with Ver on the piece of grassy verge that aproned a farm gate, while Alys roamed about, chatting to people.

"Making friends, your mum," said Ver. It was hard to tell whether or not she approved. "She's got the gift of the gab, hasn't she?"

"Yes, when she wants to. She can talk to anyone." *And does.*

"Have there been any more disturbances, back at the house?"

"All quiet for the last few days or so."

"I wish I could say it would stay that way." Ver was busying herself with plucking daisies and threading them into a chain. "But it never does. I learned that early on."

"No, it never does," agreed Luna, watching Ver's old, deft hands. Some day her own hands would look like that. She did not mind, but it reminded her of a question she had been meaning to ask for some time. "Ver, what was Sam's grandfather like?"

"His grand-dad? Oh, he was a handsome man. A northerner, from Cumbria. Black haired, blue eyed like some Irish – he had Irish blood, he told me, from Wexford way. His own dad, I think. He was a bit of a lad, got into some scrapes – I don't mean illegal things, but you know what I mean, same sort of scrapes you get into – but he was a good man. A painter by trade – I think I told you that. And a good one. Not just walls and fences. He made those cards I showed you once."

"He is – dead, Sam said." Used to fathers who simply were not there, Luna had assumed that Sam's father had also taken himself off, but when she had mentioned this, Sam had replied that no, he was dead, also.

Ver sighed. "Yes, Sam's grand-dad and his parents. Michael – that was my husband – died a natural death. Cancer of the blood, years ago. He wasn't one for going to the doctor and they found out too late. You can do only so much with herbs and that. And Sam's mum, my daughter Rosemary, and his dad – that was a lot earlier, when Sam was a kiddie. There was a fire. He was staying with me at the time or he wouldn't be here now. He doesn't like to talk about it so I don't know if he's told you. It wasn't a natural fire. I don't mean arson in the normal way – a lot of travellers end up getting burned out of their homes and it's usually other travellers or farmers or just someone who takes against them, but in this instance I mean someone who was not from this world of ours, but somewhere else. I never found out who. There was one witness: a young girl in a caravan nearby who was looking out of her window at the time, couldn't sleep one night like you, and she said it burned blue as the sky and made no sound. Like a great flash and very little left. She told me they probably never knew. I hope not."

"Has Sam ever tried to find out who did it?" Luna asked, appalled. The daisy chain was growing fast.

"When he became a young man, I think he might have tried, but he didn't tell me about it if he did. We don't discuss it. You know, in all the stories, the young boy – or girl – grows up to want to take revenge and he or she tracks down the murderers, like Batman or one of them things, and justice is done. But life isn't like that. Sometimes you just get on with grieving and decide to let sleeping dogs lie because there's bugger all you can do about it."

Luna nodded. She knew what Ver meant.

"There. Crown for my Princess Luna." Ver handed Luna the daisy chain.

"Thank you! It's so pretty."

"Not for long, though."

"Never mind, I shall wear it until it fades and then I shall put it into the compost heap and the whole cycle can start all over again – oh, what's going on?"

The inevitable had happened. Luna and Ver stood up to get a better look. A car had come along the road and discovered that its way was blocked. The driver was now out of the car and remonstrating. He was middle aged, in a tight, rather shiny blue suit, and becoming redder in the face by the minute. It was a nice car. Luna could see the azure and white BMW badge on the bonnet.

"He's not taking it well," Ver said, not without sympathy. "Mind you, it must be very annoying."

"They're telling drivers to go back round Hoxley." Alys strolled up to join them. "Another fifteen minutes. Someone's done that already."

"Ah, we didn't see them."

"Farmer in a Land Rover. He wasn't happy either but he just turned around and went."

Snatches of conversation floated across.

"Bloody nuisance… I'll call the police… ought to be banged up… load of effing anarchists…"

"Technically, of course, we are not anarchists," Ver remarked. "I think he'd find the camp rather orderly. I myself am quite an admirer of the Queen and not the only one there, either. He's going to do himself a mischief if he carries on like that." Several other cars had now backed up behind the driver. "But I can see that if perhaps you need to be somewhere urgently, like the doctor's, and you find your way impeded by a motley crew…"

"He doesn't have to be anywhere, Ver, I bet. He's just going to be an arse because he can. Look at him. He's the type. You can tell."

The great horn sounded again. From the other side of the Tor, Luna heard a more familiar noise on the wind: the shriek of a siren. Looking back along the road, she saw a hectic flicker of blue lights. The farmer in the Land Rover, perhaps, had called the police.

"That'll bloody show you!" shouted BMW Man. "Perverts!"

"Now that is uncalled for," Ver said.

"What *sort* of perverts, I wonder?" murmured Alys.

The police car was now quite close. They watched it come around the bend and slow to a stop when the driver saw the crowd. A couple of resigned policemen got out of it.

"Get them off the sodding road!" bawled BMW Man. "Do your bloody job!"

"Who's in charge here?" asked the older policeman.

"Nobody!" a voice cried.

"Echoes of Odysseus," said Alys.

"All right. Who can we speak to, then? Who owns this vehicle?" The policeman squinted up at the tractor.

"Don't know, mate."

"Haven't a clue."

"Are you the driver, sir?" the policeman said to Mac, who was closest to the tractor.

"Indeed I'm not," Mac said, with apparently genuine regret. "I'd love to help, but it's not my tractor. I don't even have a licence."

"How do you get about, then, sir?" the younger officer asked.

"Shank's pony. And the occasional bus."

The more senior policeman came over to Alys, perhaps because she was the person who looked the most respectable.

"Madam. Do you happen to know who owns this vehicle?"

"I'm afraid I don't."

"Yes, she effing does." BMW Man was now bearing down upon them, even more crimson of face than he had appeared from a distance.

"That," said Ver, sotto voce, "is exactly the sort of man who bullies women."

"Good luck with that," said Luna.

Alys said, very coolly, "I'm afraid I do not know and I can't think what would make *you* think that I do."

"Mrs Bloody Stuck Up, aren't you?"

"Now, now sir, I'm afraid I must ask you to remain civil," the policeman said, but BMW Man had passed that point. Standing within inches of Alys, he bellowed,

"You snotty fucking bitch!"

"That won't help," Alys said. The policeman started forwards.

Luna did not actually see red, but she felt it in her head, hot and bursting.

"You leave my mum alone!" she shouted. She tried to get between them but Alys was quicker. She gave Luna a quick push back into Ver's arms as the man, open handed, slapped Alys across the face.

"Hey!" the policeman cried.

Alys punched BMW man in the nose, exceedingly hard. He sat down as though someone had cut the strings of a puppet. Suddenly there was blood everywhere.

"I told you that wouldn't help," Alys said.

Much later, Luna and Ver entered the Mooncote kitchen to find Bee washing out a woolly jumper in the sink.

"Hi! What a beautiful afternoon it's been. How did you get on? Did you have a nice time?"

"Yes, well," Luna said. "Mum's been arrested."

STELLA

It was some while yet before the clocks went forwards and by the time Davy and Stella reached Richmond, it was dark. To an extent, this did not matter in the city: the ambient light of London, combined with actual lighting along the sides of the river, meant that full night was rare, as Stella had observed when meeting Davy in the nineteenth century.

"So where are these people?"

"Around here somewhere, according to my contact. What's the tide doing?" Davy peered at the river. "Ah, water's quite low. They were moving around, apparently."

"Can't see the good burghers of Richmond liking that."

"Nor me. My friend said they were in plain view, but he wasn't all that convinced everyone could see them. He said he mentioned it to a woman walking her dog and she looked at him as if he was mad. Mind you, that might have been for other reasons."

"And there were how many of them?"

"Legs eleven. If you follow the Bingo. My gran's into it; I always say that. Anyway. My friend said they looked Medieval but, quite frankly, so do half the populations of Glastonbury and Totnes, as you'll well know."

"Oh yes," said Stella.

They had come down to Richmond by boat: a small craft powered by an outboard and steered by a friend of Davy's, called Luke. He was a silent young man, who merely nodded when spoken to. Stella did not get the impression that he was a romantic contact and there was something about his sharp profile which suggested he might be a Dearly relative. Davy did not vouchsafe this information and Stella did not ask. She did, however, like her increasing use of the Thames as a highway, and said so.

"No stuffy Underground, no standstill buses, no expensive cabs… Okay, it's a bit tricky if you're going to somewhere like Hampstead or Beckenham, though there are the canals, but if you're travelling east or west it's superb."

"It always was the main artery," Davy said. "But there were other rivers, too, like the Fleet and the Tyburn. My grand-dad told me that. Evie will tell you the same."

"Evie's told me a lot about it. She says Pepys used to travel up and down by wherry and it was a way to avoid dangerous and filthy streets. Which I can now understand. But it also gives you a completely different perspective on the city."

Davy nodded. "Just that. I couldn't live far from this old river. Obviously, I've gone on holidays and so on. But I miss it, you know? I really do."

"I get that," Stella said.

Luke had remained with the boat, which he had hauled up onto the foreshore. Looking back, Stella could pinpoint him by the occasional flash of his cigarette. They were now some distance along the shore, but it did not feel remote: there was laughter and chatter and the clink of glasses from the big pubs along the riverfront. Stella could hear a car engine. Then Davy put out a hand and brought her to a stop.

"Look."

There was a tent a little way along the foreshore. This was hardly unusual in central London; Stella had seen tents and benders all along the banks up Regent's Canal and others. Housing was an unreachable aim in the city for many people and she knew several who couldn't afford rents, who had tucked themselves away in the nooks and crannies of the city. Herself, for instance. Stella's berth on the *Nitrogen* would cost her three times as much in a flat that was half the size.

"It is," Evie had once remarked, "my way of sticking it to modern capitalism."

This tent, however, did not look like a modern canvas affair. It looked as though it had been patched together from skins. In the flickering lights from the pub, Stella could see the seams. There was a fire on the foreshore in front of it, which someone crouched over with a spit.

"Yeah," Davy said. "Either they're old school New Age travellers, or someone's come from somewhere else."

The figure looked up as they approached. She was a small girl, dressed in a ragged and dirty smock. Her face was smudged like a Victorian urchin.

"Hello," Davy said.

The girl said nothing, but simply stared.

"Davy," Stella said. "Does she look – well, a bit *green* to you?"

"You're right. It might be the light?"

"I know some green people," Stella began, but at this point a man stepped out of the tent. He, too, wore a kind of smock, over leather leggings. It was a kind of rural shepherd's garb, Stella thought, but the man did not look quaint. He looked tough.

"She's of the wose kin, yes," he said, mildly enough. "You can see us then, and from your speech you know us?"

"Yes, you're quite visible," Davy said. "I'm Davy Dearly, waterman's daughter, and this is my friend Stella."

"Pleased to meet you. I won't ask you in, there's no room. But the shore is wide enough."

Davy and Stella perched on a nearby block of concrete and listened, while the child sat with her arms round her knees by the fire and watched all the while. His name was Saul and he and his companions had come from the hinterlands, he said, following the tributaries until they had come to the head of the great river. Stella got the impression, although he was vague about this, that they had started a very long time ago, but yet had not been on the move for very long, skipping from time to time, and had been making their way ever since. She did not think he was talking about the head of the Thames, either.

"But are you coping?" Davy asked. "Do you need help?"

"So kind. So many have asked me this, those who see us. We feel welcomed. We will manage. We look after each other. Not all of us are from the same place."

"Or the same time?" Stella asked, wondering if they were collecting temporal refugees as they travelled. And would they end up in some future version of the city? The thought made her shiver.

"Two have joined us, from another." He glanced down the shore. Stella saw a man staring out across the water. A crossbow dangled from one hand.

"Do you think you will return home? What made you leave?"

"Invaders. Gefliemen, from the direction of the rising sun. They burned our villages and we fled."

"Do you know a girl named Aln?" Stella asked.

"Aln? Yes. Her brother – there was trouble, with the Gefliemen, with their leader, the man they call the Helwyr. She left – last year? It is difficult for me now to pinpoint time. But I think it would have been then. She wanted to look for her brother."

"Do you know Aln?" a woman's voice said. She had crept out from the tent to listen and the green child clasped her hand.

"Yes. My sister was friends with her. She found her brother in the end but then – well, there were some problems. He is a tree now."

"Oh," said the woman, and the child repeated it, like an echo.

"She was travelling on to look for an answer," Stella told them.

"If you ever need help on the river," Davy said, "then go to the watermen and mention my name. They will help you."

"Thank you."

"What I'd suggest is keep making your way downstream."

"I'd be a bit careful, though," Stella said, thinking of the island owned by the hopefully late Cas Pharoah, on which Serena and Ward had an unusual experience at New Year's. That was further up the Thames Valley but Stella was not sure what else might be lurking, further into the city itself.

"Yes, don't be too trusting. Follow your noses."

Saul laughed at that. "I'm good at that. And in return, maybe one day we will be able to help you."

"You might be able to do so anyway," said Stella. "We're looking for anyone who knows the lie of the land. The ins and outs."

He nodded. "I understand."

"And when you moved from time to time, Saul my friend, how did you travel then?"

Through many places, it seemed. A chapel in the green, a priory, a great oak tree. A cavern whose walls were studded with shells and a holy well.

"The coldharbours," Davy said.

"What does that mean, Davy?" Stella had a vague memory that it was the name of a place.

"Secure places to spend the night. Abandoned settlements, mostly, hence the 'cold' bit. Quite a few in the otherlands, they tell me."

"I've seen one of the chapels," Stella said.

When Saul had finished his tale, the woman ushered the child into the tent and they took their leave. When Stella looked back, the tent and the group had gone: only an old upturned rowing boat lay on the foreshore and the fire had gone out. The man with the bow was nowhere to be seen. A last ember flew to the river on the wind.

"That was interesting," Davy said.

"I hope they'll be okay. I liked them."

"Refugees. I've always thought it must be one of the worst things to happen to you. This city's full of them and you wonder how well it really treats them."

"Unimaginable. Especially from another world or time."

Luke pushed them out into the river and fired up the outboard again. They set off on the evening tide, back through Richmond and Kew, Mortlake and Putney and Battersea, and on towards the city. Davy seemed lost in her own thoughts, Luke did not seem to want to speak anyway, and so Stella remained silent until they neared Vauxhall Bridge. The red paint looked almost black in the lights from nearby office blocks and the ziggurat of MI6, but Stella could see the four big statues of women, staring upstream. As they passed beneath, one of them turned to look at the boat, moving with a faint creak. Davy jumped and exclaimed. But then the outboard took them under the bridge and away.

"God, that gave me a fright. Never known them do that before."

Stella thought she would mention it to Ace, but later. There had been quite enough excitement for one evening. She sat back in the boat and let Luke run them back up to the *Nitrogen.*

SERENA

"What do you mean, Mum's been arrested?" Serena prided herself on her ability to remain calm. She tried to be as serene as her name, but on this occasion, she was failing. With dismay she could hear her voice rising.

"Don't worry." On the other end of the phone, Bee's voice was significantly steadier. "She wasn't arrested for long. Just as we were about to bake her a cake with a file in it, they let her go."

"Oh God! What was she arrested *for*?"

"Assault."

"What!"

"An objectionable man, according to Ver and Luna, was unwise enough to slap Mum so she punched him in the nose. And broke it." Serena got the distinct impression that Bee, normally so law-abiding, was trying not to laugh.

"Good for Mum! But why did he hit her in the first place? Was this in a pub or something?"

"No. Alys, despite a rather larky life and some dubious recent acquaintances, has not yet taken to brawling in local hostelries. Although watch this space. She took Luna to Ver's road protest, basically to look after Luna and keep an eye on her."

"Well, that went a bit pear-shaped, didn't it!"

"Somewhat, yes. Anyway, they've both been released and Mum won't be bringing charges, although she should. She says she can't be bothered with all the legal stuff and she's cursed him instead."

"He'd be better off up in front of a magistrate," Serena said.

"That's what I thought."

"Anyway, she's a bit cross but otherwise all right. I'm about to pick her up from the police station. How are you?"

"I have been working," Serena said. "And it's all going rather well although there has been a certain amount of stuff happening. We went to Stella's gig at Windsor."

"It was someone's birthday, wasn't it?"

"Yes, and I went too, because Stella's agent mentioned to the birthday girl that I was her sister and apparently she really likes my clothes and has some of them already, who knew? So she ordered a dress for her birthday and very kindly invited me to her party. We had fun. Sort of." She had been going to tell Bee about it, but it sounded as though her sisters in Somerset had enough to deal with. "I'll tell you the rest later, but it sounds like you've got a lot on your plate right now. Please give everyone my love and tell Mum to stay out of trouble."

"And good luck with *that*," Bee said, and hung up.

Serena went upstairs to draw the curtains. It had grown dark now and she could hear a sudden burst of rain spattering against the windows; it was time to shut out the night. She paused for a moment to look out of the uppermost panes, across the roofscape of the city. Movement caught her eye in the mews below and Serena hesitated, then drew the curtains across, turned the light off and peeked around the corner of the curtain. The person was still there, standing motionless in the shadows below: Serena's neighbour had a huge mass of wisteria across the front of the building and although this was not yet fully in leaf, the branches were sufficient to partly conceal someone at the side, where the houses were unevenly joined.

She wondered for a moment if it was the airman. But then it moved and she glimpsed a face, a white oval lit as if by a flare, from the lamp at the door of the opposite house.

Miranda.

Well, well, well, thought Serena. She was sick of being on the defensive. She ran down the stairs, snatched her keys from the table, slipped her feet into a pair of running shoes, and was out of the front door, ready for confrontation.

But Miranda was no longer there.

Serena was now furious. She ran down the mews, glancing into corners. This part of London was Georgian, and unlike newer parts of the city – all clean lines and boxes – the houses were different heights and none of it quite fitted together. She passed the Lion and Unicorn, crossed the road, and was into the next set of mews.

Where the hell had the bloody woman disappeared to? She had a sudden image of Miranda simply ascending upwards like a giant bat. A gull, anyway. She paused, looking around her, and suddenly found a hand over her mouth. Before she could start to struggle, a voice said,

"It's me. Hob. Don't kick me."

He let her go and she turned to face him.

"Miranda was there!" Serena hissed. "Outside my house! Spying!"

"Yeah, I know. I've followed her from Docklands."

"Where is she now?" Serena hoped Hob's tracking skills had improved since last time.

"I'll show you," Hob said.

Serena looked at him uncertainly.

"And I can trust you, can I?"

"Well," said, Hob. "I can see why you wouldn't. But you've got someone looking after you, haven't you?" He gave a meaningful look down the mews. Serena saw a shadow on the air. The airman? Or someone else?

"All right. Lead on."

Hob took her through the maze of mews. Serena was well acquainted with her neighbourhood and she knew that Hob, a not completely improbable Peter Pan, was leading her in the direction of Kensington Gardens. Soon, however, she realised that the street down which they were heading was not familiar: there were candles in some of the windows and the air was different. It felt more like Somerset than London; she could smell horses and hay. When they came to the edge of the Gardens, Serena was not surprised to see that they, too, had changed. Instead of the park, she was standing at the entrance to a large formal garden: a parterre, she remembered vaguely. Topiaried yews stood amidst box hedges, and the air smelled sweet with the spicy scent.

"When are we?" Serena asked Hob.

"I'm not quite sure but I think it is early eighteenth century. Miranda likes the Regency, and the Victorian period, and Elizabethan times. Not so keen on the Commonwealth, and she finds Medieval times a little rough."

"How inconvenient for her," Serena said. "She hasn't considered, say, moving permanently to the sixteen hundreds?"

"Miranda likes to dot around, you might say."

"I hope they haven't let her borrow Kensington Palace."

In the light of the moon, the symmetrical brick frontage of the palace was clearly visible. Hob said,

"No. She likes the gardens, though. I know where she meets people."

Serena glanced surreptitiously over her shoulder. Candlelight caught shadow: the person was still there. Serena followed Hob into the Gardens. If someone was looking from the windows of the palace, what would they see? A maidservant on an assignation, or a lady in waiting on some errand for her mistress? She hoped no one was watching. Being caught for trespass on Royal ground was not appealing. What would the punishment be? Beheading, or the Tower? They were closer to the palace now but Hob led her past it, away from the garden and towards an avenue of trees. Serena tried to remember if an avenue was there in her own day, but then realised that she actually did know where they were heading: towards the section of the park which in her own day was Princess Diana's memorial garden. In the modern city it also housed the Elfin Oak, a great stump in a wire cage, carved with all manner of fairy figures in the 1920s. Along with Peter Pan, Serena considered this rather twee, and said so. Then she wondered if she had been tactless.

Hob did not appear offended. He said, "Two hundred Moons in their pale course had seen/The gay-rob'd Fairies glimmer on the green."

"Sorry?"

"I wasn't much good at school – couldn't learn a thing. Miranda taught me that. Let's sit down for a minute. It's not midnight yet."

"It was a long way off midnight when we set out! It had only just got dark. Anyway, what happens at midnight?"

"She's got an appointment." Hob sat down on the grass.

"With whom?" Cautiously, Serena joined him.

"I don't know. I overheard her on her phone when she left her house. She didn't say who or when. All she said was 'I'll call you tomorrow, can't speak now, I've got an appointment this evening. Midnight, actually, so I won't be able to call you before the morning'."

"And you were what, spying on her?"

"Yeah. She got back from America yesterday. She had to go to LA for like twenty four hours – the director of her upcoming shoot was furious and told her he'd cast someone else if she didn't show up for some meeting or other."

"You seem remarkably well informed for someone who's been living in the eighteenth century."

"I've got a mole in Los Angeles. He doesn't like Miranda. So, now she's back, I thought I'd go and see what she was up to. Don't worry, I told Bill."

"And what did Bill say?"

"He said, *be careful.* Anyway, what I just recited to you – as I said, Miranda taught me that. It's from a poem. Thomas Tickell. Kensington Garden."

This rang a faint bell but Serena said, "I don't know it."

"It's about a Princess Kenna – that's where *Kensington* comes from, so they say, and she's Oberon's daughter, right?"

"I didn't know he had one."

"Ask Ward. He'll probably know. Anyway, Kenna falls in love with a mortal changeling boy called Prince Albion and their love is doomed, there's a war between fairies and people and he's killed and she mourns forever more."

"And this is what, seventeenth century?"

"Early eighteenth, around now. In the poem Kenna inspires architects and gardeners and that to building Kensington Palace and the gardens. So that's probably where Peter Pan comes from. But it was a hunting park for the kings before that – the poem's made up."

"You learn something new every day." Serena was uneasy with all this talk of fairies. And it had been a hunting chase? Would Stella's friend Noualen show up? "So was Kenna real?"

"No, I don't think so."

"And are there still fairies in the gardens?"

"What do you think?" Hob's face was white in the moonlight; his expression downcast.

"I can hear something," Serena said.

Hob looked up, sharply. He said, "Come on." He got to his feet and pulled Serena back among the trees. "Don't let them see you."

A carriage was coming up the avenue, the horse that drew it moving at a brisk trot. It passed the place where Serena and Hob were hiding. Serena could not see a driver. The horse skittered to a halt and stood, tossing its head; it was a chestnut, a big rawboned thing. There was movement among the trees and a figure walked out, caped and with a tricorn hat of the sort that Serena mentally associated with highwaymen. It was a moment before she realised that it was Miranda.

The door of the coach swung open and a man emerged. Serena saw the gleam of leather in the moonlight, beneath a heavy dark cloak. He was bareheaded, his hair drawn back.

"Hound!" Hob breathed into her ear. He gripped Serena's arm, rather painfully. "They never come here!" Looking at the Hound, Serena could see that he was really not very human at all, though he remained in his man's shape, did not become beast. He moved fluidly but there was something wrong about those movements, about the swiftness of the turn of his head, the way his joints moved. But Hound plus Miranda was not a combination Serena liked and Hob had sounded genuinely surprised.

"Can we get closer?" she breathed.

Hob hesitated, then he said, "Be very, very careful."

They crept through the long grass – no lawnmowers in these days, thought Serena irrelevantly, and a man with a scythe was not the same – to the edge of the avenue. Chestnut branches nodded above Serena's face; she could see the fat, sticky buds, shining in the moonlight like the hound's leather jerkin. She heard Miranda say, her voice shrill, "I didn't promise you anything!"

"My master hired you to do a job!" the hound said. His accent was unfamiliar to Serena and it was a moment before she understood what he said: the words were oddly emphasised. She was not even sure if he was speaking English.

"And I am doing so." *Insolent*, was the word that Serena would have chosen, but she thought she detected a note of fear. Miranda, trying to be the great lady and falling short?

"You are failing in your duties. Your services, my lady, after Windsor, are no longer required." The hound spoke lightly but then, without warning, he hit Miranda across the face. She gasped, stumbling, and he struck her again. She crumpled to the ground and the Hound took her throat in one hand and began to squeeze.

"No!" Serena heard someone shout. A moment later, she realised to her horror that the word had come from her own throat and she had torn herself free from Hob's grip.

"Serena!" Hob grabbed at her and missed. Serena was up and running. The Hound turned and Serena was looking straight into his mask-like face, at the meaningless smile and empty eyes. He reminded her for a minute of the Guido Fawkes masks of recent protest movements. She saw a long sliver of bone in his hand. He struck out, but Serena was lifted off her feet from behind and thrown down onto the grass. Something streaked past her: a big black greyhound, followed by another, this time white. A woman's voice said, cold and furious,

"Why have you come here, Geflieman of the Wild Hunt? Did the Heath-Stalker send you? This is still *my* territory!"

To Serena's surprise, the Hound whimpered and cringed, like a dog chastised. Serena glimpsed a green cloak and blazing hair: she knew who this must be.

"Go!"

Serena was enveloped in darkness, as swiftly as though someone had hoodwinked her, thrown a bag over her head. She stumbled up and cannoned into someone – Hob? A shower of sparks dazzled her and they were falling, down, down, and gone.

Serena blinked. She could now see quite clearly. The boy was graceful on his plinth, surrounded by animals and fairies and poised lightly on one foot. He held a horn to his bronze lips. Along with Hob and the huddled figure of Miranda, they were crouched by the statue of Peter Pan. It felt early, with a pearly rosy light in the eastern sky above the park, and a mist rising from the Long Water. Serena's phone pinged: she examined it to find a sequence of increasingly desperate messages from Ward and several from Stella. It was, she saw, just before six a.m. The morning after she had gone in search of Miranda.

She looked up from the phone to see the shadowy figure of the airman. A flower bed was visible through his knees. He turned and bestowed a long, ambivalent look upon Miranda Dean. His lips moved but Serena could not hear what he said. Then he was gone, winking out like a star.

Serena's first action after that was to call Ward, hoping he hadn't reported her as missing to the police. Hob was trying to rouse Miranda, who did not seem to be conscious. When he rolled her over, Serena could see the livid red print of the Hound's hand upon her throat.

"Serena! Where are you? What? Whatever are you doing in Kensington Gardens? Are you all right? I've been up all night! I haven't phoned the cops – I thought you had to wait 24 hours?"

"No, you can report it immediately. They just won't do very much before that." Memories of Alys' disappearance were still rather too present in Serena's memory.

"Anyway, I thought it probably wasn't a *mundane* sort of missing. Which has made it worse. Are you all right?" Ward repeated.

"Yes, I'm fine. I'm with Hob and –" Serena hesitated. She didn't want to wind Ward up even more. "And we're just leaving. I'm coming home. I might –" What to do with Miranda? "I might stop for a cup of tea and a bun, though, if you don't mind. I'm starving. I didn't have any dinner last night. But apart from that I am honestly fine."

"I can make you breakfast!"

"That would be lovely but I might just grab a cup of tea on the way back anyway, thanks so much Ward, speak later, love you, sorry," Serena said. God, that sounded really furtive. Ward trusted her: he wouldn't just default to thinking she'd spent the night with someone else and Hob would (she hoped) back her up but she wouldn't blame Ward if he was suspicious. Silently, she cursed

Miranda, who was now sitting up groggily. Her highwayman hat and cape had disappeared; she was wearing a silk blouse and a long hobble skirt. *Tarty secretary look*, thought Serena, who was in no mood to be charitable, but Miranda looked so bedraggled and woebegone that she had to harden her heart all over again.

"Come on," she said, going over to the actress. "On your feet!" She stuck out a hand. Miranda blinked and took it. Serena hauled her up.

"Cup of tea. It's nearly half past six in the morning. I hope we can get out of the Gardens."

"The gates are open at six," Hob said, looking shifty. "I happen to know. And there's a café just off High Street Ken that should be open now as well."

"Great." Serena marched off, without waiting to see whether Hob and Miranda were following. However, they did so, and the gate was open and so was the café. When they had sat down and ordered, Miranda, without looking at Serena directly, said in a very small voice, "Thank you. He would have killed me."

"Clearly, it's more than you would have done for me."

"I know. I'm sorry."

"Really? Pardon me for being ever so slightly sceptical."

"I know," Miranda said again. At least she had apologised, Serena thought, even if it wasn't sincere. She was an actress, after all. A plate of scrambled egg on toast arrived and she found that she had not lied to Ward: she was starving. There was something comforting about eggs.

"Look," Miranda said. She took a swig of very hot black coffee and winced; it must have burned her mouth. "I'm not going to pretend I haven't done some – *things* and I totally get why you'd hate me. But I'm in over my head. You saw that last night. I thought I could control the situation and I couldn't, okay?"

"Miranda, you know what the Hunt is like." Hob sounded genuinely distressed. "What did you say you'd do?"

"They want your sister Stella," Miranda said to Serena. "But their power in the city isn't strong. It's stronger in the countryside and in the past, but in the modern city –"

"What do they want with *Stella*?" If it had been Luna it would have been more understandable: Luna had bested the Hunt once already and she did not think they were the forgiving sort.

"Because of who she knows." She must mean Noualen, Serena reflected. Another ancient nature spirit, confined to the city's parklands. Noualen wanted the man with the Knowledge to be found: did the Hunt want this, too? Or did they just not want Noualen to be freed?

"Anyway, they don't usually come into the city, it's true. Some people do better nowadays, some don't."

"Caspar Pharoah being one of the former."

"All right, I admit I was pissed off about Ward. I don't like competition."

"What? *You* dumped *him*."

Miranda ignored this. "Cas had plans and he promised to include me."

"And what did he get in exchange?"

"I – got some things for him."

"Magical things?" Serena had to remember to keep her voice down. She did not think the group of hard-hatted construction workers across the room, in for their morning tea, would appreciate this conversation.

"I have some contacts," Miranda said.

"She's a fence," Hob added and Serena was pleased to see that he met Miranda's glare full on.

"I do little bits and pieces," the actress admitted.

"And what about these old ladies in black? The Searchers? What part do they play?"

"Oh God," Miranda said, crumpling again. "I took something. Something they wanted. Caspar Pharoah wanted it too – I didn't realise they were interested in it until too late. Pharoah had died by then – how did you kill him, by the way? I heard all sorts of rumours. Suddenly they were after me and the thing they wanted disappeared when he died."

"I laid low after Twelfth Night but then the Hunt – got in touch. They said they could save me from the Searchers. I've always tried to avoid the Searchers before now – you remember me saying that, don't you, Hob?"

"I do. Christ, I didn't realise you'd pissed *them* off."

"I didn't tell you. I thought it would be safer."

Serena doubted this.

"What was it you stole, Miranda?"

"I can't tell you."

"Have a go!"

"No, I really can't," Miranda said. She opened her mouth and Serena could see the muscles of her face trying to work, but no sound emerged. Acting? Or something else?

"That's happened to me, actually," Hob said. "It's awful. It's a spell."

"In exchange for saving your life," Serena said, "and because I think I can help you, I want to know everything you know." She fixed Miranda with a basilisk stare. "Everything that you are able to tell me."

"I –"

"She really can help, Miranda," Hob said, eagerly. "She's helped me."

Miranda looked at him, as if for the first time. "What happened to you, anyway? Where did you disappear to?"

"He's staying with someone I know," Serena said. "And I think you'd better meet him, too. Assuming you haven't already."

Ward's first response, when he met them in the hallway, was, "What the hell is *she* doing here!"

"Hello, Ward," said Miranda, very coy. Ward looked at her with repulsion. She went on, defiantly, "Serena saved my life last night. And she's going to help me now."

"Darling, have you gone quite mad?"

Serena said. "Calm down, Ward. We're going to Southwark."

There was no way of getting in touch with Ace, it still being early, so Serena called a cab and, with Ward, accompanied Hob and Miranda south of the river. The pearly start to the day had fulfilled its promise: it was now a perfect spring morning. Serena regarded at the sparkling river with pleasure as they sped over Westminster Bridge;

the old city looked young once more. Miranda, however, seemed to notice nothing of her surroundings, but stared grimly ahead. Occasionally Hob patted her hand surreptitiously. Serena had not told her who they were going to meet and she feared a row: she herself had not met William Blake and at the back of her mind was also the worry that Hercules Road would simply not admit them to its older form. Miranda might be able to choose her day and age to some extent, but Serena could not.

She need not have been concerned. They got out at the corner of the road by a large pub and the taxi pulled away. The road stretched before them: some Georgian houses with the middle of the street occupied by a large, and to Serena's eyes unsightly, 1960s block.

"South of the river," Miranda said with distaste.

"Don't diss Lambeth," Hob told her.

Serena did not know what to do. Like a child, she closed her eyes and wished, and when she opened them again, the block of flats was gone and an unpaved street of small pallid houses had taken the place of the modern Hercules Road. She clenched her fists in fleeting triumph: take that, Miranda! But perhaps the street had reacted to Hob, its house guest, and not to herself. Never mind.

"Come on," she said, steeling herself as a man on horseback ambled around the corner. But it was only an old man on a nag, hairy at the heel and placid. He mumbled a greeting as they passed.

"Where are we going?" Miranda asked plaintively, hoisting her skirts out of the way of the mud and dung.

"You need pattens," Serena said.

Miranda actually smiled at this. "I've got some, somewhere."

"The time traveller's camping kit," Ward murmured. He was looking about him with interest, perhaps gaining new insights for forthcoming costume dramas, Serena thought.

"It's here," Hob said. He stopped in front of one of the houses. This was not a particularly wealthy neighbourhood, though these places would cost a bomb in modern London. The paintwork, however, was meticulous: the sash windows looked new. Hob went up to the door and placed his hand upon it; it opened. Serena and the others followed him inside.

BEE

Bee collected her mother from the police station. On the journey to Wells, she had rehearsed a number of approaches, ranging from disappointment, to annoyance at injustice, to extreme irritation. In the end, she decided on none of them.

"Hello, Mum."

"Hello, darling." Alys was not incarcerated in a cell and clutching the bars. Instead, she was sitting in reception, cross legged and elegant, reading a copy of *Country Life*. She might have been waiting for a dental appointment. "Thanks for picking me up."

"No problem," said Bee. "Do we need to sign you out or anything?"

"No, it's all done. I'm free to go." She walked into the sunlight without a backwards glance.

"Honestly, Mother, getting arrested at your age." Bee tried to sound disapproving but she could not prevent a faint, and annoying, note of admiration from creeping into her voice.

"I know. I have been arrested before, mind you. But not in this country."

"You've never told us that! Where?"

But Alys simply gave a vague smile and remarked on the display of daffodils along the verges. As Glastonbury Tor hove into view, she said,

"Could you swing by the protest site, please, Bee? I want to speak to Ver March."

"Just don't punch anyone again!"

"No, no. Did you see any of the road protest on your way here? The diggers were supposed to be coming in this morning."

"Oh God, I hope *Ver* doesn't get arrested… No, I didn't – I came via Shepton Mallet. I didn't want to be held up."

She skirted Glastonbury itself and took the road that ran south of the Tor. It would not be long before the orchards came into blossom; the blackthorn had gone over now, like dirty snow, but the pale pink and white bird cherries and wild plum had taken its place.

As they neared the field which was slated to be sacrificed for the first stage of the new road, Bee saw that it was filled with earth moving equipment. And blue lights.

"Wouldn't it be funny if those were the same policemen who arrested me yesterday?"

"Hilarious," Bee replied, sourly.

"They were lovely, really. They made me a cup of tea."

"Did they actually put you in a cell?"

"No, I assume they've got cells but I didn't see them. They put me in a room. The only reason it took so long was because of the paperwork and they had a big drugs bust or something, so I wasn't exactly a priority. I saw some of the most interesting people being led inside in handcuffs. I looked through the window in the door. I don't know if the room had one of those two way mirrors. I wouldn't think so in Wells, would you?"

"I suspect that is only in places like Scotland Yard. Or American television dramas."

"Anyway, it was all a bit of an anti-climax, really."

"What happened to that man who hit you?"

"He had to be taken to West Mendip casualty first to get his nose seen to and I don't know what happened after that, although he is apparently from Nottingham – down here on business – so I'm unlikely to run into him again. And I'm sure he doesn't want to run into me."

"I should think not. You might break his nose again."

"Or worse. I should have just kicked him in the balls. Well, that's certainly a protest."

No one was lying down in front of the diggers. They were, however, standing before them: a silent row of women, holding hands and chanting. Bee recognised one of the goddess chants that Luna sometimes sang under her breath.

"Mum, you're going to wait here in the car. This is because I want to get lunch on and clean the kitchen and go for a walk with Ned and ring Nick and I don't want to have to come and bail you out again if the law catches sight of you." She spoke with firmness but was surprised when Alys said, meekly enough, "Okay."

Bee got out of the car and found Ver March. She was not standing with the first line of women, but some distance away, chatting to a couple of men in hard hats and hi viz.

"Bee, dear. You're here. I was just explaining my point of view to these gentlemen."

From the expression on the men's faces – mild amusement – Ver's explanation had gone down well. Bee said,

"Ver, Mum wants to have a word with you about something. Sorry."

"Least I can do. I hope she was treated well by the pigs?"

"I expect she thoroughly charmed them," Bee said. "They made her some tea."

"It's all very English, isn't it, dear." Ver came over and leaned through the window of the car. "Hello, Mrs Fallow. I think it's wise to stay in the car – the law are around somewhere. Don't buy trouble, is what I say –" that was a bit rich, coming from someone who'd been camping out for weeks in anticipation of a protest, Bee thought "– but I must say as well, that was quite a thump you gave that unpleasant man."

"He deserved it," Alys said grimly. "My cheek still hurts."

"Down with the patriarchy!"

"Too right, Ver. I wanted you to know – something's on the wind."

Ver gave her a wary look. "What sort of something?"

"I don't know. Sorry, that sounds like a thing a spy might say. But it's the truth. I was sitting in that draughty old room last night and I could hear the wind, rattling against the window, and there were voices on it. Crying out, troubled. It's not a good sign."

Ver nodded. "All right. I have noticed a couple of things myself, in fact. I think we all need to be careful. Spring tide's on the turn: it's the equinox in a bit. An Embertide, my grandparents always called it, though it's a bit different from the one the church follows, I dare say. You can always expect things to be unsettled around then and this is supposed to be a big tide for some reason."

"I don't know what to expect," Alys admitted.

"Things'll probably settle down once the equinox is past. But not till then so, as I say, be careful. Ward your doors at night, keep the animals in."

Bee snorted. "Good luck with my cats."

"Cats have too much sense to be abroad at the moment. And keep an eye on the moon. Dark of the moon over the equinox itself and then the new. Things will change then and, if I'm right, get better. The old tide of the year will carry a lot away. I hope."

Bee, too, hoped she was right. She could still hear the chanting: it would become an earworm for the next few days, she feared, unless she managed to dislodge it. It seemed to be getting louder. Ver looked up and shaded her eyes with her hand.

"Oh dear."

There was a sudden roar and shouting. Bee realised that one of the big pieces of earth moving equipment had been fired into life: she could see a man in a hard hat in the cabin, wrestling with the gears.

"What's he doing? He can't possibly be about to drive into them!"

"He's hoping to scare them off, I should think," Alys said.

But the women weren't budging. Bee could see the policemen now, marching quickly over. One of them was gesticulating and waving. The earth mover lurched backwards, its tank-like treads gouging a scar in the grass. Its long arm reared up, high above the women.

"He wants to be careful," said Alys. "If that comes down on somebody's head..."

The policeman was making 'stop' gestures, slashing a hand from side to side.

"I don't think he can see him," said Bee.

"Machismo," Ver remarked. "Always a problem."

The line of women held firm. The earth mover skidded back and the claw came down, raking a scar in the soil in front of them. Bee's attention was all on the equipment and she jumped when there was a sudden sharp tap on the window. She looked up to see a man, in a cap covered in flowers and thistles. His appearance was so unexpected that Bee gaped at him for a moment before recognising him. It was not a protestor, but Kit Coral.

"Get out," he said to Alys. "Trouble's coming."

After a moment's hesitation, Alys scrambled out.

"I told you there was something on the wind," she said.

Ver nodded. "Tide's moving."

Bee did not pretend to be as much in the loop as Ver or even her mother, but she could feel the change: the air was shivering, the wind suddenly cold and veering round to the north. A cloud blotted the sun and she saw the scene briefly in negative, the figures bright as fire, the meadow dark. A cacophony rose up from the rooks in the small patch of woodland and Bee glimpsed them whirling up from their untidy nests in a stand of ash. The ground quivered once, beneath her feet, and she heard the sound of hooves. Alys seized her hand.

"Quickly, Bee."

With Kit Coral, they ran towards the woodland. Bee could hear shouts behind them but she did not want to lose her footing on the rough ground – that was all she needed, a sprained ankle – and so she did not look back.

"Ver!" she panted. "Are you all right?"

"Save your breath for running!" Ver said. But then they were among the ash trees, sprigs of vivid, fiery green bursting out of the small black hooves at the end of each twig. A drum was beating far down the meadow, rhythmic and ominous, a war drum, Bee thought, although she could not have said how she knew.

"Well, that was more exercise than I've had in weeks," Ver said, wheezing.

"They can't have summoned the Hunt with a couple of chants to the goddess," Alys said.

"No, the Hunt were already on their way." Coral gestured into the heart of the wood. "Come on, out of sight. You don't need to see them."

"What will they do?" Bee quavered, thinking of the brave line of women. She felt terrible about running away.

"I don't know but you don't want them catching sight of *you*."

Alys might, Bee thought, but did not say.

"I got you safely home before," Coral said. "I'll do so again."

"I do know the lie of the land somewhat," Alys said and he looked at her as if for the first time.

"Yes, you are the Far Farer, aren't you? Your father lies in the churchyard and speaks to me through the weathercock."

"I don't know about that. You can trust me, though. I know Bee's had her doubts. But I want my daughters to be safe."

"Then let's go."

SERENA

Bill Blake was sitting in his back garden, surrounded by birds. Serena saw chaffinches, a blackbird, a scattering of sparrows and a handsome spotted woodpecker, running up and down the trunk of an apple tree like a mad little admiral. She looked at Blake with interest. Stella had mentioned meeting him during a nudist episode – he had followed this practice, apparently. This morning, however, Blake was fully clad, to Serena's secret relief. He wore breeches and buckled shoes, and a knee length coat, but no hat. He did not rise to greet them but returned Serena's stare with a lively interest.

"Good morning, Hob. I see you found what you sought."

"Oh my God," Miranda said. "Are you William Blake?" She gave a quick glance over her shoulder as if assessing the chances of flight, but Ward stood behind her on the path.

"Madam, I am. And you are Mistress Dean." His tone was quite neutral.

Miranda put a fluttering hand to her throat, still marked with the red scratches made by the Hound. Serena thought she was weighing up a response: defiance, explanation, or throwing herself on Blake's mercy. In the event, she did none of these things; Serena had the impression that she was entirely at a loss. Blake said, in quite a kindly way,

"Sit down. We are at an age for tea. Should you like some, I can arrange it."

"I would love some tea!" Serena said and he smiled at her.

"And you, you are the theatrical actor, are you not? Mr Garner?"

"Please call me Ward, Mr Blake."

"Then, Ward, perhaps you might go into the kitchen and ask Nellie, that being our maid, to arrange for some tea. You will find it stronger than it is in your own day, I understand. It is quite restorative."

"Certainly!"

Miranda sat down with care on a bench. Serena perched on the edge of the flower border, on a rock. She did not quite trust sitting next to Miranda and Ward evidently felt the same, for when he returned from issuing instructions to the maid, he sat down next to Serena.

"Well, Mistress Dean," Blake said. "What of it?"

"I don't owe any explanations to you!" Miranda snapped, but almost instantly deflated. "Oh, all right. It seems I have come to the attention of the Searchers."

"Dear me! I usually counsel against coming to such attention."

"Absolutely. If they find me – I don't know what they'll do. Worse than death, it's said."

"A living death, indeed."

"Sir," Serena said, "My sister met some people once, on the lych path, in White Horse Country. Coffin bearers. Are they the same? Ace said the Searchers were women who sought out the dead for the records."

"Here beginneth my history lesson, for the Searchers of which you speak come from similar origins as those on the lych way, but are different. Though both are among those who bring death, not merely seek it. They are allied to the ravens in the Tower: some say that they are the spirits of carrion birds, who remain in the city and are tasked with its cleansing and reparation. They snatch the souls of evil folk and carry them beyond the North Wind."

"I helped one of the ravens," Serena said. "From the Tower."

"Ah, I see. What made those marks on your throat, Mistress Dean? Something with claws."

"Yes. A Hound."

Blake's eyebrows raised at this. "Here, in the city? They rarely venture into the capital of men."

"It was not during this time, a quieter age, but I agree."

"Some would not call it so quiet, with all the war we have, but I understand you. And did you chance upon this Hound, then?"

"No, I had an appointment. I had a message from a – a man, with connections to the Hunt. He said they could save me from the Searchers. I was desperate. I agreed to meet him but – they asked something of me first, which I was not able to fulfil."

"That did not please them, I see."

"No. He tried to kill me."

"What was the thing they wanted you to do?" Ward asked. Miranda was silent.

"Miranda?"

"I think she means they wanted my sister Stella," Serena volunteered.

"They wanted me to kill her," Miranda said to Serena.

At this point, perhaps just as well, Serena reflected, the tea arrived. The maid placed teapot and cups on a small table and disappeared back into the house. Serena took the cup offered to her and sipped: black tea, and it was indeed much stronger than she was accustomed to. Blake said, still mild, "What has this family done to you, Miranda? For I fear you have tried to put an end to not one, but two, of the Fallow girls?"

"Spite," said Ward. Miranda shot him a nasty look but before she turned to address Blake, she had composed her expression into one of humility.

"Ward is right," she said, sweetly, "in your case. I am sorry, Serena. I tried to take your life and in return you gave me back my own. Will you forgive me?"

If she is genuinely repentant, thought Serena, then I am Queen Marie of Romania. However, moral high ground! And she felt a certain pressure to behave graciously in the presence of William Blake, no less.

"Yes, I will. On my own account. But what about Stella?"

"The Hunt were insistent. Stella has been recruited by an enemy of the Hunt in the city," Miranda said. "They want her gone. You are right, Mr Blake. Their power here is limited and the city is still in disarray after the winter. Twelfth Night did more damage than you know."

"Glad to hear it," said Blake.

"So I don't mean to sound snide, Miranda," Ward said, rather obviously intending exactly that, "but why hire *you* as an assassin?"

"I told you – the city's in disarray. A lot of people have gone to ground. I was available." She looked at Hob. "I would have asked you to help me but I don't know if I can trust you any more."

"I don't like murder," Hob said, in alarm.

"No, you don't like getting your hands dirty, do you? But you'll leave it up to me."

"That's not fair, Miranda! We've had adventures, yes, but that hasn't involved killing people."

"Petty theft," Blake said.

"If you like. There's a big difference."

"I cannot call off the Searchers," Blake said to Miranda. "I don't have that power. Once they have you in their sights, they will not let you go. I can offer you shelter here for a while, as I have done to Hob, but I cannot hide you forever and I want something in exchange – not a stolen item," he said, holding up a hand to forestall whatever she had been about to say, "but information. You will tell me everything you know, everything that Hob has not already told me, and he has told me much."

"Oh, have you!" Miranda said to Hob.

"Didn't have much of a choice, did I?"

"Catherine!" Blake called. The placid-faced woman in a headscarf who had shown them into the garden reappeared at the back door; Blake's wife, Serena presumed. "Take Mistress Dean into the house and find her somewhere respectable. She will be lodging with us the night."

Miranda looked as if she would have liked to have said more but did not dare. She rose, meekly enough, and followed Catherine Blake into the house. When she had gone, there was a sudden flurry of white and black and her place on the bench was occupied by a magpie, who looked at Serena out of one bright eye.

"Go with her, boy," Blake said to Hob. Once Serena and Ward were alone, he said, "You told me you saw a raven."

"Yes, it was on the Victoria Embankment, in the gardens. A taxi hit it; I helped look after it. I called the Tower and a woman came and took it away."

"Perhaps the Searchers are looking after you," Blake said. "Because you aided one of them."

"I don't know about that," Serena said, alarmed. "They sound frightening. But someone is." She told him about the airman.

"Why him, I wonder," the old man said. "Do you know who he is? An ancestor of yours, perhaps?"

"That did cross my mind and I spoke to my sister in Somerset, but we couldn't place anyone who was in the RAF during the war. All our male relatives of that generation were in the Navy."

"Yet he, and the Searchers, now know you. You don't need to be afraid of them, Serena. You are not their quarry and they may see themselves as being in your debt. They are not evil, but they are implacable."

"But Miranda does need to be afraid," said Ward. "Can you keep her safe, Mr Blake?"

Blake gave him a sharp look, quick as the magpie, which was see-sawing to and fro on the arm of the bench. "Do you care, Mr Garner?"

"Frankly, no. I don't want her dead, though, if that's what you mean. Even given what she's done – I have some principles. But I don't trust her. I don't like to think we've sent a Trojan Horse into your household."

Blake laughed and slapped him on the shoulder. "I am old and cunning as the serpent, as Odysseus himself. Have no fears for me. Now you should go about your day, and leave me to mine. I shall be in touch, or Mags here will, or Mr Spare." This was, Serena recalled, Ace's surname. "Good day to you. Nellie will show you out."

She did so, and, thus dismissed, Ward and Serena stepped into a quiet modern street, with contrails criss-crossing the blue sky overhead.

"Well," Ward said. "That was interesting. I can't believe I've just met William Blake."

"He was nice," Serena said.

"He was supposed to be remarkably difficult when he was alive. Always arguing with his patrons and so on, but maybe he's mellowed. Maybe death does that to a chap?"

"If he's actually dead. He looked a bit too solid. But so does Ace." Serena yawned. "I think I need some coffee."

"Talking of Ace, do you think we should speak to him?"

Serena looked at her phone. "It's still early. But I think we ought to let him know about Miranda."

"I also couldn't believe it when I saw her in the hall with you."

"She's a viper," Serena said. "But I did save her life and I felt almost sorry for her, although I know I shouldn't."

"And talking of reptiles, those would have been purely crocodile tears. I've fallen for that once too often. I told myself Miranda was sensitive. Ha!" said Ward. "She's about as sensitive as a brick through a windowpane."

"I'm wondering if she's realised she's overstepped the mark," Serena said.

"No, I don't think she's capable of learning that, even through fear. I have confidence in friend William but I must say I don't like to think of her and Hob sitting in his back bedroom plotting."

"She won't have much else to do," Serena said. "She can't go out, in case of the Searchers. And I think the Hound really scared her. He scared me. Let's go to Borough and get more coffee. And then we'll talk to Ace if he's there and then we'll go home."

LUNA

Luna looked at the clock. Midday, and her mother and Bee should be back soon. Bee had left quite early to collect Alys; perhaps they had stopped for coffee. She hoped that there had been no complications at the police station. It was the opposite of the time when Alys had gone missing, but almost as worrying. Then, no one had known where Alys was; this time everyone knew, but could she be extricated? Luna told herself that the police were underfunded and understaffed, that they couldn't keep a nice middle class lady inside indefinitely. Could they? "Stop fussing," Luna said aloud, and emptied the dishwasher.

Sam was at Amberley and she had packed sandwiches for his lunch. The kitchen was clean. Luna had intended to polish the woodwork in the van this morning, and she fetched dusters and an old cloth and a bottle of wood varnish, scented with lavender. She hoped Sam wouldn't mind that. First, however, there was housework to be done. She took the dusters into the hall and polished the bannisters and the wooden acorns that stood on top of each newel post, said to be an old protection against lightning. The house was peaceful and quiet, sunlight falling in shafts on the stairs and a cat, Fly, in a heap right in the middle of them; Luna had to step around him every time she went up the stairs and she had become too bulky to do this sort of manoeuvre with perfect safety.

Then she took the dusters out to the van. It was a beautiful morning and a pleasure to be out in the open. Luna finished her polishing and sat on the step of the van, with Moth gazing at her hopefully, to eat her own lunch, basking in the spring sunshine and admiring the blossom and the results of her efforts.

By two o'clock Alys and Bee had still not returned. Luna felt a bone of worry in her throat, tried to stop her thoughts gnawing at her. She texted both and then called Ver, but there was no reply. She rang Sam.

"Sorry. I'm fretting."

"Maybe you're right to fret," Sam said. There was unease in his own voice. "It doesn't take long to get to Wells and back even if they did stop off for lunch. Do you want me to ring the station?"

"Would you mind?"

Sam hung up, but a few minutes later the phone buzzed and they were talking again.

"They let her go this morning, and Bee picked her up. Have you spoken to Ver?"

"No, she's not answering the phone."

"I've got to see to one of the horses and then I'll ask Richard if he wouldn't mind if I leave early. I'll go over to the protest camp – see if they're there."

"I think that's a good idea," Luna said. "I hope they haven't run into trouble."

An hour or so later, back in the kitchen and making more tea, that panacea for all ills, she heard a vehicle pulling into the yard and ran out to greet it.

"Sam!"

It was not Sam's Land Rover, however, but Laura's. She jumped down with no trace of stiffness or pain. Luna had not seen her after the episode at Cheltenham, but Bee'd had plenty to say about it.

"Laura, hi."

"Hello Luna. Sorry to drop in unannounced. I was driving back from Shepton and I saw someone in your bottom field, when I was coming over the top of the hill. I thought you'd better know."

Since Luna now knew Laura's secret, it was a relief not to have to maintain the social niceties. She cut to the chase.

"What sort of person? Human?"

"I don't know. It was moving really quickly, on two legs, sort of crouching, and it was wearing something white. It was quite tall."

"Which direction was it going in?"

"West to east, more or less. I'm a bit concerned about your horses."

Luna grinned at her. "I suppose you would be!"

"Oh God, sorry about all that. I don't mind you knowing."

"Bee and Mum are coming back from the police station – did you hear about that?"

"No!" Laura's eyes were wide. Quickly, Luna explained.

"Oh God. We'd better go and have a look."

When they got down to the field, however, the piebalds were peacefully cropping the grass. The only pale thing in the hedge was a bank of primroses. Both horses raised their heads when they saw Luna, and they whickered companionably at Laura, but when no treats were forthcoming they returned to their grazing. With some trepidation, since this location had caught her out before, Luna stepped into the field shelter and looked around but nothing was out of place and when she went out again, all was as ever.

"I can't see anything."

"She's in the orchard," a voice said in Luna's ear. She jumped.

"What – ! Oh, Ned." He was standing directly behind her.

"Oh!" Laura said. Her hand went to her mouth. "You're a – I've seen you before."

He smiled. "I helped Bee look for your mother, once. We saw a white horse on a hillside, running. Then we met you. I did not think you had spotted me."

Laura looked slightly abashed. "I sneak out sometimes. Cloudy – me – isn't supposed to be out on her own. But sometimes I just need to run."

His look was kindly. "I understand. You need to run now, Laura, and so do we: there's someone in the orchard."

Luna was not as quick now as Laura and Dark, but she moved as swiftly as she could and Laura waited for her. As soon as they opened the orchard gate, she knew something was wrong. A chill wind rose up, stirring the new leaves of the hawthorn, and the day darkened.

"Look," Dark whispered.

Someone was walking along the end of the orchard. Laura had described a crouching run, but this person stood straight and tall. The white shoot had come back and now she was grown. Perhaps Alys' height, Luna thought. Her pale hair brushed her ankles and she wore a moon-coloured gown. She was singing as she walked, a cold little song, and flowers rose up within her bare footprints. They, too, glowed and the sight of them made Luna shiver. She gasped, and the shoot turned. She stared down the orchard with glittering malice: her eyes were serpent-green.

"Luna," Laura said, unsteadily, "I think we should go."

Luna thought so, too. She clasped Laura's hand and stepped backwards through the orchard gate.

"Go to the house!" Dark said, sharply.

They did. They ran, and Luna, moving with difficulty, flung herself through the open kitchen door. Laura was close behind her. It had been afternoon when they went to the field, no more than three o'clock, and now it was dusk with the church bells ringing.

"Dark –!"

"Close the door! Now!" He was already in the kitchen. Luna shoved the door shut and bolted it.

"Where are the dogs?" But the spaniels were in their basket and in response to her shout Moth appeared enquiringly at the kitchen door.

"Don't you have cats as well?"

In unspoken agreement, Luna and Laura ran upstairs. All the cats were on Bee's bed; Fly raised an enquiring head. Luna closed the door. They ran next into the spare bedroom where the wooden horse was rocking, rocking, creaking against the boards, its mouth agape.

"Don't go too close to the window," Dark said.

"I do need to see, though." The long, dark blue curtains were partly closed and Luna tugged one aside, to look cautiously out. The shoot was standing on the lawn. Her head swung from side to side; she did not look remotely human. Luna found her both repulsive and fascinating: she was like a white worm, her skin faintly wet and glistening. The filaments of her hair quested out with a life of their own. Then, as if making a sudden decision, she began to pace the lawn. She walked up its length, once more leaving footprints behind her. Sam and Bee had mown the lawn a few days before, its second cut of the year, and it was smooth and velvet green. Stars winked out in the shoot's footprints and became flowers with coiling stems, wiry and white.

"What's she doing?" Laura whispered.

"Locking us in." Dark's figure was vague in the shadows of the room. "Wait here," he said, and vanished. The shoot had gone around the end of the house and out of sight. Laura and Luna waited.

Then Dark was back.

"Yes," he said. "She's going right around the house. I don't think you ought to try crossing the flowers."

"Why not? They're just flowers, aren't they?" Laura said. "They look like windflowers. Or lily of the valley."

"They will burn you," Dark said.

"God, I hope Sam and Mum and Bee don't suddenly come back. I ought to get my phone and call Sam, warn him."

"We'll go downstairs together," Laura said.

In the kitchen it seemed much darker than it should. Luna's phone was still on the table and she had charged it that morning, but when she picked it up, it was dead. So was the landline. And this was why it was so dim: not only had the day darkened outside, but the lights in the kitchen were off.

"No power," she said. Laura, too, was looking at her phone.

"Same here. Luna, can we go back upstairs? I feel safer there."

"Yes," Luna said. She picked up a loaf of sliced bread and the butter, took milk and cheese out of the fridge and put them all in the box that Bee used for the post along with some biscuits. "I'm not going to starve, though. It's all right for *you,*" she said to Ned.

"A sound plan for a siege."

Luna peered out of the upstairs window again, this time kneeling on the window seat, but there was no sign of the shoot. The lawn, however, as far as she could see to the edges of the house, had sprouted a ring of white flowers.

"It's like spring gone wrong," said Laura.

"I think that is exactly what it is," Dark said. "I have heard of spirits who leave flowers in their wake but always they are benign."

Luna remembered the air of malice that had clung to the shoot and shivered.

"And after we gave her her own pot in the greenhouse, too," she said. "What an ungrateful plant."

BEE

On their previous journey, Bee recalled, Kit Coral had seemed concerned that they should get home before dark. Now, however, he seemed to have given up on this idea. She asked him why.

"We took a low road last time. Now, we must take the long. It's safer."

"What is on the low road, then, Kit?"

"The Hunt, as you know, and the Corpse-Bearers. There are crossroads with the lych paths, that way. The Searchers, sometimes."

"What are they? The Searchers?"

"They seek out the dead. Or so they say." His face was grim. "Others, too. Drovers, Shucks. Our best chance is to find a pilgrim band but I don't know who might be coming through. Uncertain times. I am sorry. I hoped to do better by you. It is my allotted task, you see, to guide innocent travellers."

"I'm sure you're doing your best," Ver March said. "We'll manage."

They would have to, Bee thought. The woodland was beautiful, but somehow that made it worse, more menacing. In the winter, the bare branches, snowstrewn earth and the blank white sky above had fitted the danger of this liminal world. Now, the great beeches bore spears of lime green, and windflowers and anemones were coming up at their feet. The blue sky above was dimming to a deep ocean green and Bee thought she had glimpsed a new moon, riding low amid the branches. It should have been idyllic but it felt wrong, the air humming, as though Bee might touch nettle or briar and jerk back her hand with shock. She felt on edge, jangling with anxiety. Ver was uncharacteristically quiet and Kit Coral strode scouting ahead, soft of foot. Only Alys seemed at ease. Her mother was smiling faintly as she walked, looking straight ahead. If someone came to greet them, would Alys know them? Who did she know and by whom was she known, the Far Farer, in these edgelands? That had been the question that had preoccupied Bee and her sisters throughout the winter; it returned to beset her now. She would have badgered Alys, finally ceasing to tiptoe around her mother, but she thought they ought to keep silent.

"There's a light," Ver said. They had come out onto a high ridge of track, the trees thinning. Bee looked down the shadowy slope and saw a bobbing lamp.

"More than one person," Kit said.

"Horses?"

"No."

A flame flickered up. Someone was lighting a fire.

"Wait here," Kit said. He went quickly down the slope while Ver and Bee halted. Alys turned and stared back into the trees. And Bee thought again: *is that really you, mother?* She and her sisters had voiced the thought, back in the winter, that this might not be Alys at all, returned from her travelling, but something else, something that had borrowed her skin. This thought returned to haunt Bee now. Alys had seemed so like her old self, once the events of Twelfth Night had passed; back nearly to normal. But now Bee wondered if this had merely been a dormancy, a quiescence of an alien spirit.

"He's waving," Ver said. Kit Coral was beckoning them down the slope.

They walked into an atmosphere which reminded Bee somewhat of the protest camp. A huddle of people, ragged around a bonfire. A man leaned on a staff like a shepherd's crook, talking to Kit. His coat bore a badge; it was too dark for Bee to see what it might be but then the firelight flickered up and she saw that it was a scallop shell.

"Pilgrims," Kit said. Bee thought she detected a note of relief in his voice. "Barnabas says we can camp with them tonight."

It was beginning to dawn on Bee that she really wasn't going to be home any time soon. And she didn't do camping. But it would not do to complain so with a sigh she sat down by the fire and accepted a rough blanket that a woman thrust at her. She was also given a piece of bread, which turned out to be wrapped around some fish: bland but nourishing enough, although Bee could not help wondering where it had come from. And how old it was. She voiced this thought to Ver. The other pilgrims did not say much and when they spoke, it was not in a version of English that Bee easily understood, although odd words came through.

"I wondered the same," Ver said. "But we'll just have to hope for the best. It's food and it's given freely by good people; that's all one can ever really hope for."

"Do you know what kind of fish it is?"

"I think it's smoked eel, dear. I'm going to have a wee over there behind those bushes and then try and get some sleep, and I suggest you do the same."

Bee thought this was a good idea, but before she sought her rest she went over to Kit Coral and told him their plans. He nodded, absently.

"There'll be a watch kept." He looked in the direction of a man with a great grey dog, like Luna's Moth, but larger. A bow hung by the man's side.

"Do you know these people?" Bee asked him. "Do you know where they're going?"

"Yes, they're going to Glastonbury, to the shrine. They've come from Walsingham, down the Michael and Mary Line." This was, Bee knew from local folklore, the ley that was supposed to join the south west of the country with the east.

"They're nearly there, then?"

"Near enough. I counsel sleep, it's a good idea."

"Good night to you," Bee said, who knew dismissal when she heard it. She went back to the fire, via the bushes, and wrapped herself in her coat. The ground was hard and lumpy. Bee missed her own warm, comfortable bed and the presence of Dark with a sudden physical pang. She was glad that Ver was by her side and it struck her, then, how she had been automatically grateful for the presence of Sam's nan but not that of her own mother. She raised her head. Alys sat not far away, her arms round her knees, staring into the woodland. In profile, her face reminded Bee of a hunting hawk. But what would Alys be hunting, once released from her jesses, and where would she fly? Bee lay back down.

She could not, would not sleep out here in this strange land among strangers, not even with the sideways smile of the crescent moon overhead. Bee stared at it, wondering if it was in some way the same that gazed down upon Mooncote. The moon sailed up with its companion star, Venus the evening lamp, and the star spun and grew and became many stars, and then it was the grey light of morning and Bee was waking up.

Ver was gone, but as Bee clambered to her feet, feeling stiff, she reappeared from the far side of the camp. A number of the pilgrims were already awake.

"No chance of a cup of tea I'm afraid, dear, but have some milk."

"Oh, Ver, thank you!" Bee took the small horn cup and sipped: it was goat's milk. She looked around. Kit Coral was tending the fire but Alys was nowhere to be seen.

"Yes," said Ver judiciously, following Bee's gaze. "Your mum has taken herself off."

"God! Why am I not surprised?"

"Let's not be too hasty. She might have just gone for a scout around although, I must say, I'm more into the idea of sticking together."

"So am I. But Mum does know this place. How much of it she knows is the question."

Ver gave her a sharp glance. "More than she's been telling us, I'd suggest."

"I think you're right."

"Well, as I've said before, you girls have done well, in my opinion, to be a bit cagy with her."

"The thing is, Ver, who can you trust if it isn't your own mother? I've turned this over and over in my mind and you know we've wondered if it even *is* Alys."

"I've been thinking that myself and I think it is her. Don't ask me how I know, it's just a feeling. But I think your mum's become two people: Alys Fallow when she's at home in Mooncote and pottering about in the garden or going for coffee with her friends, and the Far Farer here in the edgelands, and I have to say that I don't know that woman at all."

"Does Kit know she's gone?"

"Yes, I told him. He's not going after her, either – says she can look after herself and we can't."

"He's probably right. It's very good of him to guide us. He must have other responsibilities. But he said it was his task."

"I wonder if it has been a task laid upon him, that he must fulfil. I've come across that sort of thing before. I don't know who might have laid it, though. It's usually a penance."

"It seems a bit crass to ask."

"Well, exactly. Although I might yet. The pilgrims will be going north soon; they have a way to go yet, Barnabas' friend young Clement over there told me. Glastonbury might be close by in our world but this is harder to judge. So we'll head south east with Kit."

"I have to say, I'd love to see the Glastonbury they're going to. I bet the Abbey's still standing – they must be pre-Reformation."

"I should think so. Perhaps you'll have the chance one day."

"Or even to Avalon itself! Maybe there's a Lady of the Lake? But," Bee added regretfully, "we need to get back. Luna and Ned will be worried, so will Sam."

Ver nodded. "Agreed. What about your mum?"

"I'm assuming she left of her own free will and wasn't abducted in the night?"

They asked Barnabas, who had been on watch with the big grey dog. Kit had to translate, though Bee understood the gist.

"She left in the night. She said we were to go on without her."

The falcon had flown.

"Right," said Bee. "She can fend for herself, then. She's a grown up."

She found that she was more worried about Luna than Alys. Who knew what might be going on back at Mooncote? At least Sam was there, she told herself.

Parting company with the pilgrim band, they set off down the track. In the soft morning light, this was barely visible, despite the people who had come along it the day before. It lay faint and silver in the grass, difficult to see directly.

"Those pilgrims. Did they meet any trouble, on their way?" Ver asked.

"Some, Barnabas said. But they are sensible folk. They keep together, set watches, have dogs and weapons."

They pressed on into open downland, as the light grew.

STELLA

At the end of Hercules Road stood a pub called the Pineapple. It was an unusual building, reminding Stella of the Flatiron in New York: this was like a miniature version. Inside, however, it was pure Dublin. Only traditional Guinness from Ireland was served, said a stern notice on the bar, and a number of harp logos and shamrock hats adorned the walls and shelves. There would be, so a chalkboard announced, Music Tonight.

"An actual Irish pub would be playing Country and Western," said Davy Dearly.

"Or Elvis. But it's always nice to have a decent pint of Guinness and I now intend to do so," Ace said, "whether or not young Hob shows up."

This was intended to be a debriefing session for the last couple of days: Stella, Ace, Davy and Hob himself. Blake would not be joining them, but Ace said he would pop down the road to see Bill later: he wanted to make sure that Hob and Miranda were behaving themselves.

Somehow, Stella doubted that Miranda knew the meaning of 'behave'.

Hob, at least, was more or less on time; Ace had only drunk half of his Guinness by the time the young man came through the door and joined them in the window seat. He was clean and tidy, but his expression was worried.

"How are you doing?" Stella asked.

"All right. Sort of."

"And your new flatmate?"

"Bill and Catherine have been sooooo kind. It's almost like having a mum and dad." He sounded as if he meant it. Stella remembered that Hob had said that Miranda was like a big sister to him: here was a man in search of a family, if ever she'd seen one.

"And the divine Miss M?"

"I didn't tell her I was coming here, if that's what you mean. She's not speaking to me."

"Yeah, well, Hob," said Stella. "That might not be much of a loss."

"I know, but I still – I thought she really was my friend."

Davy Dearly nodded towards the street.

"There goes your friend now."

Ace hastily drank the rest of his Guinness. "I'm not wasting it," he said to Stella. "Not at nearly £4.50 a pint."

Davy and Hob were at the door. They lingered a little, then headed in pursuit. Miranda was heading down Lambeth Road towards Southwark, walking quickly: Stella hoped she would remain in human shape because they didn't have a chance of following her if she became a gull. The four of them were conspicuous enough as it was. But Miranda did not look back.

"She may, of course, know we're following her," Ace remarked in an undertone.

"Yes. 'Trap' had crossed my mind. Maybe a couple of us should hang back? But I'm not keen on splitting up," Davy said.

"Too late." Either Southwark had experienced a recent industrial accident or something else was going on; Stella didn't remember it smelling quite this terrible. Or being full of fields. She could have been transported back to Somerset: this was a place of meadow and tree. Tall elms swayed in the breeze and the grass along the verges was full of celandines. It still stank, however.

"That smell is something else," Stella said.

"That is a tannery," Ace said. "Lots of tanneries, in fact." He nodded. "Bankside's up ahead." Soon they were among a cluster of half-timbered houses.

A woman in a long brown skirt came out of a house with a wooden bucket, the contents of which she hurled into the road, narrowly missing Stella.

"Hey!" said Stella.

"I wouldn't even bother," said Davy Dearly. "It's not like it's going to make much difference to the general ambience."

They headed east, picking through streets which were unfamiliar, but somehow plucked at Stella's memories, of her knowledge of Southwark. She wished she had looked into the history of the city in more detail, of how it had looked before the fire. Really must find a decent history book that you could read, rather than living in. She knew that London was, obviously, much smaller than the contemporary city: not far from here were low green hills, reminding her of Henry's chase, and the glimpses of the river revealed it to be a lot wider than the modern Thames.

"It's because the Victorians put embankments in," Davy said, when Stella voiced this thought.

No one paid them any attention, although a woman with no teeth accosted Ace and, from the sound of it, offered a range of unspeakable services.

"No, but cheers, love," Ace said, shaking his head once she had gone by. Stella was reminded of the Geese: the prostitutes of the old Southwark stews, funded by the Bishop of Winchester.

She wondered if they looked out of place, although when she looked down, her legs were in jeans and sneakers as usual. Up ahead, however, Miranda now wore a long grey and white gown.

There was so much to see: Stella had visited Elizabeth's time before, but the impact of the capital was once more borne upon her: the towering, leaning buildings that seemed to have been placed haphazardly upon the streets, pleading beggars on every corner, the range of clothes and the immense and constant bustle. Also the filth. She noted again the houses with unpainted oak and honey-coloured plaster and they already looked old. Perhaps it was due to the air quality, Stella thought. Everyone seemed to be smoking. She mentioned the little boys she had seen on her visit to St Paul's, all puffing away on pipes.

"They thought it was good for you," Ace said.

"Those people look like they're all going somewhere." The crowds were heading in the same direction, like football spectators before a match. "What's that big round thing?"

"That big round thing is the bear baiting pit."

"Lovely."

But this was the age which had ensnared the Behenian stars, and given birth to Dark and Drake, to people she had met. Thinking this, Stella felt a little more at home.

They passed a church; she did not know the name, but she was sure that she had seen it before in her own day. It stood quietly in its churchyard, a small pool of green in the heart of the old city. It was this that gave Stella the nod that they had arrived at the same time of year as they had left: hazel catkins flagged in the wind from the river and there were jonquils among the graves, small and wild, unlike the bright cultivated daffodils of the twenty first century. The graveyard did not, however, smell of flowers. Stella and her companions moved swiftly on.

From the corner of her eye, Stella could see a constant skittering movement.

Davy gave a little wave.

"You all right, Davy?"

"Seen someone I know." A large rat bobbed over a wall.

"Give that house a fucking swerve," said Ace. The little old place had a white sheet on the door, with a red cross on it.

"What's that mean?"

"Plague."

"What, like the Black Death?"

"The city's had regular outbreaks. They used to nail people up in their houses. That's what the Searchers did – check out the bodies, write them down in the Bills of Mortality, summon the dead cart. I don't want to bring that back with me. They can cure it in our day. I just don't want it."

Then, after a narrow passage of streets, they came out onto the river.

"Oh my God," Stella said.

She had known that old London Bridge had houses on it. She had seen them herself, in a strange dream-like episode in Southwark, in the company of a spirit and a star. But now, in the sharp spring sunlight, the impact of the bridge caused her to halt in her tracks.

"Yeah, I know," said Davy Dearly. "Impressive or what?"

The bridge was massive. It was built on enormous blocks of stone, through which the river raced and churned. She could see a wheel turning at one end: a mill. Half-timbered houses thronged it, some balanced precariously over the river on great wooden struts, and at its entrance stood a palace, golden weather vanes creaking upon its cupolas. Beyond, Stella could see masted sailing ships all along the river, and a host of smaller craft. The bridge was so eye-catching that it was a moment before she noticed a familiar building: Southwark Cathedral, much as it looked in her own day when it hosted Borough Market at its feet. She said as much to Ace.

"Known as St Mary Overie, in this day and age." He nudged her. "By the way, if you need public facilities, this is one of the only places in London to have them."

"What, actual public toilets? I didn't think they had proper plumbing?"

"Well, they do have some – the Romans did, after all – but the bridge, well, use your imagination."

"Ah!"

"Pub's not here yet. There's a debtor's prison on the site of the Southwark Tavern instead."

"Trust you to focus on the essentials, Ace!"

"Pubs *are* essential. There is, however, the George somewhere over there, which survived the Fire. I'll take you in there."

"Not during the Fire, though!"

"No, I think we'll skip that bit."

"Have you been here before, Ace?" Davy asked.

"Once. At night. That big building partway down the bridge, over the water – that's a chapel to St Thomas. It was meant for sailors to use, but I think right now it's being used as a warehouse – they decommissioned it for some reason. It was all lit up with tallow candles in the windows. I was on a boat at the time and we didn't come that close – those big stone stands, they're called 'starlings,' channel the water. Really dangerous. Boatman said he wouldn't go near it, be taking his life in his hands. I was heading down river past the bridge, so he dropped me off and I walked round the entrance and we, the person I was with and I, got another boat on the other side. He said most people did that but sometimes young men, natch, wanted to go under the bridge. Like shooting the rapids."

"Rather them than me," said Davy Dearly.

Miranda stepped onto the bridge. Her pursuers quickened their pace.

LUNA

It was now fully dark. A crescent moon had risen over the chestnut trees but it was soon swallowed by the growing clouds. Below, around the house, the flowers glowed with a sickly, pale light of their own. Something about them felt diseased, Luna thought, rather like the shoots themselves. A wrongness.

She and Laura had consumed the bread and cheese. Dark had gone downstairs, but on returning said that he couldn't get past the flowers.

"It's still like cold fire. I could bear it, but they will not let me pass. As though the air itself has turned to ice, and hard."

"But why?" Laura asked. "What is she planning?"

"I don't – is that thunder?"

The distant rumble came again. "That's all we need," Luna said as a blue flicker of lightning split the sky. They sat silent, counting.

"It's coming closer," Dark said.

Luna had been turning over an idea for some time in her mind and now she voiced it.

"If I could change…"

Laura looked at her hopefully. "Could you?"

"I don't know. I'm not like you, Laura – I can't do it at will."

"I'd teach you," Laura said, "but I don't know how. It's like a sort of switch in my head."

"I can try."

She went to the window and opened the sash. A breath of cold air wafted in, and a sweetness, with an undernote of carrion. It made Luna's nose wrinkle and a strong resentment rose within her: how dare someone trap her in her own house and steal the cool, countryside air so characteristic of Mooncote? And she was dreadfully worried about Sam, about Bee and Ver and her mother. She stood by the window, looking out. They should find a way to protect the house better… She remembered what Bee had said about Wycholt, about the Marian marks above the front door. And that gave her an idea. She closed the window and went into Bee's bedroom, to the fireplace, ducking so that she was looking up the chimney. A great artillery barrage of thunder echoed down it and the room was lit by a livid flash. The storm was coming fast; it must be nearly overhead.

It was as though her worry and fear and the onrushing storm became a power that drove some inner engine. Her vision swam bloody and red and she felt her fists clench by her sides, her arms melding to her body, everything shortening and compacting. Luna was almost used to this by now but triumph was her dominant emotion. Changed! Good!

Luna rocketed up the chimney and out. It was meshed, to prevent jackdaws nesting, but Luna was small enough to squeeze through. She did not try to cross the barrier of the flowers but flew up, up, towards the swing of the stars. Birdsense locked her on the Spring Triangle and to the east lay the moon, though she could see neither star nor planet through the crashing skies. Luna flew higher and higher, the wren no longer perching on the eagle's back in the fable but under her own steam until Mooncote lay like a doll's house far below her, black in an aura of glow. At last she was so high, directly above the house that was almost invisible now, that Luna felt it might be safe to try to cross the barrier of the flowers. If she failed, she would just go back, she told herself, trying not to think of icy tendrils reaching up, snaring her, dragging her down… There was a crack of thunder, rolling right overhead, and lightning struck the house.

Luna cried out, hearing only the wren's warning chirk, but the lightning did not bring down the chimney pot or set Mooncote ablaze. Instead it poured like shining water over the roof and down the sides of the house, earthing harmlessly. Then Luna remembered her efforts in polishing the bannisters, the wooden acorns on the newel posts which were said to stave off lightning in the old country belief. Well, looked like that old wives' tale was true. She was reminded of Ver. Those old wives knew a thing or two.

The wind tossed her to and fro, tumbling her through the air. Luna hurtled north, there was a fleeting chill, a touch of burning snow from the flowers around the house, but Luna was free.

She dived down to the topmost twigs of a big ash. The ash thrashed in the wind but Luna clung on. She wanted to see – and she could see Mooncote behind her down the slope, the white moat of flowers and, dimly, the bedroom window where Laura and Dark would be waiting anxiously. Luna was too far away for her tiny wren's voice to carry, too far to be seen, and perhaps that was just as well, for she did not know who else might be watching.

She could see, however, that Sam's Land Rover was not in the drive. Where had he gone? Luna shoved her anxiety aside. She had a decision to make. To Ver at the protest camp? But Ver had not answered her phone or replied to Luna's texts. Neither had Bee, nor her mother. From this height the church steeple was visible, its weathercock swinging in the wind like Luna on her perch, and that was an option, too, but it made more sense to Luna, then, to drop from the twig and continue north. To Wycholt and the hunt master.

She could not seem to fly slowly. She hurtled through the air like a bullet, but maybe that was the way of wrens, Luna thought. The storm was rolling away towards the coast: if the shoot had summoned it, she had lost control. Luna did not want to fall prey to some hunting owl although she saw one, ghosting below her through the wood, and a shiver of fear, cold as flowers, ran through her. Over the grey path of the road and she could see the gates of Wycholt, the long wall of the estate. Nick had said something about protection, wards, would it let her through? But it seemed that her bird guise was good. Luna flew straight up the drive.

The door was, of course, closed, but there was an upstairs light on and the window, a sash like Mooncote, was ajar. Would a witch mark keep her out? But she had no ill intent... Above it stood a chimney. Well, it had worked before and there was no smoke emerging from the pot. Luna slipped down the dark channel as easily as a mouse and found herself, to her considerable embarrassment, in Nick Wratchall-Haynes' bedroom. It was occupied. Thankfully he was dressed, sitting at a desk with a pen in his hand. He looked up sharply as Luna fluttered into the grate.

"What? Oh, hello, little wren. You shouldn't be in here." He rose from his desk and came to the fireplace.

Luna closed her bird's eyes and made a supreme effort of will. A second later she was standing in front of the hunt master. Nick looked stupefied.

"Shit! What – Luna? Luna!"

"I'm really sorry!" Luna said. "There wasn't any other way of doing it. We're in trouble."

"Okay. Let me find my shoes and come downstairs. What's going on?"

Luna told him as succinctly as possible. Sitting in the pool of light beneath the big standard lamp in the drawing room, he was still when she had finished, contemplating her. Then he said, "The females are rare: mostly the survivors grow into males. They are, earth spirits, I suppose you might say. You find them in Welsh legends – flower maidens. Where they walk, flowers grow."

"That sounds really nice, and pretty," said Luna. "But this thing is creepy as fuck, and the flowers are horrible. Do you suppose she has somehow gone wrong?"

His mouth twitched. "Product of climate change? Genetic contamination?"

"I've no idea. I don't know what she's trying to do."

"Nor do I. Trap you? Then call the Hunt? Earn her place in it, maybe? Well, we could speculate for hours but it won't help your family. And you haven't heard from Sam?"

"No. We couldn't use the phone, either, but I think we ought to call Richard and Caro. First Ben goes missing, and now Laura – I mean, we know where she is, but they don't."

"You're quite right," Nick said. He picked up his mobile and said casually after a moment, "Caro? Nick. Hi, hi. Just to let you know we're over at Mooncote. Laura dropped in when I was there, persuaded her to stay for supper. She might stay the night, save someone having to drive her back. I made the mistake of opening the Cab Sauv. That okay? Great. Speak soon."

To Luna he said, "I didn't dare ask about Sam. Thought it would sound odd."

"It would have done. I'm sure he's fine." She was not sure at all and Nick seemed to realise this. He reached out and squeezed her shoulder.

"Don't worry, Luna. It will be all right."

Luna hoped so. "What do we do now, though?"

"Get Laura and Dark out of the house, first of all. Then I think we should try and find Sam and Bee and your other relations."

"Can you do that? Free them from the house, I mean?"

"I can try."

BEE

Bee felt as though she was losing periods of time and it worried her. She mentioned this to Ver, who said,

"I know what you mean. But I don't know what to do about it. I thought it was much earlier than this but the sun's quite low now. It's happened to me before."

"When I – visited – the past before, we came out more or less in the same time frame that I went in. That happened to you and Luna in the winter, didn't it?"

"More or less. I think we might have lost a couple of days. I've never had a Brigadoon type experience, mind you, or I probably wouldn't be alive now and I don't think it works quite like that. But rumours vary."

"This isn't the past, though, is it?"

"A very good point."

There had been no sign of Alys. Kit Coral skirted the woodland, keeping high on the hills, although the landscape occasionally opened out into long vistas: hazy blue ridges running to a brightness which suggested the coast, that chalky light above the sea. Bee, perhaps irrationally, she thought, kept looking out for landmarks but she did not recognise anything about this landscape: it was a little like Somerset, but some of the hills were more like the Dorset slopes, and sometimes she thought that the high ridged land, tree crowned, resembled the Wiltshire Downs. Thorn scrub was abundant, making the interior of the woodland often impassable, and the trees varied: towering grey-barked beech, gnarled oak, stately ash and other familiar trees in turn.

Then, far away, she saw the great figure of a white horse, outlined in chalk on the side of the hill. It was like the Uffington Horse, which some said was really a dragon, but Bee thought that the hill on which it had been carved was different: higher and more pointed than the long scarp of the Wiltshire version. She mentioned it to Kit.

"When you look again, it might not be there. Neither might the hill."

"That must make being a scout pretty challenging."

"Yes. It does." He smiled. "A puzzle, this land, always."

"But there are fixed points, right?"

Kit admitted that this was so. "Some, yes. Chapels and other buildings. The coldharbours, as they are known. A few gardens. Follies and grottoes. Standing stones and churchyards and holy wells. A palimpsest, they call it. Layer on layer, so that you may go down and across and up."

It reminded Bee of a 3D chess game she had once seen on a TV programme. Star Trek, perhaps.

"And do you hold all of this in your head, Captain Coral?" Ver asked.

"Patches and fragments. I know some of the old ways and leys, the safe roads. Well, safe as they come here, anyway."

Luna had told Bee about White Horse Country, as it was apparently known, and Bee was intrigued to see it for herself. But Luna had also told her about some of its dangers. The land seemed quiet now, but Bee did not trust it. It was simmering, deceptive, she felt, necessary to keep your eyes and ears open. Once, she heard something moving through the woodland off to the left, crashing through the undergrowth.

"Kit? What's that?"

"Deer. Perhaps."

Later, she could smell the distinctive rankness of wild garlic and they detoured to pick a handful of the pointed green leaves. Kit produced a loaf of bread: a gift from the pilgrims, he said. Bee hoped Barnabas and the others had reached their destination safely by now. Her feet were growing sore, unaccustomed to so long a walk. Had this been the real England they would have come across a town or village by now, but this was not the real England. Or perhaps it was, and the modern world was the shadow. Once she thought she could see the spire of a church steeple in the long blue haze, but when she shaded her eyes and looked more closely, it was gone. The sun was growing low again and Kit said that he thought they ought to make camp. Bee, feeling feeble, was happy to stop. She had a big blister on her heel. Ver tutted when she saw it.

"And these are sensible shoes, too!"

"It's not your fault, Bee. I'm not used to such a trek either. Hold still, I'm going to prick it." Ver removed a brooch from her shawl and did so.

"I thought you weren't supposed to puncture them?" Bee said.

"So I was told but I ignored it. I always found it was better if you do. Hang on."

She wandered off and came back with a small clump of flat green leaves. "Plantain. Yarrow's better – all heal – but I can't spot any of that for the minute so plantain it is. Pull your sock over the wad of it and it'll be better in the morning."

"Thank you! I have to say, I'm feeling a bit grubby."

"Ladies merely glow, dear."

"I'm glowing like a furnace."

"Nobody's going to worry about that out here," Ver said. "We've got bigger things to fret about."

"Too right. I hope they're okay back at the house."

"I'm sure they are. Sam and Luna have got their heads screwed on."

By this time Kit had produced the last of the loaf. He refilled the small waterskin from which they had been drinking, via a trickle emerging from the hillside.

"No fire, though. Attracts too much attention."

Bee sighed inwardly at the prospect of another night out in the open but she didn't want to complain. She would manage, she told herself, wrapping herself once more in her coat and watching the light die. She hoped that the next morning would see them reaching home.

Again to her surprise, she slept. Later, she thought that it must have been all that exercise. But in the night, she woke. Something had cried out. Bee lay blinking up at the snowstorm of stars. No moon was visible now but she could see a light, fixed and unwavering, down the valley above which they had made camp. She raised herself on her elbows and stared: it was a dim yellow square, perhaps the window of a cottage. There was a yelp from deeper in the wood; tawny owl. Bee turned to Kit to ask him about the light and found that he was no longer there.

She leaned over and prodded Ver, who awoke with a snort.

"Shhh! Ver, sorry to wake you up. Kit's gone."

"Shit!" Ver hissed. She sat up. "All right. Maybe he's just gone for a pee. We'll wait for a few minutes and then we'll have a scout around."

"I don't think we should go too far away."

"No, neither do I. And we need to stick together. I can just see us running about the place like an Aldwych farce looking for each other. And missing. He was supposed to wake me to do a shift."

This had been the plan: after Ver's shift on watch, she was to wake Bee for the final pre-dawn part of the night. Now, this plan had been thrown into disarray. They sat listening to the owls hunting for a few minutes. Bee could hear one particularly persistent bird: actual hooting, a barn owl, perhaps, rather than the tawny shriek.

Ver said, "I don't want to worry you, Bee, but I don't think that's an owl."

"Shit," Bee said in turn. "What is it, then?"

"I don't know. It just doesn't sound quite right to me. I might be losing my marbles, of course."

"I doubt it," Bee whispered. "How long have you spent living out of doors?"

"Well, quite, dear."

As quietly as they could, they rose and bundled up the few bits and pieces that they had been carrying. Kit's pack was still there, so Ver took that and Bee took the water skin. Then they crept towards the thicket of bramble that separated the ridgeway from the wood itself and crouched down. Bee could hear something but she didn't know what it was: a distant rustling? Voices? Ver nudged her and jerked her head. When Bee looked, she saw a flickering, floating light.

It was a little above head height, if you were averagely tall, and pallid. It bobbed and wove. A lamp, on a pole, Bee surmised. Someone was coming along the edge of the wood. In the flicker, she could only see a cloaked, hooded figure. Ver had grown very still.

Bee did not think it was one of the Hounds: small mercies. The figure paused beneath one of the towering beeches and set the pole of the lamp in the ground. Then it clasped its hands and waited. Bee had the strong impression that it was a woman but she did not know what made her think this: something about the stance, perhaps? There was a faint sound from further in the wood. The figure looked up and the light illuminated its face: it was perfectly blank, a dark oval, with two big round eyes. Bee managed to stifle a gasp.

Someone was coming through the wood, quite fast. They went straight past Bee and Ver, hopefully invisible behind the brambles, and through the trees Bee recognised Kit Coral. He went straight up to the figure and clasped her by the wrist. Bee heard him say,

"Mistress! What do you –"

A shadow dropped down from the beech tree. It was bigger than a man, amorphous, black. It seized Kit Coral and bore him upwards. He made no sound and a second later he was gone. The cloaked woman turned and ran noiselessly through the trees, hare-swift, leaving the lamp behind her. Bee and Ver exchanged a horrified glance and without further consultation ran to the beech, but not too close. They halted a few feet away and looked up. The beech was illuminated from beneath by the dim light. The branches, still bare but tipped with green, reached empty to the stars. There was no sign of Kit or the shadow.

STELLA

Stella was suddenly surrounded by cows. The noise, and the cloud of dust, along with the cries of the drovers, were not unfamiliar to someone who had been raised in the country. She flattened herself against the wall; Davy and Ace did the same. The cows were bonier than the ones you might see placidly grazing in a Somerset meadow and they had bigger horns, too. They were mooing and upset, having just been driven across Bankside. Their legs were thick with mud and dung and the drovers, agile young men, were not much cleaner.

"Probably coming up from Kent!" Ace shouted above the din.

"Poor old things!" *Not many options for vegetarians now*, thought Stella.

At last the herd rumbled by and they were free to step onto the bridge. Before Stella could move, Ace grabbed her by the shoulders and said, "Stella, I meant to mention this earlier. It's not just cows!"

"Sorry, what?"

"Body parts," remarked Davy, sourly.

"Where?"

"Up there." Ace jerked his head in the direction of the gateway to the bridge. Stella could see something rotting on a spike.

"What *is* that? Oh, fuck, it's a head, isn't it?"

"Hdq."

"Pardon me?"

"The clerks in the Tower got tired of writing it in their big ledger, someone told me," Davy said. "So they abbreviated it. Hung, drawn, quartered. There's an arm and a chunk of the chest over there."

"That's disgusting!"

Time to stop gawping at the head, or what was left of it. Stella, assailed by a remarkable range of odours beside cow and the tanneries, could smell something that was definitely rotting. She swallowed hard and stepped onto the bridge as the big mill wheel rhythmically thudded and splashed. The houses here looked spanking new, timbers bright in the sunlight, plaster gleaming like honey. Perhaps these buildings had been replaced? Then they came out into a narrow street lined with shops, but there was a gap between two of them and Stella could see that they were now directly over the river: she could hear the gushing hiss of the Thames as it raced beneath the bridge.

One of the little emporiums sold hats, another, lace. She could see the goods displayed behind the panes of leaded glass.

"Pity I've no money," she said to Ace.

"Yes. You could bring back a souvenir. 'Oh this'," he said in a falsetto voice, "'This little piece is from when I was visiting the Elizabethan era'."

"This one sells undies," said Davy, nose pressed to the glass.

"I didn't think they had them then. Now."

"Apparently they do, in some form, anyway."

Stella and Davy tore themselves away. The street had come to a temporary end; they found themselves in a wider section from which both sides of the river were visible. Beneath her feet, Stella saw wooden boards, not stone: it was a moment before she realised that she was standing on a drawbridge, presumably to let tall masted ships go by. She could see one such, heading down river. On the western bank, away from the drawbridge, stood the old chapel. The door was open and she could see that it was filled with crates. Behind them rose the magnificent façade of a palace. Golden onion domes crowned its four corners and its façade was covered with colourful coats of arms. Within, there was a flicker of a grey and white dress moving past a leaded window.

"What the hell is that?" asked Stella. "It's like a bit of Russia!"

"Nonsuch House."

"What do we do now?" Davy said, shading her eyes as she looked up at the palace. "Do we follow her in? Go up and knock at the door?"

But she did not have to.

"I have a key," said Hob.

"Evidently, so does Miranda."

"Yes, old Van Vliet's one of her pals. It doesn't surprise me that she's gone in there. I wondered if that was where she was heading."

"And old Van Vliet would be?"

"The owner of Nonsuch. Actually had it built in Holland, in panels, and shipped over, he told me. Then it was pegged together. Barely a nail in the place. Like a flat pack."

Stella looked up at Nonsuch, at the coats of arms which decked its beams, at the domes on each corner and the golden weathercocks which span in the river wind.

"Like a flat pack," she echoed.

Davy Dearly seemed equally astonished.

"I've not seen one of those in Ikea," she said.

"So this van Vliet – if he's in residence, what's he going to say?"

"I'm more worried about Miranda. Do you want me to open the door or not?"

The short answer was that there was only one way to find out.

"Lead on," Stella said to Hob.

LUNA

Nick had driven down to Mooncote but parked the Range Rover further along the road, close to the churchyard and down from the house, which lay in shadow. They locked the car.

"Nick? Do you think we should risk the drive or go round by the horse field and through the orchard?"

Wratchall-Haynes, almost invisible in black parka and a stocking cap with a scarf around his face, hesitated for a moment. He looked like a commando, Luna thought, and it occurred to her to ask Nick about his actual background, in a calmer moment. His title was 'doctor' and Bee had said something about him having a qualification in history but he did not look like a historian now.

He said, "Field and orchard. Will your dogs bark?"

"I don't know. Will it matter?"

"Probably not."

"The spaniels are terrible guard dogs, actually. They always bark at Bee and me but once the plumber let himself into the house and they didn't even wake up."

Nick grinned. "That's so dog."

"I know. I bet yours are better behaved. Moth might know it's me – Moth's really intelligent."

"Lurchers usually are."

They climbed the stile and set off up the field. The horses were down at the bottom, dozing, and barely looked up. Now that they were coming closer to the house Luna could see the wan glow of the flowers. Nick moved fast and silently; Luna had to scramble to keep up. He opened the orchard gate carefully, holding the bolt back so that it did not snick. Luna looked carefully around the orchard, but she could not see anything untoward within it. Only that eerie glow, closer to the house. She peered at the bedroom window but saw nothing. Then there was a flick of movement out of the corner of her eye: the dining room curtain. She thought someone had stepped back.

Nick put a hand on her arm.

"Luna," he whispered, "I'm going to try something. Stay here. I don't know if it will work."

"All right."

From the shelter of one of the apple trees, she watched as he stalked forwards. Luna found that she was clutching the trunk, as if leaning on an old friend. It felt quite safe, here amid the trees, although orchards could be chancy places and Luna had not always felt so secure here. Perhaps it was a mistake to do so now.

Nick paused at the gap in the hedge. He opened the gate into the garden, very carefully. She saw him take something from his pocket: a bag. He opened it and tipped the contents into the palm of his hand. A powder? From Luna's less than optimal vantage point it looked like a handful of iron filings. He raised his hand and spoke, the words rapid and tumbling and not English. A spell? It made the back of Luna's neck prickle. The contents of his palm began to sparkle darkly. She saw him tense as he took a breath, then blew. The glittering powder gusted over the lawn in a cloud, moving under its own power like the dancing gnats which filled the wetter parts of the orchard on summer evenings. When the cloud reached the glowing flowers, it fell softly downwards. The flowers shrank, blackening, melting into the lawn.

Something screamed. The sound made Luna start and she clutched more tightly at the trunk of the apple tree. The French windows of the dining room banged open and Moth hurtled out. She heard Ned shout his name.

"Moth!" Luna cried. "Moth!"

The dog gave a great arching leap over the flowers. There was a burst of light; Luna saw his long form outlined in fire, then he vanished into the air.

"Moth!" she shouted, despairing. But the shoot was running around the side of the house, her skirts hoisted in one hand. She did not look human at all. She reminded Luna of the comet that had visited them in the autumn: her face pointed and insect-like, her hair a flame. Of her free hand, one long finger pointed bone-like at Nick Wratchall-Haynes.

The ring of flowers was withering. When the shoot crossed it, it flared up. Nick sprang over the dying ring in the opposite direction and Luna saw Ned Dark reach out and pull him into the dining room. The French window banged shut. Luna found the shoot looking straight at her: she had been seen. The shoot gave a terrible smile. The French window opened again; Luna heard her own name – Nick must be explaining to Dark that Luna was still out there. Luna's hair stirred in a vast cold wind, a wind that made her shiver from head to foot and her teeth chatter. But it came from behind, not from the direction of the shoot. She tried to turn round but could not move. Ice ran down her spine; she felt her fingertips shrivel.

"Help me," Luna whispered. She thought of the stars, the spirit that had watched over her cradle, and she prayed. "Arcturus, help me!"

Someone brushed past her – no, more than one.

Arcturus, Spica and Regulus were walking through the orchard gate. Arcturus and Regulus paused, politely, to let Spica step through first. Luna could see their calm, inhuman faces: all were smiling mildly. Someone had turned on the dining room lights now – the power must be back - and she could see the emeralds glinting in Spica's hair. The star spirits glided up to the shoot, who stood, frozen upon the lawn. Regulus and Arcturus went through the gate, Arcturus' golden skirts brushing a path through the frosty grass. Luna was suddenly warm, circulation returning to her fingertips. She breathed out, a breath that she had not known she had been holding. Starlight shimmered. The three Behenian stars reached out and took one another's hands. They encircled the shoot. Luna, freed from her frozen standpoint, thrust her dismay at lost Moth as far away as she could, which was not very far, and ran through the gate. She would not interfere but she did want to see. Beyond the stars, Nick, Laura and Dark clustered by the French windows.

Over Spica's shoulder, Luna saw that the shoot had become enclosed in shimmering light. She began to diminish, dwindling. Her arms disappeared into her sides. Her head was tipped back in a silent shout and her face, mouth agape, was the last thing of her that Luna saw. A white bundle lay on the grass. Spica, breaking the chain, bent down and gently gathered it up. Then the stars filed back through the orchard gate. They did not look at Luna, watching by the hedge, but Luna saw that Spica was carrying the bundle: a pale peaceful face, a sleeping baby, lay within it. The air shuddered, the stars were gone and so was the ring of flowers: in their place, plants had sprung up, not a solid border, but scattered. Mugwort, plantain and sage. The spicy scent of the sage filled the mild air. Luna took a breath and ran for the dining room.

"Bee's going to be cross," Laura said, "when she gets home and finds her lawn all full of weeds."

"Tough! She might have found it full of creepy flowers that act as a prison." Luna took a sip of hot tea. She could not seem to stop shivering, whether through chill or reaction, she did not know.

"I think you've done brilliantly," Laura said.

"Thanks! It could have been a lot worse."

"Do you know what happened to the shoot?" Luna said to Nick.

"I think those women – they are some of your star spirits, aren't they? – have taken her back to some kind of dormant state, maybe? Made her into a child again? Who was that other woman behind you, Luna?"

Luna stared at him.

"What other woman?"

"There was a fourth woman standing behind you, Luna," said Laura. "You were watching the stars so I don't think you saw her. She was very beautiful. In a long dress, all green and gold, and she had roses in her hair."

"I had no idea anyone else was there."

"I have seen her before," Ned said, from across the kitchen. "Walking in the orchard, in each season. Not often. Bee has seen her, too. She is not a ghost. I don't know who she is."

"Yes, Bee told me you saw her a while ago – I remember now. Is she another star spirit?"

"No, there's a difference." Dark smiled. "I couldn't tell you what it is, though. She was holding a sprig of apple blossom when we saw her before, though it was not the time of year for it."

"I'm sorry about your dog," Laura said.

Luna could no longer hold back dismay. She felt tears come to her eyes and wiped them fiercely away. "I know. Moth was so brave and – and –" Laura reached out and clasped her hand.

"He could be all right," Nick said. "Just somewhere else. He'll find his way home, I'm sure."

"Maybe he's gone to find Sam. I wish we knew where they all were."

Laura looked at Nick. "Do you want to go and look?"

"Ordinarily, I'd say yes but I think something's just gone to great effort to trap you in this house and even if that something has been – neutralised, I don't think it's a bad plan to keep our heads down until daylight."

"You can stay here," Luna said. "I'll make up a bed."

"Okay. I just don't want all of us running about. Enough people are AWOL without that."

Luna hated to think of her sister, mother, partner and de facto grandmother in danger and who knew where, while she sat drinking tea in the kitchen or comfy in her bed, but there was the baby to think about, too. Reluctantly, she agreed.

"All right."

"I can go and look," said Dark.

Nick nodded. "Yes, that might be a good idea. You've got resources that we haven't."

Dark grinned. "I can hardly be slain, after all."

"No. But be careful, Ned. There are other fates, you said."

"Yes. And I shall take great pains to avoid them!"

STELLA

Inside, Nonsuch was cold and dim. They were in a narrow entrance hall, with a flight of stairs at the end; Stella could see daylight coming in through an upper window.

"Follow me," Hob instructed.

Stella and Davy exchanged glances and along with Ace, did so. Inside, the house was pokier than it looked from the outside, divided into quite small rooms, glimpsed through half open doors. Somewhere upstairs someone was playing an instrument – a lute? The melancholy song drifted downwards, as though perfuming the air.

"Who's that, Hob? Playing the tune?"

He looked puzzled. "What tune?"

Another staircase. Stella paused to peer out through the diamond leaded panes. They were on the western side of the house and she could see all the way upriver. St Paul's dominated the city, the jumble of buildings along the banks of the Thames. The river was crammed with boats. It surprised Stella that any of them would have room to move. She squinted down through the old thickening glass and saw the churn of the water through the big buttresses which supported the bridge.

Nonsuch smelled of beeswax and lavender: more salubrious than the stink of the city beyond. And apart from the lute and the rush of the river, it was very quiet. Stella felt herself breathe out a little. On one of the upper landings, Hob stopped and opened a door.

"In here."

They followed him into a long gallery, panelled with dark wood. Carpets made pools of colour on the oak boards and, above, the white plaster between the beams was painted with flowers, scarlet and gentian blue. Two long doors stood slightly ajar and Stella glimpsed a little balcony running outside, along the length of the room. A long table stood in this room and on it sat candlesticks and a small covered box.

Other than this, the room was empty. Miranda was nowhere to be seen, but the doors were open…

"Why has she come here, Hob, do you think?"

He went to the table and took the velvet cover from the box.

"She keeps something in here – she's got stuff all over this house. It's for her messages. Her drop box in these times. Van Vliet lets her use it." He opened the box, held it upside down. Nothing fell out.

"What's in there, Hob?"

"I don't know. Whatever it was, if it was a message, she's taken it. Or someone else has."

"Does Van Vliet have servants?"

"One. A man. Van Vliet's a magician, he doesn't like having too many people around the place."

"But he gave you a key."

Hob gave a sidelong smile. "I *have* a key, anyway."

Stella went to the double doors and, after a moment's hesitation, stepped out onto the balcony. A wind whipped past her; she looked down straight into the mill-race of the river.

A barge was coming downstream towards the bridge, swan-prowed, decked with an azure blue awning; she could see the oars dipping rhythmically in and out. Little specks whirled around it, leaves blown on the wind, but they were not leaves, they were birds. A great herring gull shot along the surface of the Thames, pursued by others – ravens, grey-headed jackdaws, and a magpie. At the doors, Hob was shouting.

"Stella! Get inside!"

Stella saw the gull swoop up onto the rail of the balcony. She glimpsed the powerful beak and cold yellow eye but then it was shifting, changing, flouncing into layered grey and white skirts and a tangle of hair. Miranda stood in its place.

"You fucking traitor, Hob! No more chances!"

Everyone was shouting then, Davy, Ace and Hob and then Mags the angel was at the door, in a black dress and a white ruff. Miranda slapped Stella across the face and she fell against the door frame.

"Leave her alone!" Mags snapped, but Miranda whirled up into her gull shape and, as she had done on the night on the *Nitrogen,* flew straight at Stella's face. Stella ducked and clutched at the frame of the door, but she had lost her balance and her grip. She staggered backwards and the gull struck her a great blow with one wing and then there was nothing under her feet. She saw the turrets of Nonsuch whirl up, the weathervanes creaking in alarm, and then the river below as she went over the rail of the balcony. There was nothing to stop her fall, nothing except the great stone buttresses of the bridge, and Stella plunged towards them.

BEE

Bee and Ver did not say much to one another. They walked instead, as fast as they could down the path which led away from the woodland. After a long time, when the ridge was far behind them, Bee said,

"I feel terrible about Kit."

"So do I, dear, but there is, as my friend Jane is wont to say, fuck all we can do about it."

"What *was* that thing in the tree?"

"I don't know. I've never seen it before, or heard of it, although there are some dark things around, that's for sure. That woman was wearing a vizard, I know – they used to wear them for travelling. They cover all the face except the eyes. Gave me quite a turn. As for the thing in the beech tree, my best guess would be some kind of shuck."

"I thought that was a big black dog?"

"It is, but they can take various forms. I've never actually seen one. Thank God."

Bee still felt cold inside at the thought.

"Well, I never want to see one again. I keep hoping he somehow escaped it. But where did he *go*?"

"To be quite frank with you, Bee, I'm less concerned about where he went than about where we're going. I don't like to sound so selfish, but we've lost our guide."

Bee nodded. "I know. Do you think it's getting lighter?" She was not sure if this might be wishful thinking. She felt ragged from lack of sleep and fright. Even Ver looked strained, she thought, though in the moonlight it was hard to tell.

"Yes, I think you're right. Good."

They stopped for a few minutes beside a stream, where Bee scrubbed her tired face with cold water and drank, once Ver had gone upstream to check that nothing dead was floating in it. It made her feel slightly more awake. She raised her head as a sudden, familiar sound made her jump.

"Ver! Do you hear that? Church bells!"

"So it is!"

The bells tolled six times and, as they did so, the sun rolled up over the eastern horizon. Bee and Ver stood in a bowl of downland, its chalk bones showing through the close-cropped grass. Sheep country, gently configured and reassuring. The stream was green with watercress and as Bee looked into one of the pools eddying around the rushes, she saw the silver flicker of a trout. Looking back, the ridge of woodland was far away but still visible.

The bells tolled into silence.

"Where there's a church, there might be a village," Ver said. "I'm not sure if that's a good thing or not."

"Depends who's living in it. Or what."

"We can only go and see."

"I wonder if we're back in our world?" Bee said.

"It feels a bit too clean, at least as far as the air quality's concerned."

Bee thought she was right. They climbed slowly from the bowl and found themselves standing on a high hill. The sun was fully up now and a lark rose in a flutter from the grass, singing as it soared. Its high bubbling cry was also reassuring to Bee. Beyond, the land still rolled away in waves, but she could see the little triangle of a steeple in the distance.

"I wonder if that's the church I saw before. I don't think it is – that steeple's not so high."

"Hard to tell. Things jump around so much here."

"But it's a church, right? That can't be bad. Can it?"

"I *hope* not, dear – whatever the deficiencies of the Christian religion, their buildings are usually well protected."

But Ver did not sound entirely certain and, remembering the tales that Stella and Luna had told of otherworldly chapels, Bee did not feel completely confident either. But she did not want to find herself wandering this land forever. She wanted a hot bath and a proper cup of coffee, for starters. Keeping the steeple firmly in view – like a steeplechase, Bee thought – they set off down the hillside.

It was not until they were halfway down that Bee realised there was a chalk figure cut into the side of the hill. Its edges were fringed with long grass, so it was not immediately obvious from the path itself, and Bee was not able to make it out properly until they came to the bottom of the slope and looked back. Then she saw that the chalk had been cut in the shape of a man. His head was a blank oval, encircled, and his feet were pointing in the same direction like a carving on an Egyptian tomb. His arms were outstretched and he held two long poles or staffs.

"The Long Man," Bee said. She had seen something very like him before, on the Sussex Downs.

"Yes, Wilmington, isn't it? But he's not quite the same, somehow. Those 'v's on the end of the staffs and he has a halo – is that what it's supposed to be?"

"I'm not sure. They don't know how old the Long Man is, do they?"

"No. But I do know that he is very old, like the White Horse. Some of them are not so ancient. Cerne Abbas, the giant with the giant – well, he's supposed to be a mockery of Oliver Cromwell, so he's not that old, really."

They walked on. This landscape reminded Bee a little of Sussex, but they could not have been coming off the South Downs themselves, or they would have been able to glimpse the sea. The church itself had stayed put, though, a low building with a little tower and a pointed roof.

"That's Saxon," Bee said.

"Small and friendly."

"Yes, it does look it, doesn't it? There don't seem to be any houses nearby. It's all on its own."

"It does have a churchyard, though. If you don't mind, I think we should try and find a side gate, not go in through the lych gate, just in case."

"Agreed," said Bee. "If there is one."

They were lucky. A small snicket gate was set into the wall, which like the church itself was studded with flints. Bee ran her fingers over one as she went through the gate; it was cool and smooth, ancient rock worn down by the sea and cast into the chalk. The churchyard itself had many gravestones, but all the names had long since been worn away. Some of the dates could be made out: 1417, 1600. It had that abiding sense of peace that Bee associated with churchyards and there were primroses out in the lee of the wall, pale yellow faces turned towards the sun. On the far side of the church stood a huge yew.

"I bet that's older than this church," Ver said.

"Some of them can be thousands of years old, so they say?

"It's grown to quite a size. Let's see if the door's open," Ver said.

Bee put her hand on the ring. It reminded her of the church door at Mooncote, but here there were no parish notices in the porch, no reminders of services or dates. She turned the ring and the door swung inwards.

Unlike the Arts and Crafts interior of Hornmoon, this church was plastered but plain. White walls, oak beams, clear leaded glass. There were none of the elaborate flower arrangements that Bee's fellow churchwardens, and sometimes Bee herself, took pride in producing. An altar stood at the end of the nave, before rows of polished pews. Bee looked for a cross and did not find it. A labyrinth, carved in stone, stood on the altar instead, facing the pews. Ver was at her side. Bee had the sudden, strong impression that someone was watching her. She glanced over her shoulder; there was no one there. When she looked back, a fossil stood on the altar, some ancient curling sea creature, an ammonite trapped in grey gold limestone. Bee blinked and the carved labyrinth stood there once more.

"Did you see that?" she said to Ver.

"See what, dear?"

Apart from this, nothing seemed untoward. Bee looked around the church, hoping to find a memorial which might give some clue as to the date, but the walls were bare, the floor unmarked by tombstones. In silence they went back outside and found that the day had blown over, rain threatening on a chilly wind and clouds concealing the sun. Moreover, a manor house had appeared by the church, a handsome half-timbered building in creamy plaster with pale oak beams.

"That wasn't there when we came in," Ver said.

"I don't think we could have missed it."

"Hardly."

"All right," said Bee to the manor house, tired of the tricks this landscape seemed to be playing upon them. "Let's take a look at *you*, then."

She took a step towards the gate in the wall, but there was a sudden shout, a blur of movement, and something struck Bee in the midriff, knocking her flat. She fell among the primroses and looked up into a mouth, full of teeth.

STELLA

The stone buttress was coming up with alarming speed. Stella flailed in mid-air, it was like a bad dream, but she could feel the rush of the wind all around her and the dank smell of the river. She was suddenly conscious that she was still wearing her little backpack: it felt much heavier than it should have done. Maybe if she twisted it around it would protect her – she clutched at it and at her touch it burned like fire; Stella jerked her hand away. She felt a flicker of relief as she missed the buttress and hit the water with an icy gasping shock. Immediately she was sucked under and carried beneath the bridge. She glimpsed the weed-racked stone supports through the bubbling water, the flickering light from above, and she struck out strongly, angling between the jutting stones as the race carried her through. Stella shot out from under the bridge, uncorked, and into the wide green expanse of the Thames. The water was much calmer here but she wanted to be back on the other side of the bridge: Davy and Ace would be looking for her there.

If they'd survived Miranda.

She dived, turned and swam back through the race between the starlings, struggling a little against the current but swimming strongly. Impressive, she thought, surprised and pleased, remembering Evie's warnings about not falling into the Thames. She was a good swimmer, but she hadn't realised she was quite this competent: she could feel the tide tugging at her but she was able to overcome it and it didn't even seem that cold… She swam on through the murky water, paddling furiously until a shadow passed overhead and cut out the filtered sun. Something large dipped past her – an oar. Her breath was running out. She surfaced with a sneeze and found herself at the end of the barge with the blue covering, beyond the oarsmen. She looked up into a group of women's faces, fringed with multicoloured ruffs and glimmering pearls.

"Oh! See, my lady! An otter! How sweet!"

Stella opened her mouth to say, *I'm not…* and looked down at her hands.

They weren't hands any more.

And she seemed to have acquired a tail from somewhere.

She blinked up, treading water, and met a pair of dark eyes in a face like a sliver of bone. Red hair curled around the face, under a tiara. The face was chilly, calculating and amused. Not to mention familiar.

"Oh my God," said Stella, but the words were an animal chatter.

"It is trying to greet you, your Majesty!" said one of the women. "See, the very beasts come forth from the depths to pay their respects to their Queen!" and everyone laughed.

Elizabeth smiled thinly but Stella thought the Queen knew exactly what she was looking at, if not who or why.

"Shrovetide is gone, is it not? Best dive down deep, little otter, before my men seek the bow."

Stella didn't understand that but she got the general message: time to get the fuck out of here. She ducked gratefully beneath the concealing waters of the Thames as the great barge glided on.

When she came up again, she was running out of river. She felt mud beneath her paws and fought her way up onto the foreshore. A glance over her shoulder told her that the royal barge was almost at the bridge by the entrance; she could see men on a small jetty, ropes uncoiling to bring it in. But there were Ace and Davy, running along the wall along the shore. Stella stood, shook herself, felt something fall away, and found herself standing, human again, her Converse embedded in slime. A short distance away, two filthy children were staring at her, wide-eyed.

"Jesus fucking wept, Stella," said Ace, slipping on the mud. "I thought you were a goner. Do not do that again! It's put years on me."

"Ace, you're already dead!"

Davy was close behind. "Mate! You changed into a bloody otter! I am so proud of you! Did you know you could do that? I bet you didn't."

Stella hugged her in relief. "Sorry, I'm all wet. And no, I didn't."

She had given no thought to the fur that Bee had sent her. She had forgotten Evie's friend Jas with the secondhand shop, so the fur was still at the bottom of her backpack. She tugged the bag from her shoulders and shook it out onto a stone piling. Phone, keys, wallet, Oystercard. No soft fawn skin. Well, well. Was that part of her now, absorbed? Stella felt that it was. She was aware of a small sensation of odd pride. Bee, wren, hare and now otter. She couldn't wait to tell her sisters.

"Like a selkie," she said aloud.

"I think that's seals," said Davy.

"It is, yes. I meant something else – I'll tell you when we're safe. What happened to Miranda?"

"We lost sight of Hob when we went after you." Ace said, "There was a massive avian kerfuffle and then they all flew off and I think the other birds were chasing her but by that time we were more concerned about fishing your drowned corpse out of the river. Davy saw you swimming up onto the shore and you changed shape."

"I saw ravens going after her," Stella said, and explained. But she could feel herself sinking into the foreshore.

"Come on," Ace said, giving her a hand out of the mud. The mudlarks were still staring, in silent shock. Or maybe they saw this sort of thing every day, who knew? "There's got to be a tavern somewhere. I mentioned the George, didn't I?"

But as they made their way up onto the stone path, the sun went behind a cloud. Stella felt herself shiver. Davy turned and stared.

"What is it?"

"Look."

There was a boat readying to leave from the wharf nearby. Black caulked, black sailed. As they stared, a herring gull flew down the Thames and alighted on the deck. A moment later, a woman in a grey cape was standing there. With a shout, the rope was uncoiled and the boat turned swiftly about, heading into the middle of the Thames.

Davy turned to Stella. "You up for it, Stella?"

"Go for it." To Ace, she said, "See you back in Southwark."

"Hang on! What are you –?"

But Stella barely heard him. A rat was running for the wharf and the little flurry of magic in its wake pulled her with it. She dropped to all fours and was running, too.

BEE

Bee took a gasping breath. She recognised those teeth, and that tongue.

"Moth! Whatever are you doing here?"

"He came to find me," a voice said. Sam helped her up and drew her into the shadow of the old yew. "Keep your voice down. Hello, Gran."

"Well, I *am* pleased to see you. We were going to go and look at that old house."

"I wouldn't," Sam said, grim faced. "Look over the wall. But be careful."

Cautiously, Bee peeped over the wall, with Ver at her side. She was now looking into the land that surrounded the manor. A knot garden, trim with herbs, lay at the front of the house and beyond she could see parkland running into the distance. The stands of oaks and beech reminded Bee a little of Wycholt, but the house was definitely Tudor.

And the whole Hunt was there, occupying the sward of grass at the back of the house. Bee, mesmerised, realised that she had never seen them so clearly before. There were a lot of them, perhaps fifty people, if one could call them that. The Hounds occasionally flickered between dog and man, but the big horses bore riders, leather clad and masked. Two had antlers; it was hard to tell at this distance if they were attached to the heads of the riders or whether they were part of a headdress, but Bee thought that the former was more likely. Another man, in a tricorn hat, had the coiled horns of a ram: *I've seen* you *before*, Bee thought to herself. A horse moved, delicately sidling, and Bee heard Ver stifle a gasp. There at the side of the hedge crouched an enormous form with the head of a bull. Serena's minotaur. Bee knew that Serena had felt pity for the beast at the last; she hoped the Hunt were treating him well. He wore no yoke or bridle. The bull's head was bent; he stared down at his great hands.

Bee glimpsed a shadow from the corner of her eye. She tried not to look directly; she did not think she would see anything there. Trying to maintain her sidelong gaze, she saw a figure in black, a long coat, a top hat, holding two leashes. Shadows squirmed and strained, moving patches of darkness. She thought of Ver's comments about a shuck.

Then Bee saw a familiar figure, in her cloak of hide. Alys was not wearing a mask. She moved purposefully amongst the Hunt and Bee saw the man with ram's horns reach down to clasp her shoulder. Alys twitched free and spoke, angrily, Bee thought, but then she smiled. A lover's tiff? *God, Mum, what have you got yourself into?* A horn sounded, the summoning horn of the pack. All the Hounds' heads went up on the alert.

Very softly, Ver murmured "What do you think they might be hunting?"

Bee did not like to think. One of the Hounds was not far from the wall. She saw his head turn; he was sniffing the air. One of the Lily White Boys, she thought, and there was an ugly ragged scar across his forehead, the scar that a flailing hoof might have made. She ducked back beneath the wall but a shout went up.

"In the churchyard!"

Bee heard Sam swear.

"Sam?" Ver said, urgently. "We ought to get back into the church."

They ran around the yew tree, but this time the door of the church would not open. Bee tugged at it frantically but the church remained resolutely shut. The Hunt was milling outside the lych gate. Bee, Ver and Sam stood at the porch, in plain view.

Bee looked towards the house. A face had appeared at an upstairs window, shouting something.

"Is that Kit Coral?" Ver said.

Bee thought it was. He had no cap and wore a white shirt. He raised his hands in a despairing gesture. A prisoner, like themselves? Bee remembered then what Serena had said about her experience with the labyrinth: that it had been anger, not fear, that had finally overtaken her.

"Right!" she snapped.

"Bee –" Ver started to say, but Bee was marching down the path towards the lych gate.

"Mum! Come here. I want a word with you!"

She could not read Alys' expression, but her mother detached herself from the Hunt and walked towards the gate.

"Bee, I know –"

"Shut up!" Bee said. Distantly, as though watching herself from some unknown vantage point, she felt her anger boil over, a simmering pot overflowing the stove. "How dare you put me in this position? And Ver, and Sam. What happened to Kit? We're in hostile territory and you just fuck off on a whim and leave us here."

"It wasn't quite –"

"And your new friends. Or are they old friends, by now? If you think you can run with the hounds and hunt the hare then you have another think coming."

The man with the ram's horns urged his chestnut mount forwards. The tails of his coat draped over the horse's glossy withers. Close to, beneath the half mask that he wore, Bee could see a proud, handsome face. The insolent yellow gaze was familiar. Not just a goat's face, but a highwayman's, she thought. She remembered Nick's mention of Adam Ant. Well, stand and bloody deliver, then.

"My dear, we have not had what you promised us." An English drawl, light and affected, Bee thought. But there was an accent underneath it, not Northern, something else. "And I would be on the move, before the church bells sound."

"I didn't promise you anything," Alys said, quite evenly, but Bee thought she was annoyed. "I made that quite clear from the outset. I told you I wasn't going to help you snatch the Amberley's mare. You saw something you wanted and you tried to frighten Bee and Luna off, then you tried to take it, and you failed, and that didn't work, so you attempted punishment and that didn't work either. I think, Aiken, enough is enough. You really need to accept defeat on this one. And let my daughter go."

"Not just me," Bee said. "There are three of us. And Captain Coral."

The man named Aiken looked down at her over the wall. "I find I've taken quite a fancy to your dog. Tell you what, you can go and I'll keep the gazehound."

"No," Bee said. "We all go, including Moth."

"And what do we get for our side of the bargain?"

"What? You get fuck all, pal."

"Your daughter is most uncourteous and unkind," said Aiken to Alys. He flicked his fingers. "Shall I take offence, or shall I choose to be amused?"

"Bee," said Alys, in that 'I am trying to be reasonable' tone that Bee remembered from childhood. But Bee was not a child. She looked Aiken in the eye.

"No, I shall not apologise. We did not ask to come here. If we are trespassing, then I regret it, but we did not come here of our own free will. We were taken, snatched by the land itself. Perhaps *it* wants us here?"

"If I said to you…" Aiken's horse gave a restless sideways step and he restrained it. "If I said to you that there is something we might want, that we cannot take. Would you consider it?"

"Depends what it is!"

"If, then, I told you that we should like free access, over the field that runs down from your house in the world of men, where you keep your horses, would you give it?"

"What gain would that be to you?"

"A bridleway. You live on ancient land, as do most in your modern country. It was all ours once, but then men came and they hedged it round and fenced it in. Selling England by the pound, my lady tells me, but that I already knew. They cut across the leys and ways with their churches and chapels and crosses. They parcelled up the land with their laws and spells and hedges and gates. We do not have a clear run across country and we want it back. Your land is a little part of that plan."

Bee looked at him. "So – you don't want a magical ring that will give you unlimited power, or anything? You just want a hedge?" Less like Sauron; more like a neighbourhood dispute, and Bee was used to those, living in a village.

Alys' mouth twitched.

"Why can't *you* give it to him, Mum? It's technically still your house."

"It's in your name, Bee. I made sure of it when I first came back."

"What? By a spell, or something?"

"No, I wrote to my solicitor and the Land Registry."

"You did? What happens, Mother, if I do grant these – hunting rights, are they? Or just a bridleway? I want to talk to you alone."

Alys looked up at Aiken. "Let me pass."

After a moment, he nudged the horse aside. Alys came through the lych gate and into the churchyard.

"Oh, Bee. I've not done a good job of explaining myself, have I?"

"Putting it mildly, Mum. Can you make him just let us go?"

Alys sighed. "He is an old man and a proud one. He's not a bad man – well, not very bad. Opinions might vary. I'm sorry about the episode with the knife; he wouldn't have hurt you. It was just for show, to frighten you and Luna, and I was very angry about that. He does listen to me but he's lost face recently. They wanted Laura and they wanted the land spirit, too."

"Why Laura?" Bee stared at her. "Like a prize mare or something?"

"Well, actually yes. Exactly that. And I need you to know, Bee, that I didn't know Laura and Cloudy were the same. If I had, I wouldn't have even considered helping Aiken. I thought Cloud Chaser was just a horse and I still refused. Aiken and I – well, never mind that now, but one of the reasons I came back home was to keep an eye on Amberley. Shapechangers are rare, although I must say one wouldn't think so around us, and she is one of very few. It runs in the family – you know the Amberleys are supposed to be our distant relations?"

"I think I did know that, yes. I thought it might just be 'we've all been here ages and so we must be related' things. I mean, the entire country must be related if they've been here a couple of hundred years, I would think. It's probably a bit closer than that around

Hornmoon. Mum, you lied to me, that night of the dinner party when I saw that face in the hedge: you told me you'd never seen anything like a man with goat's eyes. And then he had a crack at me with a knife! I know what you've just said, but how sure are you? This sort of thing does not inspire trust."

"I know. I – I wimped out of telling you, frankly. I thought I could handle Aiken myself."

"I'd watch your over confidence on that one."

"I was very cross with him indeed about the incident with the knife. Anyway, about Laura. Aiken wanted her for the Hunt. They wanted the land spirit as well, as I just said."

"Do you mean the shoot? The thing in the greenhouse?"

"Yes. She's the same kind of being as the Lily White Boys, but female, obviously. She's what's known as a white track spirit: they're usually benign but this one clearly isn't. Aiken wants passage across Amberley as well and probably Wycholt – I don't think he'll get that. He can't just take it. Power in England is all locked up. You heard what he said. It's not just wealth with a lot of country estates: it's ancient bargains and tithes and land rights. If you asked most country gents if they knew that their Norman or Tudor or even Restoration ancestors had cut a deal with a supernatural hunting pack, they'd be calling for a psychiatrist, but that doesn't mean that the Hunt itself isn't still bound by it. Think about fox hunting packs. Piss off the farmer and you suddenly have to go round the long way. And they can't just knock on the front door and ask. Most people can't even see them."

Bee, remembering what Nick had said about diversity, about connectivity and rewilding, nonetheless did not want to find herself in a situation where she actually started feeling sympathy for the Hunt. She said,

"If I do let him use the field, what's the downside? Do we have to have them milling about in the yard? Stirrup cups and tally ho?"

"No, no. You'll need to keep the animals in – the horses, particularly, unless Luna wants to move them. Let Sam know. The Hunt rides at the beck of the moon and at certain times of year. I can let you know what those are or Ver might know. And you will find that Aiken is grateful. They are not – pleasant, by modern standards, but they can be loyal, in their own way."

"What do they hunt, Mum?"

"They hunt souls. And other things, sometimes."

"Souls of whom?"

"Not of good people. You can be reassured about that."

Who had given the Hunt the right to police souls? Bee wondered. The thought made her shiver, but it seemed too big a question to ask now. "And if I say no?"

"They might take you with them or not. Bee, they can be very dangerous. They will kill and death is not the end."

"All right," Bee said. "Let me talk to Aiken."

She walked back to the lych gate. "Very well. Free passage for all of us," she said to the man with yellow eyes. "And in return I grant you use of the field path. But you leave my house and my family and my friends and my animals alone."

He hesitated for a moment, then he held out a gloved hand. "A deal, then. We'll come no more after mare or wren or hive, or beast or man, if we are granted free passage along the bridleway. And if none gets in our way."

"A deal," Bee said. She took his hand, as briefly as she could manage. He tried to hang onto it and squeeze; that typical male trick. But she was already withdrawing her fingers.

"Not quite the full deal, yet. Your sister, in the city? Tell her to call off her search."

Bee thought she knew what he meant by this. "I'll do my best," she said.

"Very well. You're free to go. Through the gate and onto the lych road. We won't come after you but you may not be alone. Take the left hand path after the thornbrake and onwards to moonset."

"Wait," Alys said, surprising Bee. "Let me say goodbye to my daughter."

She hugged Bee tightly. Bee felt one hand slip down her side, inside Bee's coat.

"Be careful."

"You too, Mum. When will we see you again?"

"I'll pop by. I want to see my grandchild."

"You're always welcome," Bee said aloud.

Alys released her. "You're all good girls. Now go."

With Moth at her side, Bee let Ver and Sam go through the gate ahead of her. She heard the gate snick and looked through. They had gone.

"Good bye," Bee said to Alys and the Hunt. She stepped through the gate into darkness. The stars were up and when her sight adjusted, there was the thornbrake. Sam and Ver were waiting for her on a path over the hills. Bee went to join them but as she did so, she put her hand inside her coat, to the inner pocket. There was something there, something hard, about the size of a pencil. Bee took it out. It was a flute, made of bone.

STELLA

Stella had forgotten that rats could swim so well. Not as well as otters, though: she streaked under the little paddling form and rose up beneath it. Sharp claws dug in. With Davy clinging to the back of her neck, Stella swam for the boat. She did not dive down again, not wanting to drown the rat, but the two man crew and Miranda were at the prow, so Stella sat up in the water, scrabbled for one of the ropes, and hauled Davy and herself aboard. Rat and otter hid behind a barrel.

"Is he planning to go under the bridge?" Davy whispered.

"Must be." The boat swung around and Stella felt the surge beneath it as the river sucked it forwards. She knew now how powerful that pull could be. There were shouts from above. She looked up and saw the golden domes of Nonsuch overhead. What had happened to Hob? *Stay off the back of the fucking deck, Miranda.* They clung to the rope holding the barrel in place as the boat shot through. Stella had a fleeting glimpse again of the huge stone legs of the bridge, green with weed, and the frothing water below and then they were clear. The tide and the wind were in the boat's favour: soon the bridge was falling behind. As they moved downstream Stella, looking back, could see St Paul's, high above the city, then ahead the Tower on the northern bank, blinding white against the blue sky.

"She's making good time," said Davy, "wherever she's going."

Stella knew that she was still in her otter shape, and Davy was a rat, but when she looked at her friend, it was as though she was seeing double: the little rat behind the barrel, bright eyed and whiskers twitching, but also Davy Dearly in her human form, looking around her with interest.

The Tower was now behind them, too. Along the river, the warehouses and wharves were busy: loading and unloading ships. Stella wondered what the cargoes might be. The boat swung around. Davy said,

"Look, you can see the pub!"

The Prospect of Whitby crouched above the river, its eaves overhanging the water.

"You're as bad as Ace," Stella said.

"We ought to try going back a bit further. Pity we can't drop in now. I could do with a pint."

The boat followed the bends of the Thames. A huge building came into view on the southern bank, not far from where the *Nitrogen* was moored in the present day, on the opposite bank. Water steps ran down into the river.

"Greenwich Palace," Davy said. Further on Stella saw a forest of masts: the naval dockyards. She looked in wonder at the big sailing ships: was Ned Dark, alive and well, even now boarding one of them? She must remember to tell him.

The boat was still moving at a quick clip. It was not alone: the river was thronged with water traffic.

"It's like the M1," she said to Davy.

"As you said when we went to Richmond, best way of getting around."

Used to the endless industrial estates, cranes, and suburbs, Stella was interested to see how close to the city the marshes were now, and the low green hills in the distance.

"Is she heading out to sea?" Stella asked. They could not be that far from the mouth of the estuary.

"I hope not! She must be pulling in soon. There's fuck all between here and Holland."

"Tell me about it," Stella said, remembering the Maunsell forts.

At last the boat started to turn and tack towards shore. Stella peered around the barrel. Nothing to see but saltmarsh and water, and a tiny wooden dock. The boat drew close; the boatman cast a rope and pulled the craft in. Miranda stepped briskly onto the down and headed into the marsh, followed by the boatman and his mate.

"Right," Stella said. At a safe distance, she and Davy, still in animal form, followed. The marsh was a maze of waterways and expanses of mud: tussocks of tough grass and samphire lay between. The marsh was littered with the bones of boats; old wrecks had been washed up by storms.

Not just the bones of boats, either. A white knobbed shape rose up out of the grass, and when Stella looked more closely a skull grinned at her from a tussock.

"Davy, this isn't that place they call Deadman's Island, is it?"

"I thought that was further round the Medway. And the bones there are more recent than these times – men who died on the prison hulks. But you know, Stella, the land and the day and age can be very shifty."

A flock of sandpipers wheeled up, disturbed by the three humans. Davy and Stella were not having any difficulty keeping up: lighter and more agile than Miranda and the boatmen, they found it easier to pick their way through the saltmarsh. Above, the sky was a hazy blue and the sun was bright, but this must be an exceptionally bleak place in winter, Stella thought.

"Why isn't she a gull?" Stella asked.

"It's probably because of her mates. She must need them for something."

"What's that up ahead?"

"Not something Elizabethan," Stella said. "It's a pillbox."

The little concrete hut rose out of the marsh, sited on an island of its own.

"You're right," said Davy. She paused for a moment to clean the mud off her whiskers. "There's quite a few of them out here. Leftover from the war."

"Do you know this part of the river well? If things have stayed put, that is."

"I know the area a bit. My aunty comes from the Hoo – near Allhallows. We used to come out here when I was a nipper and I've been back and forth since then. You wouldn't think it was so close to the city. Even in our day it's like the arse end of the moon out here."

Stella rather liked it. Perhaps that was the otter in her, she thought. It might not be so appealing to humans. Miranda, still wearing her grey cloak, was poking about the pillbox. She turned and said something to the boatman.

"Closer," Davy said. She and Stella took a circuitous route along the edge of a channel. But the boatman had sharp eyes.

"What's that?"

"It's just a rat, Rafe."

"That's not a rat," Stella heard Miranda say, sharply. Then she spoke again. The air hissed and sparkled. Once more Stella found herself pulled out of her body and seconds later she and Davy were floundering in the marsh, ankle deep in mud. The man named Rafe uttered a startled oath.

"I thought I'd got rid of you," Miranda said.

"Yeah, well."

If asked, Stella would have classified Miranda as the type to make long rambling speeches about her own superiority, Bond villain style. But she did not.

"Kill them at once," she said to Rafe.

"A pleasure, mistress." A long knife whisked out of his belt. Grinning, he came quickly forwards. Stella thought of otters, swimming, diving down, and nothing happened. She heard Davy say, "Shit!"

Then Rafe looked surprised. His eyebrows went up, his mouth opened into an O. He stopped. The knife splashed into the marsh. Rafe fell forwards, face down, and lay still with a crossbow bolt quivering between his shoulder blades.

Miranda whipped around. A small green skinned girl stood on a tussock of seagrass, beside a man with a bow in hand. Stella heard a whistling rush; the boatman's mate, too, stumbled and fell. Miranda gave a harsh cry. A gull shot up into the air above the pillbox.

Someone shouted but the gull was moving too fast to be brought down. She skimmed over the marsh but there were ravens coming in from the south, a flank of six. It was like watching dogfighting planes. The gull banked, dropped and turned, flying as fast as a falcon, but the ravens overtook her. They surrounded her, carried her upwards.

Then the gull broke free. She soared across the rivermouth, heading back towards the city, but the ravens were close. They harried her, driving her back. Stella followed their passage with her hand shading her eyes. They were a speck and then gone. But moments later a white wing feather spiralled down, followed by a spatter of red on the lintel of the pillbox. Inside, all was shadow.

Stella recognised Saul. He picked his way along the channels and gave a nod.

"It's been long since we saw you," he said.

"Only the other night, to us," Davy replied. "Thank you."

"We owed you a debt of kindness. And we've met the gull witch before, not in good favour."

"Do you think you can get home from here?"

"Maybe. These are the edgelands, close to the northern sea."

"Davy," Stella said. "I think there's someone in that pillbox."

Cautiously, she stepped through the door. The person had their back to Stella. His head was resting on his arms. He was fast asleep.

"Hello?" Stella said. The man stirred. "Hello?" Stella said again. This time, he woke. He turned to look at her, blinking. He was young and wore a faded blue uniform; his cap lay on the desk beside him.

"You're Serena's airman," Stella said.

"Who is Serena? Who are you, miss?"

"My name is Stella Fallow. What's yours?"

"Lieutenant Oliver Knight, at your service."

"How long have you been here?"

"I don't know," he said. He looked puzzled. "I was dreaming – my plane was shot down, into the Channel, and I drowned. A nightmare… then I was on the shore and a woman was standing over me. She had fair hair. She said she wanted to help me. I followed her."

"That's my sister, Serena."

"In my dream I knew I had to find someone, but I don't know who. A woman who carries a coin in her pocket."

"Like this one?" Stella said. She reached into her pocket and took out the Huntress' token. "Here, catch!"

She threw it at Knight and he snatched it out of the air. Stella saw the coin glow, brighter than the sun. She flung a hand over her eyes and in the glare saw London below: the city streets outlined, the great river running through it. She saw wells and churches, statues and palaces and parks, and the map was covered in sparks: the entry and exits of the city.

But only for a moment. The coin lay flat and dull in Knight's hand.

"Oh!" he said.

"Stella," said Davy Dearly's voice. It held a distinct note of warning. "I think you'd better get out here."

LUNA

When Luna woke the following morning, she had a moment of complete disorientation. She lay, blinking, wondering if it had been a dream. She was still not entirely sure when, washed and dressed, she ventured downstairs to find Laura making toast in the kitchen.

"Nick's gone down to see to your horses. Ned Dark says it's been a quiet night."

"No sign of anyone else? Or Moth?"

Laura gave her a sympathetic pat on the shoulder. "Not yet. Don't worry. They'll come safely home."

"Oh, I hope so." She went into the dining room with a mug of tea and pushed open the French windows. The garden was sunlit and filled with birdsong: across the lawn, blue tits squabbled with chaffinches for the feeder. She could hear a woodpecker hammering in the orchard and pigeons cooing on the roof. The birds were unconcerned, thought Luna: perhaps that counted for something. She wandered down to the drive and met Nick Wratchall-Haynes coming up.

"Luna! How are you today?"

"I feel all right," Luna said. "A bit sad. And sort of empty. And worried, obviously. But I'll be all right. How are you?"

"Fine. I've been talking to Ned. He's worried, too, about your relations and your dog."

"Who is there!" Luna cried.

"What?"

"Moth! Oh, Moth!" For the lurcher was running full tilt up the drive. He hurled himself at Luna and put his front feet on her shoulders. She staggered. "Moth, get down! I love you but get down!"

"Moth! Come here!" Sam and Ver and Bee were behind him. Luna flung herself on all of them, like the dog.

"I wouldn't," Bee told her. "I think I stink."

"I don't care. Are you all right? Where's Mum?"

"Mum stayed behind. Long story. She's okay, though. And at least I won't have to fight her for the bathroom. What day is it? What's been happening here?"

"Long story," said Luna.

Later that morning Nick had gone home to sort out horses and dogs and Laura, too, had returned to Amberley. Sam said he would run Ver back to the protest site.

"Does anyone else want to come?"

"Me," said Luna. "I'm not letting you and Moth out of my sight for a couple of days at least." She kept thinking about the shoot. Would it return? What had it been trying to do? And who was the woman who carried an apple? If she met a star, Luna told herself, she would ask her.

"Not me," Bee said. "I have a hot date with the bath."

"You've already had a bath!"

"I want another one."

So after lunch, cooked by Luna, they got into the Land Rover and set off. Spring had fully arrived now and the day lay gently over the land, with high white clouds and the hedges filled with wild cherry. Luna noticed that the hawthorn, too, was starting to bud: the may would be out before long.

Sam took the back road to the farm and found the gate to the campsite wide open. Ver's tent stood in lonely state, surrounded by dandelions. No one else was there.

"Oh!" said Ver.

"You come to pick up your tent?" a young man said. He was coming up from the farmyard, holding some arcane piece of machinery.

"Yes. Has everyone else gone?"

"Yes, all tidied up."

"What about the road protest?" Sam said, but the young man just smiled, in a vague and puzzled way, and said that he needed to sort out the tractor, adding in that inevitable Somerset way, "Over by to."

"Is the bypass not going ahead, then?" Luna asked.

"Don't know of any bypass planned round here." He wandered off, leaving them staring after him.

"You get your kit together, Gran," Sam said. "We'll go and have a look."

Where the big earth movers had been, so short a time before, the field was now untroubled. Luna thought she could see faint marks in the earth, but the dandelions and plantain had taken over. They went down to the road. No sign of anything.

"I hope they're all right," Luna said, uneasily. "What if they were all – swallowed?"

"Did you listen to the news this morning?"

"Yes, Nick put Radio Somerset on – you're right. Nothing was mentioned. It was all about some band dropping out of the Glastonbury Festival and someone else taking their place. I'd never heard of either of them so I didn't pay any attention."

"But no mention of a mysteriously disappearing road crew and vanishing protestors?"

"Definitely not."

"Bee told me she didn't want to start feeling sorry for the Hunt. I don't want to start feeling grateful to them, either."

"I don't like the thought of them having so much power," Sam said, uneasily.

"Maybe they don't. Maybe it was the land itself."

"Then why doesn't it rise up and swallow HS2 and the Stonehenge Tunnel?"

"I know. I don't have an answer to that, Sam."

They walked back across the field. Halfway to where Ver was dismantling the last of her tent, Luna felt eyes on the back of her neck. She looked around. Kit Coral stood by the hedge. When he saw her looking, he smiled.

"Sam! Do you see him?"

"Are you well, Captain Coral?" Sam called.

"Free, and that's good enough for me! Thank your sister from me." He touched a hand to his cap and was gone.

Ver was stuffing a tin cup into her backpack. "All done. Nearly ready."

"Captain Coral was there."

"Oh, was he, now? I hope he's all right. I did like him and he was ever so helpful."

"Perhaps we'll see him again," said Luna.

"Perhaps we will. No, I can manage quite well, thank you, Sam." She slung the tent into the boot of the Land Rover. "Can I camp in your garden, Luna?"

"Yes, or you can have a spare room or our van. Would you prefer the van, Ver? It's nearly the same as outside."

"Do you know, I think I would. Well, then. Let's go home."

STELLA

The Searchers stood outside the pillbox, in a semicircle: old women, dressed all in raven black. At their feet, Miranda Dean's crumpled body lay, staring up at the sky. She was, Stella thought, quite dead.

"Oh dear," said Stella.

"She was trying to kill us," said Davy.

"I know. I rather hoped Bill Blake might, I don't know, rehabilitate her somehow. Hob will be upset."

"We have done what we came to do," the Searcher said.

Davy went over to the body. "Sorry, not much respect. It's a rat thing." She rifled quickly through Miranda's pockets while the Searchers watched without expression.

"She's not carrying much," said Davy. She fished a key out of Miranda's pocket and a purse. There was also a small roll of parchment. Davy and Stella studied it:

This is where you need to seek, the note read. It was signed VV and on the other side was a map of the river, well drawn. The pillbox was marked with an inky dot.

"This must have been what she went back to Nonsuch to get," Davy said. "Van Vliet must have sent her a message."

"I suppose she thought she had nothing to lose by trying to hijack my quest," Stella said. "*My* quest, by the way. The one *I* got given."

"Let's face it, she did thieve and fence for a living. Not that I have great moral objections."

"Young man," the Searcher said to Knight. "You are free of your burden. That which you carried has gone. Where would you go?"

He looked nonplussed. "I don't know. Back to the airbase at Eastchurch, I suppose, and see the chaps."

The Searcher's face was sad. She said, "Would you like to go home, Lieutenant Knight?"

"Am I allowed? I can't just go off on leave without asking, you see."

"You have leave." She raised the bone staff that she carried and tapped it on the earth. Stella watched as a gate opened in the air: a gate in a wall, leading into a summery place. A lawn, with a house beyond, and two women sitting at a table with tea. From the facial resemblance they were mother and daughter, Stella thought. Beyond the garden, she saw other buildings: the familiar red and white striped brick of London.

"Oh!" The airman's face lit up. "My mother, and Barbara. They'll be surprised to see me."

"They're waiting for you," the Searcher said, and they stood back as he went quickly through the gate. But before he did so, he turned and put something into Stella's hand: she looked down and saw the coin.

"This is yours," he said.

"Thank you!"

The gate snicked shut behind him and the last thing Stella saw was the young man running lightly across the lawn, as the girl put down her book and stood up.

The gate was gone. "So must we go, too," the Searcher said. They bent and picked up Miranda's body. The bone staff tapped the earth once more and another gate opened, but this time everything beyond it was dark. The Searchers hoisted Miranda's body onto their shoulders and went through; the gate closed behind them. But it remained, standing upright in the marsh.

"We can try," Saul said, to the group who clustered around him.

"I don't think you want to go where they just went!" Stella said.

He smiled. "Let's see." He put a hand on the latch of the gate and opened it. Beyond was a green and watery world, the sunlight slanting golden on the willows. The little girl gave a curlew's cry.

"Good bye," Saul said. "If you see Aln again, tell her we have been lost, but found our way home."

"I will. And thank you. I hope the Gefliemen never come back."

"We hope so, too, and we thank you," he said, gravely. The group filed through the gate and Saul closed it behind him. Only the rushes stood there now; the pillbox, too, had disappeared.

Above the marsh, the day was starting to die and the wind was cold. A flicker of blue fire appeared, far out across the channels. Stella looked away from that unchancy light, westward, towards London. The sun was low.

"Davy? Would you be able to sail that boat?"

"Absolutely."

There were groups of people sitting on the grass around a little tent, which looked to Serena like the kind of tent one might see on a jousting ground. She looked back at the city. St Paul's Medieval spire still dominated the city. Across the river, she could see the tower of Southwark and a handful of houses, and the bridge still spanned the Thames, but on the north shore a wall had sprung up around the city.

Stella heard a murmur spring up as they approached.

"She has come! She has come!"

"You have brought the Knowledge," someone said. The antlered woman stepped from the tent with her greyhounds at her side. Her hair was braided down her back and she was all in green. Flowers starred her cloak. Serena felt very small.

"Yes," Stella said. "I've done what you asked me to do. I think. You asked me to find a man, and I found him, but he was a ghost."

She and Davy had discussed this at length on the way back up the river.

"So Knight was the one with the Knowledge, but he was killed and his ghost got – what, trapped? In the pillbox? Along with the Knowledge."

"Presumably. It might explain why no-one's heard of him, if he's been there since the 40s. If the pillbox is the first entry point on the river, perhaps the Knowledge took his spirit back there? To wait?"

"I hope the Knowledge actually has been transferred into this thing. Otherwise it's going to be embarrassing."

"It's going to be even more embarrassing if we can't work out where St Pancras is in this day and age."

"Part of that old hunting chase is now Regent's Park," Davy said, trimming the black sails. "So I'm taking her straight up the Tyburn."

And this is what she did, sailing the captured boat up from the Thames, through the waterway which cut through the developing city, to the greenness of the park.

Now, Serena became aware that the crowd had risen to their feet and gathered round. She saw all manner of faces: bronze skinned and black, blue eyes and dark and fiery green, and all kinds of dress, from Roman tunics to Medieval hose, Elizabethan ruff and gown to Regency foppery and powdered wigs. Not all the faces were quite human.

She took the coin and dropped it into Noualen's waiting hand.

A haunting, quavering note fell upon the air. Like the wind in a wood, Stella thought, or the cold sea wind that blows over the shore. There was a flash of light.

She took a step back. Suddenly, she was high over the old city. But there was nothing there any more, only forest and the immense span of the river. A drift of smoke spiralled up. Then she saw buildings: red tiles and a temple on the place now occupied by St Paul's. A ship was at anchor in the river and then the buildings were on fire, and then houses rose from the ashes, reminding Stella of the vision in the *Book of London*. The cathedral rose up again and a bridge spanned the Thames; she watched as fires raged once more and the city burned and grew and changed. Mud lands became the seat of skyscrapers and the Shard dwarfed Southwark; she heard the rattle of the Tube and the sound of buses.

The map of the changing city lay below her and on it, Stella saw tiny lights. There was one here, in Regent's Park by the big oak tree. There were several along the river shore, beneath churches. She recognised the place where, in the cellars of All Hallows near the Tower, Serena had slipped back into Roman times. She saw the place where Cas Pharoah's office had been, off Cannon Street, and the entrance to Hercules Road. She knew all the entry ways of London: the hollow ways, the snickets and smeuses, that ran between times.

She closed her eyes and saw the map imprinted on her eyelids. She opened them again and found it there, fading, but clear as polished glass inside her mind. She smiled. For a moment, she'd had the Knowledge, trying her on for size but it was moving on.

"Oh!" Davy gasped.

Stella found she could still remember bits and pieces but the full Knowledge had found its new home. Waterman's daughter, rat-child and London-born, Davy Dearly stood with her river and land eyes wide, staring at nothing.

"Davy!"

"Got it! Safe and sound!"

They were back on Primrose Hill. The city hummed below. A jet made its arching path towards Heathrow. The dome of St Paul's was tiny in comparison to the Shard, but still clear on the skyline. Docklands glittered in the sunlight. Stella looked around. The tent had gone and so had the oak tree and the crowd. Davy Dearly sat on the grass, looking contemplatively at a plucked daisy. She said,

"*To see a World in a Grain of Sand, and a Heaven in a Wild Flower, Hold Infinity in the palm of your hand And Eternity in an hour.* Bill wrote that."

The crowd had disappeared.

"And now can I be free?" Noualen asked.

Davy rose from the grass.

"Yes, let's sort you out."

Stella saw another little gate, appear like a garden gate with a lock.

"That's it, is it?"

"That's it."

So Stella went to the gate and reached into her backpack. She knew what she had to do now. She took out the antler prong and it was again an ivory key. She put it into the lock and opened the gate. Then she looked back. Noualen had vanished but a white hind stood on the grass, with a golden chain around its neck. Beside her were two young men: one with white skin, one with black, and both in hunting green. But their hands were at their sides; the chain around the hind's neck was her own. She looked at Stella with a grassfire gaze and leaped through the gate and was gone, with the young men running behind her. Stella stood, looking out over the park for a moment, but no white hind ran down the slope.

"I haven't made a daisy chain for years," said Davy. "Here you go!"

"Very pretty! Thanks!" Her phone pinged. "Text from Ace," Stella said. "You've probably got one too. He's back in Lambeth at Blake's house and so is Hob."

"What's the time? My phone ran out of battery last night."

"Eleven."

Stella smiled. "Opening time, then. I'll text him back, tell him to meet us in the pub. Are you coming, Davy? You said you could do with a pint."

"I could do with a walk as well," Davy said. And so they went down from Primrose Hill, over the green sward to the city: down Baker Street and through Marylebone, through Soho to St James, and Westminster Bridge and over to Southwark. They did not take any of the byways that they now knew: by mutual agreement, they went on foot and in full.

"Shanks' pony," said Davy Dearly. "Best thing next to a boat."

By the time they reached Southwark, the sun was at its height: noonday in London, with the city all around, and they paused for a moment and turned back the clock and walked around the old cathedral to find their friends.

BEE

On Good Friday Bee went down to Hornmoon church to help with the flowers. Very traditional: Easter lilies and paperwhites, and hyacinths and narcissi, some from the bulbs that Bee had taken to Wycholt. She met their donor in the vestry.

"Morning, Bee. How's things?"

"Morning, Nick. All well and good, thank you. All ready for Easter?"

"Yes, more or less. I'll be in here on Sunday, first service. Caro and Richard are coming for Easter lunch."

"Lovely. We'll be cooking, too."

"I meant to ask if you'd had any, let's say, visitations in your lower field?"

"No, but Luna and I have been doing some calculations and also doing a bit of poking about in the folklore, and we think it might be tonight."

"Are you worried?"

"A bit. Actually, a lot. But I think we can handle it. Sam's taking the horses over to Amberley in a loose box and I'm keeping the dogs and cats inside. There aren't any sheep in the neighbouring field. I don't even know if the Hunt would bother, but Aiken did say…"

"Best to be on the safe side."

"Exactly."

Early that evening, Laura dropped by to return a book that Bee had lent her, and was persuaded to stay for supper and then the evening. This was in part because Bee felt that they should keep an eye on Laura: the Hunt's interest in her had unnerved everyone, and Luna said that perhaps Laura might be safer at Mooncote. Aiken had given his assurances, but still…

And it was they, not the Hunt, who had not fulfilled their side of the bargain. For Bee had spoken to Stella by now and she knew that Stella had not called off her search. Instead, she had fulfilled it, so

Bee had broken her promise. And what this meant, Bee did not know.

When dusk fell they went up to the spare room and looked out across the field. Sam had gone down to the van with Ver, to watch from there. Dark, Bee, Laura and Luna waited, while the stars came out one by one. They sat in silence, until Bee heard a faint creak.

"What was that?"

"It's the horse," Dark said. "It's rocking."

It was. The white rocking horse was starting to move, to and fro, to and fro. Bee looked out of the window. The field was suddenly alight and she saw very briefly the Hounds running beside the grey horses, the man called Aiken with a woman in a spotted cloak on the back of his chestnut, riding pillion. The Hunt sounded like geese, flying south for the summer. The great bull-headed man brought up the rear and then they were up and away on the track laid by the moon. Up and over and out. The field lay silent under the stars. Aiken had kept his word. This time, at least. Bee breathed out.

Beside her, Laura said, "I've got to go."

"Laura?"

"Sorry, it's – something's calling me. I've got to go." And she was running down the stairs.

Bee, filled with dreadful misgiving, called, "Laura, wait!"

With Dark and Luna at her heels, she followed. Laura had gone out through the dining room; Bee heard the bang of the French windows. She ran into the garden.

Laura was there, but so was someone else. A woman wearing a green cloak, with two dogs by her sides. Her hair fired around her shoulders; her eyes were green flames. Small antlers were entwined with the white flowers of wild woodruff. She was smiling at Laura. Bee knew from her conversations with Stella who she must be. She made Bee's bones feel like water but Bee plucked courage from the air and said,

"If it's the Hunt you want, Lady Noualen, you're a bit late."

"It's not the Hunt I'm after. Not yet, though I will take back what's mine. But I'll ride my own path for a time, now I am free from my bonds, and a huntress needs a mount. Will you carry me?" she said to Laura. "Not forever, but oft times?"

Bee turned and saw the grey mare, Cloud Chaser, standing on the grass. She nickered once, bent her head and pawed the ground.

"Careful of my lawn, Laura," Bee said.

Noualen grasped the mare's mane and sprang onto her back. She laughed aloud and the mare wheeled about and cantered down the lawn. She leaped the hedge. Bee ran back into the house and up to the spare room, where the rocking horse was once more still. She looked out of the window and saw the mare and her rider running fast, along the bright line which now crossed the fields, under the stars and far away.

About the Author

Liz Williams is a science fiction and fantasy writer living in Glastonbury, England, where she is co-director of a witchcraft supply business. She has been published by Bantam Spectra (US) and Tor Macmillan (UK), also Night Shade Press, and appears regularly in *Asimov's* and other magazines. She has been involved with the Milford SF Writers' Workshop for 20 years, and also teaches creative writing at a local college for Further Education.

Her previous novels are:: *The Ghost Sister* (Bantam Spectra), *Empire Of Bones, The Poison Master, Nine Layers Of Sky, Banner Of Souls* (Bantam Spectra – US, Tor Macmillan – UK), *Darkland, Bloodmind* (Tor Macmillan UK), *Snake Agent, The Demon And The City, Precious Dragon, The Shadow Pavilion* (Night Shade Press) *Winterstrike* (Tor Macmillan), *The Iron Khan* (Morrigan Press) and *Worldsoul* (Prime). The Chen series is currently being published by Open Road.

Comet Weather was published by New Con Press in 2020.

A non-fiction book on the history of British paganism, *Miracles Of Our Own Making*, was published by Reaktion Books in 2020.

Her first short story collection *The Banquet Of The Lords Of Night* was also published by Night Shade Press, and her second and third, *A Glass Of Shadow* and *The Light Warden*, are published by New Con Press as is her recent novella, *Phosphorus.*

The *Diaries if a Witchcraft Shop* (volumes 1 and 2) are also published by New Con Press.

Her novel *Banner Of Souls* was shortlisted for the Philip K Dick Memorial Award, as were three previous novels, and the Arthur C Clarke Award.

ALSO FROM NEWCON PRESS

Queen of Clouds – Neil Williamson

A fast-paced tale set in a richly imagined world. Wooden automata, sentient weather, talking cats, compellant inks, a tower of hands built from the casts provided by the city's many visitors, and a host of vividly realised characters provide the backdrop as yokel Billy Braid becomes embroiled in big city politics and deadly intrigue.
"Superb characterization and fascinating worldbuilding. There's plenty to enjoy." – *Publishers Weekly.*

On The Brink – RB Kelly

Luchtstad: the city in the sky. Beacon of hope. Place of refuge, of acceptance. At least, that's what the rumours say. Reborn as Françoise Marechal, Danae Grant is trying to build a new life and disappear into the cracks. Nothing and nobody will ever touch her again. She's going to make sure of that. Until that is, Adam appears with an agenda of his own, one that threatens to expose Danae and put her at risk once more.

Night, Rain, and Neon: All New Cyberpunk

Editor Michael Cobley has compiled and curated a collection of stunning new visions of our future, published as tribute to Williams Gibson's masterpiece *Neuromancer*, with stories by **Ian McDonald, Justina Robson, Gary Gibson, Jon Courtenay Grimwood, Louise Carey, Al Robertson, Simon Morden, Keith Brooke and Eric Brown, DA Xiaolin Spires, Gavin Smith, Danie Ware, Jeremy Szal, Tim Maughan, Stewart Hotston** & more.

Saving Shadows – Eugen Bacon

Prose poetry and speculative micro-lit pieces by renowned author Eugen Bacon. Forty-eight pieces in all: twenty-six previously published and twenty-two written specially for this book. Complementing the written word are a series of full page illustrations commissioned by the author from artist Elena Betti; thirty-five stunning images that enhance the reading experience.

CPSIA information can be obtained
at www.ICGtesting.com
Printed in the USA
LVHW111819070223
738786LV00006B/180

9 781914 953217